Rabbit Heart

Rabbit Heart

COLLEEN HITCHCOCK

POCKET BOOKS

New York   London   Toronto   Sydney

In memory of

Eve & J. D.

who taught me the godliness

of the rabbit

Rabbit Heart

Prologue

August 4, 1891
London, England

THERE WAS A DEAD MAN IN MY BOUDOIR. HE LAY SPREAD-eagle as I dressed his still figure in the midmorning's dark. It was a difficult task, as he was a tall man to manage and death seemed to have doubled his weight. I had to rock him back and forth to re-dress him. And with each cumbersome move, I stopped to mourn the loss of my lover with a prayer or a tear.

"Dear Father in heaven, help me," I cried.

But I don't think he was listening, for I saw no sign of his holy presence, nor do I think he was anywhere nearby. Perhaps my God had another commitment overseas, or was involved in the creation of a better world than this one. In any case I interpreted his absence from my crisis as a godly commentary about my person and a direct reflection of my soul.

I wished for the outcome of a fairy tale: my tears would fall upon my pale lover's cheek; my longing sentiment would enliven him. And then we would ride off together to his castle, where our embraces would have no consequence other than pleasure.

I hoped my lover could still feel my loving caresses as I pressed my cheek upon his. I wanted my lively blood to make him gasp a reborn breath and his cool cheek rush to its rosy color. And then I thought if I pressed his hand, I might invite his dormant blood to again flow freely within his body. But none of my wishes materialized in my loving partner, and my hopes dwindled with each moment he rested on the other side of death's veil.

My maid had prepared my room that day with bouquets of roses and scented my bed with Parisian lavender talc. Now the sweet air of flowers and lace was fouled by the creeping pallor of death.

Once a horror has taken place in a room, the room is never the same. It forever bears the mark of the event's sadness, and I felt my boudoir respond to its recent trauma. Though I was alone, I didn't feel alone. I sensed a thousand eyes examining me—even the lamp, bed, and chair were witnesses to my lover's expiration. And if they were not enough, I had Denton's sweet face seeing all. All of it. His eyes were startled, yet his lips still smiled, as if he might come back from the dead to resume our courtship. That smile made me shiver in my abandoned state—and daggered my guilty soul deeper still.

Oh walls, do not tell of me. Lace curtains, do not proclaim my wrongdoing. Let my shoes hold their tongue. Please, none of you tell of my crime—

I heard footsteps coming to my door and a quick hand rattle the doorknob.

"Don't come in. I'm—"

"Mademoiselle Nicollette, do you have need of me?"

Marie stumbled on the garish scene. It was too late to wish her away.

She was my confidante and closest friend. She would have the right to be horrified at the demise of the vital man she knew to be alive just moments ago. Instead, she closed the door quietly, took my hand, and knelt next to me. So calm was her demeanor that the pause settled me.

She looked at me with a pure heart, not that of someone who would endanger me or spill my secrets—with no mind to their scandal or consequences. I trusted her.

I didn't know what to say to explain my dilemma, and so I remained kneeling near the body—as if I were praying over Denton.

But I did not pray for Denton. I prayed for the impossible: an understanding spirit that could soothe my soul.

CHAPTER 1

Dear Friend

THERE'S A REASON WHY I'M NOT MARRIED. THERE'S A secret that has caused me to move from town to town throughout England. No one must find out what haunts me. If I tell the secret, it will threaten my freedom. Instead, I'm packing my bags once again.

Denton is still a handsome man—my deed has not yet spoiled his appearance. He had such fresh boyish looks, fine manners, and wealth. He looked so beautiful with his Derby horses. I would never have wished him to be my thirteenth victim. Thirteen beautiful men gone—through no one's fault. For I can't take the responsibility for their deaths, it's too great a burden for me to bear.

For he had that persistence men have. They ask to call on you—and then ask again and again, even when you decline them so graciously. They decide they want you more and keep pushing you.

I always say no when they ask. I say it quite firmly. But they try again. And eventually I have to smile and accept their invitations, for they've beaten me down. And, I'm afraid, have become somewhat pitiful to me.

I try to look after them. I'm thinking of their safety—*their lives*. But they pay no mind. I try to save them, but they don't listen.

When they visit that first night, I let them know that we shouldn't see each other again. I try to leave it at a "Thank you for a lovely evening," but they push me. The next time the dinner is nicer. Or they take me to the theater. I try to resist, but they're charming. They open the doors for me, pull out my chair, put their arms around me, and I know what they want. They want to do all the right things to guide me into their beds. I still say no, trying to protect them. But they don't listen.

The first time it happened, I was in love—for the first time. I was enjoying the world, viewing it through glasses that could see no wrong. My heart was beating with desire and passion.

I would be lying if I told you that he noticed me first. I noticed him the moment I came around the corner on the Champs Elysées in Paris and saw a striking man with the gentlest eyes. I was not alone. Other women on the street watched him walk toward us as if a young Adonis were approaching. And he seemed oblivious to their attention. He had his head down in a book, repeating terms as if he were preparing for an exam.

Twenty feet before me he raised his head, as if told to look up, and his eyes locked with mine.

But his mouth had not stopped moving. He continued to mutter medical prefixes in Latin and biological terms.

"Cardi. Pertaining to the esophageal opening of the stomach or the heart . . ."

"But the heart is connected to everything that matters," I said.

He said nothing. He continued to look at me, then walked by me—right into a brick building that was closer than he judged.

"Are you all right, sir?" I knelt next to him and took a handkerchief from my purse.

"Allow me to help—you're bleeding."

"Who could refuse?" He sighed with a blissful smile. "You smell like a lavender field on a fresh spring day."

He seemed to inhale my scent. I could tell he loved my nearness as my body pressed against his shoulder.

"Thank you. I've never seen you before. I'm Robert, Robert Moneter. Who are you?"

"I'm Nicollette Caron."

He had a small scratch on his nose, and I pressed the linen cloth on his wound until the bleeding stopped.

"I'm on my way to take a medical examination, may I call on you later?"

"I'm just fifteen—I don't court yet."

"I will wait. Let me stop by and learn more about you. Where do I find you?"

He took out a pocket watch and checked it as he stood up. "I'm going to be late. Where do I find you, Nicollette?"

"I don't . . . I mean I don't know where I will be—"

"I will find you. If you're anywhere in France, I will find you," he said as he ran to his exam.

Robert did find me, at church on Sunday, and over the next year we began to see each other secretly.

"My friends would think you too young," he said.

So we met as often as we could. He told his friends he was at the library studying, I told my chaperone I was reading Shakespeare at the library.

"I treasure every moment I'm with you, Nicollette," Robert said every time we met.

And I would nod shyly in agreement. Our love continued to

grow over the next year. When I became sixteen, he started borrowing his father's carriage and taking me to the countryside.

Oh, the kisses! Oh, the sweetness of the sun as we rolled in meadows, the fresh scent of the grassy hills as we courted beneath the clouds. For a long year we had desired each other. And now I knew it was time to give my virginity to my beloved.

Robert was so aroused his hands were shaking. My dress fell off easily at his touch, and there were only he and I on the blanket with only God's eyes to watch, as he studied my nakedness. He took his time at first and slowly slid his hands down my sides, in no hurry to remove his own clothes. He cupped my breasts with his hands and when he sucked upon them I felt my body moving in a new direction for me.

My body grew heated with our passion and my mind broke through into some euphoric state I had never experienced. Almost a delirious state in which my soul and spirit were empowered and overruling my thoughtful mind—I could no longer think, only feel. Even though his jacket was a bit scratchy, his metal buttons rubbing into me, I felt only the pleasure of his touch. And soon he was peeling his clothes off to the sweetest pleasure yet. He was pressing his firm young body into mine.

Robert was strong and he pulled me underneath him. Lifting my bottom with one hand, he positioned me on the blanket where he wanted me. Then his legs pried mine open and he entered me. He was gentle—the man with the gentle eyes, just as I'd imagined, for he entered me slowly, pausing—to allow me to adjust.

At first he couldn't enter me, but his patience prevailed as he let me ready myself for him. And then when he had managed to penetrate me fully, he did so with strong rocking movements that took my breath and made me shudder with bliss. I moaned my pleasure in our union, and *I loved it. Dear God, how I loved it.*

And that is how it began.

I wanted more. More. Oh, so much more. I wanted to consume my young lover. I wanted our movements to never end. And I heard a voice come out of me. "Don't stop. Don't ever stop, my darling!"

And so he didn't. As if I had put a spell on him, his body continued to pump on top of me. Again, and again.

Robert loved me—until his death. He collapsed after loving me, his life force sucked dry by my insatiable appetite.

"Robert, Robert!" I cried. I tried to save him. I tried to revive him by rubbing his arms and legs. But they were lifeless as I touched him, and he no longer felt like the eager young man I loved. He was growing stiff as I watched the nightfall, hoping that he would come around.

But he didn't. He never did. And I cried my heart out to the heavens.

Ah, my poor love. My first sweet love. I sat still on the hillside in the dark. The wind howled eerily, as if it were singing to the world about my wickedness. And I would have left, for I was scared and alone and devastated by the loss. Yet I felt I deserved this additional torment for his death, for I was certainly guilty of *something*. But nowhere had I been told that making love could kill.

I didn't know what I was doing—and I'd done it wrong, somehow. I wondered if I would be beheaded for his death if someone found out. And when I felt I had inflicted upon myself a lengthy enough emotional beating, I took the carriage back to town without Robert's body.

I left him on the grassy hills—so he would be discovered by a shepherd before the animals could find him. Though some may have known of his affection for me, no one knew we had gone off together. I was never suspected of being the last person his eyes smiled upon.

I mourned him. I sat on the cliff the next day, thinking I would dash myself on the rocks to join my love waiting for me on the other side. I pictured him smiling on me and assuring me that he was well. In my thoughts he forgave me as he led me through heaven's gates and into the peaceful eternity we would share.

But I was young. And I decided I was not ready to give away my life. Perhaps Robert whispered in my ear to go on.

I didn't have the courage to open death's door for myself, and I tormented myself over this shortcoming. For surely if the love were true, then like Juliet I would jump to join my Romeo. Alas, I could not.

I spoke to no one for a week. I cried myself to sleep each night—for my loss, and for my wanting. But even as I lay sobbing, I felt my desire building. I had no place to release it—and it was growing, like some insatiable beast within me.

The next time I went to town, I met Collin. Although I firmly suggested we not pursue our relationship, he didn't listen. We found ourselves upon some blankets, and my desire mounted. And again I continued loving in the only way I knew—until it happened. Collin expired also, in the early moments of our intimacy, with a frightful gasp that terrorized me so much I galloped away from our scene of passion without taking a moment to retrieve my buggy's blankets or ponder the gravity of Collin's loss of life.

Oh, holy heaven, help me. For loving and lying down became a habit I could not break. Each young suitor would fail to listen when I discouraged him. He would be perpetually aroused whenever he was near me. We would become locked together, as we loved. He would try to pleasure me, as good lovers do, and would continue until his death.

They had their smiles, all of them. They courted with jewelry, exotic gifts, horses, and other property. They ordered valuables for me, or collected beautiful fabrics from their travels to please me. So my dowry has grown. But it was never their moneys that I wanted. I sought only the satisfaction of my physical needs met, my desire rewarded.

And so I will flee for my safety. I will ride to the west tonight, perhaps to Wales to hide. When the bobbies come, someone can tell them I have gone to Sussex, or perhaps fled to France. Where, surely, they will believe it best to have me wounding the French instead of the English.

"Please hand me the low-cut black dress, Marie—I'm certain I'll need it. Thank you, Marie. And I do have one last favor . . .

"Could you take care of Denton's removal? You are my very dearest friend."

CHAPTER 2

The Plan

W HEN I TURNED BACK TO SEE MARIE STANDING OVER
Denton's body, I had a feeling I didn't expect—a sudden attack of
such distress and sorrow that my knees almost buckled from their
burden. I realized that leaving the small woman with such a task
was unfair. The body did need to be hidden and, after all, I did
need to have the task done well.

I'm small, weighing under eight stone, but Marie wasn't
much bigger than I, and I knew I would have to help her before I
ran for my own safety. Come morning, Denton's servants would
wonder where their master was. An inspector would be certain to
query me, since we had been seen together last at the Queen's Ball
by every eye worth anything in London. And no one could forget
my gown, as I was the only one dressed in red.

"Dear sweet Marie. I can't leave you so troubled."

"It's all right, Miss Nicollette."

"No, I must help with the situation. But I don't know where
to dispose of such a thing. Do you, Marie?"

"Well, perhaps you could make it look like an accident."

"Oh, Marie! You're brilliant. How do we do that?"

"What if it looked as if he were thrown from his horse, or a buggy ran over him?"

"I rather like the idea of the buggy. His carriage is just outside." I paused, working out the details. "What if we make sure he has a broken neck and leave him on the London trail that leads to his estate? The trauma would be attributed to his accident, and no one would wonder about it."

"Of course," Marie said. "I'll break his neck, miss."

Marie was a small, strong servant, and she squatted without flinching near the body—until she was about to touch the cooling corpse. She then crossed herself three times and gripped Denton's chin to twist his head toward her. As she did, Denton's eyes stared right into hers. Marie held her gaze upon him. I could tell she was thinking too much about what she was doing and at risk of losing her concentration.

She let out a cry and fell back on the floor. "Oh, my. I'm sorry, miss."

"It's all right, Marie. I'll help you."

Here I was, still wearing my red-velvet brocade dress with my bare shoulders and inviting cleavage, squatting next to the corpse.

"Come, Marie, we'll accomplish this together."

Marie positioned herself so that she was on the body's left side, and I was on the right. I pulled Denton's darling face toward me so he was looking into my eyes. And as I put my left hand under his head to turn it, the action lowered his chin so it looked as though he were taking a last look down my neckline.

After leaving the ball, Denton had instructed his driver to deliver us to my estate. In the back of the buggy, he couldn't take his hands off me. He wanted to touch everything. The silk fringe on my dress, its velvet, the ruffles under my skirt, everything feminine enraptured him, as if he were hypnotized. The first time he brushed against my breasts he pretended it was an accident. I could easily have stopped him, but I didn't.

And when he was able to get by with this sly gesture, he became bolder. For each time he reached to fondle my bosom, he was encouraged by my throaty appreciation of his forward touch.

He looked gallant in his formal black suit with matching gentleman's hat, golden-tipped cane, and white gloves, and at the ball he had paraded me as if I were royalty. I had to sustain the jealous glances of several ladies who no doubt yearned for Denton's affection. And who had no idea why he would prefer to have a Frenchwoman on his arm when he could have had an Englishwoman.

I invited him in for a glass of brandy, which he accepted with a knowing smile of anticipation that what was to happen with us had nothing to do with drinking. Though it may have slightly accelerated our loving pitch, cognac did not steer the course we had now set for ourselves.

I thought about not taking him to my boudoir. I really did. I knew I should kiss him good night and send him on his way. But I couldn't. Not after the buggy teasing. For he had spent the hour's ride fondling me, and I was now so aroused that I could have drowned in my want of this man.

We entered my parlor room. I stood with him before my magnificent oil painting of a large Paris night scene by an artist named Caprioli. The painting is impressionistic and bold, with dramatic blues and reds, done in a style that ignites the evening light and praises the excitement of Paris. It has a large two-by-three-meter frame tipped with twenty-four-carat gold, and it takes most viewers' breath away. No matter how often I look upon Caprioli's masterpiece, it takes away mine and reminds me of my thrilling Paris nights.

When I offered Denton a drink, he set it down after just one sip.

"Extraordinary."

"I think so too." Then I saw that his intense look was directed at me. "Do you mean the painting, Denton?"

"That, too. But I meant the woman, Nicollette. *Extraordinary.* Quite extraordinary."

Then he walked to me—and kissed me. He pushed me against the fireplace hearth, his hardness pressing against me. I felt him there. Aroused and ready and wanting me.

"You really are a bit naughty, aren't you?" he said.

I looked innocently at him and smiled with my eyes. And then he lifted me and carried me up the stairs as I pointed to the correct room.

"You're very strong, Denton," I said as he put me down in the candlelit bedroom. He liked my comment, for I saw his chest expand proudly. And he kissed me. *Excellently*—he kissed me.

"I would love to see your dress hanging on that mannequin." He pointed to the dress form that usually wore my next day's attire.

"Then help me out of it, Denton. I must have help with all the buttons."

He turned me around and looked at the twenty-five small pearl buttons that ran in a line down my back.

"Yes, my darling, gladly."

It was a joyous task for him, I could tell. "Someday there will be a faster way for men to undo their ladies' dresses," he said, "and if someone doesn't hurry and invent it, then I will."

Now he had my dress open in the back. But he still had ten matching pearl buttons on the inside of each wrist, and he continued gleefully with his job. When he was done, he helped me slip the dress off and took a step back to feast his eyes on my womanly charms. I liked his not rushing the moment we shared. We looked deeply at each other, spellbound by our attraction and enjoying the romance of my boudoir.

"Nicollette, you take my breath away, more than the greatest work of art at the Musée du Louvre. Seeing you there in the candlelight, I don't believe there's a man alive who could look on you and think of anything but love."

I smiled at my handsome suitor, utterly open to our fiery anticipation and desire. Then I was flooded with the dread that I should disclose my fatal secret to my unsuspecting lover. I was about to tell him when he interrupted my thoughts by lightly flicking my corset's ruffle with his fingers.

"I like casting my eyes on your feminine ruffles—I've never had a woman allow me to do such a thing. Perhaps they fear their mystery will disappear, but they're wrong. A man only wants a deeper drink when he's near such lovely waters."

He reached out higher to run his fingers softly along the fine lace on the bust of my corset. "I never imagined that a Victorian lady could be so free."

I lit another candle even closer to me, to shed more light for him. *There it was again—I must tell him.*

"You're a rare one, Nicollette." He reached for me, but I stepped back and turned away from him. I hoped that by not looking into his eyes, I would find the strength to do the right thing. I would save this charming man. But I believe that when I turned, he only became more aroused by the laced-up back of my corset and perhaps the roundness of my derriere.

"Denton, there's something I must tell you. When you know, you will want to leave and never see me again."

"There's nothing you could say to me, Nicollete, that would turn me away from you. Are you a married woman?"

"No."

"Are you with child?"

"No."

"In love with another man?"

"No."

"Then hush and let's only hear the sound of our love, unless you would like the promise of my intentions now. For I can ask you right now for your hand if you'll have me."

He reached for me strongly, as if he would cross time for me. And he craned his neck to try to see down my bustier. As if he wanted to see more clearly the breasts that teased him so.

The lover's neck that bent then to kiss my lips, nuzzled softly against my own neck, and craned so that he might see inside my bustier, was now the very neck I was trying to break.

I waited for Marie to see that I was comfortable holding the dead man's head in my hands, and for her to assume her position. I turned the head with her help, but nothing happened. *Ninety degrees.*

He was getting stiffer, and his neck was hard to turn, but we continued to press further—until the body's head faced the floor. *One hundred eighty degrees.*

Still, we knew it was not broken. We pushed and pushed. *Two hundred degrees.* The head was now turned past Denton's right shoulder, more than halfway around.

As I said, both of us were small and together totaled his weight. And the weight of his body was resistant to our actions, for ours was a difficult task. *Two hundred forty degrees.* Still we struggled with our brutal effort, not having anticipated its difficulty.

Marie was pushing with all her might, as was I, yet for some reason Denton's neck still didn't break. *Two hundred seventy degrees,* and a little more. And then we heard the *snap* we waited for. Ah! *Two hundred seventy-five degrees!*

"Oh! Marie, it took more than a three-quarters turn to break his neck."

"Mother Mary of Jesus."

We sat for a few minutes, worn out from the wretched ordeal.

I did not want to involve another, but we needed assistance.

"Will Wilbur help us?" I asked.

"I'm certain he will, miss. I'll wake and fetch him."

Marie was gone several minutes to rouse Wilbur, the strongest man at the manor, which gave me time to contemplate the state of my life. I didn't like what I saw, and I bowed my head in shame. But then I realized I was doing what I had to do—to protect my life.

It was an accident, for God's sake, I couldn't be held accountable. It wouldn't be fair. Not after doing all I'd done to deflect Denton's intentions. I must have refused him ten times before allowing him to call on me. A woman can't be held responsible after that, can she? *I think not.*

As I awaited my servant friend's return, I stood and looked in a mirror. I love to smile and laugh, but I saw worry. I'm blessed with a soft, even complexion, but I looked pale. My small nose had a smudge of dirt across it from groveling on the floor with the corpse.

My eyes are brown with hints of amber and green that catch light and flicker like a candle flame, or so I've been told. But I couldn't see any shine as I looked at myself in the mirror. I could only flash back to the dead stare in Denton's eyes.

I wear my hair many ways, but always neat. Now long brown strands had fallen down to my waist in disarray. Goodness—I'd need to repair it before going out, for no lady would be seen in such a state, even after three in the morning. And my uncoiffed look would surely cast suspicion on me if I were seen in my current state. So I primped my hair in the mirror as I waited for Wilbur and Marie, the whole while fearful that my face might reflect the horror of Denton's death.

Then I turned with compassion to my resting friend. I knelt close to his violated form, turned his head back to its resting place, smoothed his lapels, and whispered, "Forgive me," softly in his ear.

But he lay there motionless, silent, and unable to release me from my guilt. Every cell in my body shuddered from the aftershock of Denton's death. And I wept over the loss of yet another lover.

Marie and I sat next to the dead man. When Wilbur approached us, I could tell by his expression that if he'd had his choice, he would still be sleeping. But these were not his choices. If he wanted to keep his job and make a good penny, he would have to sell a bit of himself this evening.

"Good evening, Wilbur, so kind of you to awaken for us."

"Yes, miss."

"Wilbur, good sir, we have a bit of a problem. Can you assist us?" It somehow helped to include Marie, as if I were not the sole cause of the situation.

"Miss, I think I understand the difficulty."

"I'll make it worth your while, Wilbur."

I reached under my red dress and showed him my long-stockinged leg. I did not put my skirt down immediately but instead held it up as I reached for a small pouch secured in the top of one stocking. I pulled out its basted string and tossed the pouch to him. When my skirt was down, Wilbur still stared at the area he'd seen and paid no mind to the money's bag.

"It's full of gold coins, Wilbur. I ask for your help and your silence. The money is not yours unless I have both promises."

Wilbur's eyes widened as he looked in the pouch. "Yes, miss, I'm at your bidding."

"This is what you're to do." I explained to him about the staged death scene and told him we'd need his help to carry the body and lift it out of the coach. I also needed him to drive the buggy and leave it behind as I rode off with the other.

Then he asked a question I hadn't thought to answer. "Where's his driver?"

Marie ran to check on his whereabouts and returned to inform us that he'd fallen asleep in the stable waiting for his master to return.

I reached in the liquor cabinet for one of my best bottles of whiskey and handed it to Marie.

"Marie, please go entertain our visitor. And see that he has so much liquor that he awakens numb to his evening."

"Yes, miss."

"Marie, I don't know what will happen. Would you please secure the painting for me as we planned?"

"I will, miss."

"Hide it well."

"When will you be back?"

"I don't know."

"What about the manor?"

"Contact Mr. Ferguson, the estate manager. He'll look after it in my absence, as he does my other properties."

She turned to leave, but I touched her arm gently.

"Marie, if I were somewhere safe, I could send for you. Would you like that? I trust you so."

"Very much, miss. I would come without hesitation."

"Thank you, Marie, for I'll miss you." Our eyes spoke to each other, not as mistress and servant but as woman friends who wished each other well. I saw the compassion in her eyes for me—and thought that perhaps only a sensitive Italian like Marie could understand me at all.

Then she took the bottle and scurried down the long hall to the stable. I knew in my heart that she would accomplish her tasks, and thus had no worry of Denton's driver.

Wilbur was a strong, stocky man who, with only slight assistance, was able to get under Denton and carry him to the carriage. As I watched my handsome lover flung over Wilbur's back, my heart was pained, my stomach wrenched, my soul quivering. I wanted to cry out in my suffering.

I'll never forget walking through my manor, following Denton's swinging head as Wilbur carried him down the long hall toward the mock tragedy that awaited his corpse. Denton's neck wobbled loosely, like a doll's head about to fall off. And I couldn't take my eyes off his face. His face smiled while his eyes looked upon me.

Then I swear his face became animated. I saw it. I swear I did. His head lifted to me with a struggle, as if the movement of his dangling neck were an earthly task that was harder to maneuver. And the fact that his blood was still, his body had stopped, and he was now a dead man unable to move by all laws of nature and God was not a factor when he had words left unspoken to me.

A dead man with a neck injured from my own doing—I feared what he would say to me. What thoughts must he have to offer, if he could speak? My lover was off to his grave when he had done nothing but tender me his love. What accusation might he have for his murderess?

Denton gasped, at first, as if the wind he was trying to force through his larynx was not there. He twisted his neck in adjustment to say his words to me. I stepped back in fear and raised both my arms in defense of the attack I knew must be aimed my way. And then I heard him say, *"Nicollette, you take my breath away."*

It was a twisted guttural sound wheezed through his broken neck. And the sound forced a cold shudder through my spine. It was a wonder I could still stand. Yet I continued my walk behind Denton's remains. I imagined myself a soldier of sorts, wearing invisible armor that would protect me from any harm or bullets fired at me. I was strong. I wore a war bonnet, and countries depended on my strength.

Once Denton's body was secured, Wilbur hurried back to the house to gather several of my packed bags and the basket of food, wine, and grapes Marie had prepared for me. When I told him I had chosen Glastonbury as my destination, he jotted down a quick map for my travels and swore he would keep my plans secret. He drove the carriage with Denton's broken body, and I followed in my packed buggy.

About two miles away from my manor, Wilbur stopped at a roundabout. I held the buggy still while he removed Denton from the carriage and laid my lover in the road.

"Like this, Mademoiselle Caron?" Wilbur nodded toward Denton's still figure, lying obvious to the next passerby.

"Wilbur, I think you should drive over him with the carriage. As if the horses were confused and ran over him."

Wilbur looked at me, aghast. "Yes, m-m-miss," he said.

He drove the carriage up to Denton's body and stopped. I believe I watched him gather his nerve in that pause. I fancied that even the horses sensed the evil deed and thought it best not to be a part of this labor. But the harnessed beasts did not have the opportunity to move of their choice. Wilbur slapped his whip and drove the carriage over my once lively lover.

Its wheels bent poor Denton's body so that his arms and legs flew up, almost as though he were trying to walk away from it all.

I heard the sound of the hooves pounding his flesh. The sound repeated again and again in the stillness of the early-morning darkness.

Wilbur decided not to follow the road but walked through the meadows as the raven flies, so as not to leave tracks on the road leading to my manor.

Denton's carriage was in place. My deceased lover lay in the road, displaying to the next one down the path his broken neck and misfortune.

I hoped to reach Glastonbury by noon or possibly midmorning. When I snapped the reins to move my horses, Denton's horses startled and pulled the driverless carriage down the path toward his stable.

I could neither stop nor tether them, or it would not look like an accident. As I watched the carriage grow smaller, I prayed that this deed would not be found out.

For I knew that if the truth were ever known of my night, a court would not tarry with my case—an unforgiving rope would close about my neck. I reached up to touch the pearl-and-ruby necklace at my throat. Reassured that the necklace—and my neck—were still there, I urged the horses to go faster.

CHAPTER 3

Walter's Pub

ENGLAND'S TOP CRIME INSPECTOR, JACKSON LANG, STOOD at the bar buying a round for his whist table. He gathered his change and stacked some shillings for the bartender's tip.

From the back he was the fittest man in the room. He had broad shoulders, strong arms, and a well-tailored suit to show off his silhouette. From the front he was startlingly handsome, with dark brown hair, keen green eyes, and a brightness to his whole face.

"Congratulations on your capture, sir."

"Thank you, Peter."

Walter's, named after Sir Walter Raleigh, was a popular London pub with an upper-class clientele. Carved mahogany moldings of extraordinary quality were polished to perfection. Framed dueling pistols and swords and antique breastplates decorated the walls. Full suits of knights' armor guarded each door.

In the entry was a piece of metal nailed to the carpet that appeared to be a puddle. It was a subtle thing men stepped over without notice. But when a woman entered, the doorman would ring a bell and lay down his cape for her to step on. He would bow low and tip his hat. "Walter's welcomes _____." And then he would give the woman's full name.

Female guests felt amused and honored. Male patrons in the bar were called to attention to notice a new woman in their midst when they heard the tinkle of the bell. So the prank satisfied both genders, and Londoners flocked to enjoy the friendly ambiance.

An attractive woman brushed against Lang's arm at the bar. "Excuse me."

Lang tipped his hat to her and smiled. "That's quite all right."

"I'm Daphne Dabber of Seven Devonshire Terrace," she said.

"Jackson Lang of Scotland Yard. It's a pleasure to meet you, Miss Dabber."

"I heard all about what happened to you today—that you were involved in a gunfight with a lunatic and saved five hostages' lives. How exciting. You're so *brave.*"

"Thank you."

"Your wife must be so glad to have you alive and well tonight."

"Actually, I'm not married."

"Well, your *fiancée,* then. She must be so relieved you weren't hurt."

"I'm not promised."

"Oh, my," she said.

Lang noticed she was pretty, with violet eyes and a tiny heart-shaped beauty mark on her cheek. He also noticed that talking to him seemed to make her quite tense. She wrenched a hankie in her gloved hands and continued.

"Did I mention that I live at Seven Devonshire Terrace? Near Hyde Park?"

"Yes, you did. I know that's not far from here."

"No, it's not far, perhaps you'll stop by for tea sometime? I mean, if you were to find yourself in my neighborhood. It's just that . . . we have lunatics in our neighborhood, and we may need you to, ah, keep them in check."

"Miss Dabber, I appreciate your cordial invitation."

"Well, I wasn't asking for just myself. I know my father would like to meet you. He owns a hotel and told me about your rescue today."

"I'd be most happy to meet your father, Miss Dabber, and to accept your invitation, but we've been so busy lately that I can't commit to a visit. I'm on call at all hours, which creates a difficult schedule for a woman to accept."

"I'm very understanding," she said.

"I'd wager you are."

Edward Wilcox approached and tapped Lang on the shoulder. "Jackson, do you need help with the drinks?"

"Edward Wilcox, may I introduce you to Miss Daphne Dabber? Miss Dabber, Edward is one of the CID's new detective recruits."

"My pleasure to meet you, Miss Dabber."

"Pleasure to meet you, Mr. Wilcox."

"It's difficult to play whist with three, Jackson," Wilcox said. "Not only do we depend on you as a fourth, but more importantly—you have our drinks."

Lang sighed. "I'd best get back to my table, Miss Dabber. Good evening."

"It was very nice to meet you, Mr. Wilcox and Inspector Lang. Seven Devonshire Terrace—remember, tea *anytime.*"

Lang tipped his hat and gathered the drinks.

"We send you on a simple errand, and you use it to hustle an invitation to tea?" Wilcox said. "Meantime, you've left your friends high and dry."

"Emphasis on the *high,*" Lang said.

"Sir Bart complained you were gone so long there's dust in his empty glass."

"Well, he's mostly made of dust, so that's fitting," Lang joked, as they walked back to join the two men at their table.

Lang handed around the glasses, took a sip of his tea, and the game resumed. To Lang's right were his two young recruits, Ulysses Peavey and Edward Wilcox. Hired to sergeant rank, the new detectives followed Lang around as part of their training. To Lang's left was Sir Bart Marshall, chief of the Metropolitan Police.

"Don't you feel *dinky* drinking tea when you're in the middle of a celebration?" Sir Bart asked.

"I like to think I can celebrate without spirits, Bart."

"Well, we concede that you have the magic touch at solving criminal cases by day," Sir Bart said.

"But we're exhausted at the taxing stress of being the clever ones after hours," Wilcox said.

"Exactly," Peavey said.

"What assures you of your cleverness in the evenings?" Lang asked.

"Because you're not drinking, and you just bought our last two rounds."

"Touché."

Tinkle. Tinkle. The sound of the entrance bell rang, announcing the arrival of a new female.

"Walter's welcomes Miss Martha Whiteley," the doorman called out.

"Who's she?" Peavey asked the men behind their cards.

"A young gold digger looking for a wealthy husband," Wilcox said. "Save your effort, Ulysses, unless your wallet is larger than you've led us to believe."

• • •

Daphne returned to her table to join John, her older brother. Her father, Dominic Dabber, arrived and took a seat with his children.

"Hello, Father. I met Jackson Lang."

"Were you introduced?"

"You don't think I'd just go up to him and start speaking, do you, Father?"

"Well, I certainly hope not. Your mother and I have schooled you on your proper etiquette."

"He's very attractive, Father."

"That isn't why I thought him an interesting suitor, my dear."

"He's the one right over there"—Daphne pointed inconspicuously to Lang's table—"with the dark mustache."

"All the CID are clean-shaven with well-trimmed mustaches. Which one is he?"

"The one with the green eyes, Father."

"I can't see the man's eye color from here. Wait, I can. They're quite green, aren't they?"

"He's tall, Father."

"So are all the men with the Metropolitan Police. It said in the paper that the chief believes the height and size of the men matters, so they can effectively intimidate and overpower the criminals."

"Father, I think Jackson Lang went to Oxford or somewhere. His English is quite proper."

"Yes, he did. But he wasn't a privileged child, he worked hard to get where he is. He's a self-made man. Now, you're just beginning your courting period, Daphne. Remember, you only need one good prospect. Don't go hog-wild."

"I won't, Father."

"Your brother and I will look out for you. The men must have the best intentions when they call. You're a beautiful girl, Daphne, and you must remember this is the most important decision in your life. So you would be wise to have your mother and me involved in the matter."

"Yes, Father. But we're in modern times, and women do get to select whom they marry."

"Well, yes, within reason. I won't let you marry the neighbor boy."

"Father, how did the man seated next to Jackson lose his arm?"

"That's the Scotland Yard chief, Sir Bart Marshall. He's a close friend of Lang's and appointed Lang to the number two position. Lang's title is senior detective inspector of the detective force. That means he's next in line to be the chief. The chief has responsibility for eight hundred men and one woman, a network of constables, police, detectives, and clandestine groups whose job it is to stop felons and terrorists."

"But what happened to Sir Bart Marshall's arm?"

"I'm afraid I read that it decomposed long ago in India, where a tiger mauled him, when he was in the military. He's highly decorated and was knighted after he saved Queen Victoria from an assassination attempt. He has excellent political connections and has become a close friend of the queen's."

"Do you think Jackson Lang is looking this way, Father?

"Your brother brought the newspaper article," Dabber said. "Go ahead and read it to her, John."

John opened the paper and read:

> Jackson Lang is part of the new breed of enforcers who are educated and intelligent. He has an analytical brilliancy that has earned him respect. Even before he spoke to me, this reporter sensed his astute abilities.

"I like his dark mustache," Daphne said as John read on:

> He's polished, well-bred, and so well
> trained by barristers that he could have
> excelled in the legal profession. Instead,
> Lang told this reporter, "I'd rather work
> for smaller pay, just to intrigue my mind
> with the criminal puzzles set before me."
> He employs deductive reasoning and
> creative logic in each criminal arrest he
> makes.
>
> And his persistence and perseverance
> in tracking criminals have won him
> awards. He does not give up once he be-
> gins a case. He *always* gets his criminal.

"He has a captivating smile, doesn't he?" Daphne said, dreamily.

"His hair is quite thick." Dabber touched his own thinning hair as he studied Lang. "But it's orderly. His clothing looks to be the best. I wonder which haberdasher he frequents."

"His complexion has such a healthy glow to it, as if he exerts himself physically, doesn't it, Father? I mean, he doesn't have the pale complexion of most Londoners."

"I'm interested in him for you because he would elevate your status, Daphne. He's said to be a candidate for knighthood. This would reflect well on us—on *you.* "

"Father, look at how all the women in the pub turn their heads toward him."

"Well, he has a fine reputation. No doubt they know of it."

It was true. When women scanned the room, their eyes rested on Jackson Lang. And they did this frequently, hoping to catch his green eyes, whenever their escorts looked away or went for drinks.

Although Lang liked the women's attention, his primary focus was on his profession and the tasks of his day. Even when he ate a meal or played cards or enjoyed a social evening such as this one, he thought about tomorrow's puzzle.

"Uh-oh, I suspect Peavey's going to perform," Wilcox said.

Peavey wobbled to his feet and hovered over Wilcox with both hands near his face. "Wilcox, what's this? This looks like a halfpenny honker you have here." He grabbed Wilcox's nose, and a stream of halfpennies issued forth as Peavey caught them with his other hand.

Sir Bart cackled. "That's quite good."

"They were hired for their comedy antics and had no idea they'd be solving homicides," Lang said.

Peavey stared at Sir Bart's nose as if studying a rare fossil in an archeological dig.

"What are you looking at?"

"The amazing lines of your nose, sir."

"What's different about it?"

"This looks like the grand shilling nose. Quite rare, sir." He reached over and squeezed Sir Bart's nose, from which a stream of shillings poured—twice as fast and twice as long as Wilcox's coins.

Lang picked up a couple of coins that fell to the floor. He studied them carefully until he had all their attention.

"I'm sorry, these coins appear to be counterfeit. Sirs, I regret to inform you that I'll have to place your noses under arrest for the counterfeiting of the queen's gold."

They all laughed. "I'm not sure I've seen you loosen your cravat ever," Sir Bart said. "Come on, have one drink, Jackson."

"No thanks, I like the full use of my faculties at all times."

"But Jackson, today you single-handedly took a loaded rifle away from a deranged lunatic. You saved the five hostages from certain death. The night belongs to you—one toddy won't hurt you."

"Sir Bart, I swore off the grog long ago. Perhaps one day other people will see the folly in alcohol."

The men laughed. "Not likely."

Sir Bart still had a smile on his face. "Jackson, you have one eye on knighthood; don't get it confused with sainthood."

Lang had grown tired of defending his beverage choice. Nor did he think it necessary to celebrate the solution of a murder case. The discovery of clues, the chase, and the criminal's arrest were the climax for him. The elevated pitch during the trial and the perpetrator's dance at the end of a rope were not—even though he was in the front row at all the hangings.

A prominent model for England's criminal justice system, he welcomed the recognition and respect from Scotland Yard, the public, and, most importantly, Queen Victoria. His upstanding reputation was *paramount* to him.

"When is he coming to tea?" Dabber asked.

"Well, he didn't actually agree," Daphne said.

"He declined tea?"

"I did invite him, but he said he may not have time, so we'll have to see, Father."

"That's rather impolite."

"Maybe he didn't think I was pretty enough."

"What? I'll just go see about his intentions."

"But, Father—"

Dabber was off like an angry bull. He approached Lang. "Excuse me, sir. I'm Daphne Dabber's father, Dominic Dabber."

Lang stood and extended his hand. "Very nice to meet you, Mr. Dabber."

"I understand you told my daughter that you had no time for tea with her. She just began courting, and I'd like to ask your intentions in regard to her."

"Mr. Dabber, I'm not in a position to court."

Dabber gritted his teeth to hold back his anger.

"My profession is most demanding of me right now, and it simply wouldn't be fair to your daughter."

Dabber's arm moved back.

"So quite candidly, I don't foresee time for a visit. But should my current schedule change—"

"You rogue!" Dabber shouted, then blindsided Lang with a jab across the left side of his face.

Lang slightly blocked the punch but took part of the blow.

"Sir, perhaps it's just as well," he said, rubbing his sore cheek. "I'm not looking for difficult in-laws."

"You would be lucky to have us," Dabber said. With that, he strutted out the door, John and Daphne trailing behind him.

"Father, I don't think Daphne was properly introduced to him," John said. "She just went up and did it herself."

"No wonder this didn't go well, Daphne. Don't you remember your etiquette?"

"Ulysses, do you think Lang will ruin our reputations?" Wilcox said. "You know people will think we're cads just because we're in his vicinity."

"I don't know, but I think I'll take the young lady and her father off my list," Peavey said.

"Why do these things happen to me?" Lang asked.

"It's hereditary, Jackson. You have a handsome-devil ancestor somewhere in your family tree."

Jackson picked up his teacup and drained it. "Peavey and Wilcox, thank you for your help today. I couldn't have done it without knowing you had me covered."

"Jackson, did you think our guns were loaded?" Wilcox said. "I never load mine—do you, Peavey?"

"Oh, no," Peavey said. "I find firearms quite threatening. Someone could get hurt."

Sir Bart chuckled at the recruits' antics. He had hired them after strenuous interrogations and testing. And he knew that both were expert shots.

"In any case, then, I'm grateful I didn't need you," Lang said. "Gentlemen, I'd best check on Pegasus. He needs a good brushing. Will you be all right?"

"Oh, yes, once you and Sir Bart leave, then Peavey will cry about not having a nice girl in his life. I'll tell him about the compromising women I met while in the French Foreign Legion, which perks him up some. Then I walk him around the square to sober him up, tie him to a horse, and get him back to his room."

"Is this true?" Sir Bart asked.

"We have witnessed Peavey's first drinks tonight, sir. He never drinks. He only had three tonight."

"Thanks, again," Lang said.

Sir Bart got to his feet. "I take great pride in your success today."

"I appreciate that, sir. See you in the morning." Lang tipped his hat and promptly left the pub.

Sir Bart said, "He's the best—the absolute best. But brushing his horse at midnight is just *not normal.*"

CHAPTER 4

Silence Is Golden

"We're about two miles east of Glastonbury now and approaching the most spectacular manor in the area." The Staffords were in their buggy, showing off the English countryside to their cousins visiting from Belgium.

"It's owned by Blake Williams, Lord Baston, who is known in several counties for his extraordinary gardens. The manor boasts a full staff of gardeners who tend the lush flower gardens you see here."

"Oh, my—look!" one of the visitors said.

"This man lives better than most kings. And to our English perception, Lord Baston has secured a habitat just this side of heaven. Don't you agree?"

"It's surely a remarkable one. And Herbert, you're a fine tour guide."

"Well, I think a lot of Lord Baston. He's quite a great man. And we all appreciate the spectacular improvements he's made on our countryside."

"I don't think I've ever seen so many lilac bushes."

"Yes, his perimeter of the estate is lined by rows of lilacs. And he has roses and bulb flowers in striking arrangements near the manor."

"Oh my goodness, look at the fountains."

"Quite extravagant, aren't they? And so artistically placed, with such dramatic effect. He also has fish pools with fish from as far away as Asia."

The buggy continued around the property onto the long drive that meandered to the estate. Down the drive they could see brilliant greenery carved into animal sculptures.

"There's a rabbit!"

"I see a lion!"

"There are many others. They fascinate Lord Baston's visitors, tourists, and travelers. And there's more, as you'll see . . ."

Lord Baston glanced at the buggy approaching the manor house.

"It looks like the Staffords and some friends. Motion them up if they'd like to visit and have Chi show them the grounds and give them some large bouquets to take with them."

"I'll take care of it at once, my lord," Bertrum said.

"I'll greet them, then I'm ready to go."

A few minutes later, he extended his hand to help the women step out of the buggy.

"Very nice to see you again, Mr. and Mrs. Stafford. Are these friends of yours?"

"Yes, this is Herbert's cousin from Brussels. Mr. and Mrs. Archibald Stafford."

"This is my very fine gardener, Chi. He'll show you around the grounds and make sure you have your favorite flower bouquets to take home with you."

"How very generous of you, Lord Baston."

"Herbert, may I speak privately with you for a moment?"

"Certainly." The men stepped aside, Lord Baston towering over his guest.

"Is your business thriving?"

"I had a special order for a table and four chairs I carved. It's perfect for whist or a board game. Anyway, the people haven't paid me a shilling for it yet, and it's been nine months, so I'm holding it in wait of payment."

"How much are you asking for the set?"

"Twenty-five pounds."

"Quite ornate?"

"Yes. It took me two years to complete it."

"Would it go well in one of my rooms?"

"I'd think it would look well in your study, my lord, or in the alcove near the study."

"I'll take it—bring it by at your convenience. Next time, make sure on your special orders that you get at least half of the money down."

"You mean before the people get anything from me, sir? That doesn't seem fair."

"It's more than fair. You should be paid for the commitment of your time."

"I don't know if anyone would do that."

"They will if they want your craftsmanship, Herbert. I'm very pleased with your other work."

"Thank you, sir," Stafford said, his voice trembling a little.

"The world does not appreciate artisans as it should, Herbert. So you must teach people how to treat you."

"Thank you, sir. You have no idea how much this means to me."

"Bertrum, would you call Clive for me?"

Clive Satler, manager of the house and servants, arrived in a moment.

"Clive, kindly pay Mr. Stafford thirty pounds."

"Yes, my lord."

"Twenty-five, my lord," Stafford said.

"I think you're mistaken, Herbert. We agreed on thirty pounds. I'm sure of it."

"Thank you, my lord."

"I regret that I have a prior commitment in London and must leave. But you should be well hosted without me."

"We understand, my lord. Thank you for your kindness."

Archibald Stafford's wife crooked her head to peer inside the manor.

"Would you like to see my home, Mrs. Stafford?"

"Oh, could I?"

"Of course. Chi, it will be teatime soon, but tell Clive to give all the Staffords an early dinner with my best wine."

"Yes, my lord."

"Good day, Lord Baston."

"Good day. Thank you for the visit. Bertrum?"

Lord Baston's trusted servant opened the carriage door and held it for him to enter.

"Very well, my lord. Shall we go southeast again today?"

"Certainly."

Bertrum took his place behind the four tethered black horses and slapped the reins. The sound of the crack stirred the horses quickly down the road, away from Lord Baston's estate with its rainbow flower gardens and toward his destination—a city pub.

The Mare's Head Pub was nearly a four-hour buggy ride for Lord Baston, but he enjoyed visiting the pub of ill repute in London's East End at least twice a week. It was located in Buck's Row, near the site of the first Jack the Ripper murder just three years earlier. And it was still not considered safe from the butcher's reign of terror, since the murderer was still unknown and at large. But Bertrum would take his master there in any kind of weather. For the nights when Lord Baston wanted to go—go he must.

He told Bertrum that it was for the home-brewed ale the pub featured, but Lord Baston hardly drank ale, preferring wine at all times of the day. And this Bertrum knew.

It was a motley group that gathered at the pub, mostly easy ladies of the house and poor folk. Lord Baston had to hang on to his wallet there, for thieving hands were so expert at picking a pocket that their touch was never felt in this part of town.

The Mare's Head's most distinguished patron stood six feet six inches tall, tall enough that his height—and striking demeanor—kept him safe. He often dressed in different clothes on these outings, not the formal attire befitting a lord. One could call it a disguise, since tonight he had glued an artificial beard to his face, wore spectacles for which he had no need, common clothes, and a wig. These props almost covered up his piercing good looks: a manly jawline and a straight nose, a strong brow with well-shaped eyebrows that framed sea-blue eyes. And when he spoke, or turned his direct eyes upon others, his voice or glance took ownership of them, holding them captive to his intentions.

To him it was a game. Some mental exercise like the board games Fox & Hounds, or Go. Only there was no game board, the bar folk became the marbles, and he the player. A harmless game that afforded a wealthy baron a chance to step outside his mansion into his own production starring himself as a new character, untethered from the inhibitions, stature, and grace of his position. Blake enjoyed being able to watch others react to him as a man rather than a lord.

Bertrum was a loyal servant, who considered himself fortunate to have two square meals a day, a comfortable straw bed, and fair pay for his dedication. He was treated well by his master.

Even allowed to see a doctor on two occasions that cost five pence. In exchange, Bertrum proved his dedication with silence and discretion. He never spoke of where they went on their outings or what might or might not have taken place. He had learned to keep quiet, for his thievery had once earned him time in Newgate Prison.

Lord Baston was never recognized when he was in the pub. Bertrum watched him and did not have answers for his master's strange behavior. He thought Lord Baston might be some sort of double personality, not unlike a man he had seen in prison who had talked in two voices. The strange behavior had so confused the prison masters that the man was taken to the Press Yard for the penalty of his nuisance. There the crazy soul was laid on the ground and his torso covered with rock—until he was crushed to death. That's where Bertrum learned that in England, madness doesn't get you anywhere.

Lord Baston was in good spirits tonight. As usual Bertrum purchased him a drink and then keep himself busy in the alley waiting until Lord Baston chose to leave—usually at daybreak.

"Here's your wine, my lord."

"Thank you, Bertrum."

"I'll be near, my lord."

Lord Baston nodded and looked around the room. If he squinted his eyes in the dim light, the women scattered around the room were *almost* pretty. The pub's fiddle music was loud and the crowd boisterous. The air smelled of pipe smoke and ale. Everyone was talking and laughing. Some of the men had whores on their laps, the women in deep negotiations as to their next business step. Sporadically, couples ascended the stairs to the rooms above.

A pretty young woman with red hair, luminescent green eyes, and ivory skin caught Lord Baston's eye. She had a few freckles scattered on her nose and wisps of hair that strayed from the arrangement of curly hair atop her head.

She had the look he sought, the essence that seemed to call to him. She looked *vulnerable*. And when he saw a vulnerable woman, he knew she would be putty in his hands. She looked alone and a little afraid as her eyes darted around the room, as if perhaps she thought she shouldn't be there. Or didn't want to be. She looked up at Lord Baston as he approached her.

"Good evening, my dear. You looked so lovely across the room—would you mind if I join you? I thought you might be in need of protection from some of the vagrants here."

She looked up at him and smiled.

He pulled out the chair next to her and tugged her chair close to his.

"Allow me to introduce myself. I'm Franklin Darnell. And what do I call you, other than lovely woman?"

While he spoke Carrie was studying his lips, as if weighing each word in her head. She reached into her fabric purse to retrieve a small notepad and a pencil, a gift from a patient priest who taught her basic grammar. She scribbled a few words on the paper and handed it to him.

The note read, "I'm Carrie McMurray. I'm a deaf-mute. I'm sorry. I cannot hear or speak to you. I can read lips."

Lord Baston was taken aback, but only for a moment. He looked at her and guessed her age to be only seventeen or eighteen.

"You're very beautiful, Carrie."

She fluttered her lashes at him.

"Where are you from?"

"Ireland," she wrote.

"Why are you here?"

"I want work," she wrote.

Lord Baston's eyes shone as though he had found the end of the rainbow.

"What is it you do?"

She shrugged.

"Are you alone?"

She nodded.

"Where do you stay?"

She pointed to two o'clock on his watch, to show that she stayed until closing. She shrugged and wrote, "streets." And Lord Baston nodded that he understood.

"Who knows where you are?"

She shook her head to indicate no one and wrote, "I ran away."

"Perhaps I can use your services." He smiled at her. "It's quite noisy in here—too difficult to talk out a business arrangement. I have a room upstairs, where we won't be disturbed."

Carrie looked deeply into his eyes. Lord Baston saw no trace of fear in hers and was boosted by her trust.

She wrote on the pad, "May I work for you, sir? You're the kindest man I've ever met."

"You don't find me fearsome?"

Carrie laughed and shook her head.

He smiled and took her hand. She picked up her full burgundy skirt as she walked up the steps, balancing on her high-button-top shoes and carrying her small fabric handbag. No doubt, patrons thought of them as just another couple who had successfully concluded negotiations.

Bertrum kept a close watch on the horses and carriage. Once in a while someone would pay mind to him or the finely made black carriage with gold lion insignias. But usually the alley was filled by scam artists and drunks with pickled memories, riffraff so far gone that any description of the carriage or himself would elude them the next day if not moments after sighting them.

Bertrum found a quiet place on a back step. He reached into his pocket for his knife and a reed, and began to whittle a new whistle. Carving a woman's nude body into the dried willow's shaft, he passed the time quietly in the night.

At sunrise, Bertrum noted that Lord Baston was taking longer than usual. Soon the streets would change and the work-ing-class folk employed on the docks would replace the passed-out drunks and thieves. The sailors would be spent. Even the whores would be in bed for the night, with the blokes who'd paid the highest for their services.

An hour of daylight passed. Still no master. The servant was getting nervous. He knew Lord Baston's habits. He had followed this path for more than five years. Never before had his master been so late to return from a sexual interlude.

Bertrum had started another whistle when he decided he should check on his master. He knew which room was rented since he had arranged for its use. He secured the horses well, then climbed the outside steps that led to the back door. He proceeded down the corridor to the room with the number 15 scratched into its wood. He stood outside the door a moment, listened, but heard no sound.

Perhaps something had happened to Lord Baston, for never did he sleep here. Then he heard a faint rustling inside and some-thing that sounded like an endearment. He knocked on the door anyway.

"Who knocks?"

"Bertrum, my—sir. It's so late, I thought I should check on you, sir."

"Don't think, Bertrum. Go wait with the horses."

"Very well, sir."

But Bertrum didn't go right away. He stood listening at the door, suddenly curious about his master's affairs.

"I see your feet, Bertrum. Go wait with the horses."

"Yes, sir. Sorry, sir."

This time Bertrum walked back to the horses and waited.

Inside the room Carrie hadn't slept. Blake had begun by explaining his fantasy to the young girl and agreeing on a price. She was cheap—she wanted money for one night's stay. She couldn't talk, so it was mostly a quiet interlude with Blake directing the activity.

They'd had sex in numerous positions around the room. Once while standing, once on the bed, in a chair; he'd even had Carrie on the dresser.

"Is there something wrong?" He caught her staring at his face when he awoke. She pointed to his beard, which had come off one side of his face.

"Ah, this . . . ," he said, pulling the beard off completely. "Carrie, I'm not Franklin Darnell. I do this as a little game for myself. Not to mock anyone. It's because I'm bored mostly. But I'd like to help you . . . if you will help me once more this morning." He ran a finger down the side of her neck. "Turn over," he whispered.

It was another hour before Lord Baston appeared before Bertrum at the carriage. He was not alone.

"Bertrum, this is Carrie McMurray, of Ireland. She will be a new servant at the manor."

Bertrum had known an Irish lass when he was a young man, and looking at the young girl he thought of her for the first time in years. He was startled by the resemblance—and by this young woman's beauty. He barely regained sufficient composure to tip his hat and bow.

"Lovely to meet you, miss. You surely will brighten up the place."

She smiled at the gangly driver as he assisted her into the carriage, and Lord Baston followed her. He looked exhausted, and disheveled from a hurried dress without the help of his valet.

Bertrum made a few adjustments to the horses' bridles and bits, then pulled himself up to the driver's seat and cracked his whip. The wheels of the buggy began rolling toward the manor in Glastonbury.

It occurred to Bertrum that this was the first time he'd ever seen a woman the next morning when Lord Baston had been with her the night before. In fact, once a woman had been with Lord Baston, she was often not seen or heard from again. Bertrum couldn't help thinking this woman must somehow be special, even though she looked much like all the others.

CHAPTER 5

On to Glastonbury

THE CRISP EARLY MORNING AIR SLAPPED MY FACE WITH its chill, leaving me no time for fatigue. I could only think, and feel, and drive my horses harder than the beasts deserved.

The tragedies I have experienced might have left me cold to my soul. But I'm not a heartless woman, nor one to carelessly leave dead lovers in my path. I'm sensitive. I mourn. I'm torn by each loss.

I cried almost all the way. I felt so alone in the darkness before the day's break, so pierced by regret. As I traveled I cried for the young men, and then for myself—as I'm the one who suffers the losses. Death is harder on those left behind. For the dead go on to a brighter place, I'm sure. Or I rather like to think they do, and that I will.

I sobbed for Collin. I sobbed for my first love, Robert. Oh, how I cried for Robert. I cried for all the others. I even cried for Allan, who seemed to go the quickest—and who, truth be told, didn't satisfy me at all. Which is why I went out immediately that night for another. I couldn't help myself. Honestly, I couldn't.

I don't know what I can possibly do to cage myself, though perhaps that is the only way. Were I to be caged, the bars might contain my passion. They might tether my free spirit so that my energies could be turned to painting, or writing, or some worthy art.

I have written poetry. I have painted meadows. And I sculpted with a friend once. I was not sure if I saw talent within my work, for these were my first attempts, but perhaps there is something else I could do other than tempt men. But then I seem to have been drawn on God's board for the role I play.

Perhaps I shouldn't dress the way I do. Showing that inch of cleavage in my bodice. For I have to admit that if I like a frock for its fabric but don't feel that the neckline is right, I'll have it altered to my taste—just so when I bow to my gentleman caller he will catch a glimpse of my feminine charms.

I have only an average bosom, but my corset is loose enough for me to breathe freely, thus my breasts jiggle slightly in any dress. They rise above my bustier and rouse men's eyes.

I'm not tall, so as they talk with me they can look down into my dress and see slightly more of my breasts than someone standing at eye level. I see them drink me in with every lingering glance. I don't blame them, for the bosom was made by God to tantalize. It is the way of the world, this dance between the genders.

Other women feign innocence and show no curiosity about the size of a man's wares that lie buttoned and restrained within his pants. But I do. I wonder about his look, his feel, and his personality.

Ah! Yes, they do have a personality. Men cannot pretend their love. They either respond to their lover's touch or they recoil.

And if a contemporary woman's lover responds, entertained by her touch, then she's sure to be pleased if she can learn to surrender to his attention rather than dread the ordeal.

Most women today believe their attitude has nothing to do with their marital happiness. But I know better. Other women believe that a sexual union is something they must suffer if they are to have their man's provisions. I don't. For I know of another suffering—that of too much desire.

Such were my thoughts as the day broke into sun while I rode on to Glastonbury for a new start. Hoping I wouldn't repeat my pattern of love and death but settle with a stalwart spirit who would dance easily with our attraction. Hoping that somewhere there might be a man strong enough to hold me still, and say, "There, there, Nicollette, I understand and love you despite it all."

Could there be a mate who would let me be the woman I am and protect me, even as I am? I wonder. Above all, I wish a man could love me heart and soul, yet somehow survive my passion.

Oh, sweet dreams of life, I reach for you as the new day reaches for the sun.

I was still several miles east of Glastonbury. I was exhausted, and the horses were lathered and hungry. I knew I'd have to find a stable for their care, so I stopped the first man I saw for his advice.

He was atop an apparatus such as I had never seen. It had a small wheel in front with two large wheels at least a meter in diameter in back. He sat almost as high up as I on my buggy, each of his feet resting on a small metal footpad that moved the wheels forward. As we neared one another, he stopped the odd vehicle and tipped his hat to me.

"Good morning to you, beautiful lady."

"Good morning, kind sir."

"Am I dreaming you? If so, you mustn't wake me."

"You flatter me—I must look a sight after my journey."

"I never flatter when it isn't due. You're very striking in your red frock."

"Thank you for your generous compliment."

"I'm Frederick Bothem, and whom do I have the pleasure of addressing?"

"I'm Nicollette Caron. It's a pleasure to meet you, sir." I stretched out my gloved hand and shook his like a lady, holding just three of his fingers. They seemed to fill my small hand. I could tell that Frederick was charmed by my offering a handshake when etiquette didn't require it.

"I've never seen a contraption such as this. What do you call it?"

"It's a tricycle," he said. "I find I get lovely legs from my rides, and require no hay throughout my day."

I laughed at his humor. "Lovely legs?"

"Yes, would you like to see? I'm quite proud of them. Excuse my boldness, Miss Caron. I'm well-known as the town clown."

"I can see why. Have you lived here long?"

"Born and lived every day of my life in beautiful Glastonbury."

So, I found it helpful to gather information before entering a new town. There was much I might learn from him about my destination.

"Forgive me if I'm too forward, Frederick, but I wonder if you would like to share a picnic with me? I have a basket with cheese, wine, and some lovely grapes."

"Well, Miss Nicollette, I'm a married man. Thirty happy years. But if you don't tell my missus on me, I see no harm."

"It will be our secret, Frederick."

"I know of a more secluded spot for our picnic, miss, but I paid ten pounds for my tricycle—so I'd best conceal it from the road." He hid the cumbersome machine behind some nearby trees, where it wouldn't be seen by travelers who might covet it. Once assured that his tricycle was protected, he stepped up onto my buggy and took the reins.

"Allow me." And I settled back, happy to have a gentleman in control of my destiny for the next several minutes.

He took the buggy about a quarter mile closer to town, then down a dusty lane that led to a bank on the side of a stream. A group of large old trees shaded and protected the creek.

"This is lovely, Frederick. How did you know of such a scenic spot?"

"Well, there's very little in these hills that I haven't known. And actually I courted my Mamie on these same grounds."

He helped spread out the blanket, then retrieved the basket from the back of my buggy. He uncorked the wine and poured a glass for each of us. I placed the cheese on a plate and decorated it with the grapes.

"What a delicacy," he said. "I haven't had grapes for years."

"I love them so." I noticed that Frederick was looking into my eyes—in a new way—and that he found it hard to break his glance.

"I'd help you in any way that I could, miss." His voice, which had been jolly and friendly, had changed. He was now more serious.

"I'll need a place where I can stay for a bit," I said. "And, of course, a stable."

"Well, there's a stable just as you come into town, on the west side of the street. And there's a lovely rooming house called Miriam's Cozy Inn adjacent to the stable. Miriam Bestell is a wonderful hostess, I'm sure you'll be quite comfortable there. I'll be happy to show you."

"Thank you. Can you tell me about the town?"

"Glastonbury won't offer you the social excitement of London, but it has a rich history mixed with mystical legends. It's the land of Avalon, King Arthur, abbeys, and retreats in Bath. Stonehenge and Avebury are nearby historical sights that draw a great number of visitors. It's surrounded by beautiful hillsides and offers several pubs, restaurants, and planned events all year long.

"We're not far from a beautiful coastline overlooking the bay, where you can embark on beautiful day trips to Wales—and, Miss Nicollette, you'll find great friends here. The people are marvelous. There's a riding club, and there are several available wealthy gentlemen who will love to hear of your arrival. I don't expect once we know you that we will let someone like you leave us."

My mind wandered a moment as he spoke. I drifted in and out with my thoughts of Denton's death, my flight, wondering how Marie was faring, yet I needed to keep the conversation flowing and cordial. So I blurted something out in the pause where he stopped.

"Tell me, who's the most dashing gentleman in town?" *Why did I ask that? I don't need another man—what's wrong with me?*

"Oh, that's easy. There's a nobleman here by the name of Lord Baston. He's quite a figure in our town, miss. You may find him of interest. The ladies do, although I understand that he's quite elusive. Most of the unmarried ladies have tried to interest him—without any 1 luck."

"None of them has impressed the gentleman?"

"Well, we heard there was one long ago—Jenny something, I think. But she moved away immediately after their brief courtship. And no one has heard from her since."

"What is this man's pleasure, and where would I meet such a fine fellow?"

"You'll find him at most of our events and parties, and he belongs to Glastonbury Foxhunt Club, which hosts excellent fox-hunts in season. But Lord Baston is not the only wonder that awaits you. Have you been to Bath?"

"I haven't had the pleasure."

"They have a most impressive abbey in Bath, with bells that will resonate throughout your soul when you hear them ring each day. And the mineral springs have an interesting history. It's there that the Romans rested after battle."

We spoke for several hours about Glastonbury and its people. He told me of meddlesome folks and those I should befriend if I wanted success in the town. He also related several incidents from the town's history and whispered gossip about a few of the townspeople. Within a short time I felt as though I'd ride into a town in which I had already lived.

Frederick was a handsome man, for an older gentleman. I guessed him to be not yet fifty. His eyes were quite vibrant as he told me about his town. He struck me as a decent man of average breeding who appeared to be a pillar of the community. I never troubled to ask, since my interest was not in him.

He tried to acquaint himself with me, but I was so tired that I wanted to leave and offered little more than cordial conversation.

"Do you know the time?"

"Yes, it's one o'clock," he said, putting away a fashionable pocket watch. "You certainly are beautiful, Miss Nicollette. I don't believe we've ever had a woman as beautiful as you in Glastonbury."

"Frederick, you shouldn't speak to me so. I believe you're flirting, and you told me you're a happily married man."

"I thought I was. But I didn't know you then—when I thought that, I mean. Miss Nicollette, I've never wanted to commit adultery in my life. Ever. But I can't even remember what Mamie looks like now."

"Frederick, I wouldn't be a good thing for you—if you want to continue *to live."*

"You're right, Miss Nicollette. Mamie would kill me."

"That's not what I mean, Frederick."

"Miss Nicollette, perhaps one kiss would satiate my sudden desire for you."

"I think not, Frederick."

"I'm not to your liking, miss?"

He looked so sweet and sincere. The mouth beneath his gray mustache smiled with a bit of becoming insecurity. And I suddenly wanted to pull him to me. But I wouldn't. He was too kind, too sweet. I'd fight the urge. For my own urge, though feeble, was growing.

"Please don't persist, my dear sweet Frederick. It isn't to be."

"Say that again: 'My dear sweet Frederick.' Coming from your lips, it sounds like a melody."

"If it arouses something in you, then I won't say it again. For we aren't to be."

"Are you a soothsayer? How do you know? I fear I may persist until I have you."

He looked into my eyes with that desire and drive I've come to know—intimately. For many women, it's an exciting dance. For me, it's a waltz with the devil.

He reached for me and held me firmly, but I twisted and turned for my freedom.

"Frederick, don't—you're hurting me."

"Oh, I won't hurt you, Nicollette. I only want to love you."

I felt his warm breath on my neck as I turned away from him. I was afraid. He pressed his whole body against mine and pinned me with an aggressive kiss. He was breathing harder.

"Frederick, please. You're not invited, you're a married man. This overture is wrong—stop it at once."

"I can't. I can't!"

"You must. This isn't how a woman wants to be held."

I started to scream, but he put his hand over my mouth.

"Please. Don't cry out."

We were in the wilderness, and unless an animal came to my rescue, I knew my shouts were useless. I had no intention of an involvement with him. This was not a union that interested me, and I shoved him from me and stood quickly. *Although his strength had surprised me when I was in his arms.*

"Frederick, I must get into town. I'll put away the basket."

He turned over on his back, cemented to the ground as if he were trying to let Mother Earth's mud draw out his passions like a poultice. I quickly gathered the glasses, and while I was putting the basket into the buggy, I couldn't see what he was doing.

I turned back for the blanket, only to find that it was walking toward me. Frederick was holding the blanket flat out before him. All I could see was his mischievous smile above the blanket.

"I told you of my legs, Nicollette. How fine they are."

He lifted up the blanket and slowly showed me his bare legs. Then he began doing some Irish jig—I found it comical to see a man's hairy legs sticking out from under a blanket.

"Allow me to introduce my infamous legs, Miss Nicollette. Lucky you, Miss Nicollette, to meet the Extraordinary, the Incredible, the Amazing Legs of Mister Frederick Bothem of Glastonbury. How fortunate that you didn't need to purchase a ticket to this eighth wonder of the world.

"Frederick Bothem of Glastonbury is on call for whatever job may have need of his Amazing Legs. The Amazing Legs of Frederick Bothem can dive deeper, swim farther, and come up drier than any legs in the universe—because these are the most Amazing Legs in the universe."

His commentary on his legs and their movements were so

funny that a wave of laughter overtook me—until he dropped
the blanket, and I learned that Frederick was completely nude.

He did have beautifully muscled legs, as he boasted. His skin
appeared to sparkle in the light, somehow finely tended and not
at all like the older man's body that I had imagined. Though he
had gray in his mustache, his body hair was dark. And I gazed
upon the straight line as it moved thinly down the center of his
body—until I looked upon Frederick's member. It was aroused,
ready for interaction.

"Oh, good Lord, Frederick, dress yourself!" I got into the
buggy seat to drive myself away, but he threw the blanket in the
back, jumped into the buggy's other side, and reached for me. I
pulled away and crawled on my knees to the back of the flatbed
buggy.

I tried to get away from him—but he grabbed me around my
waist with both hands and pulled me to him. He had dropped
the blanket in an unpacked area of the buggy and then fallen
upon the blanket's cushion. Still he held me and pulled me with
him.

His movements were gentle—yet forceful. I couldn't get away
from his grip, because he pressed most of his body against my
side. Holding me down firmly whenever I struggled.

"Please, Nicollette. You must give us a chance."

"Frederick, don't. Don't. You shouldn't force yourself on me."

"Nicollette. I'm so wrong—I see this now. Settle me. Let me
hold you a moment in my arms and long for what can't be.
Please."

"Frederick, you must let me go." I tried to push him away
from me, but he was too strong and held me fast to him.

"Nicollette. Let me have just a moment to hold an angel."

I struggled some more but finally fell limp in his arms. I was
still in my red brocade dress and felt somewhat protected by its

bulk. But if I were to think about it, a naked man was clutching me flat on the back of a buggy. How strange the scene must look to the heavens.

"Frederick, please release me. I want to leave now."

"I can't. I need to hold my angel longer. Please indulge me, Nicollette. I've never experienced a woman as beautiful as you, and for me this moment is the apex of my life. I'm at my highest right now. I could die a happy man, holding you."

He lifted his head to kiss my cheek. I looked at his dreaming eyes and thought about his persistence. And the way he was making such a fool of himself. He had humiliated and embarrassed himself in his quest—for just a moment of love with me. I felt pity for him.

As I lay there in the buggy with Frederick holding me, I thought about the silliness of love. And the misdirected drive it often exhibits. I tried to gather a second wind to fight him off again, but I had no strength, and my muscles once again became limp. I was exhausted from the struggle.

My head fell back, and I closed my eyes to rest. But Frederick read my movements as a surrender in his arms. His body, still pressed against me, held me down in the buggy. And one hand reached to pull up my hem. He began to rub my leg and for a moment his touch felt like Denton's. A sensation of pleasure traveled up my leg and seemed to ignite wherever his hand fell. And then he kissed me on the lips. The kiss fanned the flames that stirred within me. And I moaned.

I found certain areas of my body now craved attention. They were fighting the restraints of my clothing. And so when Frederick started to remove my dress with such tenderness and anticipation, I found myself participating in the movements, as I never imagined I would.

He took off my dress with surprising grace, though his movements were hurried as he tossed my red ball gown out of the buggy. My undergarments followed, until he had me naked in his arms. He pressed himself against me and rubbed his stiff member on my thigh to ready me, and I felt desire stirring throughout my body.

"Wasn't it worth it, Nicollette? To get to this moment? You arouse me so. Oh, Nicollette. Oh, Nicollete!" He was barely able to catch his breath.

"Frederick, listen to me. If you make love with me, I believe you'll die doing it."

He looked into my eyes. He saw I was in earnest. I think he perhaps even believed me.

And he said, "If I die, I die, my love."

Now I had warned him. I couldn't fight him. I felt pleasure from him and I surrendered.

I felt him enter me. I felt his hardness between my legs, then he moved deep within me and withdrew—and then moved deeper again. Thrusting his passion into me, with a delirious smile that bespoke his ecstasy.

I held on to him tighter as he labored over me.

"Nicollette, you're so lovely. This feels so—so lovely. Oh, Nicollette. Oh, my God."

He kept pumping himself within me. And I moved so that I was thrusting and reaching for him as he entered and re-entered me.

I fell into an altered state. And I no longer was thinking in a rational sense when I said, "Don't stop. Don't stop, my darling!"

"I won't," he said. "I won't."

And just after he answered me, I heard a terrible gurgling noise from his throat.

I cried out, "No, no, no! God no, please no!"

It didn't take Frederick long to expire over me. I rolled him onto the blanket. I rubbed his arms, as if hoping the circulation would enliven him, but of course it didn't.

"Frederick, don't die. Please, Frederick, come back. I warned you. Oh, Frederick, please. Please, God."

But I was already confronting the realization that I had caused yet another death. "Oh, dear Lord, why, why?" Praying for forgiveness and bemoaning the curse I bore in my life, I lamented the loss of Frederick to the skies.

I slipped on a different dress from my bag and packed my red frock. Then I held Frederick's head in my lap and rocked him, talking to God with a fury of prayers. I wished for a miracle to enliven the newly dead man I held tenderly. But there was no spirit in his body. It was gone. With yet another's blood on my hands, I started to cry.

CHAPTER 6

Caught in the Act

A HAND STARTLED ME. IT WAS PATTING MY BACK AS IF I were a child. I looked through my tears to see a man wiping his eyes.

"Don't c-c-cry."

The sight of him clarified my thoughts. Once again, I was caught with a dead man in my arms. It was one thing to have an understanding Marie as my witness—and quite another to have a stranger who could convince the authorities that I should hang for my murder.

"I didn't mean to hurt him. You must believe me. I beg of you, kind sir, please believe me."

"Don't c-c-cry."

The stranger was a burly man of about thirty, roughly dressed. He had a coarse face with a high, thick forehead, shaggy hair, thick lips, and puffy cheeks. Yet I saw sadness and empathy in his expression.

"Don't c-c-cry." He patted my back again. "Don't c-c-cry."

"I'll stop." I wiped my tears. "I'm Nicollette. Who are you, dear sir?"

"Don't c-c-cry." There was a shallow look in his eyes. I saw that he might not have his full faculties.

"Do you have a name?"

He nodded. "Um."

"What's your name?"

"Um."

"Um. That's an interesting name. You seem like a nice man."

He climbed up on the wagon and helped lift Frederick's body from my lap.

"Um, I need to leave him somewhere. If I do, will you promise not to tell anyone?"

He nodded. I doubted he knew what he nodded about. But the reins slipped as I moved, and the slack slid over the horses' rumps. They began to move slowly, straight ahead toward the creek. Rather than reacting as an ordinary man would and grabbing the reins to stop the horses, Um curled up in a ball and whimpered.

"It's all right, Um. I'll stop them." I scrambled to the front of the seat only to find that I couldn't reach the reins. But we were moving slowly enough for me to jump on the ground, and I stopped the horses by grabbing my lead horse's bridle.

By the time the buggy came to a rest, it was very close to the creek and the small waterfall Frederick and I had enjoyed.

I crawled back into the buggy and patted Um's back. "Don't cry, Um. Don't cry."

He looked at me with a childlike face. "Pretty."

"Thank you, Um. I like you, too. Now, will you help me carry this man to the creek?" I showed Um I wanted him to pick up Frederick. I was then able to roll Frederick to the end of the buggy and fold the gate down so that Um could carry the body and lay it on the creek's waterfall.

When I stepped back it seemed a hollow grave to me, so Um helped me gather brush and flowers to make a shrine of sorts around Frederick.

When we were done, I gave him money and told him not to tell. I don't think he understood much that I said.

"Remember, you promised me you won't tell, Um."

"Pretty."

It was dusk by the time I arrived in Glastonbury. It was a quaint town, just as Frederick had described. I turned my buggy into the stable near Miriam's Cozy Inn and handed my horses' reins to an eager stableboy. Though I had never been in this town before, the men that walked the streets looked familiar to me.

When I looked closer, I saw that *one of the men to my right looked like Robert,* my first lover who had expired upon the hills. When I focused clearly, I saw that it *was* Robert.

Over my left shoulder, *I saw Denton and Collin cross the street,* quickening their gait toward me.

I blinked my eyes in a hope that my vision would go away. But when I looked again, *they were still there. And then Frederick was straight ahead, approaching my buggy.*

"Frederick, I'm so glad you're all right," I whispered.

He remained in motion, coming closer toward me. I couldn't see his legs move—he floated to me.

The buggy shielded me and I felt protected. *Until I saw him move through the buggy as if he were vapor and the buggy a light breeze to him.*

"Frederick, I tried to tell you. You wouldn't listen. Why didn't you listen to me, Frederick? Why? Why?"

The ghostly apparition came closer, then I felt ice pierce my skin.

I looked down at my hands: my flesh had turned gray and now was darkening before my eyes to a light blue and then shades of darker blue.

The fine veins on the back of my hand turned white, as if ice rushed through my body instead of my warm blood. Frederick moved through me, and I felt a shooting pain as if someone were icing my heart, slowing it down. I felt light-headed and nauseous. My legs were suddenly unstable, and I thought I might fall. I went down in a heap next to the buggy as I lost consciousness.

"Miss. Miss. Are you all right?" It was the stableboy, who had rushed to my aid.

"Yes."

"Miss, you look white as a ghost. May I take you to your room?"

"I was going to rent a room at Miriam's."

"I can help you there, miss. I'll bring your bags over for you after you register."

"Yes, thank you." The stableboy was strong, and he propped me up and supported me as we crossed the street to the Cozy Inn.

"Welcome to the Cozy Inn. I'm Miriam Bestell."

"Lovely to meet you, Miriam. I'm Nicollette Caron."

"So nice to have you stay with us, Miss Caron. What brings you through our town?"

"I'm going to visit my aunt who recently moved to Wales."

"Usually one leaves Wales," she mumbled under her breath. "But I have a wonderful room for you, Nicollette. It has a cozy bed that you may never want to leave."

The quaint room at Miriam Bestell's inn was attractive, with lovely pink-flowered wallpaper and a bed with a luxuriously down-filled mattress that cradled me. The bed felt so comfortable as I lay on top with my clothes on that I didn't even move when the stableboy appeared. As he brought in my last bag, I lifted my head up to look around my room. It was haunted by my dead lovers. *On the chair was Robert. Denton stood near the window, and Frederick sat on the end of the bed. And I gasped as Collin walked toward me.*

"Are you all right, miss?" The young man looked concerned and a little frightened by my appearance. It was apparent that he couldn't see the men haunting my room.

I stared at him between the ghosts, trying not to see them. But I *could* see them at the corners of my vision.

"Miss? I asked if you were feeling better."

"Ghosts aren't white."

"You've seen a ghost before? I'd be afraid to meet a ghost, miss."

"They're in the room now. All around you."

"There's nothing here."

"Yes, there is. They have black eyes that see right through to your soul. And if they come near, they'll try to ice you and take you with them."

"You're scaring me, miss. Can I get you a doctor? Dr. Ignat is very good."

"No, I'm fine. I was, just—jesting. There are no ghosts, of course. I like to jest with young boys, I guess. I shouldn't."

"Oh, no, that's all right, miss. I knew you were having fun with me. Well, you should sleep. I'll take good care of your horses, miss. Good-bye."

"What's your name?"

"Alexander is my name, miss."

"Thank you, Alexander." He turned to leave. *Stay, please stay.* I wished anyone alive would sit with me and hold my hand. But I dared not ask for help in my defense against the afterworld, or I'd be thought a lunatic.

With so many voyeurs I couldn't take off my clothes as I readied for bed. As the apparitions were near me I could smell a disturbing must, a dankness of their ghostliness—and when they moved through me, I felt the ice of death. When I moved my hand near them, I relived their deaths again and again in my mind.

And when I closed my eyes, the spirits didn't go away. My nerves held fast to a sustained string of nervous tension, waiting for resolution or solution of my ghosts' suspense. If they could just put a dagger into me, to finish the tense movement that surrounded me, perhaps then I could rest. Rest in eternal silence—a bounteous gift for any soul so tortured as mine.

Their stillness screamed in the dark. Yet perhaps their presence would free me from my curse. For how could I court with a free mind, if with me were horrible phantasms when the lights went out? What man could survive the gruesome bedmates I brought to the boudoir?

The ghosts of my dead lovers remained in my room, their soulless stares provoking a malicious echo that resounded within my mind. Why? I yearned for slumber, yet feared the dead men would do something to me in my sleep. What?

What could they do to my resting body? All of my thoughts were too heinous to dwell upon. But what else could I think—*when I felt cold hands lifting my hem and touching my legs? When they stroked my inner thighs, even as I flinched from their touch? They reached their hands to paw at my bosom, their dead flesh still lusting for me. Still trying to reach for me with their cold body shells, still trying to complete the act of love. All the while they stared into my eyes without their souls.*

I denied their presence. I muttered to myself that they were gone. The dead men were not with me. I was alone in the dark, and nothing could touch me. Angels sheltered me, and God's wing was my protection. I kept talking to the air in whispers, in hopes that my prayers would be answered.

I reached for a moment without torment. Let me sleep. Just one night. Please, dear God, let me sleep. One moment of peace in a deviled life. It didn't come easily, but finally God granted me what I so desperately needed. Finally, I slept.

CHAPTER 7

What Ails Her

CARRIE COULDN'T BELIEVE HER GOOD FORTUNE WHEN she arrived at Lord Baston's manor. The meticulously groomed yard and gardens had an iridescent glow from the morning dew as their carriage turned into the long drive. Carrie thought it looked as if crushed crystals and diamonds were scattered all over the grounds.

The flowers in full bloom this August morning made the picturesque setting so vibrant that she could barely take her eyes away, or even take the time to blink. Her world was a silent one, and her eyes had developed a sharpened sense of beauty. Now the vision before her made them widen to drink in the luscious colors of the gardens. The oranges were so orange, the yellows so bright, the purples amazing. Even the white flowers were purer than the whitest bridal gown.

Lord Baston stopped the carriage to survey his property as Carrie daydreamed. She quickly imagined herself the lady of Lord Baston's manor with her own servants. But even being a servant for Lord Baston was better than sharing a home with her nine brothers and sisters and a father who drank too much Irish whiskey.

In Ireland they struggled for the potatoes they lived on, going months without a taste of meat. And because she was known as the town deaf-mute, she had been teased for as long as she could remember, by insensitive louts who poked fun at her disability and set her up for cruel pranks. The harassment had made her believe that no one in Ireland could ever have a loving interest in her.

With no hope of finding love, and scarred by the brutish ridicule, Carrie had made her Irish exodus, only leaving a note for her family. She prayed there would be more opportunity for her in England. And at least her absence would allow more resources for her starving siblings.

"Hold it, Bertrum."

Bertrum came to a halt halfway up the drive. As Lord Baston stepped out of the carriage to speak with his gardeners, Carrie used the opportunity to reach into her small handbag for her bottle of Dr. Goodman's Elixir. She took a quick sip and let the drug run down her throat. She felt the tingle rush throughout her body, then raised the bottle to her lips again for a longer sip, welcoming the euphoric sensation.

This morning she wanted to feel that rush, to be numb throughout her body and soul. She wanted to blot out her past sexual liaisons and the other things she hoped God didn't see. She sought a peaceful existence, away from the dangerous street life of thievery and prostitution. After last night she would no longer have to endure encounters filled with her mute cries as a man had his way with her.

Her highest goal was to be provided for by someone with substantial power and greatness, someone like her new lover—who she now knew was a lord. As she waited in the carriage, still surveying her surroundings, she believed that goal to be within her reach.

She could do what was required of her. In the past she'd had to close her eyes as she longed for a man to get off her—in the knowledge that she couldn't tell.

She hoped she'd done the right thing. That in time Lord Baston might come to care for her, perhaps even love her. Yes, she even thought of his loving her, because then she could be the lady of the house. That was in her dreams—only in her dreams. And she slid the elixir bottle into her handbag.

Lord Baston climbed back into the carriage. "My dear Carrie, I hope you feel at home here. I'm most happy to have your company."

Carrie smiled at him—wondering if she could ever rise in his home to a feather bed, and how she was going to get the next bottle of her precious elixir. She had always wanted a feather bed. As for the elixir, she simply couldn't do without it.

Carrie's room was in the attic of Lord Baston's west wing. To a girl from Ireland who had shared a two-room shanty with eleven people, it was luxurious. She lightly touched the softness of the quilt's fabric on her double bed. She ran her hand over the feather pillows with embroidery trim on each case. She walked around the room touching every item to imprint its feel and texture, twirling from one object to the next.

She sat by her dresser mirror fingering her personal grooming aids. And she smiled at herself and squeaked barely audible sounds she had no idea she was making. They were not to communicate. They were just the unheard noises of a girl who felt too much excitement over her good fortune not to express it.

But if anyone wanted to know her thoughts, they could have translated them by looking at her face. Carrie never wanted to leave her mansion—not ever.

Many of the items a lady might desire were provided. She had a silver horsehair brush, with a matching mirror and comb, and a dusting puff and fragrant talc powder, for after her bath. Soap and tooth polish and a toothbrush. Scissors to trim her hair, with a golden swan handle. All of these items were arranged on a dressing table that held a huge mirror in which she could check her appearance for the day. She studied her appearance, for she had never had the luxury of staring at herself so long in a mirror.

Her room had a comfortable cool breeze when she opened the shutters. She found the sweet countryside air exhilarating. There was a straw bed, much softer than the one she'd shared with three sisters back in Ireland.

She had a place to sew. There was a hand-painted pitcher and bowl with yellow roses on it, so she could wash in the room. And she fancied that. All in all, her situation was delightful.

Her morning began with Roberta knocking on her door. She was given her work attire: a black dress with a white apron, a cap, and a basket of accessories to complete her tasks. She had appeared before Bertrum in the master's kitchen on her first morning.

"Carrie, there are certain rules you must be aware of." She nodded her understanding.

"You aren't to bother Lord Baston for any personal needs. If you want anything, come to me."

She nodded.

"If you receive mail, visitors, or anything delivered for the master, you must come to me."

Carrie didn't understand what Bertrum said—he'd turned away, and she couldn't read his lips. And she couldn't ask, not having a notepad in her pocket. But he turned back to her and then she understood his conversation.

"You'll receive your pay once a month."

She nodded.

"Stay out of sight and do your job."

She nodded.

"If you see Lord Baston come and go, at any time of day or night, take no note. His affairs are his own and not to be mentioned to anyone."

She nodded.

"If your imagination runs wild, and you want to share information with anyone, don't."

Then he must not know of her condition, that she was unable to share anything with anybody.

"You will be serving Lord Baston his meals. He likes to dine at nine, one-thirty, and eight. Tea will be served at four o'clock every day. Roberta and Clive will go through Lord Baston's preferences with you in the kitchen. No departure from his preferences is tolerated—so learn his particulars, miss."

Carrie nodded again.

"Clive and Roberta are waiting for you in the kitchen. Run along now or you'll be late." Bertrum's last words were still sinking into Carrie's mind as she transposed the ones she now saw on his lips. She looked at him and his features softened.

"Everything is going to be all right, Carrie—you'll be just fine. I'll be here to help you along."

Carrie came from a loving family. They were poor, but they freely expressed their affection for one another. And so it felt natural to her, when Bertrum spoke his kind reassuring words, to reach for her fellow servant and hug him tightly to show her appreciation. He was shocked—and pleased—by the hug.

"Run along, Carrie. You don't want to be late. Run along."

CHAPTER 8

Roundabout Dead

Peavey, Wilcox, and Lang rode into the roundabout. A heap of what looked like rubbish blocked their path ahead. On closer inspection they could see the pile was covered with aggressive black birds, feasting on a carcass.

"If that's our body ahead, Lang, we'd best hurry, or we'll be dissecting the birds for our clues," Peavey said.

Peavey and Wilcox dismounted and scattered the protesting ravens to nearby trees, where the birds watched and waited to get back to their banquet.

The white horse Lang rode was a white Lippizan stallion named Pegasus, an Austrian horse of rare breeding trained for exceptional jumps, trots, canters, and gallops. The show horse had almost as many tricks under his hooves as his master had up his sleeves. He dipped to help Lang dismount, without a command. The simple act of the horse's intelligent aid emphasized Lang's mastery, to have his beast anticipate his wishes without a visible signal.

Lang checked the body for any sign of life and, as he expected, found none. And the ravens had already pecked upon the man's neck, starting their natural process of returning the dead man's remains to the earth.

"He's been dead for several hours," Lang said. "I'm surprised this late in the day that we seem to be the first on the scene."

"How do you know how long he's been dead?" Peavey said.

"You tell me."

The young men crowded around the dead body, trying to mask their distaste for its condition.

"His possessions are still with him," Wilcox said. "He has a watch, ring, a money clip with at least five pounds in it, and his first or last name, 'Denton,' stenciled on his pocket comb."

"Good," Lang said.

"The freshest horses' trails went west," Peavey said.

"With a buggy," Wilcox said.

The men continued to study the carriage tracks around and over the body. Peavey took out a pencil and some paper and began to draw the scene. Wilcox paced the distance from the body to the trees, and Peavey noted the numbers. Lang was most interested in his study of the body. The men remained for several minutes, each intrigued by their own tasks before finally lifting the corpse over the rump of Wilcox's palomino.

As the three mounted their fine animals and rode off, two persistent ravens dived straight at them. Their first dives and chatter were meant to frighten and halt the men. The next few dives and squawks demanded that they drop their large meal. The ravens' swoops grew shorter and more urgent, accompanied by pleading squawks. Finally, they returned to the trees to protest among themselves the theft of their feast.

CHAPTER 9

Dead Man's Meeting

THE RECRUITS SHOWED THEIR IDENTIFICATION TO ENTER the New Scotland Yard offices that had just opened. Lang signed in a notation of the dead body and turned to face them.

"I'll be leaving in the morning," he said.

"Without us, Jackson?" Wilcox said. "We would have terrible withdrawal from you. We'd miss you."

"Oh, yes," Peavey said, "I'd like to marry you, if you hadn't met your horse first and left me without a chance."

"Even if I'd met you first," Lang said, "I'd have waited for the horse. He never has a smart tongue to me." He turned and rested a fatherly hand on Wilcox's shoulder. "I believe Peavey needs some female companionship in the near future. Will you take care of that?"

"Yes, sir. If I might ask, sir, where are you going?"

"I plan to attend an event I enjoyed last year in Glastonbury—they invited Pegasus to perform again. It's a quaint town and a nice ride. I'll be leaving in the morning for just a day."

"Are there women who attend this event?"

"A few. All witches. Most men are afraid of them."

"Edward, have you tamed any witches?" Peavey asked.

"One. But then she wanted to marry me."

"What did you do?"

"I enlisted in the militia within the hour." The men laughed.

"Gentlemen, you're welcome to come along. It will be only for the day."

Angus, the front desk clerk at the door, said, "Good afternoon, Inspector Lang. What have you got there?"

"A strange case found on the road. Would you order me a wheeled table for the body?"

"Yes, sir.

"Accident?"

"Unknown cause of death. Is the chief here?"

"I'll get him, sir."

The wheeled table was in an old storage room in the Scotland Yard basement. The corpse, now naked, lay on its metal slab surrounded by Lang, Peavey, and Wilcox. Sean, a young volunteer who worked for an occasional shilling, approached them with a sheet to partially cover the body.

"I did what you asked, sir," he said. "He did just what you said he would do."

Lang held a magnifying glass over the body. The room had a bare bulb of light hanging over the corpse and a small lamp at either side of the slab.

Lang looked up. "You asked Dr. Lindsey to come, and he said his job as a doctor is to look after the *live* people, right?"

"Those were his exact words. He did say he would come over this weekend if he could find a moment. Then he told me to go away."

"And then you said what I told you to say?"

"Yes, I said the corpse had a broken neck that looked self-inflicted."

"And then you left, as I told you?"

"Yes, sir. He called after me, and said, 'Son, what did you say?' I said, 'Well, I got to get back. Inspector Lang is over there and several of the other detectives are fascinated, and no one can believe their discoveries.' By this time, he'd pulled his stethoscope off his neck. So I told him I had to race back because I didn't want to miss a thing."

"Then you waited for a moment outside the door?"

"Less than a minute. He already had his coat and hat on. I walked him over, and he's just getting his clearance now. He knows where to come."

"Well done, Sean." Lang reached in his pocket and tipped the boy some coins. Then he picked up his magnifying glass and began to study the dead man's neck.

"One day, Sean, this will be a science. There'll be doctors who specialize in the condition of a corpse. They may get so good that they'll be able to tell us the actual cause of death."

"Men who become doctors to study corpses? You think that will happen?"

"I do."

"Well, wouldn't that be something."

"Dr. Lindsey's coming, I hear him."

Ian Lindsey was a short man whose right leg had a bit of a drag to it from an injury he never referred to. He claimed it was nothing, but obviously a part of his right leg was made of wood, for he stepped with his left foot and dragged his right sideways as if it were deadweight.

Perhaps it was the wooden leg that made his face look weary and sad. Or the demanding life and schedule of a physician. Or the nonpayment for the services he performed for the poor London townsfolk. Dr. Lindsey had been heard to say that he realized he didn't like people. And though he had a Mrs. Lindsey who cooked, cleaned, and bore him children, he had trained her to curb her tongue and quite enjoyed silence whenever possible. So the idea of scientifically studying a corpse had a certain appeal for him.

Lang, who had found Lindsey to be quite brilliant at discovering things no inspector would think to notice, had come to rely on him for his insights. And though it was apparent that Lindsey didn't care for most human beings, he seemed to respect Lang as a fellow intellect who also excelled in his field.

"I can't stay long," Dr. Lindsey said. "Whenever I'm here I don't leave until after midnight. And I'm getting too old to do these late-night investigations anymore."

"Ian, I understand. We certainly appreciate your visit. It's just that we're so baffled."

Lindsey came closer to the body. "I believe I recognize this young man, Jackson."

"You do?"

"My wife dragged me out to the Queen's Ball, the only affair we attend each year. Yes, he was squiring a spectacularly beautiful woman in a red dress last night. Everyone noticed them. Brickman, I believe. David or a D-name. I'm not sure of his first name, but I believe his last name is Brickman."

"Could it be Denton? We found a comb engraved with the name Denton in his pocket."

"Yes. I believe that's it."

"Sean, can you see if there's a Denton Brickman who's been reported missing?"

"Yes, sir."

"What do you have here?" Lindsey asked.

"This young man was found in the road, Ian. It appears as though he may have fallen from a horse. But we believe he may have been riding in the carriage with a driver earlier that evening."

Sean returned. "Denton Brickman of London. His servants reported him missing this morning."

Lang addressed the corpse. "Well, hello, Denton. We're going to try to figure out what happened to you. Feel free to help us any way you can."

"What else, Jackson?" Lindsey said.

"He could have fallen from the carriage and broken his neck. And then the carriage rolled over him—or some carriage did. Perhaps we can see wheel marks here. The injury broke the skin."

"He'd been dead a while, then." Lindsey took Lang's magnifying glass and peered intently at the marks on Denton made by the wheels.

"Why do you say that, Ian?"

"He would have bled had he been alive. I'd say he was dead by the time the carriage rolled over him."

"Yes, I thought you might think that."

"In fact he may have been dead quite a while, because the blood was settling, pooling to the bottom of the body—as happens when we die. Most interesting." Lindsey inspected Denton's neck. "It's clearly broken."

"But look here." Lang showed him the other marks on the neck.

"What are these?" Lindsey said. "Pick marks?"

"Raven. He was covered in ravens."

"Yes. But these other marks?"

"What do you think? They're all around the neck."

Dr. Lindsey studied the marks. The left side had a gaping dark hole where the birds had dined. Around the throat area were many bruises. Lang noted that they covered the 360-degree circumference of the neck.

"Made by hands, Jackson. Someone was pushing with all their might for this outcome."

"Indeed. How much strength would it take to break the neck of a corpse?"

Lindsey sighed. "As you know, most of the time I'm forced to spend my appointments with the live ones. I don't have the luxury of testing the elastic quality of dead necks—so I'm afraid your guess is as good as mine."

Lang turned to Peavey and Wilcox. "Gentlemen, do you have any ideas for potential suspects?"

"A vagrant or a thief," Peavey said.

"His driver, his escort, or someone from the manor," Wilcox said.

"Someone from the dance or a jealous suitor."

"All excellent suggestions. Please note them," Lang said.

Lindsey looked up from the body. "I believe his neck was most definitely broken after he was dead. Perhaps someone laid him on the road, then rolled over him with a carriage."

"But what did the young man really die from? No bullet holes?" Peavey asked.

"None."

"Knife or other wound?" Wilcox said.

"None."

"But there's a question I have that is lower on the body," Lang said as he pulled down the sheet that covered the lower half of the corpse. "See if you see it. I value your opinion, Ian, and I'm not a medical man at all."

Lindsey seemed mesmerized as his eyes moved down the body.

"Ah-ha!" he said. Then he knocked a lamp over. "Drat it."

He bent over to pick up the lamp, obviously reluctant to take his eyes away from the puzzle that tantalized his mind.

He used the magnifying glass to study the young man's penis. "I've never seen a penis so engorged. It's also more reddened than is usual, as though blood has locked there rather than drained."

"Yes."

"And he has a color characteristic of a cardiovascular attack. Yet he's a young man. All highly unusual. I've never seen anything like it before."

"Nor have I," Lang said. "Anything else you've noticed?"

"Take a close look at his face," Lindsey said. "The corpse is smiling."

"Yes, I saw that too."

CHAPTER 10

The Missing Piece

THE MORNING WAS CRISP AND I WANTED TO FEEL AS clean as the hillside air. So I arranged with Miriam to have a bath drawn for me, which was accommodated nicely by her house servant.

I soaked my body and washed my long hair. Gone were the perspiration and soil from my long buggy ride. No more grass stains from Frederick's attempt to roll me in the meadow by the creek. I even fancied that my hands were cleansed of breaking Denton's neck.

I returned to my room and applied my fragrant after-bath talcum, then my lip paint and rouge. I dressed in a royal blue frock that had hints of purple in the print and a tiny ruffle around the neckline. I put on my sapphire locket and matching earrings, then glanced at myself in the mirror. The woman in the mirror made me feel confident of my appearance as I went downstairs to have breakfast with other guests I assumed were staying at the inn.

Instead, Miriam sat alone at the table. She stared into a cup of cold tea.

"Good morning, Miriam."

"Good morning, Nicollette. I trust you slept well."

"I did, and the bath was lovely." She barely looked at me. I was expecting a comment on my dress, or something more.

"Is everything all right, Miriam?" With her golden brown hair and deep blue eyes, she was a lovely woman. She had an infectious friendly smile, and had seemed warm and kind when I arrived. But her warmth was not evident at the moment.

"Well, there's quite a bit of sadness today, I'm afraid," she said.

"What do you mean?"

"One of our most beloved townspeople is missing, and there's a group out looking for him."

"Oh? Who's that?"

"Frederick Bothem."

This was too soon—I was caught off guard. Most often they didn't show up for days, even weeks. Now this was in my face. I said nothing.

"You didn't know him, but he's been our constable and mayor for more than twenty years. He's birthed babies, protected us from bank robbers, and been relied upon in so many ways. We all truly love him." Tears welled in Miriam's eyes.

"And *I've* loved him since we were just twelve. Thirty-six years ago. Now I'm a forty-eight-year-old spinster.

"But he chose Mamie. Damn, Mamie. She's so mean. She's even hit him—and he takes it. I only loved him. He knows he should have picked me, but he married until death doth them part. He thinks he's made his bed and has to lie in it." She reached for her handkerchief and cried into the small square.

"I loved him so. I guess I never stopped . . ."

I put my arms around her. "How awful for you. You must

mourn like the widow, without the rights. I understand, I truly understand." And she cried in my arms for the man she loved but never had.

Finally, I said, "What do you think happened to him?"

"They don't know, they haven't found him yet. But he rode a new mechanical device, and I wonder if he didn't fall off and lies injured somewhere."

"Well, perhaps he's all right," I said.

"Do you think so? But he came home every night."

"Hunting or fishing?"

"No. He left his equipment behind."

"Perhaps he had an affair and ran away for a weekend."

"Oh, you don't know Frederick. He would never have an affair. He wasn't cut out of that cloth. Or he would have been in my bed long ago."

I'm sure she didn't see my eyebrow lift as I quickly looked away. "Well, he'll turn up, then."

"You're so kind. You feel like a sister, when we've only just met."

"You would do the same for me."

"You look so lovely, Nicollette. I must invite you to the Glastonbury Foxhunt Club dance tonight. It will be a fine chance for you to meet everyone in the town."

"I'd love to go."

"Wonderful. But now, let's pray for Frederick."

And as Miriam bowed her head, I prayed with her. God help me—I said a prayer for my protection.

I did think fondly of the sweet man who had assisted my transition into his town, but only for a moment. Because I couldn't afford to weaken; for the path of suspicion might lead to me.

I thought of leaving right then. I thought perhaps I should just move on to another town. After all, a man had just died, and I had just arrived. But there was a carrot set in front of me that I needed to reach. Lord Baston. The man no woman seemed able to entice. Was that not a challenge befitting a princess of temptation?

I rather thought so.

I was about to look around the town when Miriam grabbed my arm.

"Nicollette, will you please go with me on an errand? I need you." She sounded so desperate, how could I refuse?

"Of course, Miriam. How can I help?"

"Come with me, I'll explain in the buggy." Miriam's buggy was brought around for us, and she took the reins.

"We're going to the edge of town. To the Fog Cave. It's well-known. She only sees people on Fridays."

"She?"

"Gabriella. The reader."

"She's a seer?"

"She sees things, she knows the future. But she will select just a few each Friday. Many people have traveled great distances to see her only to be turned away."

"Have you been to her before?"

"As a young girl, when I wanted Frederick. She told me it was not to be, and she was right. Have you ever been to a seer?"

"I've never wanted to go."

"Well, we may not be chosen."

We rode about five kilometers south past the hill known as Tor. We continued down some worn roads, finally stopping on the side of a small, sloping hill. Miriam secured her buggy with several other horses and buggies, and we entered an opening to a cavern that tilted into the earth's rock.

A woman in a brown sack dress who had a pleasant face welcomed us graciously.

"Good morning, my friends." She carried a paper on a stiff

board, and she entered our names on a list. We noticed an attached waiting room filled with others we assumed were on the list ahead of us.

"She's going to choose soon," Miriam said.

"Miriam Bestell and Nicollette Caron," the woman read from her list. "And the subject?"

"We're trying to locate a missing person, Frederick Bothem."

I stood next to the woman and looked down at the list. I was surprised to see almost thirty people listed. Some came with clues to find a missing daughter. Some asked who had killed a relative. Lovers wondered if they should marry. One young woman wanted to know if she should participate in an arranged marriage to an Arabian prince. A man who had journeyed from Italy was tracking a killer.

The woman in brown disappeared and returned moments later.

"Gabriella wants to see only one person for the day. Nicollette Caron. I'm sorry. Everyone else should leave. If you would like to stay in town until next week, you can stop at the Foxhound Inn, and if we should have a special session, we can reach you there."

Sighs and cries went up around the room. "My God, please help us," one woman said between sobs.

"I'll gladly give up this spot to the others who came so far," I said.

But the woman in brown said, "No. Gabriella has words for you."

Miriam hugged me. "Nicollette. Make sure you ask about Frederick. I'll wait right here for you. Good luck, my dear."

"Come with me," said the woman.

I followed as she led me deeper into the cave. Oil torches shed a little light in each of the cavern rooms. We went into a third cave, then a fourth. Finally, we reached the seventh room, where

Gabriella sat behind a round table. She didn't rise or even move as I entered. Her eyes were closed, and she appeared to be meditating, with her hands palms down on a large plate of sand. I was led to a seat across from her. The woman in brown disappeared from my side, leaving Gabriella and me across from each other in the cold, dark cavern.

I sat silently, having no idea as to what a lady should do or say in this situation. I'd have thought she would greet me, but she didn't. So I looked at the strange sand. I looked at her face, then looked away. But I found myself drawn to looking back, studying the strange woman across from me.

Her figure was bulky and draped with layers of different colors, but it was her face that drew my eyes. It was large and round, topped with matted orange hair that showed no luster or care. Her eyes were closed, her nose large, her lips protruding and full. Most remarkable was a deep crease down the middle of her forehead, as if her mind might be segmented.

I stared at the crease, a deep groove that began at the top of her forehead and created a vertical division two inches into her nose. Then, suddenly, her eyes opened, and I gasped. Her eyes had a film over them, a web completely covering each eye. I was not expecting the ghostly whiteness of the eyes, which suffered without a colored iris.

"I'm sorry," I said. "You startled me. I thought you might be resting."

"Don't you think I'm used to this? It is why I hide. Why I only see people once a week. I can't take their shock more often."

"Perhaps, if people knew you more, saw you more often . . ."

"I have no need for people. There are other realms than the physical one."

"I understand."

"Well, aren't you sweet."

"Thank you."

She laughed, and I realized her remark had been facetious.

"What does the plate of sand do?" I asked.

"The sand is from holy ground. I read the answers to any question on tiny grains. Each one tells me a story."

"I see."

"No, I see all, Nicollette. I see backward, forward, now. I see above you, below you, around you, and through you—and I understand you. More than you understand yourself.

"I know that coming here was not your idea and that you're afraid to be here. You're afraid that I'll know of your past, and I do. I know this with or without you here, so your being here makes no difference. The answers to everything about you are mine, and you will learn some of them today."

"Why me? So many others have come so far, with important questions for you."

"I know you don't believe in people like me, but I do this so that you may save yourself and others. December 4, 1870."

"That's my birthday." *How could she know this? We have only just met.*

"I know you. You have a freakish condition that causes death to the men who love you. Robert. Collin. Allan. Ethan. George. Nathaniel. Jacques. Pierre. Paul. Antonio. Armand. Gino. Denton. And most recently Frederick. I count fourteen beautiful men. Am I correct?

I could not speak. How could she know? But she knew, *she knew about all of them.*

"You have wondered why you love your partner until his death, Nicollette. You have to understand this so you can learn how to live with it."

I sobbed into my hands.

"Listen to me, Nicollette. For many men this isn't the worst way to die. If you advertised everything you do, there might be a long line of men of all ages waiting to go."

I lifted my head up at her bit of understanding. But her lightness on the subject of my plague made me uncomfortable.

"This isn't something you could have helped," she said. "You have a rabbit heart."

"And what is to become of me?"

"You'll meet your match."

"There's a man for me?"

"Oh, yes."

"Can you give me a clue?"

"He's trained as a barrister."

"But what would happen if we were to have a union?"

"You will learn. You will have to find a way."

"When will I meet this man?"

"Sooner than you think."

"How will I know him?"

"You will know."

"I don't understand."

"You will know."

"What if I abstained?"

"You can't."

"What if I were caged?"

"You would ascend your cage."

"Will I have a happy life?"

"Happy and sad, like all the other lives."

"Will I survive my past?"

"The past is right next to the now. It can surprise you when you least want it. You hid your past well, but perhaps not well enough."

"I'm not sure what you mean."

"No games. This is enough. I'm tired. You must go. You will

learn more in the future. Just remember this for a time when you will need it: Go north to the ferryman."

"North to the ferryman?"

"Yes. I'll walk you out now."

She lumbered around the table and took my elbow to lead me through the maze of cavern rooms to the last room, where Miriam sat patiently. She stood up, excited to see Gabriella.

"Please—where's Frederick?" she said.

Gabriella said, "Nicollette can help you find your friend."

Miriam and I left quickly to return to Glastonbury.

I didn't want to talk at all on the way back to town. And I suffered as Miriam hounded me about where her Frederick could be.

"Tell me everything she told you. Every word."

I shrugged. "There's not much to tell."

"You were in so long with her. Tell me what she said."

"We knew people in common in France," I said.

"I didn't know Gabriella had spent any time in France."

"Tell me about her crease," I said.

"It happened at birth—caused by the metal tongs the doctor used to remove her from her mother's womb. The doctor squeezed too hard, to pull the baby's head out. And she was born with a caul, a web covering her face. Such a web is supposed to signify a true mystic."

"I see."

"If only she had told you where to find Frederick. . . ."

Miriam began to sob, and I couldn't bear to hear her. I covered my ears with my fingers to drown out her sounds and told her my ears ached when she asked me what was wrong.

I was so exhausted from the outing and the pressure of Miriam's grief that I decided to go back to my room and miss the hunt club dance that evening. I needed rest and I needed to think about what I had just learned, so I put myself to bed even though it was only midafternoon. But even as I entered my room, I smelled a hellish dust—a preview of another haunt.

When I opened my eyes for a moment, *I saw Denton sitting on the chair across from me. He stared at me with empty eyes.* I couldn't scream, for the appearance of my ghost tattled the blood on my hands. And if he were only a vision, then to call for help would be an exposé of my mental imbalance. I closed my eyes to close him out of my mind, and pretend my apparition couldn't be.

But as I lay in the midafternoon's shaded darkness, I felt a cool breeze coming from his direction. A dank musty odor came with it, and I opened my eyes to find that *Denton's apparition was moving closer to me.* I again closed my eyes and tried to race to the only haven I felt could harbor me: sleep. I sought to dream of a better life I might reach. And if I couldn't attain it in my haunted life, then perhaps I could find peace within my dreams.

CHAPTER 11

Notes and Dreams

Upon his seating the linen napkin should be opened and handed to Lord Baston. Next, he should have his main course set before him, followed by his wine." Carrie carefully watched Roberta and Clive as they demonstrated the structured order of service.

"After he has sipped his wine and it is to his liking, his tea should be served with the small sugar cube bowl. He must *never* need to touch the sugar cube bowl himself. *You* must add the cubes for him to his taste—which, luckily, never changes."

Clive held up two fingers. "Lord Baston likes his tea with two lumps of sugar per cup. And if his tea should cool, don't attempt to warm it. Give him a fresh cup of hot tea. And *always* remember to give him the two cubes of sugar." He waved the same two fingers at Carrie. "Always, always. He doesn't like to ask for either hot tea or the cubes.

"I find a fresh cup every twelve minutes is a good rule," Clive continued. He was happy to be handing the responsibility of the master's hot tea to someone else. He thought of it as a twelve-minute tether he had been bound to five times a day for longer than he cared to remember.

Carrie didn't ask any questions or talk at all, Clive noticed. It was no matter to him. If she could do the job of a top servant, that was all he cared about.

The mansion had a spacious kitchen with an island in the center to store bowls and cooking utensils. There was a large cooking stove. The kitchen's newest addition was an indoor water pump, which, when primed, brought underground springwater inside. It was the first one to be installed in the county, and Lord Baston was convinced it would catch on.

Attached to the kitchen was a dining room where a magnificent cut-glass chandelier hung over a seventeenth-century hand-carved oak table and matching chairs. The table seated forty-eight people, but Lord Baston usually sat alone at the head. He rarely entertained inside his home, preferring his privacy.

He employed twenty-five servants to care for the grounds and the manor house, only a few of whom had direct contact with him.

He met with Roberta and Clive about the menu for the day. Clive managed most of the staff. Bertrum was Lord Baston's main driver and was also in charge of his large stable of horses bred for pleasure riding, foxhunts, and racing.

The manor house was filled with rare art. Large paintings from the Renaissance period and Oriental artifacts Lord Baston had brought back from his Asian travels were displayed in every room and hallway.

Lord Baston sat beneath a large oil landscape painting of a foxhunt, waiting for his breakfast. Carrie brought his tea first.

"Good morning, Carrie."

She set a tray down on the sideboard and poured some hot tea for him. Her hands shook. He noticed, and said nothing. She went back to her tray, retrieved a bowl with sugar cubes, and carefully used a pair of tongs to drop one cube, then another in his tea.

"Excellent, Carrie. You did that perfectly."

She was watching his mouth, to read what he said to her. He remembered how she had looked the night they first met. How she had let him remove her clothes easily. And when the corset and layers fell away, how luminous her white skin had been.

He remembered looking at her womanly charms, his passion quickly aroused. He suddenly felt aroused by her now. He could smell the scent of roses she had behind her ears, the same scent she'd worn when he panted over her.

Carrie picked up the tea tray and moved out of the room. She returned with another tray and served him a breakfast of waffles and berries. There was also a hard-boiled egg with the shell removed, in an eggcup. She set down the salt and pepper to his right, near his glass of wine.

"Carrie, are you happy here?" Carrie heard nothing and couldn't see his lips move. So he grabbed her hand and held it tight.

Carrie looked at Lord Baston and felt her heart beating. Oh, the confusion. She wanted this man, but it made no sense. Was it because of her need to have a place?

The truth was, she wasn't sure why she wanted him. She had never before connected with a man who had been on top of her. Usually she never saw the men again.

She looked down at her seated lord, whose gaze remained steadfast on her. *Yes, God help me, I want him again. If I had him again, I could tell. I'd feel then.*

He looked back. She smiled, curtsied, and left the room.

She found her handbag in the kitchen and hid in the pantry

to write a note on the stationary she had lifted from Lord Baston's desk.

She took from her bag the elixir, opened the cap, and swigged down a huge gulp of the golden brown syrup. The jolt shot through her body and her mind raced. She wrote the note quickly and put the paper in her pocket.

When she grabbed her bottle for another drink, she saw that there was just a drop left. She drank it, letting the bottle hover over her mouth, hoping that more drops along the sides would unite to give her the full swallow she craved. But there was not enough—though she waited a moment. Nothing. The bottle was clean.

She licked into the bottle as far as she could reach her tongue. She licked the outside of the grooves where the top screwed on. She put the cap on, returned the bottle to her bag, and walked back into the kitchen.

Clive was watching her. He lifted an eyebrow and pointed to the pocket watch held in his hand. She nodded and quickly gathered the tea tray to go to Lord Baston.

She served him a fresh cup with two cubes of sugar, then reached into her pocket and passed him her message. She turned back into the kitchen, where she saw Clive waiting for her.

Lord Baston fingered the note that had been discreetly slipped to him. He opened the hurried gold-waxed seal on the back of his own parchment paper. The note read:

Dear Lord Baston,
You're all I can think.
  Be with me again, my lord.
  Love,
  Carrie

The handsome lord smiled. *I will, Carrie. I will.*

• • •

I was afraid to open my eyes. I was afraid I'd see Denton's ghost haunting my room. It was afternoon, and I'd fallen asleep in my dress.

I dreamed I was in my bed in the Cozy Inn—in the very room I occupied, but in the dream I felt myself rise out of the bed still able to look at my resting body as I slept upon it. I walked through the house, past Miriam, who seemed not to see me. I continued out of the house—through the door, down the walk, along the street, and past the shops.

I went by two businesses, then turned into a quaint bookshop stacked with current and older books. As I walked through it I was drawn to the back of the store. A woman wearing a dark shawl turned to me. As I approached her, I could see the woman was without a face. But as I got closer, I saw Gabriella's distinct facial features.

"It's time for you to learn," she said as she handed me a book: *A Rabbit Heart.* I walked out of the store. Then, realizing I needed to pay for the book, I returned to the store, but it was no longer there. The door to the shop was now the door to an undertaker's, displaying Frederick's corpse in the window. His dead body sat up and spoke to me.

Am I dreaming you? If so, you mustn't wake me.

I screamed in the dream and awoke in my bed. My body was perspiring. My breath was short and rapid, and it took several minutes for me to figure out what was real and where I was.

On my nightstand was a small thin book with gold-edged trim. I looked at its title: *A Rabbit Heart.* There were some printed pictures scattered through the book. I looked at the 1795 publication date in the front of the little volume and searched for an author but couldn't find a name. The book, though a hundred years old, looked brand-new.

I opened it, wanting insight into myself yet fearing what I might learn. I began to read the introduction: "You're not the first, the story is old. Just follow along as the story is told. It's impossible for a rabbit's heart to rest or hide its desire. And rabbits must race or stand in the fire. For the world is a dream, and life has its beauty, then passion is icing upon love's—"

I was interrupted by a knock on my door, and I slid the book under my covers. "Come in."

"Nicollette. You simply must go to the dance tonight. It's the biggest event of the year—you simply can't miss it."

"I was just resting."

"Oh, you can rest all weekend if the handsome men of Glastonbury will let you." Miriam sailed into my room. "You have plenty of time to get ready, and I hate to go alone. I'm so tired of being the town spinster."

"Very well, I'll join you, Miriam. Thank you for the invitation."

"Wonderful. We'll have such a fine time. I'll fetch you a pitcher of warm water and leave you privacy to freshen up."

When she left the room I reached for the book to hide it, but it wasn't under the covers where I had put it. I checked under the bed, near the headboard, rechecked the covers. There was no book.

It made no sense that a solid object, within my grasp minutes ago and being read by my eyes, had disappeared. No physical sense at all.

CHAPTER 12

The White Horse

THE DREAM STILL VIVID IN MY MIND, I DECIDED TO WALK
the streets in search of the bookshop. I passed the familiar shops I
had noticed upon my arrival, but where the bookshop had been
in my dream last night—there was only a stable.

I was fixed on the boardwalk when a young boy, not watching
his path, smacked right into me. He was a fine boy of about ten,
with bright eyes and long straight hair. He was well dressed for
his age, even sporting a hat and a cravat at his neck.

"Good day, young man."

"I'm sorry—did I hurt you, miss?"

"Not at all. Are you all right?"

"Oh, I'm fine, thank you."

I smiled at him. "And who might you be?"

"I'm Thomas Taylor, miss."

"Very pleased to meet you, Mr. Taylor. I'm Nicollette Caron.
Could you tell me if there's a bookshop nearby?"

He tipped his hat, bowed deeply to me, then, when he raised

himself, gave a little cry as he looked up. He recovered himself, and said, "Miss, there's no bookshop in Glastonbury. But look at that horse—I've never seen anything like him. He looks like a horse from a legend."

I turned to look in the stable. A stream of sunlight streaked through an open window and struck a horse that looked as if God's light had illuminated him. The young boy was right—this animal was the stuff of legends.

"I've never seen such a horse," I said. "He's breathtaking."

"Bet you that's Pegasus, the horse everyone's talking about. He's supposed to be able to fly like the wind, and dance, and jump—and he's really smart. He can understand anything we say to him."

"Really?"

Thomas ran to the stable and stood near the horse. I followed him, ignited by the young boy's curiosity, but I saw no stable hand tending the animal.

"Perhaps we shouldn't be in here," I said.

"I don't think they care. Come on, I must see if the horse understands what I say."

I followed the dark-haired boy because I found myself resonating with his excitement over this magical horse.

As Thomas studied the horse's build, I was more interested in his expression. For when he turned to me with intelligence in his eyes that I couldn't miss, he seemed to confirm that he was, in fact, allowing me to understand his thoughts. He came up near me and nuzzled me in a deliberately affectionate manner.

"And this horse loves," I said, delighting in his sensuous nuzzle. I began to pet his neck with long, soft strokes. "This is an extraordinary horse," I said. "Perhaps he's for sale."

"No, ma'am," Thomas said.

"Well, he could be for the right price."

"Oh, no. The man that owns him, he's really close to his horse. He and Pegasus perform all over together—they're performing here tonight. He'll never sell him."

"I don't give up easily. Perhaps I could barter with something the man might want."

"What could you have that a man would give up a horse like this for? Oh, I don't mean to be unmannered, miss, but a horse like this? No man is going to sell *a perfect horse.* Why, he could never find another horse like this—in a million years."

"Perhaps you're right, Thomas."

A voice in the distance called out, "Thomas!"

"Oops. That's my mother. I better go. Nice to meet you, Miss Caron."

"It was lovely to meet you, Thomas Taylor." He bowed deeply, remembering his manners, and tipped his hat. Then he ran off in the blink of my eye. I turned back to the horse and continued petting his neck softly.

"You truly are a splendid animal. Were you dealt so fine a name as you deserve? Perhaps you could be mine. Would you like that? I fancy you so, I'd baby you like a child."

"Grand Rexford Pegasus of Austria." The voice seemed to come from his stall.

"Well, that *is* a grand name," I said.

"But you can call me Pegasus."

"Thank you, Pegasus, I'm quite taken with you. Do you know if you're for sale?"

"He isn't." A man stepped out from behind the stable's support beams—a very handsome gentleman, with green eyes that seemed to pierce my own.

"Since you already know my horse, and he's shy about introductions, I should be the forward one." The man tipped his hat to me. "I'm Jackson Lang. I heard you introduce yourself. Miss Nicollette Caron, is that correct?"

"Yes. I'm happy to meet you, Mr. Lang. I'm sorry, I shouldn't be here. It's just that . . . is he yours?"

"He is."

"He's a spectacular horse."

"That he is."

"Where did you acquire such a fine animal?"

"Years ago I saved the life of an Austrian count, who gifted me with the horse. Pegasus is bred from a fine lineage of horses called Lippizan." Lang stroked his horse's neck. The animal leaned in slightly, in appreciation of his touch.

"Oh. I've never heard of that breed."

"He's quite an entertainer, and I do show him to townsfolks when I visit. He'll perform tonight at dusk—if you'd care to watch, I'd be honored to have you as my guest."

"Perhaps."

"He's an excellent ride, well trained for tricks and stunts, but beyond that he's my confidante. When I have puzzles in my mind, he helps me figure them out, for he quite fancies what I do."

"And what might that be?"

A young man entered the stable. "Sir, Wilcox and I'll be at the far end of town. We'll be back at dusk to watch you and Pegasus."

"Very well."

The young man left, without an introduction. Jackson Lang's green eyes seemed to look so deep inside me that I wanted to turn away.

What was it about him? He was a fine-looking man with a strong brow and jaw, a straight nose, and just a tip of gray in his sideburns. I found his mustache interesting to watch as he talked. Not so long as most, but trimmed to frame his lips. And those eyes.

A part of me was unnerved, which suggested that I move away and leave this man. But he was quite charming as we stood next to the finest horse I had ever seen in my life.

"I have some time before the show," he said. "Would you care for a spot of tea and conversation?"

"I'm afraid I'm not in a tea gown."

"Please come. I like you quite well in your present frock."

"Very well. We could go to Miriam Bestell's for tea."

He gently took my arm and walked on the outside, protecting me from the street. In a short time we were seated on Miriam's porch, where her personal servant served triangle apple pastries with our Chinese green tea. It was a lovely warm afternoon, with a gentle breeze that tossed wisps of my hair.

There was silence between us as we sat, and neither of us seemed able to break it.

Finally, I said, "Tell me the story of how you saved the Austrian count and came to receive such a beautiful horse."

"About seven years ago, I was meeting daily with barristers. I had chosen a law career for myself when my life was suddenly changed.

"My mother and father lived in London, and I went to visit them for a Sunday dinner as was my weekly custom. Instead of their welcome embrace, I found my lovely parents dead. Slaughtered for a bag of my mother's jewelry and a small sack of my father's gold.

"I searched for clues as to who had done these senseless murders and found out who the two men were. When they knew I was after them, they fled on horseback to the shore and took a boat. Once on board, the thieves on the ship promptly robbed them of my parent's bounty. But they landed safely in France and continued to flee. I remained on their trail, through France, Germany, and into Austria. There they believed they were far from me—and that I had given up the chase. But I wasn't far away. I was studying them, waiting for my chance to overpower them.

"In need of money, they set out to rob and kill again. I

watched them as they broke into a castle in Salzburg, followed them in, and discovered they'd tied up the royal family. As they were about to torture the count for access to his safe, I managed to shoot both of the men and set the family free.

"The count was so grateful that upon my departure he gave me a fine colt. Pegasus was all gray then. Lippizans are gray at birth and for the first three years, then they become their noble white color.

"The count also sent an experienced trainer to train the colt for me. For such a fine horse must be trained with great patience, never threatened. Lippizans are too intelligent for any example of negative training. They learn total trust of their owners.

"And that's the story of Grand Rexford Pegasus of Austria."

I found myself so pulled toward this man. We continued to talk for almost two hours, though it seemed like minutes. I shared a few things about myself but didn't inform him that I had lived in Hyde Park with London's society, nor did I tell him about the cities where I had lived.

The only truth I disclosed about my background was that I was French and had spent my youth traveling to many cities in France. I did share some of my true feelings. And after a time, when we had gotten to know each other somewhat, I asked, "Is there any price I might pay you for your horse? Just name it, and it's yours."

"Dear lady, Pegasus will never have a price—he's beyond money. I couldn't imagine an amount of money or a cause so great that it would part me from him. One cannot sell greatness. Ever."

Two young men approached us from the street, leading Jackson's magnificent horse. Both tipped their hats to me and bowed. "Excuse us, miss."

"It's quite all right."

"Jackson, it's time for your show. The townspeople have arranged quite a crowd."

"I hadn't realized it was so late. I must go. Would you excuse me, Miss Caron? Please come and watch."

"Yes, of course."

"Ulysses Peavey and Edward Wilcox are trusted assistants. Please allow them to escort you." They bowed and tipped their hats again.

Jackson mounted his horse, and Pegasus stood on his back legs and walked for me. He seemed in no hurry to return to four hooves, as if he were quite used to walking on two legs. When he was back on all fours, he began to prance slowly down the street toward the waiting crowd.

Peavey and Wilcox sheltered me between them and offered their arms. Miriam appeared and asked to come with us. Wilcox gave her his arm, and the four of us joined the crowd of towns-people.

Everyone in Glastonbury seemed to be there for the show. I saw clergy, business owners, working people, men and women of all ages—even Um. He danced a jig alone with joyful abandon, as though he heard a song within his own mind, not the chatter of an excited crowd. Nor did he seem to have any awareness of what brought the crowd to the event. I don't believe he even noticed the fine white horse in the center of the street or recognized me.

I noticed that Jackson Lang had a different posture when mounted on Pegasus. He had a straighter back. Instead of leaning forward, he seemed to levitate above the horse as Pegasus picked up his hooves. With every step, the gentle breeze ruffled his tail and mane and he looked as if he were flying.

"Bravo!" The crowd shouted, and applauded.

Next he gently stretched his forward legs before him and to-gether, as if he were in prayer. We then saw him walk on his hind legs, rider intact, as he stood straight up, then actually jumped off the earth on his two back legs.

"Bravo! Bravo!" Wild applause followed each stunt, and no one in the crowd dared to blink during the performance. Jackson Lang and Pegasus were so in tune that their movements seemed perfectly synchronized, as if they were one being.

Pegasus would curve his neck and walk as though he knew that he was special. Very special. And so, as I was beginning to think, was his master—when I looked just beyond the performers and saw a tall, breathtaking man across the crowd.

I worked my way around Peavey and whispered, "Miriam, who's that gentlemen there?"

"Which one?"

"The tall man."

"Oh, yes, Nicollette. That's Lord Baston."

I willed myself to attend to the final stunt of the show. Pegasus galloped and leaped into the air while he kicked his back legs out. He seemed to remain still and airborne so long, I was sure that if you took his photograph, there wouldn't be a blur at all.

It was amazing to watch. I loved this horse—his beauty and his talent—but suddenly I caught the tall man's eye, and he mine, across the crowd. All images of Pegasus and Jackson Lang were wiped from my mind like school sums from a slate.

I saw only Lord Baston, and he saw only me.

CHAPTER 13

In Bertrum We Trust

CLIVE ENTERED THE LIBRARY WHERE LORD BASTON WAS reading a book. Lord Baston closed the book and set his hand down on it, as if to hide its title. Clive made no attempt to see it. The large windows in the study were open, and a gentle breeze made the draperies rustle a bit over his shoulder.

"Good evening, my lord. How was the horse's showing?"

"Extraordinary, Clive. Lovely breeze tonight."

"Yes, smells of lilacs, sir. Very pleasant. We thought you might dine a little earlier this evening, my lord. We assume you're planning to go to the affair at the club."

"I hadn't decided, Clive. I thought of staying home."

"My lord, if I may say, I know they look forward to your attendance. You have such a presence when you attend any social affair."

"Perhaps you're right, Clive. I may put in an appearance."

"Would you like to dine at seven-thirty, then, sir? Roberta has a lovely roast she has marinated in cognac."

"That will be fine. Will you lay out my best black suit?"

"Yes, my lord. I'll see that Jeremy's ready to dress you after dinner."

"How is the little Irish girl doing, Clive? I want her to fit in here."

Lord Baston had tipped his hand. Had he asked the question open-ended, Clive might have shared his reservations. He might have told his master that he had searched Carrie's purse without her knowing, that he thought she might be an addict. But he was an experienced servant who knew that just as often as not, the messenger can be shot. And he valued his job.

"Clive?"

The best thing to do was wait for her to show her true colors. "You made an excellent choice, my lord. Were you pleased with her service today?"

"Yes, I was. Thank you, Clive."

Clive turned to go, satisfied that he had done the right thing in holding his tongue. After all, he had seen the way they'd looked at one another, and he'd read the note Lord Baston had tossed in the waste.

Carrie didn't know how she got through dinner. She served Lord Baston his vegetable broth, then returned to the kitchen. Sitting down, she wiped the sweat from her brow. Why did she feel this way? She was hot and cold, then hot again. *Her brain had an animal running through it, pressuring her skull as the exotic beast tried to escape. A big bird. Huge. Flapping its wings. It had a needle-sharp beak, and it was nibbling her brain from the inside out.*

Her balance was off—she wobbled around a corner. *The pain from her head raced down her spine.* How could she hold the tray? She was going to fall, or drop the tray. *A shooting pain ricocheted through her head, piercing her skull like an arrow, and then another arrow. More arrows. She had more holes in her head, and her brains could leak out any moment.* What did he say? Who said that?

"Good evening, Carrie," Lord Baston said.

He said something. She didn't care. She couldn't focus on his lips. She barely knew where she was. *I'm in Ireland and should walk home now.* That's it. *I'll walk back to Ireland tonight to gather more brains.* Wait, I can't, I'm in England. *Help me, Jesus. Help me!*

She felt the bird again—flapping its wings harder. Leave me alone, *bird.* She concentrated on serving Lord Baston roast, his breads. Poured his tea. She took it away quickly to bring him a warm cup. *I forgot the sugar cubes. Remember the sugar cubes. He likes four cubes in two cups. So he wants six cubes in this one.* She started to give him six cubes, but he stopped her on her third attempt.

"Thank you, Carrie. That's enough." Lord Baston was looking into her eyes. He saw her sickness. He saw through her. He knew.

She ran to the kitchen and hid behind an apron on the wall.

Clive snapped his fingers at her. "Lord Baston is ready for his dessert."

She took rice pudding to him, but he waved it away. Oh, oh. He didn't want dessert. *I did it wrong. I did it wrong.* Carrie dropped the dessert, shattering the bone china dish into shards. She ran into the kitchen as Clive stepped forward with a broom and pan to clean it up.

Carrie held the side of her head to keep her brain from falling out of the hole.

Bertrum was waiting for his dinner in the kitchen when he saw Carrie run out the back door toward the hills. He followed in pursuit of her and when he caught her, he held her so she couldn't run.

"Carrie, I want to help you. Let me. What can I do? What's wrong?"

The first time he asked she couldn't see his lips, then he faced her and repeated his question.

She pantomimed that she couldn't speak. That she couldn't hear. She pulled out a pencil and paper and wrote: "I can read lips."

"I didn't know," Bertrum said. "I'm sorry, Carrie. I didn't know."

She calmed when she realized that someone was trying to understand. She wrote, "I need elixir. I need cocaine."

Bertrum nodded his understanding. "I'll help you—I'll find it for you. I'll be taking Lord Baston to the dance. I'll get some for you."

Carrie cried with relief, and Bertrum held her in his arms. He hadn't held a woman in his arms for years. And he liked it.

Perhaps she could be mine. I'd look after her, and take care of her. Yes. That's it. I'll take care of her and protect her. Just as soon as Lord Baston is done with her.

Or maybe I'll need to protect her from his lordship. Yes. That's it. I know what can happen to Lord Baston's women. I'm silent, but I'm not stupid.

Lord Baston was never ignorant of what happened on his grounds. Even with a waning moon, he saw his driver holding Carrie on the hill.

"Not smart, my trusted Bertrum," he whispered.

CHAPTER 14

The Dance

THERE WAS A KNOCK ON MY DOOR. I WAS WEARING ONLY A corset and stockings.

"It's Miriam."

"Sorry, I'm not dressed yet."

"That's all right, I'll help you. Let me in."

She carried a glass of wine with her and was already tipsy.

"I'm *too* excited about the dance," she said.

I was just beginning to powder my arms and shoulders with talc. Miriam looked at me in the mirror. I set out some of the grapes from my basket for her.

"You're welcome to nibble on these."

"Oh, I haven't had grapes in years. We don't have them in Glastonbury. They're such a delicacy—so expensive."

"I indulge myself from time to time."

As she gobbled grapes, I listened to her talk about Frederick and the wicked Mamie, who'd stolen him from her when she was forced to visit out-of-town relatives for a year. Finally, after listening to her history, I managed to change the subject to the people who would be at the dance.

"Tell me about Lord Baston."

"He'll probably be there, but he never dances with any women or pays any mind to them. So the women of Glastonbury have come to realize that he's like a beautiful dress in the window, one they can't have. Or they rationalize his lack of attraction to them by whispering that he may prefer a *male* companion."

After the look we'd exchanged, I believed such speculation to be ludicrous.

Miriam helped me tighten my corset, and I put on my lowest-cut dress.

"Nicollette, I'm not sure the men of Glastonbury have seen such a black-velvet gown. We may have injuries over it. All the men will be hoping you turn your head their way."

"Do you think it's inappropriate?"

"Let's see. Low-cut back with tiny black pearl buttons, hugs your bare shoulders, tiny sleeves that slip almost halfway down your arm, an inch of cleavage . . ."

"Is it wrong for the dance?"

"The gown cannot be at fault, Nicollette, it's merely the hood for the cannon. The true artillery is the woman in the dress, her motives, and her desires. I'll guess this will be an adventurous event tonight. And you're dressed perfectly for the affair."

"I'm relieved to hear you say so."

"You show an inch of cleavage. An inch is all it takes to attract men. Any more than that, and the women will snub you. Believe me, I know."

"I do like to be welcomed at events and not treated as if I were preying on other women's men, for I'm not." *I don't need to, for they'll all be after me.*

"Your diamonds are beautiful, Nicollette." Miriam filled her wineglass and drank it down without taking a breath.

I wore a diamond necklace with matching earrings and a bracelet thick with diamonds. Originally designed for the queen, it was to have been an addition to the crown jewels—until Robert ambushed its destination as a courting gift for me.

I also wore a tiny diamond fox pin, hidden on my dress near my décolletage. No one would find it without studying my bosom for some time.

My hair ornament of diamonds was another courting gift. And my hair was piled atop my head. Finally I applied some lip paint and rouge, and Miriam said, "You look like an exquisite doll."

"Thank you—and you look stunning in your frock. That shade of rose is my favorite, and it makes your complexion glow."

"Why, thank you, Nicollette."

"I'm sure we'll have a wonderful time," I said.

Giddy on wine, Miriam's feet flew out from under her when she started down the stairs. She dropped on her derriere and skidded the rest of the way. I ran down and helped her to her feet.

"Miriam, are you all right?"

"Well, I believe my bum has been getting larger just for the protection of this very moment."

And she laughed at herself. Apparently she was so "relaxed" that she felt little effect from her fall.

"I've arranged for a carriage ride so we can arrive in style rather than in our buggy," she said.

Sore arse or not, intoxicated or not, Miriam was ready to dance.

"How thoughtful, Miriam. Thank you."

We chattered and laughed all the way to the dance. Within

minutes we stood before the Glastonbury Foxhunt Club, listening to the music and laughter pouring out of the clubhouse.

Three well-dressed men stood together near the front door. I overheard them speaking about a racehorse, but as we came closer they stopped talking and fanned out in a gallant line with their hats tipped.

"Miriam, introduce us to your friend."

"Who's the new girl, Miriam?"

"Miriam, me first."

"Gentlemen, I'd like you to meet Nicolette Caron. Nicollette, this is Charles Faraday, Douglas Pfeiffer, and Oliver Davis."

"It's a pleasure to meet you." I smiled but didn't offer my hand, as protocol left the choice up to me. And I find when meeting several people that it's awkward to pump hand after hand. Instead, I studied each gentleman. Charles Faraday was a tall slim man with red-brown curls flat to his head and large, luminous eyes. Douglas Pfeiffer was dressed in a fashionable pin-striped coat, had a gold watch chain draped across his front, and in general seemed quite affluent.

But it was Oliver Davis who captivated me, on my first look, with his radiant smile. His eyes called to me. His dark hair and flashing smile seemed to light up the whole front entrance. When he looked at me I felt as though he were trying to see through my dress to my corset, even while he made direct contact with my eyes.

Charles interrupted our moment. "Will you dance with me?"

"No, me," Douglas said.

"Dance with me, please," Oliver said.

"I'd love to dance with all of you, gentlemen." The three men swarmed around me, jostling each other to be the closest one leading me into the club. And as I knew I'd have choices once again, I couldn't help feeling aglow with anticipation.

• • •

At the other end of the dance floor Inspector Lang leaned against a post observing the activities with Peavey and Wilcox.

"She's a beautiful woman, isn't she?" Peavey asked.

"I think she's as grand as a woman gets," Wilcox said.

"And you, Inspector?"

"I received a telegram this afternoon. Denton Brickman was with Nicollette Caron on the evening of his death, so the woman who's making you two drool could be our killer."

With that, Lang walked away to refill his punch cup. He settled into a quiet area of the club where he could see but hardly be seen.

"Did you get that, Wilcox?"

"Yes, I got it. But I have to adjust my trousers just looking at that woman. And I make no promises for my behavior if she shows me her ankle."

"Miss Caron, we have to keep dancing—for I don't ever want to let you go," Oliver Davis said.

He was moving me as smoothly around the floor as if dancing were his profession. I felt covetous eyes upon us as we danced—and why not, for Oliver was a handsome man with personality and humor who had his own manor and stables, specializing in Derby racehorses.

He flashed me his wonderful smile. "Would it help me at all if I told you that Charles and Douglas are not fully recovered from cholera?"

"Really?"

"Miss Caron, you wouldn't believe their nauseous afternoon and what they coughed up. And Charles was pale as a ghost, too."

I looked over at the two men. Both removed their hats, bowed, and danced a little dance. A demonstration that they were ready for their promised dance with me.

"Oliver, they don't look so very ill," I said.

"Charles is quite an actor. He's probably wearing his mother's rouge for color. Believe me, they won't want you to know—it would ruin their last night." Oliver cocked an eyebrow at me. "I'd say you have only ten or eleven hours left, if you fancy them."

"You like to win, don't you Oliver?"

"I always get what I go after, Miss Caron. When I have my eye on something I want."

"Well, I rather like that confidence in you." I smiled. "Is your eye on me?"

"I must confess, it is. You are my fox." He pulled me tight to him and dipped me deeply. I'd have lost my balance as he bent me backward had he not held me tightly in his strong arms. The song ended, giving me time to straighten myself out as Oliver led me back to Charles and Douglas.

The two waiting for me had become four. "Hello, will you dance with me, Miss Caron?"

"May I have this dance, Miss Caron?"

I nodded to them, assuming each would take his turn for a dance. And Charles confidently offered his arm to me and led me onto the dance floor. "Did Oliver speak ill of me?"

"He did mention your recent attack of cholera."

"Oh, yes, I fixed that." He smiled. He put his arm around me, just as smoothly as Oliver, and we began our dance.

"Say, I saw you got fairly close to Oliver on the floor there. Don't let his mother see that. She's quite jealous of him with other women, you know. I hear they sleep in the same room still."

"Oliver told me his father is the ambassador to South Africa and his parents live there and he rarely sees them."

"I heard he was trying to start that rumor, but one mustn't discount what the servants confide."

"Oh, so you've heard this from a good source, then."

"Quite good."

I didn't meet any other women at the event. I had no time. My night began with ten men taking turns for my dances, all of them trying to undermine one another. I laughed so hard, because I could tell that, underneath it all, the men were good friends.

Nor did Miriam want for male attention. She danced, drank, enjoyed the music, and had a grand time.

Lord Baston stood on the porch and looked in to the dance floor. He saw Nicollette and immediately recognized her as the breathtaking woman he'd noticed at Jackson Lang's horse performance. He was captivated by her, but she was surrounded by his horse racing friends.

As he contemplated his next move, he felt a tap on his shoulder. "Good evening, Lord Baston." The shorter gentleman tipped his hat. Blake recognized the man as Herbert Stafford, the woodcarver from whom he'd bought the table and chairs.

"Good evening, what brings you to Glastonbury?" Blake asked.

"You know I don't visit this far west often. But I brought some sketches for a possible carving job, and my interested prospect resides in Glastonbury." Stafford lifted a leather satchel he carried with him. "Would you like to see them, Lord Baston?"

"Not right now, Herbert, but I wish you success in your sale."

"Lord Baston, I can't tell you what you did for me that day when you purchased my table and chairs. I will be able to pay my debts and feed my family for more than a year with your generosity." The woodcarver started to tear up.

"My good man, don't do that. That's what we're here for—to help one another. Say, would you like to return a favor?"

"Anything, sir."

"Have you ever acted before?"

"I was in a school play once. Played the lead in it. They said I was quite believable."

"Excellent. See that beautiful woman there?" He pointed through the doorway to Nicollette.

"Oh my, yes—she's stunning, isn't she?"

"Yes, quite. Now see those three pesky men that hang around too closely?"

Stafford nodded.

"Do you know any of them?"

"No."

"Would they know you?"

"I'm hardly in this area at all. I'm sure they wouldn't know me."

"Here's what I'd like you to do." The men huddled for a moment before Blake snuck to his position.

Stafford entered the dance hall. "I'm looking for Oliver Davis?"

A young man pointed. "He's over there, dancing."

Stafford walked across the dance floor as if on a heaven-sent mission. "Excuse me, but are you Oliver Davis?"

"Yes, I am."

"I'm sorry to bother you right now but this is a matter of extreme importance for you, Mr. Davis. I'm also looking for two other gentlemen that I understand might be here, a Mr. Charles Faraday and Mr. Douglas Pfeiffer—do you know them, by chance?"

"Yes, they're right here." Oliver motioned the men to his side, and now Charles, Douglas, Oliver, Stafford, and Nicollette were standing together. "This gentleman apparently has some news for us," Oliver said. "Very well, who are you?"

"I'm James Weatherby V. My family has been the accountants

of the General Stud Book for the Jockey Club since 1791. As you know, we meticulously record the pedigree of every foal born, so it's critical that our records are accurate.

"The question I bring to you is of great importance. For it involves the lineage of your stallions and will affect your stud fees—and I would only need a few moments of your time to set the record straight. If not, I will have no choice but to revoke the registration on your top stallions."

"What? I've never heard of such a thing. We've registered appropriately."

"Very well." The imposter shrugged. "Consider that your stallion, Royal Prince of Glastonbury, is no longer in our General Stud Book, Mr. Davis. And this could happen to all your horses. I think we should discuss this somewhere private—it will only take a moment for me to verify our records with you. Come with me."

"Nicollette, I'll be right back. Will you be all right without an escort?" Oliver asked. "I feel like I'm leaving you in a den of thieves here. All the men desire you."

"Nonsense," I said. "I'll be fine, I'll join Miriam."

I watched my gentlemen vanish with Weatherby. And then, I wasn't sure from where, a man appeared so quickly before me that he startled me.

"They say that abandonment can scar someone for life. Perhaps I'm the remedy. May I have this dance, miss?"

When I looked up I saw that it was Lord Baston. I almost gasped. I hadn't seen this charismatic tall man walk in—he must have taken his position from behind me. For had I seen him, I would have had a hard time taking my eyes off him.

"I'm Lord Baston."

"Nicollette Caron." He took his dance position with grace and strength.

"French?"

"Yes."

"A nervy one."

"What do you mean?"

"It appears that you're trying to corner the market of available lads here, while the English women sneer at you from their sidelines over there."

"That isn't my intent . . ."

"What is your intent, then? Are you interested in quantity—or do you seek a suitor of high quality?"

"That depends. Sometimes those who consider themselves of high quality have low shortcomings. Then I'm forced to settle for quantity," I jested.

I had to reach for this man, who towered over me. My arms almost went numb from holding them above my shoulders as we danced. But I wouldn't let go—nor did he.

There was no relaxed coupling as with Oliver. I didn't meld with Lord Baston's movements. Why? I wondered. Then I realized that this man actually made me nervous. I felt anxious. On edge. Unsure. I lacked my confidence. I didn't know what to say. My God, was this what suitors went through with me at times? How awkward I felt.

I followed his steps. But I don't believe he had danced so often as Oliver and the other gentlemen. And then I looked at the crowd.

Those who had been dancing were now standing and watching. I saw Miriam and her friends. My suitors were on the sidelines, even the musicians stood to watch us dance as they played. Why? Were we that awkward together?

Then I remembered Miriam's telling me that Lord Baston never danced. Ah! It was this rarity that had the attendees so awestruck.

Finally, I decided to reassure him. One of us *had* to speak. "You're a wonderful dancer, Lord Baston."

"I'm not known in Glastonbury for my ability on the dance floor."

"What are you known for then?"

"My knack for accumulating wealth and my honesty."

"Admirable qualities."

"Well, as an example of the latter. I must say, you're the most beautiful woman I've ever seen."

"Thank you. I'm flattered I please your eyes."

"More than my eyes are feeling pleased as I look at you . . ."

"Lord Baston, this is our first dance. Perhaps we can save some conversational territory for future dances."

"Come home with me," he said in a low voice.

"Lord Baston . . ."

"Blake."

"Lord Baston, we met only moments ago."

"Let's go for a buggy ride then, some fresh warm country air will—"

"I came to the dance with Miriam. I will go home with Miriam."

I was attracted to everything about this man. His strong, tall physique, his daring conversation. I loved his blue eyes, his strong nose, and the way his nostrils flared, as if ready to charge me, but his arrogance made me stubborn.

"We should leave, Nicollette."

This time I ignored him, and said, "I'd love to hear the story of how you became a lord. It must be an interesting tale."

"It's a simple one."

"How does one achieve the honor in England?"

"Two things are required. One—you need to catch the eye of the queen."

"And the other?"

"Wealth," Lord Baston said.

"A lordship can be bought?"

"Sh-h-h, don't tell anyone. It's a secret."

"Of course."

"Money is boring, don't you think?"

"Then, pray, introduce a more interesting topic."

"All right. Beauty."

"And what do you think about beauty?"

"Well, I've known some very beautiful women in my day."

"You have?"

"Quite. And they grow tired of hearing how beautiful they are. Do you think that all beautiful women are exhausted by their own beauty?"

"I . . . I wouldn't know. Perhaps they would be."

"Well, it appears you can't help me at all on that question, can you? I'll have to track down one of those other beautiful women I used to know to learn the answer."

"Are they still around?" I felt a bit jealous. Why was he bringing up other women while he was dancing with me?"

"Well, one is, one isn't."

"I see." When he saw I had some concern, he smiled—and the most wonderful twinkle was in his eyes. The light concentrated their deep blue color and seemed to pull me in deeper.

"One was my grandmother—and she's not around still."

"I'm so sorry."

"Oh, don't be. She's on safari in Africa."

"And the other?"

"My mother. And she won't be returning soon."

"I'm sorry."

"As am I. But in all honesty, Nicollette—your beauty is bewitching me. I want to stare at you and dance, but I'm not coordinated enough to accomplish both tasks at the same time."

He looked into my eyes with great sincerity and warmth. I felt energized to be in his arms.

He turned me in his arms so that he leaned in behind me as we swayed to the music. I thought I should pull away and return to our original position, but he held me tightly in front of him.

I liked the way his strong arms felt around me, but then he leaned his right arm over my right shoulder and draped his forearm across my bosom. As we moved to the music, his arm moved lightly back and forth across my bosom. It unsettled me and excited me. I searched the crowd, but no one seemed to notice his bold move. Lord Baston acted as if he were unaware of what he was doing, as if the unusual way he held me was all part of the dance. But I could tell he was aroused and wanting me. And I found myself wanting to fall into him.

Instead, we danced.

"Charles, Douglas. Find anything?" Oliver asked.

"Nothing here," Charles said.

"I don't see anything this way," Douglas said.

"Mr. Weatherby, are you sure you dropped your logbook in the woods?"

"Quite sure. Oh my goodness, this is just awful. That logbook had all the registrations back to 1848."

"Well, Mr. Weatherby. What did you want us to see? We've properly filled out forms on all our horses. Charles, Douglas, and I send in our forms promptly to confirm each foal—don't we?"

"Yes, of course."

"Yes."

"It wouldn't be beneficial to our sales if we didn't keep our paperwork in order. We have the finest Thoroughbred lines in all of England. We sell to the queen, for god sakes."

"As you know, we've had five generations of registering horses for the Jockey Club, so my visit should not be taken lightly. We could look farther down this road. I'm sure we'll find it."

"Mr. Weatherby?" Oliver squared off with the smaller man. "I was having the most wonderful night of my life. And I don't see why this can't wait until the morning. You'll find your book easier in the daylight and you can come out to my manor, where I have all my foals' birth records, and we can correct any errors first thing in the morning."

"But . . . just a while . . . right down this road—"

"I'm going back to the dance. But Charles and Douglas, don't let me speak for you."

"We'll join you, Oliver. I think that Nicollette fancied us and may need our protection."

"Wait a minute," Oliver said. "May I see your identification, sir? Certainly a man of your credentials will have it with him."

"Actually, I . . ." Stafford said.

"Anything, show us anything with your name on it," Oliver said. Then, as Stafford began backing away from him, "You're not from the Jockey Club. Gents, I believe we've been duped." He grabbed Stafford by the back of his suit collar. "Who put you up to this?"

"I . . . it was in fun. He told me you do this all the time to each other. And . . . well, he's a lord, how could I refuse?"

"Baston!"

Charles laughed. "Well, that's a good one."

"Easy for you to say," Douglas said. "You didn't have a chance with her."

"*Au contraire.* She told me on the first dance with me that she'd come to my home by 3:00 A.M. to crawl in my bed," Charles said.

"Yes, and she was coming to my bed by 1:00 A.M.," Douglas said. "She wanted me first."

"You deluded buffoons, she was mine," Oliver said. He turned in a rather intimidating manner to Stafford. "Drive us back."

"Yes. Yes, of course."

I stopped dancing and stepped back from my partner as Oliver, flanked by Charles and Douglas, rushed toward us.

"You're a cad and a bounder and should be horsewhipped for your deceit!" Oliver said. He tried to shove Lord Baston with both his hands, but Lord Baston dodged and hit Oliver's jaw with his elbow. I couldn't tell if the strike was accidental or done on purpose. It wasn't a hard blow, but it was enough to catch Oliver off guard and send him toppling to the floor.

"Oh, Oliver." I knelt next to him.

"Nicollette, the man that fetched us earlier was an imposter—set up by Lord Baston," Douglas said.

"Lord Baston, I'm shocked!" I pretended to be miffed.

I felt a spectacle. I decided for the first time of the evening that I didn't want the eyes of the town watching me. Suddenly I wasn't at my most charming—and after all, this was my introduction to the people of Glastonbury. What would they think of me?

Lord Baston led me away from the others.

"I had better go back," I said. He looked at me as though I had just slapped his face.

"I want to bed you," he said.

"You *what?*"

"You heard me."

"Well, I'm not interested, sir. Not interested at all. Your manners are atrocious. Nor are you the gentleman I heard you to be. Quite frankly I find you—appalling."

"I'm sorry." He bowed his head.

I looked at Lord Baston. His head was still down. When he

lifted his blue eyes to mine, a beam of light shot through me like nothing I had ever experienced.

"Please let me start over," he said in a low voice. "I'm truly sorry for my behavior. You must believe me. I've never met anyone like you."

My heart raced. *Who was this man?*

I said nothing.

"I'm a gentleman. I assure you. Oliver, Douglas and Charles are old friends of mine."

Charles stepped forward. "I'm certain he's sorry for the punch and will make it up to Oliver, won't you, Baston?" Oliver joined them and faced Lord Baston squarely.

"Yes, I will." Lord Baston turned to Oliver. "I'm sorry, Oliver, it was an accident. I'll be over on Monday to pay you too much for that racehorse you have for sale."

Oliver rubbed his jaw. "Hardest horse sale I've had." But he waved his forgiveness to Lord Baston.

The crowd relaxed, and their casual conversations resumed. Everyone but Lord Baston and me.

"Don't make me say it again," Lord Baston said. "I won't."

I looked closely at this man, sensing that he was by no means someone I could manipulate as easily as the other men who pursued me. *I knew this.* He would be important to me. *He knew this.* I was already important to him. *We both knew.*

But I turned away. "I've had enough excitement this evening," I said over my shoulder.

"Don't go, Nicollette. Stay with me." He pulled me closer to him. I saw his eyes search me, his passion crave me, and felt his full-scale erection pressing against my hip.

His arousal was a tease and I wanted it to go deeper, feel it intimately. Yes, his taunt had aroused my desire, and the situation grew dangerous. But I did the right thing.

"Even if I wanted to, Lord Baston—I couldn't," I said. "Charles," I called, "would you please escort me back to my table?"

"Certainly," Charles said.

"Play your games with the small change," Baston whispered in my ear before Charles led me away.

I turned back, straightened the train of my dress, and disappeared from his sight.

I found Miriam with a man inappropriately wrapped around her and taking too many liberties.

"Miriam, I'm fatigued. I'd like to leave now."

She pushed the man off her. "I'll go with you, Nicollette."

"Oh, you've got me going now, Miriam," he said. "Don't leave me so worked up for you."

Miriam gave him a gay smile. "Oh, Harry, I can work you up another time."

"Good-bye, Charles," I said. "Oliver. Douglas. I've had a lovely time with you all." I smiled graciously and left the dance without seeing Lord Baston again.

CHAPTER 15

Bertrum's Good Deed

Woman, quit horsing around, just hand me the jug,
You can kiss me later, if you top off my mug,
Don't ever expect that I'll make you a bride,
Mention marriage to me, and I ship off to sea,
But I don't mind a little filly for a ride . . .

THE SINGING MAN WITH RAGGEDY CLOTHING LAY IN THE street. He clambered to his knees, then choked, gagged, and puked, spewing yellow vomit on the front of his torn trousers.

"Quite a gob you did there," Bertrum said. He had just dropped off Lord Baston at the dance.

"I'm on a program to clean out my liver. This here's yesterday's bile." The man pointed to dried spots on his trousers. He retched a couple more times, finally spitting the vile taste out of his mouth. "Need something, Captain?"

Bertrum pulled out Carrie's empty bottle. "I'm looking for some elixir. Like this."

"You want to go see Doc, then. The American. You got to admire a guy like that with so much going for him. Told us he was Abraham Lincoln's best friend for years. Told us he wrote the Gettysburg Address for him, then Lincoln used his ideas and didn't pay him anything for it. Doc's a great guy."

"Where do I find him?"

"Go north on Gooney Road a few miles. He's in a shack just outside of town on the west side. Just look for the big leech."

Bertrum found the place in record time—after all, who could miss a leech ten feet high in the front of the shack?

"Got bad blood, do you?" asked Doc.

Bertrum stood in the entryway looking at a large trough of leeches. "No, I don't believe I do. I'm looking for elixir."

"Ah. That'll get you."

"It's not for me."

Doc smiled. "Sure, it ain't."

"Do you have this kind here?" He showed him Carrie's empty bottle.

"Real close. I got the copy of that stuff, but most like it better. Got more cocaine in it. You'll like it, you will."

"It's not for me."

"Sure, it ain't."

Bertrum didn't want to argue.

"I'll give you a free taste."

"No. It's not for me."

"One taste? Are you that pure of a guy? A little euphoria never hurt anybody."

"No. Well, just one."

Doc poured a small shot glass for Bertrum, who took a sip. He rolled his eyes, caught off guard by its bitter taste.

"What's in here?" He choked as he squinted to see the liquid in the bottle.

"It has some opium, too. A bit of a bitter taste, but the effect is worth it."

"How much?"

Doc looked out his window at Bertrum's expensive carriage. "Six bottles is a pound."

"A pound? That's too much."

"Well, you're a nice gentleman with your suit and all."

"My threads belong to my boss man."

"How about six bottles for half a pound?"

"All right."

The man bagged the bottles after holding them up to the light to make sure they were full. He uncapped a few of them and took a sip or two, then screwed the top back on.

"There. They're even now."

Bertrum paid him and reached into the bag. He decided to take one more sip before he hit the road. This second sip seemed smoother. He knew what to expect, was ready for the taste. He liked it.

"I don't have to tell you, you forgot where you got this, right?"

"Right. Until I want more?"

"Right."

"Need some leeches for anybody you know? There's not an illness exists can't be improved by leeches—and that's a scientific fact."

"No, not this time."

Lord Baston was furious when he walked out of the Foxhunt Club dance and found that his carriage was not waiting for him. As he paced impatiently, people glanced his way and gossiped over the evening's events. He wasn't sure if he was angriest at the whispers, at Bertrum, or at himself for his behavior at the dance. He slapped his gloves in his hand.

He waited only ten minutes for Bertrum to arrive, but it seemed like an hour. No one came up to chat with him. People steered clear of him. And that infuriated him even more.

"Sorry, my lord," Bertrum said when he drove up in the carriage. "I had to relieve myself."

"I've been waiting ten minutes, Bertrum."

"Well, my lord, if I may be candid with you, I have to say the shepherd's pie didn't set well with me. I'm feeling poorly."

Lord Baston got in the carriage, and said, "Quickly."

Bertrum seemed to think it best to keep quiet after his apology. And on the way back, he drove the horses quickly, as commanded.

He dropped Lord Baston off at the manor. "My lord, can I do anything for you this evening?"

"No, Bertrum, you've done quite enough."

Bertrum stayed outside and looked up to see Carrie waiting in her bedroom window. Even from the ground she looked sickly. And Bertrum knew the cure in his pocket needed to reach her fast. He nodded to Carrie from the ground and slapped his pocket. She nodded her understanding from her window, and he headed into the mansion.

Several servants had stayed up waiting to see if Lord Baston would need them once he returned.

"How was the dance, my lord?" Clive asked.

"To bed, everyone. It's late," Lord Baston said.

"Yes, my lord."

"Yes, my lord."

The servants scattered as Bertrum walked up the stairs.

"Where are you going, Bertrum?" Lord Baston said. "Get to bed, it's late."

Bertrum stopped. "Carrie found my reading glasses, my lord. I like to read a few pages before I nod off. They're upstairs. I'll get them first if that's all right with you."

Lord Baston studied Bertrum for a long moment, then nodded.

Carrie was waiting at the top of the stairs.

"Here it is." Bertrum took the bottle out of his pocket and handed it to her. He followed her a few steps into her room.

She fumbled with the cap but drank the nectar down in seconds. Bertrum looked around while she took a second, longer sip. On her dresser stood an antique silver box, beautifully detailed, one of Lord Baston's prized possessions.

"What are you doing with that box, Carrie? It can't be to polish it—Roberta does that. Why is it here?"

Carrie closed her eyes. She didn't read Bertrum's lips or pay any mind to him. Carrie had what she wanted. Euphoria.

Bertrum came downstairs, pulling his glasses from his pocket. "Got them right here. Good night, my lord."

"Good night, Bertrum." Lord Baston had heard Bertrum speaking to Carrie at the top of the stairs. His most trusted servant had lied to him. And this lie put a second notch on Bertrum's tally sheet. That made two in one night.

The house was dark and the servants asleep. Lord Baston went to his room to retire for the evening but found that he was stimulated from the dance and quite restless. Perhaps a sexual interlude would help him sleep.

He went quietly down the hall. Carrie wouldn't be able to hear a knock or his call, so he slipped into her room. She smiled as soon as she saw him. She wore a sheer nightgown, her long auburn hair fell loosely down her back, and she raised her arms, as if she had been in wait for just this moment.

She stepped toward him. But before he kissed her, Lord Baston looked down and saw his sterling silver piece.

"Carrie, what are you doing with my box?"

She flashed a wide-eyed look of surprise, then ran across the room for her paper but couldn't find it and pantomimed polishing the box.

"Roberta always does the polishing." Lord Baston paced the little room. "They would have told me."

She tried to put her arms around him, but he pulled away.

"Carrie, you're a beautiful girl, but if you weren't to polish the box, then you're a common thief. And I won't bed a common thief, as much as I want and need you now."

She pulled at him and desperately pressed her head to his chest, then clutched at his arms as if begging for his mercy. But he grabbed her wrists firmly and pushed her away.

"In the morning we will talk to Roberta. If she told you to polish it, you'll stay. If you've taken it in order to steal it, you won't be welcome in my home. You'll be given a boat ticket to Ireland, or returned to the tavern where I found you."

She began to cry.

"Carrie, we shall know first thing in the morning. Roberta will have the answer for us. I'll see you at sunrise." Then he turned and, without looking back, went to his bedroom.

CHAPTER 16

Marie's Interrogation

FREDERICK'S NUDE BODY WAS DISCOVERED LYING ACROSS the creek. It was covered with leaves and sticks and dirt, but various wildflowers decorated his resting place as if someone had taken great care with his interment. The wildflowers were arranged with darker colors near the bottom and lighter colors at the top of a rainbow-like arch.

Frederick's best friend, Niles Morgan, stepped in as the new acting constable. He was a good friend to both Frederick and Mamie Bothem, and he led the posse that found Frederick.

"It looks like quite a nice place for Frederick to rest," he said. The men, who had searched all day in the creek banks, agreed with Niles.

"And I don't see any wound or injury," he added.

Mamie cried when Frederick's dead body ended their turbulent love story. Two men had to escort the distraught widow over to Niles Morgan's house, where Niles's wife, Rachel, consoled her.

"Mamie, give yourself some time. Your wound will heal."

"Not with the mystery. My God, what could have happened to my love?"

There was nothing to look at in the Scotland Yard meeting room, which was often used for interrogations. The walls were gray. There were no windows or curtains, no prints or anything else hanging on the walls. There was a plain wood table with six hard chairs around it, and three extra chairs for observers. Lang and his recruits sat around the table with their chief for a briefing about the case.

"What is it you know, Jackson?" Chief Bart Marshall asked.

"Denton Brickman, a man of considerable means, was last seen with a Frenchwoman at the Queen's Ball."

"I was there," Sir Bart said.

"He escorted a woman named Nicollette Caron," Lang said.

"Red dress?" the chief asked.

"Yes. You know of her?"

"No one wearing a pair of trousers that night could have missed her. She's quite memorable."

"We know she left with Denton in his carriage, to return to her manor," Lang said. "And just a few miles distant, he was found dead in the road. Mr. Brickman's carriage returned to its stable on its own."

"What about his cause of death?" Sir Bart said.

Lang slid Dr. Lindsey's report to him. Sir Bart studied it closely. Lang knew how important it was to keep his superior well-informed on his cases. He also knew that this was a high-profile case that would be scrutinized by many eyes, including Queen Victoria's.

"Quite unusual, Jackson. Do you suspect this vision in a red dress?"

"Possibly. We met her accidentally in Glastonbury. She may still be there or have moved on. It's still early in our investigation."

"What do you require to get the job done?" Sir Bart said.

"Five pounds in advance for our expenses. I'd like to take Peavey and Wilcox."

"Would you rather have more experienced men with you?"

"They have strong morals. They follow orders. I think they will be fine detectives, Bart. Both of them."

"Glad to hear that. Much better than Fergus Jones, the fellow who cried when he saw a gun?" Marshall smirked at the mention of their former recruit, then rose from the table.

"Well, he wasn't my pick, Bart."

Sir Bart extended his hand. "Can't win them all, I guess. Sign out your cash, keep in touch with me by wire, and good luck to you, Jackson. You know there's a lot of pressure here on this one."

"I'll do my best."

"That's always good enough for me."

The day was overcast with an intermittent sun that poked out to warm the road in front of the three detectives. They had already been to Denton Brickman's manor and interviewed his staff, including the driver who'd been left behind on the evening Denton died.

They arrived at the estate of Nicollette Caron about noon. Marie opened the door for them. She gulped when she learned they were Scotland Yard detectives, there to question her about the night of Denton's death. The driver had admitted that he'd fallen asleep in a drunken stupor and couldn't recall a moment from that evening.

The three investigators told Marie they wanted to speak to her. She agreed, and the four of them sat around a small table in the living room. The maid brought them tea with some small pastry cakes.

"Non parlo il pozzo Inglese."

"What did she say?" Peavey asked.

"She doesn't speak English well."

Lang looked at Marie. He knew this game from other interrogations. "I was schooled in Italy," he said. "You'll find my Italian quite understandable." He watched her reaction and could see she understood his English with ease. "Would you like me to query in Italian?"

"No, I try to fit in with the English talk, please ask as you wish."

"So that evening you helped Miss Caron prepare for the ball in London?"

"Yes."

"And Denton picked up Miss Caron before the ball?"

"Oh, yes."

"They attended the ball together and returned here in Denton's carriage?"

"Yes." Lang noticed that Marie tightened her posture.

"Did he come in?"

"Yes." He saw the lump in her throat.

"Were you present in the house that night?"

"I was in my room."

"And did you dress when you knew they were coming in?"

"Oh, yes. I thought they might want tea or some sherry."

"And did they?"

"No. He said he had to be going." Her eyes darted.

"Why?" Lang said.

"It was not my place to ask."

"And did he leave right away?"

"Yes."

"And he was healthy and well, when he left?"

"Oh, yes."

"And all of you were shocked when you heard the news?"

"Oh, yes."

"Anything else you want to tell me?"

"No, sir." *She knew more.*

"Think. Perhaps you will remember something."

"No, nothing."

"Was there a chance that they were courting, or doing what lovers do?"

"No. Well, maybe a brief kiss, then he left."

"So it would have been impossible that they went to bed, or had a deeper intimate connection that night?"

"It would not be possible. He left right away."

"Very well, then. That should be all I need for my notes."

"Is there anything wrong, Inspector? It was an accident, wasn't it?" She shifted uncomfortably in her seat.

"We're not sure what caused his death. We do think he may have had a sexual encounter before he died."

"Oh, my."

"Do you think he could have gone to a house of prostitution after leaving here that night? You know, have became so aroused that he went to a house?"

Marie's face flushed. "Perhaps. That could be."

"It's just that a house of ill repute is so far away. About fifty miles' round-trip—on the other side of town. About the same distance if he went into the city's East End. So he would have had to drive for several hours and have been on a different road from the one where he was found. We think this unlikely."

"I see."

"Are you sure it isn't possible that Miss Caron and Denton had an intimate affair?"

"Oh, no, sir. She's such a fine woman."

"That's what I hear." Lang looked hard at Marie, who looked away. "Here's my information, Marie. If you think of anything further, please get in touch with me."

"Oh, yes. I will."

"Where is Miss Caron now?"

"She's traveling. She loves to travel."

"Where did she go?"

"France, I think. She's from Nice originally."

"I see. Do you know how to reach her?"

"No, I wish I did—I'd be most happy to be in touch with her. But we haven't heard from her since her departure."

"Thank you."

Marie escorted Lang and his colleagues out after showing them the manor.

"I didn't know you spoke Italian, Jackson," Peavey said.

"Lei amerebbe per dormire sopra perche lei sono cosi bello, ho qualcosa lei puo sedere su?"

"I'm impressed. What did you say?"

" 'Would you like to sleep over, because you are so pretty, I have something you can sit upon.' It's the only sentence I know."

"You tricked her?"

"I did."

"She's lying about something," Wilcox said.

"That she is."

"What do we do about it, sir?"

"We follow her."

CHAPTER 17

Morning After

I THANKED MIRIAM FOR THE WONDERFUL EVENING AND went to bed, exhausted, as soon as we got home. But Miriam woke me up with tea at the first rooster crow. She couldn't wait to talk about the Foxhunt Club dance.

"Well, you're going to be the gossip of the town today, you know," she said.

"I hope not."

"You'll have no choice. Nothing this big has happened since Frederick's father dueled for his mother fifty years ago. It will be interesting to see if Oliver and some of the others decide to pursue you—now that Lord Baston has shown his interest in you."

"Well, why wouldn't they, if they're of a mind to court?"

"Lord Baston is the largest landowner in this county, and many of your would-be suitors share boundary lines with him. Some are involved in business with him."

"I hope they don't let that stop them. After all, I'm not interested in Lord Baston. Wouldn't you say he made a great fool of himself last night?"

"Yes, he did. But it was all in the cause of love."

"What?"

"The most handsome, desirable bachelor in the county spends years never paying attention to a female. He's never even danced with a woman, at any of our dances. *Never!* Then he sees you and flattens your dance partner, one of his best friends, to lead you off the floor."

"Well, I thought the other fellows were much more charming."

"Trust me, this man can be the most charming you'll ever meet. Lord Baston is an elegant man who was a bit out of his element last night—acting beneath his elegance, you might say—but it was because he wanted you, my dear. Lord, how he wanted you."

"I believe I'll go about my business."

"My guess is you won't have to wait long for him. He'll let his intentions be known."

I lay back in bed, thinking a little more sleep might be nice.

"Oh, get up, my dear—I think you're going to have a big day, and you'll wish you had an early-morning jump. I'll fetch you some water for your pitcher, or if you'd like a bath, I can have one prepared for you."

"All right, then. I'd like a bath."

Miriam disappeared to order my bathwater, and I arose to greet the day.

I had a lovely view out my window in any direction I looked. The beautiful town of Glastonbury seemed to float in a mystical mist, with the inspiring hill of Tor to the south. The sun was shining down through the early-morning mist. The setting was so picturesque that I felt safe in a storybook world.

I slipped out of my nightgown and into the tub of hot water that was brought to me. Miriam stood nearby as her servant girl poured in the last of the water.

"The temperature shouldn't be above one hundred degrees. Hot baths can sap your strength."

"And I need mine. Thank you, Miriam, this temperature is perfect."

Miriam wanted to stay with me as I bathed, but I asked if I could have my privacy and sent her away. I relaxed in the bath and felt wonderful for my soak. Downstairs, I heard a knock on the door, and Miriam came running up.

"Oliver is downstairs and asks if you would go for a drive with him today."

"Can he wait? I'll be an hour."

Miriam left and returned to me. "He says he would wait not only hours but days, weeks, months, years for you."

"Silly boy. Tell him I graciously accept his invitation and will try to hurry my grooming."

"Nicollette, I'm going to have to keep a calendar for all your social invitations."

I was ready to stand, and she wouldn't leave, so I did rise from the bath. Miriam stared at me as I stood naked in the tub.

"Well, now I know why the men are all mad for you—I believe they must be able to see through your frocks. I pity them, Nicollette. They haven't a chance."

She closed the door behind her as I dried myself. I dusted talc on my body, then put on a pink corset and my custom-made pink stockings. I donned a pink-and-white summer frock with a matching spencer coat trimmed with white eyelet. I put on a hat with a soft pink ostrich feather, applied my rouge and lip paint, and was ready in less than forty-five minutes. When I walked downstairs Oliver smiled and reached for my hand.

"My lady. You look even lovelier by daylight. I'm not sure I'll be able to keep my heart from leaping out of my body to your side."

"What a charming compliment, Oliver. I think I rather like you all put together in one piece."

"Then I'll do my best to stay intact. I've packed a lunch, and I thought perhaps we'd have a picnic, and I could show you my land. I have to go to London by train late this afternoon to see my brother on some business, but I've saved my day for you."

"Your plan sounds delightful, Oliver."

He helped me up into the buggy, and I took my place by his side.

"Oliver, I had a lovely time with you last night. You're such a good dancer."

"It was easy to dance with you, Miss Nicollette—may I call you Miss Nicollette?"

"You may call me Nicollette, Oliver."

"Oh, Nicollette, being with you lifted me so high." He gave me his irresistible smile. He had beautiful deep-set eyes, high cheekbones, and a bewitching dimple.

So much had happened the night before that I had hardly taken the time to see him closely. He was a few years older than I, strong and tall with some lovely color to his cheeks. And long dark eyelashes. Why is it men who always get the natural blush in their cheeks and the long eyelashes? When he closed his eyes, I wanted to kiss him right there.

His land was to the east, and as he drove toward his destination he told me he had a special place for our picnic on the way. He went a bit out of town and turned down a barely driven road—near the very same road Frederick and I had traveled.

"There's a beautiful creek with a waterfall that is quite scenic," he said. I was quiet.

We reached a lush green area about a quarter of a kilometer from the spot where Frederick and I had stopped. Oliver spread the blanket on the ground, then gathered his basket and squired

me a short distance to a clearing where the panoramic view of the
falls excited my eyes. With gentle patience he assisted me to a
comfortable position on the blanket.

"Nicollette, I've never met a girl like you before. You'd complete my dream if I may kiss you."

"No, Oliver. We mustn't. We hardly know each other."

"Ask away. What do you want to know about me? I'm single,
available, and a good man. The women here tell me that I'm a
catch. But I've been waiting for a special woman to love. I want
the right woman to share my estate, accompany me to the Der-
bies, and travel with me. I hear you like travel."

"I do. And I can see who you are, Oliver. But I'm no good for
men—I mean, any man. If you knew all there is to know about
me, you wouldn't like what you knew."

"Impossible. I already love the woman I see before me."

"You mustn't."

"It's too late. I didn't sleep five minutes last night."

"Perhaps Lord Baston's blow rattled something in there?"

I touched his head in jest, but he was staring into my eyes.
"I'm going to keep asking to kiss you until I'm allowed. So you
might as well kiss me now, Nicollette."

"I'm sorry, Oliver—don't ask again." I rolled back on the
blanket, propped up on my one arm. *Oh sweet Lord, here we go
again. No. No. I'm telling him no.*

He rolled over on top of me and looked steadily into my eyes.
He licked my bottom lip, catching me off guard.

"I won't kiss you, then. I'll just lick you." He slowly licked the
corner of my mouth, then the other corner. He breathed into my
neck and licked my earlobe. I could feel his warm breath quickening in my ear and knew I had aroused him. And he was arousing me. He sheltered me tightly as if I were made of solid gold
and he was protecting me in a den of thieves.

"Oliver, you must stop. Please, *please*."

"I can't, my darling. You've tantalized me so." He reached down to my high-top-heeled boot and started his hand at my ankle. He touched me firmly all the way up my stocking, on the inside of my leg, and rubbed my inner thigh—his fingers close to my most personal area.

I gasped at his forward move, but after that I couldn't stop him. He rolled me over and undressed me from my frock. Soon I was down to my corset and stockings, and Oliver was looking at me in the sunlight.

"Nicollette, do you know how beautiful you are to a man's eyes? Please understand that mine have overcome me—they won't see again unless I have you now."

"Oliver, you must stop. You *must.*"

"My dearest love, Nicollette, I don't know what has gotten into me. I've always been a patient man. But I must have you, or I'll go mad."

"Oliver, you mustn't. *Or you will love me to your death.*"

"Damn right I will!"

He loosened the rest of my clothes as I pleaded with him. Tears slipped down my cheeks, but Oliver didn't see them.

My corset was now on the grass next to my stockings, and Oliver, too, was naked. He had a well-muscled body, with strong shoulders that felt beautiful to the touch of my fingers. And I acquiesced to what was about to be. I held on to Oliver as he entered me, feeling him suddenly pulsing inside me. *I felt him move in and out. And my God, he felt so good. Beautiful. He felt beautiful inside me.* And then I heard my words, "Darling, don't stop. Don't stop."

"I won't," he said. "I won't."

CHAPTER 18

Flowers, Milady

L ORD BASTON CALLED BERTRUM INTO HIS STUDY AT DAY-break. "Bertrum, please sit."

"Yes, my lord."

"I value our relationship. Do you?"

"Yes, my lord. Very much, sir."

"I've noticed that you have an interest in the Irish girl. Do you?"

"Just as a fellow servant, my lord. Nothing more."

"I've noticed a couple of bouts of dishonesty from you, Bertrum. I can't have that. I can't distrust you. Do you see that?"

"Yes, my lord."

"Now, you must share something with me. If you speak honestly, you will secure your job. If you lie, you will forfeit it. Do you understand?"

"Yes, my lord."

"What did Carrie need from you, and where were you with the carriage last night?"

Bertrum told Lord Baston the truth.

"Do you understand that with my position in the community I can't have my carriage seen at the site of a drug purchase?"

"Yes, my lord."

"That can't happen again, Bertrum. Ever."

"No, my lord. You have my word on it."

"I believe you, Bertrum. I caught Carrie with a silver box. She claimed she was going to polish it, but Roberta tells me there was no such arrangement. Carrie has shown herself to be a common thief, and she's to leave at once. Would you see that she's taken back to the pub where we met her?'

"Yes, my lord. Will you worry about her down there?"

"I don't believe I will, Bertrum."

"Well, my lord, to be candid, if I may, I'll have concern for her."

"What do you propose to ease your conscience?"

"I was thinking that you've enjoyed that pub, my lord, but perhaps you are weary of it now. We could find another place to frequent."

"Yes, we could."

"And perhaps I could reimburse you for the flat down there. Just so Carrie has a roof, sir. It's paid up for another three months, and I could pay you from my salary."

Lord Baston studied his driver. "Do you fancy her, Bertrum?"

"I suppose I feel something for her, since she wasn't given natural abilities like most folks. I'd feel bad if she fell to a Jack the Ripper down there. It's not really a safe area for a young girl."

"Bertrum, thank you for reminding me of grace. You're right. I couldn't recommend her for a neighboring manor when she's a thief, or I would have done so. She asked to go back to the pub. When you take her down, please give her Flat 15 to stay until the lease is out. Take some blankets and bedding, food, and incidentals to get her started there."

"Thank you, my lord, that's very generous."

"Take her now, Bertrum."

Bertrum drove Carrie to London. She cried most of the way. He hurried back in record time to Lord Baston's manor after he made sure she was settled in the flat.

After sending Bertrum off to take care of Carrie, Lord Baston gathered the servants around him.

"I want you to cut all of the flowers in bloom, on all sectors of the grounds. They are to be collected and beautifully arranged. Only select the flowers that represent perfection, or are about to bloom. I don't want to see any flowers acceptable for an arrangement left standing."

Soon eight male servants were outside, cutting and gathering flowers on the grounds. Nine female servants were inside, creating the arrangements as soon as the fresh flowers arrived. Lord Baston closely observed and critiqued as they worked.

Flowers were arranged in vases of various types found throughout the house. A driver went to town and bought vases from every store that sold them. When the servants ran out of vases, they were told to use water pitchers or anything they could find that would hold flowers. Finally, they loaded over a hundred bouquets on three flatbed buggies and delivered the flowers to Miriam's Cozy Inn, with a note from Lord Baston to Nicollette.

Miriam was overwhelmed when she opened the door and saw the extraordinary demonstration of Lord Baston's courtship. Flowers filled the house and Nicollette's room, with barely a space to step. Others spilled outside, down the front steps, and into the front yard of the boardinghouse.

There were roses, in reds, fuchsias, yellows, and whites; heathers and other wildflowers in pinks and purples; carnations, tulips, snapdragons, gardenias, lilacs, lilies of the valley, sprays of baby's breath. Every kind of flower England has to offer. The scent was wonderfully fragrant and the colors seductive.

Miriam put the note from Lord Baston on Nicollette's bed, barely able to wait for her return. Bertrum showed up at about three in the afternoon and asked if there was a reply to Lord Baston's dinner invitation for that evening. When Miriam explained that Nicollete had gone out with a gentleman caller and hadn't been seen since the late morning, Bertrum tried to find out about Lord Baston's competition. Fearing for Oliver's safety, Miriam told him nothing.

Bertrum went back to report to Lord Baston that there was no reply as yet. Lord Baston remained anxious while the staff went about their tasks—all of them wondering what would be the outcome of their master's ostentatious courting gesture.

Just before dusk I drove Oliver's buggy into town—it took me that long to hide the body. I didn't want anyone to question where he might be if they should recognize his horses, so I let them off just outside town and slapped them in the direction of Oliver's manor.

I strolled into a few shops, greeting anyone I recognized, as if I had been shopping for the day. When I returned to the board-inghouse Miriam was waiting for me on her porch, surrounded by huge bouquets of flowers.

"Where have you been?"

"Oliver dropped me off hours ago, and I've been walking around the town."

"If I'd known, I'd have looked for you."

I walked past flowers covering the porch and entered Miriam's house to find flowers creating an electric splendor everywhere. I went up the stairs to my bedroom, which was lush with flower arrangements. But I was still preoccupied with the loss of Oliver and the blood of another dead man on my hands.

"Oh, Miriam, I'm so tired. I haven't had any decent sleep."

"Notice anything?"

"What?"

"The flowers."

"I'd have to be blind not to notice them; they're magnificent." I stretched out on my bed and closed my eyes.

"Wait, before you rest, you have to tend to your invitations. It's only proper etiquette, Nicollette."

"Yes, of course."

"First, Lord Baston cut every flower from his land for you and delivered them to you with this note."

"That was sweet, wasn't it?"

"He's Lord Baston, Nicollette. This isn't sweet. This is a momentous courtship gesture."

"So it is." I was impressed with the magnificence of the gift. The flowers' beauty and variety were mesmerizing. The bouquets were all arranged with great care, but a few details felt wrong to my eye. I rearranged some of them so that the reds were on the lower part of the stairs and the colors gradually changed to the lighter shades in my room. When I was done with my task, I said, "They're quite spectacular, aren't they?"

"Quite. Open the note. He has sent for a response three times today."

The letter was on heavy stationery, with an impressive gold seal. It read:

Dear Miss Nicollette,

My apologies for my rudeness last night—it was an unfortunate beginning.

If you would be gracious enough to give me a second

chance, I'll change your crude opinion of me. I'm not the bar-
barian I have led you to believe. Please accept my flowers and
this invitation for dinner tonight at my manor.
  Event: Dinner
  Place: Lord Baston's manor
  Time: 8 PM
  Respectfully,
  Lord Baston
  R.S.V.P.

"I'm too tired to go."

"I'm sorry, you can't decline this. You simply can't. I won't
let you."

"I'm dirty and tired."

"Well, you'll bathe again."

"Twice in a day?"

"Twice in a day. Whatever it takes. I'll send a servant of mine
to let Lord Baston know that you accept."

"If you insist."

"Where is Oliver?"

"He took a train for London. He has business with his
brother there."

"Did you have a nice time?"

"Very nice. But I don't know if I shall see him again."

"Well, if things don't work out with Lord Baston, you have
these to fall back on." Miriam held up nine other envelopes from
suitors.

"Oh, my goodness."

I sat in a chair by the window's light to read about each gentleman's interest in courting me. Through the window I saw a
new buggy riding into town. I stood up with surprise when I saw
that it was Marie.

My dear sweet friend, Marie. I was filled with delight as I watched her stop to talk with someone on the street, who pointed to Miriam's. By the time Marie arrived, I was at the door to greet her with a warm embrace.

"Marie, I'm so happy to see you here. How are you?"

"Very well, mademoiselle, I have missed being with you. But we must talk." She was breathless and her hair in disarray.

I didn't want Miriam to overhear our conversation, so I closed the door behind us and suggested we walk to a nearby park bench. We held our conversation until we had crossed the street, some distance from anyone who might overhear us.

"Miss, I've been visited by three Scotland Yard detectives. They want to speak with you about Denton's death. I told them he left after returning you home, but I don't know if they believed me. Perhaps we should leave before they come here."

I had looked away, as if searching for answers in the breeze, when a man caught my eye. *He looked like Oliver Davis walking down the street.* I turned back to Marie, not wanting to look closer at the man's resemblance to my recent love.

"Marie, I think I need to stay for a bit longer here. I must not act as if I were in a hurry to leave this community. It might look suspicious if I were to leave suddenly again."

"Do you want me to return home?"

"No, now that you're here, I think you should stay—I've missed you terribly. I'll get a room for you next to mine, and we'll decide when we can slip away from Glastonbury without too many questions."

"The town looks lovely."

"Yes, it is. I'd love to stay here," I said wistfully, for I knew I would never be able to remain for long in a town.

I glanced back at the street. The man who looked like Oliver turned to me, and I saw that it wasn't just a resemblance to

Oliver. *He was Oliver. He stared at me as my eyes widened.* I was, once again, seeing a sweet lover as the phantasm of a man I had held in my arms. In the height of our passion, I had felt my heated lover change to a cold and still corpse. I had felt his spirit go out of his body, leaving me with his empty shell to hold at our highest moment.

And now I searched for the Oliver Davis who charmed me and found not the man I knew but only an outline of him, with hellish eyes that burned me to my soul.

"Marie, do you see that handsome man with the dark hair walking toward us?"

She was tugging at a dangling thread on her dress, but she looked up and studied the street. "What man?"

And then Oliver became vapor and disappeared. I composed myself and turned back to Marie.

"I'm invited to Lord Baston's tonight. I'll send a message that I'll bring you along to chaperone."

"Lord Baston?"

"Oh, Marie. My insides flutter when I'm near Lord Baston. He looks at me like I'm the only woman in the world in a crowded room. I can't wait to introduce you to him. You'll come, won't you?"

"I can't wait to meet the man that makes you swoon. Of course, I'll attend. I'll bring the smelling salts in case we both get a case of the vapors." Marie giggled like a schoolgirl, and her infectious laugh lifted me and made me more excited about our outing.

"I'm glad you're here, Marie."

I was lucky. Her constancy and understanding had brought me peace of mind often. "We must get ready, Marie. Did you bring some clothes?"

"Very few."

"Would you like that royal blue dress of mine you've admired?"

"You know it's my favorite."

"Very well, it's yours."

"Thank you." She embraced me, then pulled back and looked in my eyes. "Miss Nicollette, I don't want anything ever to happen to you. Please stay safe."

"I've come this far, but you must know something, Marie. If you stay with me, you may risk your own neck."

"I know. But my life is sadder without you in it."

"You should think about this carefully, Marie."

"I have. It is why I came. I want to travel with you, Miss Nicollette."

And we hugged again.

Across the street Miriam was peering out of her window. I knew she had observed our public display of affection because I looked up and saw her watching. And I sensed she would talk about us.

For I had begun to sense a change in my relationship with Miriam. My charming hostess who reached for a friendship was becoming envious of all the male attention I was receiving. I felt that I could no longer trust her and that my days at her boarding-house were numbered.

Still, I couldn't abandon my Glastonbury residence too suddenly. I'd need to set up my next move carefully so as to avoid speculation about my travels or the reason for my departure.

Miriam was happy to rent out another room and seemed to accept my explanation that Marie was my personal assistant and closest friend. Still, I knew I must keep my guard up for an ambush in the dark.

CHAPTER 19

Miriam's Tongue

WHEN THE THREE INSPECTORS ENTERED THE GLASTONbury constable's office, Niles Morgan sized them up immediately as serious professional men.

"Good morning, Constable. We're with Scotland Yard. I'm Inspector Jackson Lang. These are my colleagues, Peavey and Wilcox."

"Niles Morgan, temporary constable."

"Temporary?"

"Our former constable, Frederick Bothem, was just discovered yesterday, dead."

"I'm sorry to hear that. What happened to him?"

"We aren't sure how he died. We found him in a creek, but there weren't any marks on him. It could be that his heart just gave out. Of course, we have to look at this death very carefully. He was in good health, and there are suspicious circumstances."

"Why do you say that?"

"Well. He was nude in the woods. And we found a dam built around him."

"By animals?"

"Not unless the animals laid his clothes carefully over him and arranged wildflowers at the site."

"I see. Did you photograph him?"

"My God, no. Who would ever do a thing like that? It's sacrilegious, isn't it? I never did buy the Prince Albert postcard of him in his casket. Quite morbid, I say."

"May I see the body?"

"Well, he's already at the undertaker's. Sam Benson may cooperate with you. I'll go with you."

The men walked across the street. The sign on the door read: SAM BENSON & SON, UNDERTAKERS OF THE HIGHEST ORDER, WE DO THE BEST JOB IN TOWN.

The four men entered the small funeral shop.

"Sam, this is Inspector Lang from Scotland Yard and his detectives. They'd like to look at Frederick's body."

"Certainly." Sam led them to the back room. "I'll give you time for your respects."

"I didn't know the fine fellow," Lang said. "I merely want to inspect the body."

"Go right ahead, sir."

"Well, I'd like him undressed."

"We just dressed him for the service."

"I'm afraid we need to observe him without attire."

"Why? We put a lot of time into preparing him."

"Please cooperate with them, Sam," Niles said. "We're sorry about the extra work for you."

"Very well. But I've never had this request before."

Sam called for his son to help and explained Lang's odd request. The two removed the dead man's clothes down to a thin suit of long underwear.

"There you go."

"More. We need the body without any attire."

Sam and his son removed the underwear, leaving Frederick nude on the table.

"Notice anything, gentlemen?" Lang said.

"Yes. Same engorged member."

"Anything else?"

"Yes. I see it."

Lang continued to look, but he had seen the same suspicious signs he'd observed on Denton's body. Wilcox made notes in his book.

"I think we need to question Nicollette Caron," Lang said. "Let's go find her."

"I don't think she even likes men at all," Miriam said to the audience at the Crown and Thorn Pub. She'd had enough wine to be quite outspoken in her opinion. Among her eager listeners were the Scotland Yard detectives, who were seated at a nearby table.

"But we all saw her dancing at the Foxhunt Club's dance," a woman said. "She certainly seemed to take quite a fancy to the men."

"Not like the fancy I saw her take to her assistant, Marie. They hugged and kissed like long-lost lovers. I think she's *airy*, that one."

Douglas and Charles rose to Nicollette's defense from a table nearby.

"Miriam," Douglas said, "I danced with Nicollette several times and found her quite responsive to *this* male."

"Perhaps you're confused, Douglas, and it was your hand that was responsive to your male."

The crowd laughed.

"I danced with her also," Charles said. "In my opinion, there's no more feminine woman to be found in all of England."

"Oh, what do you men know? Why, when she was bathing, she flaunted her body to me, in hopes I'd act upon the offer. I didn't, of course, but I couldn't believe it. Her preference must be her woman friend. I'd put money on it."

"I'll match any bet," Charles said.

"Double that here," Douglas said.

Lang walked over to Miriam. "Excuse my interruption. My name is Jackson Lang."

"Yes, Inspector Lang, I remember you. Nice to see you again."

"May I speak privately with you for a moment? Would you care to join us?"

Miriam eyed the handsome detective. "I'd be delighted."

"May I offer you a drink?"

She didn't need to be asked twice. "Lovely," she said as she took a seat with the detectives.

"You remember Peavey and Wilcox, my assistants?"

"Of course, from the horse show. They kindly escorted Nicollette and me. What brings you to Glastonbury?"

"We're assisting with the investigation into Frederick Bothem's death. We understand you knew him quite well."

Miriam squeaked out a little cry. "Knew him? I loved him. More than Mamie—I loved him. Do you suspect me?"

"Not at this point, but we consider all paths until we find the correct one."

For the cost of a glass of wine, Miriam told the inspectors everything she knew about Frederick, his marriage, the townspeople, Nicollette, and anything else they wanted to query.

"Where is Miss Nicollette Caron this evening?"

"Having dinner with Marie at Lord Baston's. Don't tell him. Let him find out—*that she doesn't like men at all.*"

"The men quite disagree with you, I believe."

Miriam leaned in toward them, as if proximity to their ears meant closer vicinity to the truth. "The bumpkins of Glastonbury? What do they know? The only girl they've had experience of is Missy Corchoran, and that's because she's like an old county fair mare. Anyone gets a free ride."

"I see." When the detectives felt they'd gotten all they could out of Miriam, they rose to leave.

"When do you think would be a good time tomorrow to call upon Miss Caron?"

"Get in line early. Or if you come at teatime, perhaps that would be best."

Lang touched her shoulder. "Would you not mention our talk, Miss Bestell? I'd like to keep our visit a surprise."

"Of course, I'll not say a word to her."

She looked at the hand that rested upon her and smiled up at him. Then she primped her hair with her hand, stuck out her chest a little, and said, "Might you gentlemen like a special invitation this evening?"

Carrie woke up on the cold wood floor and reached for the bottle of elixir. But it wasn't there. The sailor she had traded sex for a bottle had taken back the elixir, robbed her flat, along with her blanket and the handful of personal items she still possessed.

Her eyes moved from wall to wall as if hoping the comfortable room she'd been given might reappear. But it didn't. Her room was stripped bare. The bedroom set, the lamps and knick-knacks, the blanket she'd been sleeping in on the floor, and even her lucky burgundy dress and bag—all were gone. What remained was one outfit in need of repair. The one she slept and lived in—in hopes that it not be stolen in this neighborhood of thieves.

There was one place that beckoned to her. She left her room and walked down the street in search of a horse not under a watchful eye.

CHAPTER 20

Dinner at Lord Baston's

"THIS IS THE MOST BEAUTIFUL CARRIAGE I'VE EVER SEEN. It has a lion in the front of the carriage, and it looks so royal, Nicollette. Is that Lord Baston's?"

I ran to the window and looked down the street, my heart pounding in anticipation. "Yes. That's his, Marie. Right on time."

"Oh, my. I'm going to feel like Queen Victoria, I am."

"As I mentioned, Marie—Lord Baston has apologized, but I don't intend to be so easy for this man. He still has to demonstrate his manners, charm, and good taste, or I'll show no interest in him."

"Of course, Miss Nicollette."

I wore an emerald green dress with black beading and matching waistcoat. At my neck was a pendant of emeralds, diamonds, and pearls—a gift from Robert. My neckline was a deep u shape that flattered the lines of my neck and molded to my bustier. Had I worn a dress that exposed my shoulders, I'd have been too obvious, so I had not.

I wore my long hair up, and Marie had placed tiny simulated diamonds in its strands. They were woven in, as if diamonds just happened to grow in my hair naturally.

Lord Baston looked slightly surprised when he saw Marie, but he recovered well.

"Ah, two beautiful women? I'm twice blessed." He offered his arm to steady us as we entered the carriage, and his driver assisted us from the outside.

I introduced Marie and Lord Baston and, following proper etiquette, he seated himself in the front of the carriage, across from the two of us.

"Nicollette and Marie, I'm so pleased you could join me this evening. But I don't know if I can handle double the beauty at my table. You remind me of two bright shining stars."

I smiled, and Marie giggled, a habit she had when she was nervous and charmed. My mind wandered throughout the carriage ride. And Lord Baston's must have wandered also, as we said nothing to each other. I felt his stares, but I looked out of the carriage and into the night's darkness. Not, of course, to see anything in the night but to avoid Lord Baston's intensity.

He scared me, as no man ever had. I feared he could pierce my most vulnerable self in his search to know me. And that would mean he might learn of my soul's great haunt.

When we reached his stately drive, Marie whispered, "This is strange, Nicollette. There should be conversation."

"I know."

The driver stopped the carriage along the drive when I begged to see the manicured bushes. There were a dragon, lions, a rabbit, and several other animals. The precision and artistry captivated me. Though most of the flowers were cut, many were still flowered, with buds about to open. And then I was charmed by the mansion's design—no king could have asked for a more beautiful castle.

"Who does the animals for you, Lord Baston? They're delightful."

"I have a team of gardeners who work every day grooming my property. My head gardener, Chi, is from Japan. It's most kind of you to mention the animals. I'll share your compliment with him."

"Please do."

As we reached the manor, we waited for the driver to help us out of the carriage. And once on the ground, Lord Baston offered me his arm, and the driver offered his arm to Marie.

I've seen many impressive manors—castles, even. But Lord Baston's manor had an elegant entrance with a sheltered overhang and a most tasteful decorative foyer that demonstrated both status and warmth. It was clear when you crossed the threshold that this home had great attention to detail and was cared for with great affection.

I walked in with Lord Baston, making small talk, but there was such light from his eyes when he gazed down at me that I was almost afraid to look. When I did, his eyes were fixed on me, and I had to look away.

A servant he addressed as Clive stood properly at the door to take our wraps. The driver, whom he called Bertrum, asked Marie if she would like to meet some of the staff, and Lord Baston and I were left alone in the foyer.

I marveled over two majestic artifacts that stood vigil before his grandest room. The life-size horses were made of small tiles of lapis and ivory, with exquisite gems handset in each horse. These Asian antiques were like nothing I had ever seen before, even in the finest museums, and Lord Baston admitted they were his most prized possessions from his travels.

"You may call me Blake," he said.

"I may, I may not."

"I assure you that what we're going to do this evening wouldn't be my first plan," he said. "Just my idea to make up to you for my behavior last night."

"I'm sure I shall enjoy your plans."

"I want to hold you, Nicollette, and more—quite a bit more. But I'll demonstrate my restraint, for restraint must be what you want from me."

"It is."

He offered his arm to me and led me into his den. The front wall displayed foxhunt, horse, and hunting trophies. There were also photos of Lord Baston in different countries.

"Where are you here?"

"Japan."

"And here?"

"China."

"This one?"

"South Africa. Our boat almost didn't make it. The sea was rougher than the North Sea."

"How about here?"

"This is the bridge in Florence where the poet Dante first met Beatrice. I'm standing there."

"I've only been on Italy's northern shore. I'd like to go to Venice and Rome."

"I'll take you."

"Perhaps."

"Perhaps? You give me only *perhaps,* Nicollette?"

"Last night, you intruded on my dances and hit a new friend for no reason. You've chopped a houseful of flowers, courted me to your home, and I presume will feed me, Lord Baston, but I'm not ready to commit to a foreign trip with a man I don't know"

"I'm—"

"We were doing so well. If you let things develop, perhaps they will. But your bullish method of courting isn't to be tolerated. Where did you learn this? Are you used to women who have no mind? No voice? Women who don't see a choice to bed you? Or not?"

"Yes, I am."

"You'd be unwise to count me among them. Now may we continue to get to know each other? Allow me to question you. And you may ask questions of me."

"Yes, Nicollette. Please—"

There was a gentle knock on the door.

"Come in."

A girl stumbled into the room. Her dress was threadbare and her face and hair unkempt, yet underneath I could see that she was extraordinarily pretty. She seemed quite curious about me. She eyed me woman to woman, as if sizing up her competition. Her eyes darted from me to Lord Baston, then she stepped up to him and tried to give him a note. He refused to take it, and it fluttered to the floor.

"Carrie. What are you doing here?"

She grabbed Lord Baston around the waist. He pulled her arms off of him.

"Nicollette, my apologies for this scene. Clive! Carrie, you don't work here. You don't belong here; you aren't welcome here."

Clive entered the room. "Yes, my lord?"

Clive took a step toward Carrie. "What are you doing here?"

"Take her away," Blake said. "She's not to return."

"I don't know how she got in, sir." He grabbed the girl by both elbows behind her back and pulled her toward the doorway. She gave Lord Baston a desperate look over her shoulder. "Should I have Bertrum take her back to London tonight?"

"No, call the authorities and let them deal with her."

"I'm so sorry, sir." Clive muttered as he ushered Carrie out the door.

"Blake," I said, when she was out of the room, "what was that all about?"

"She was in service here, but I caught her stealing."

"She never said a word to you."

"She's a deaf-mute."

"I see. A woman without a voice. How perfect."

He looked uncomfortable.

"What about the note?" I asked him. "Are you going to read it?"

"No." He picked up the paper, crumpled it, and tossed it in an Asian gold basket near the desk. "Let's begin again, Nicollette. I want to begin as many times as you will let me clear my slate. One day I hope to win you."

"Very well. I was asking about your travels. Where is this picture from? And who's the girl here?"

"My other trip to Japan. She's a geisha girl. A Japanese woman trained to please men."

"Oh, my. And you *know* her? Or do you know *of* her?"

"That's Kimi. I know her."

"What is this in her hand?"

"A most unusual book she gave me."

"What is the book?"

He went to his desk and unlocked a drawer. He removed a gilt-edged leather book and handed it to me.

It was a beautiful book with the title, *777*, stamped in gold. I opened to a page in the middle of the book and saw an anatomically correct sketch of a nude man and woman twisted together like a sailor's knot.

"I've never seen anything like this, Blake. Close your

study door—don't let anyone see me looking at this. But I must."

Lord Baston locked the door to the study, and I sat on a comfortable rose-velvet love seat to study the pictures. He was silent, waiting for my reactions.

"Why is the book called *777?*"

"There are 777 different positions."

"I see," I said calmly, as if a professor had just explained to me that one and one is two.

"Oh, Blake—look what they're doing here! Do you think it would hurt to unite like this?"

He came over to sit next to me on the love seat and looked at the picture. It showed a woman lying faceup on top of the man's front. It appeared as if he had entered her.

"Can a man's member bend this way?"

"Yes, it can." *One plus two is three.*

My voice shook a little from asking such direct questions, but I had to know. "Could he move it in and out?"

"Yes, he could." *Two plus two is four.*

"Are you sure about this?"

"Quite sure." *Yes. I see, professor.*

Our eyes met, and I said nothing for a moment.

"Let me ask it this way, Blake. Have you done this before?"

"Perhaps. Would you like to see some of my other favorites?"

"Yes, I think I would. I often try things when they come highly recommended."

"Have you ever heard of the *Wild Horse* position?"

"No."

He turned to a page with a sketch of a man hanging off of a bed with his feet square on the floor with the woman straddling him. I read the paragraph below.

The man disrobes and has his upper body on the edge of the bed, his knees bent, square to the floor, with his feet on the floor. The nude woman perches herself upon his penis and rides him like a wild horse. This position gives the man a lot of thrusting power as he has such free movement with his legs and allows the woman to control her own pleasurable ride.

"Ahem."

"What?"

"Nothing. I just cleared my throat."

"Would you like some more wine?"

"Yes, some wine would be lovely."

He freshened my drink. I realized I had no idea how I should be reacting as I read this most intimate book in mixed company—let alone my suitor, who was surely quite ready, willing, and experienced in the techniques featured in this unusual book. He apparently had felt such drive to learn these lessons in love that he'd traveled halfway around the world for them.

"This is another one of my favorites," Blake confided. "It's called *Walking the Wall.*"

"What a strange idea. Against a wall?"

"No, the wall is actually the man's chest. The woman positions herself to walk her feet up his chest."

"Oh, my."

As he turned to the page, his hand brushed lightly against my inner wrist. I felt such excitement from his touch it was as though he'd stroked a more private part of my person.

The woman will sit on the edge of the bed. The man will enter the woman as she places her feet on his chest and as he thrusts into her, she will place one foot ahead of the other as

she "walks the wall (his chest)" until she finds her most suit-
able angle for penetration.

"Wouldn't this hurt the gentleman, if she . . ."

"No. That doesn't hurt at all. It's quite pleasurable."

"Ahem . . ."

"Did you say something?"

"This is quite fascinating. It would be interesting to, ah . . ."

"Experiment with this?"

"Yes."

"Your partner could then be an infinite number of experiences."

"Yes." The whole while I felt such titillating pleasure being
near him. He was softly stroking my inner wrist, and I was suf-
fused with excitement, anticipating his full touch.

"There's another move that I know here . . ."

But instead of going to another page, he turned my face gently to face his and said, "This isn't what you think it is."

Then he kissed me. It was a different kind of kiss. He
softly breathed on my lips and lightly ran his tongue over my
bottom lip. Then he gently pressed my lips with his parted
lips. He opened my mouth with his tongue, thrusting his tongue
gently in and out of my mouth in a rhythm that simulated
sexual thrusting so perfectly that my whole body was instantly
aroused.

I closed my eyes and pictured Lord Baston strong and naked, par-
tially hanging off a bed. In my mind's eye I saw a vision of me stand-
ing before him shamelessly nude and coming toward him as I
watched my suitor become more aroused. I straddled his legs and
began to ride him as I had seen in the Wild Horse position. Sliding
up and down on him, his member sliding in and out . . . just the
thought of this was making me feel moist. The mere mental sugges-

tion of sex was sending signals to my body to ready itself for a sexual romp.

Blake's tongue continued to move in and out of mine, and I was quite breathless. I felt his breath quicken, his body heating up—as was mine. My lips closed to grab his tongue, but he pulled it away from me. As if he wanted to tease me. And I found myself naturally trying to suck his tongue in an effort to get it to stay inside my mouth, so that we could stay joined if only at our mouths. Then his hands slid down the front of my bodice and I pushed myself away. I didn't want to—I had to.

I stood up. "What was I supposed to think that was, Blake?"

"I thought you might *think* it was a kiss, and that it would have been too soon for me to kiss you."

"Well, yes, it would have been too soon for that. Yes." What a hypocrite I was—for my thoughts were as wicked as his. Just a moment ago I had ridden his body in my daydream. "What was it, then?"

"I merely wanted to taste you, Nicollette."

I laughed at him. "You're so clever."

"Why do you say that?"

I sat back down next to him. "Because while you had a taste, I had a taste. And now I see the banquet before me."

He kissed me again, and I knew that no kisses had ever aroused me so. I thought I'd merge with him, without our clothes even being off.

My bodice was tied protectively, and near impossible to get in and out of quickly, but that impediment was not stopping Lord Baston. As we sat on the love seat, he slid his hand from my ankle up the inside of my leg. He found that if he twisted his fingers just so, he could take them as high as my waistband and then, entering my undergarment, reached my personal area.

And as he continued to kiss me with his deep throbbing kisses, he stroked me there and slid the third finger of his right hand in and out of me. He massaged me in a way no one had ever touched me. And I found myself holding him so tightly that nothing could have pried us apart.

I didn't want to let this man go. For that moment I had no thought of my plague. No thought of what could happen to my lover, as I usually did. This was a man who could take care of himself, who could rise to any occasion. Lord Baston was different. He didn't feel like any of my boyish suitors.

And he made no movement to stop. I had no plan to continue until a sexual union, I thought such an early relationship was very advanced to be as forward as we were. But there was no denying our attraction; nor was either of us first-time contestants in the game of love. But I was a bit shocked when he found a way to undo the bodice of my dress.

"Blake, you mustn't do this."

"Oh, but I must."

"I mean it. This isn't good . . ."

"I think it's marvelous, my darling." I stood up and moved away. "Come back here, Nicollette."

"But what about your staff?"

"What staff? Do I have staff?"

"Yes. There are other reasons to halt our affair."

"I wouldn't want to hear them."

Blake walked over and picked me up. Then he tenderly laid me down on a comforter that had been draped over the love seat.

He lifted away an exterior corset that was made for the dress and slid it down to the floor, then quicker than I had put it on, my undercorset was removed, and he was caressing my breasts.

"You're so beautiful, Nicollette. So lovely," he murmured to me. "How I want you."

He opened his shirt and vest and I saw his chest and abdomen. He had a muscled stomach with strong chest muscles that were lightly haired and tickled my fingers as I moved my hands over his body. I had but a moment to reach out, then he knelt before me and started to suckle my breasts in the most tender and erotic way. He loved them slowly, with such a faint teasing that I found myself turning inside out from his touch.

He had found a way to suck on my breasts as if they were connected to my most hidden womanhood. For when he cupped his hands around them and caressed and nibbled them, my nether lips felt wet and aroused and waiting for him.

I wanted him to fill me. I wanted him to make love to me in every position he knew. I wanted to feel my upper torso aligned with his, I wanted us to lie chest to chest, heart to heart.

I desired him close and inside me, and I wanted him to never leave me. To stretch this most intimate moment into the next and the next. But how could we ever, when the ultimate closeness meant death to my lover?

We heard a gong for dinner from another room. Still, we continued our sexual play. Blake unveiled more of my body, but he did it slowly with a passionate urgency underlying a gallant restraint. It made me hotter still for his touch.

I could not get enough of his fondling my breasts, it moved me in such a way as to obliterate thought. Never had a man spent so much time arousing my body.

The dinner gong sounded again, and Blake continued to touch me—until enough time passed that they might be worried about us. Lord Baston was the one with restraint. He stopped. I don't think I could have, or would have. We had managed to arouse each other without a lethal end, but how long could I tempt Blake's fate?

He locked the book back in his drawer and handed me a mirror. I used lip paint and rouge from my bag to repair myself.

"Nicollette, you look ravishing. If you spend another moment on your grooming, no woman in the county will speak to you. I'll show you the rest of the rooms later, darling. For now, I have a surprise for you."

He led me to the dining room, where I saw a long table that would seat close to fifty people. It was filled, except for two seats at one end.

I was shocked, as I had not heard anyone else enter. Nor had I heard any sound from the extravagant party. But I was a bit put off by the crowd. I would rather keep our courtship more private.

Lord Baston picked up champagne flutes for us both and toasted me:

> *Last night I was an idiot, who tripped upon my toes,*
> *'Twas because of your beauty, now everybody knows,*
> *So here's to my apologies, to Nicollette, and friends, and*
>   *foes,*
> *That this party does charm her, and that she never goes.*
> *Nicollette, welcome to Glastonbury.*

I could hear the titters of a number of guests and their commenting on the toast, which conveyed Lord Baston's interest in me. For the toast became his public statement of his intentions.

He seated me on his left with an affectionate kiss on the cheek, his guests murmuring at the familiarity of his public display.

As I watched my host it dawned on me that he'd had forty-six guests waiting for us while he fondled me in his den as if he had all the time in the world to do so. His savoir faire made me smile, as did the reasons for it. His well-trained servants were ready to carry on without his presence. And Lord Baston had found enjoying me of more importance than greeting his guests.

The dining was festive and merry. Our meal had seven courses, each partnered with its own wine from Lord Baston's cellar. The people of Glastonbury were quite rowdy for a formal dinner party—I'd never heard so much laughter. I thought perhaps it was the sprinkling of a few Irishmen in the party that elevated its mood, but on study the Englishmen were just as entertaining.

There were guests of all ages, but most of them were in their twenties and thirties. Charles and Douglas had brought each other's lovely cousins, Andrea and Sandra, who hung on their escorts' words. Miriam was engaged in conversation with Jackson Lang and his two apprentices, Peavey and Wilcox. I wondered how they'd come to be invited—how Lord Baston knew them—but Miriam sat so close and acted so familiar with the Londoners that I deduced she had brought them along.

Lord Baston had left me so aroused, I could have taken off all my clothes and had him take me right there, leaving the people of Glastonbury with no unanswered questions. But he was so calm and collected, no one would have known that he was aroused at all.

About an hour into the dinner, as we began our fourth course, he was engrossed in conversation with several women on his right who gazed longingly in his direction. I felt disappointed, as he seemed to have forgotten our recent intimacy—until I noticed something. Most of the time, he locked his fingers together and rested his chin on them in a thoughtful pose. But every few minutes, with the faintest of smiles, he raised the third finger of his right hand near his nose, to recall my scent.

Men are often put off by our complicated female apparatus, and they can make a woman feel as if she were a soiled doily—especially if she has had several lovers. But Lord Baston paid no mind to my experience in the bedroom, and reached in the air for me. Not for a woman's lavender behind her ear, her soft body talc, or the rosewater dabbed on her bosom. This man wanted inside me. And I wanted inside him.

As the dinner progressed, he shared the glints of light in his eyes with me. The dinner guests seemed to disappear. They were there; I just no longer saw them. And he reached to hold my hand. He would look unafraid at me and lift his eyebrow in my direction. It was a look he had already found, to melt me.

But in the middle of the meal I heard Charles's cousin Andrea whisper, "Jackson Lang, Peavey, and Wilcox are all Scotland Yard detectives. Isn't that exciting?" Then, after staring a few minutes at Wilcox's strong biceps next to her, she spoke up during a lull in the table conversation to capture his attention by speaking around him to Jackson.

"Mr. Lang, did you come to Glastonbury for your performance with Pegasus?" Andrea asked.

"Yes, I come here each year for the show—and enjoy my visits very much. This year I invited Peavey and Wilcox, my newest recruits, for a well-deserved break."

"But there was a rumor that you have police business here. Is that true? Glastonbury never has anything exciting going on," Andrea said.

My evening of charm and seduction was now fogged with my fear. I remained calm on the outside, I had to—or someone might suspect me. But inside I was a nervous wreck, replaying my conversation with Jackson and wondering if I'd said anything to give him clues about the real me.

"Well, we have been told to work the murder case of Frederick Bothem and actually have a suspect, but we need to learn more about the case before it will lead to an arrest, a trial—or a hanging."

After several glasses of wine and the mention of Frederick's murder, Miriam ran out of the room crying with her handkerchief in her hand.

"I'll go check on her," Sandra said, and she followed Miriam.

Andrea said, "I've heard that you've been responsible for bringing many men to justice, is that true?"

"If you mean have I led a man to hang on a rope? Yes. I have. Many times—without a quiver to my soul."

"What if the killer was a woman—would you still hang a woman?

"Without question. If there is a crime, then the criminal must pay. It doesn't matter if the killer is male or female."

The discovery that Lang and his men were from Scotland Yard made me wonder what Miriam had told them.

"You look pale, Nicollette," Lord Baston said. "Are you all right?" He reached for my hand and sheltered it protectively in his hand.

"Yes, thank you for asking. I'm fine—it's just the excitement."

"I'm right here. Always. I'm right here."

Over the last course of our meal, Lord Baston stood up. He lifted an aperitif glass to me and whispered a toast:

Here's to a fine woman,
The best of God's inventions,
And here's to my love, Nicollette,
May you guess of my intentions.

Then he kissed my cheek and turned to the guests, who had not missed his display.

"I want to thank everyone for coming. Please join our orchestra for a dance in the ballroom. Please, stay as long as you like."

The fourteen-piece orchestra played a series of waltzes starting with Charles d'Albert's "Sweethearts" waltz, followed by Mendelssohn's "Wedding March" from *A Midsummer Night's Dream.*

Peavey and Wilcox amazed the crowd with a new dance called the two-step. It was set to 2/4 time, but the dance partners all had to move so fast together that it was humorous to watch us fall all over ourselves.

"You dance closer to me tonight," I said.

"I feel closer to you tonight," Lord Baston said. "Stay with me," he whispered.

"Blake, I can't do that."

"You can and you should."

"I should?"

"You don't intend to ignite me and leave me tonight, do you?"

"Perhaps I could cool you off in a water trough?"

"Mmm . . . walk the wall." He sighed.

"Oh, Blake."

If the room knew of our tease, some would be appalled. But his guests danced happily. Some showed off their nimble talents, and a few too merry from the wine sat still, convinced the room was moving too fast.

It was as if Lord Baston had taken dancing lessons during the day. I didn't want to call attention to it, but I wondered.

"I didn't care for the music last night," he said. "They're playing my favorite tunes now. Do you like them?"

"Yes, very much."

After the dance he led me out to his balcony, which was connected to his den, then slipped me in the back way to the den. Closing the drapes behind us, he guided me to the love seat.

"I'd like to see more of you, Nicollette. I mean that in every way. Does that alarm you?"

"A bit. But not for the reason you think. Blake, I've had a lovely evening, but I think it's time to take me back to Miriam's."

"Stay with me, Nicollette."

"We've only met, Blake. Give me time."

He tried to coax me to stay. And I wanted him, oh, *how I wanted him.* But I remained steadfast. Not for my reputation. Not for the pace of our courting. But because I had come to my senses.

I didn't want to kill Lord Baston; I already loved him too much.

Bertrum returned Marie to Miriam's Cozy Inn about midnight. I watched Marie sit rather close to Bertrum as their carriage departed.

Blake's second driver took us back about an hour later. By the time Blake and I arrived at Miriam's, it was too late to go to bed at a decent hour, and the whole village was asleep.

Lord Baston took me to a place in the yard, sheltered a bit by some lilac bushes and a tree. He bent down on one knee before me, as if proposing.

"This was the best evening of my life. I'm in some kind of heavenly intoxication over you, Nicollette. And you must see me again, or I'll perish. Tell me you have no mind of Oliver, Charles, Douglas, or any of the other scurvy that lingers in our town, or on this earth. Tell me you will see only me, because I see only you."

"I see only you, Blake." He sat down and pulled me to him, laying his head on my bosom a moment, and then with his knee still out, he set me on his knee and drew my arms around his neck.

"You're funny, Blake. I quite enjoy you."

"Am I? Well, I didn't hang around with barristers every afternoon for years without learning angles."

"Angles?"

"Yes. There's a reason I have you sitting on my knee this way."

"And what is that?"

"Well, I need to make sure that everything's put together properly back here." He reached under my dress and stroked me. Then slid his hand up to the top of my undergarment and down into them to touch me while he kissed me deeply with his tongue. His finger probed me in and out—in the same cadence as before—and I could tell I was moist where his finger slid, and that I was ready for him to enter me.

Oh, yes, I was very ready.

I was the one who stopped this time. "Blake, we can't. There are neighbors."

"They're all asleep."

"All it takes is one who is awake to spread the news around the town. You would prefer a reputable woman, wouldn't you?"

"It isn't a requirement. This is where Victorian men have gone all wrong. I want a responsive one. I want you."

I stood up to wander in the yard and stopped near a large tree. Blake followed and picked a small bunch of leaves from a sleepy branch just over my head. He arranged a small group of the leaves in his fist, dropping those with a sign of imperfection before presenting the bouquet to me. And he smiled at me with such sexy promise in his eyes that I thought about our interlude in his den and fluttered.

"We must stop," I said.

"Why?"

"It's just time to stop, that's all."

"What is time?"

"I must go in."

"A little longer . . ."

"We must. Stop, please stop," I said again.

"Quit saying that, Nicollette," Blake said. "Stay here and just glow with me."

"I must go." I dashed away from Blake and ran tiptoe through Miriam's garden. Blake chased me, and when he caught me, he pressed me against the trunk of a tree.

"How can you sleep when we've found each other?"

I wish I could say that I went inside then. After all, it was late and I had been gone long enough. But I didn't. We kissed goodbye, then tried to part, but he would pull me back for another kiss and begin the cycle over again.

Neither of us wanted our time to end. Finally, I convinced him there would be another day for us.

"I have meetings tomorrow most of the day, but I want to see you for dinner."

"Of course," I said.

He kissed me again. And then before I left him I asked a question I had been wondering about.

"Blake, are you a barrister?"

"Yes, but I don't like to talk about it."

"Why is that?"

"Because barristers are all pond scum, and I like to think I'm a step above them. Perhaps at least of the caliber of some friendly bacteria, who aren't so parasitic."

"Did you have a bad experience with law?"

"All of my legal experiences have been disappointing. There's no justice, darling. It's all about what the queen wants. If she judges a thing shall pass, then it shall. If it disagrees with her, someone will be hanged."

"I hope I never displease the queen."

"You're above man's law to me. There's nothing you could do to warrant the law ever to pay you mind. So leave the worry of hanging and prisons to those worthy of the sentence."

He looked at me with such tenderness as we said our good-byes. Yet if he only knew, I could be closer to needing the best barrister in all of England than anyone of his acquaintance. My multiple crimes were murder. And in England, even one murderous event was neckworthy.

I went to Miriam's door to unlock it, then thought to watch the carriage loop around to return to Lord Baston's manor. I felt spellbound in my romantic moment and tried to sustain the glow until I could no longer hear the horses' hooves. And I clasped my hand to my heart as if to keep its flutter within my bosom. But in the silence, I sensed an alert of some sort in the fresh country air. Eyes watched me from somewhere.

I scanned the darkness for movement, but the world seemed unnaturally still. The wind had died and the foliage's rustle was mute. And a fear overcame me—where I stood a moment ago protected and loved, I now felt vulnerable and alone. I wanted to reach for a strong, loving hand, but there was none to shield me.

I hurried to my room, took off my frock, then thought to look upon the street a last time. I stood in the window wearing only my corset and stockings—and I saw him. There was a man who watched me from the street, but I couldn't see who it was. My eyes aren't their best at a distance, and I could see only that the man stood motionless in the near dark.

I realized my oil lamps were burning bright, and he could see me in my state of undress. So I extinguished the lamps, put on my nightdress in the darkness, and tried to put the nocturnal voyeur out of my mind. I wondered who he was. I wondered how long he had been there—watching. And why he was not moving on.

Since I had the answer to none of these questions, I tried to distract myself from my fear by feasting on my evening with Lord Baston.

Oh, sweet Blake. For all he had done for me tonight, the hosting of a beautiful party, the erotic book, the orchestra, and a new awakening for me with that special kiss. He had inflamed my body and touched my soul. And I found the opportunity to learn from him wonderfully seductive.

I thought again of *777*, the stimulating book. I had never seen or heard of it, but I sensed that Lord Baston didn't need to have the book near. That he might already know it all.

Go away, voyeur.

CHAPTER 21

Dead Man Down

"We're down here, Doctor," Lang said.

The bespectacled balding man stumbled down the cellar steps to the mortician's basement. Halfway down, he stopped. Had he been a child, Dr. Sidney Ignat wouldn't have gone down, even if he were double-dared. But he was an adult, a man of medicine, and a group of professional men awaited him. He continued down the stairs, coughing for clear air the last few steps.

"Oh, my," he muttered through his coughs.

Frederick Bothem's body lay on a large-slabbed table. The nude corpse was a pasty blue-gray color. The heavy stench of decomposing flesh hung in the air. Yet a roomful of men ignored the thick nauseous odor that filled the basement. The detectives extended their hands in greeting, but Dr. Ignat kept his to himself.

"Dr. Sidney Ignat."

"Jackson Lang. These are my colleagues, Peavey and Wilcox. Thank you for coming, Dr. Ignat. We won't have the opportu-

nity to study the body in London before its burial, and I welcome
any observations you might make. We like to have a doctor
schooled in this sort of thing take a look."

"Well, now, Inspector, I only had to cut on a dead man once
in my studies. Although I've had a few die on my table—more
than I care to remember. So though this isn't a preference of
mine, I stand willing. What do you want to know?"

"We'd like to know if you could determine the cause of
death."

"You want me to open him up? I'd rather not."

"We won't insist on that, Doctor. Perhaps you can share your
observations."

"He's quite odorous."

"Yes, there's a lot of flavor in the air. Peavey, Wilcox, ask Sam
if he can spare some of his floral bouquets for a bit." Peavey and
Wilcox disappeared.

"Dr. Ignat," Lang continued, "Frederick Bothem's death may
be one of a series of murders that has occurred in other countries
and now in England's counties. We're most interested to appre-
hend this criminal and prevent the loss of more innocent lives.
We need your help.

"This is a case that Queen Victoria studies, and she may decide to recognize the physician who helps solve the crime. I don't
promise this, of course. I tell you only that she will be pleased
when the perpetrator is no longer a threat to England."

"I understand," Ignat said. "I'll do this for you pro bono. My
last name is spelled I-G-N-A-T."

"I will note that. Now tell us, what do you observe?"

Peavey and Wilcox reentered the room. They balanced several
bouquets each and walked awkwardly, as though they were
flower arrangements with legs. They set the cut flowers and
plants near Dr. Ignat, but they did nothing to mask the stench.

"I must say, I believe this is the first case of priapism I've encountered."

"Priapism?"

"Yes. His penis isn't normal for a dead man. Or a live one, for that matter."

"We noticed that too. What causes it?"

"The member is still engorged with blood. My guess would be that the blood was not flowing upon his death. It's blocked there—no opportunity to release the blood that has pooled in his penis. There's very little study of this condition. It's a rare one."

"Could that kill a man?"

"I'd think it could, yes."

"What's happened in previous cases where a man has suffered from this malady?"

"Without immediate surgery, the patient could die. And so far, surgery has not been pleasant. Twenty years ago there was a case related to an overdose of a man's elixir. They could only castrate him to save his life. He was never able to accept his cruel fate and killed himself shortly after the operation."

"I see."

"This man here shows signs of cardiac arrest. Either from the blood blockage or some sort of simultaneous overload on the body."

"Anything else?"

"He doesn't look as if he struggled against his fate."

"What do you mean?"

"His pleasant facial expression. He's not horrified by his death. I'd also surmise that death was not as sudden as one might expect. He had a moment to accept it, I'd guess."

"We noted the smile."

Ignat stepped back. "Well, that's about it."

"Wait. Can you give me any off-the-record comments or thoughts?"

"Well, I've known Frederick a long time. And he confided to me that he was cut off from intimacy with Mamie long ago. Yet if I were to guess, I'd say he had intercourse before he went. Considering his smile, I'd surmise that it was with a pretty woman. I think that's it, sir. Where can I wash?"

"There's a sink there."

Ignat walked over to the sink and washed his hands. He studied Benson's wall, which was hung with all sorts of tools. Sam Benson entered the room as Ignat completed his task.

"Gentlemen, did you find answers to any of your questions?" he asked.

"We did," Lang said. "Thank you, Sam, for your hospitality."

"Mr. Benson," Ignat said, "I like this saw you have on the wall here. It would work well for amputating infected toes or fingers. It looks sharp. Where'd you get it?"

"Oh, that's a good one. But not like the Wilkins saw over here, which would actually work better for your purposes. I got it from a peddler who comes around to undertakers—when he comes again, I'll be happy to get you another."

"Thank you. Anything for scraping skin after lancing a boil?"

"Well, this tool has a curved scoop on it."

"Oh, yes, that's perfect."

"I'll just send the peddler your way when he comes by. He may have other items you'd find useful."

"Many thanks, Benson."

In that moment, as he observed the undertaker and the doctor conversing, Lang decided the care of the living and the dead might not be so far apart as one might expect.

When Lang and his assistants got back to the hotel, there was a telegram waiting. It read:

TO: INSPECTOR LANG

                CATHERINE HOTEL GLASTONBURY

FROM: PIERRE COLTIER,

                NICE POLICE, NICE, FRANCE

DATE: AUGUST 8, 1891

WANTED: NICOLLETTE CARON STOP

I UNDERSTAND FROM YOUR CHIEF YOU MAY BE
INVESTIGATING A CASE OF INTEREST TO US STOP

NICOLLETTE CARON A SUSPECT IN MURDERS OF FOUR
MEN IN NICE AND ITALY STOP

DO YOU KNOW WHEREABOUTS STOP

REWARD OFFERED FOR HER CAPTURE STOP

DETAILS IN LETTER SENT TO SCOTLAND YARD STOP

WATCH CLOSELY STOP

RUNNER STOP

INSPECTOR PIERRE COLTIER

Lang returned the following message:

TO: PIERRE COLTIER,

                NICE POLICE, NICE, FRANCE

FROM: SENIOR DETECTIVE JACKSON LANG

                CATHERINE HOTEL GLASTONBURY

DATE: AUGUST 8, 1891

YOUR PROMPT RESPONSE APPRECIATED STOP

WE KNOW WHEREABOUTS OF NICOLLETTE CARON BUT
ARE INTERESTED IN HER FOR INVESTIGATIONS OF OUR
OWN STOP

WILL COOPERATE FULLY WITH YOUR INTEREST AS OUR
CASE UNFOLDS STOP

FURTHER DETAILS AND COMMUNICATIONS TO FOLLOW
WITHIN A WEEK STOP

REWARD UNNECESSARY TO OUR FORCE STOP

WILL CONTINUE ON OUR JOBS STOP

JACKSON LANG SENIOR DETECTIVE

"Do we pick her up now?" Peavey asked.

"We don't have a case yet. But it's time to fan the flames,
gentlemen."

CHAPTER 22

Discovery

I WAS IN MY ROOM GIGGLING WITH MARIE AS IF WE WERE schoolgirls.

"*777?* I wonder if this is known in Italy."

"I'd be surprised if somewhere, someplace, there aren't Italian men who've traveled and acquired this book."

"I wonder . . ."

"What do you wonder?"

"I wonder if Lord Baston has Volume Two and Volume Three."

Marie and I laughed so hard we cried. I was holding my sides when Marie said, "Nicollette, look out the window!"

The three detectives were walking toward Miriam's. Even from that distance I could see the determined look on Jackson Lang's face.

"Nicollette, you should leave for a day-trip somewhere. Take the buggy and go."

"But the buggy's not ready. They'd stop me." Marie crossed herself. "Let's pray they go away."

"Marie, they're almost here." We heard the knock, and I did the only thing I could think to do. I combed my hair, in hopes that doing something ordinary would slow everything down. The world was moving too fast.

Miriam was answering the door downstairs.

"Undress," Marie said. "Tell them you aren't done with your grooming."

I flung my dress on the bed and put on a dressing gown. Miriam came up the stairs and knocked on our door. Marie, who had planned to spend the day cleaning and repairing my wardrobe, opened the door with a pile of my dresses over her arm.

"Inspector Lang wondered if he could ask you a few questions," Miriam said.

"I'm not dressed yet," I replied. "Perhaps another time."

"He said he would wait."

"I could be a while." My throat clenched. "Tell him I could meet him in an hour."

"Of course."

Miriam scurried down and back up the stairs. "He said you could meet in the constable's office at noon, then."

"The constable?" My stomach churned.

"Where Niles's office is located, next to Dr. Ignat's office on the corner."

"Oh, yes. I know where he is."

"He said it's nothing serious—just routine questions."

"Thank you, Miriam."

"Nicollette, have you answered questions before for the police?" Miriam asked.

"No," I lied. I'd gone through several questionings in other countries, but I could barely breathe. "What would they want to question me for?"

"Who knows, but they always get their man—or woman. So if you're guilty of anything, they're sure to find out."

"Yes, that's good, then."

"When they even suspect someone of wrongdoing, they take them to jail straightaway."

"Do they?"

"There's no time for a good-bye. They take them in chains to jail, they do." Miriam eyed me for a reaction, but she didn't see me tremble at all—yet I knew she wondered.

She went back downstairs. Had I seemed calm with her? I was storming inside.

I lay down on my bed to think. I needed to prepare my mind. What would I say about Denton's death? Or Frederick's? Or my beautiful Oliver? *Relax, relax, relax. Think calm. Calm.*

I paused to pet Pegasus before I entered the constable's office—as if the strong horse might strengthen my mind were we to commune for a moment.

"Pegasus, you look so beautiful today. I think I've fallen in love with you. If you would be so kind as to indulge me with even the slightest nudge of affection, I believe I could get through my ordeal."

The magnificent animal nuzzled me slowly.

"I wish I could spend the next hour with you instead of your master."

I entered Niles's office at exactly noon. He was there with Jackson Lang and his two assistants.

"Good to see you again, Miss Caron," Jackson said. But his voice held an edge.

"Good day, Mr. Lang."

"I appreciate your coming down on such short notice."

"My pleasure. Anything I can do to help the police. What is this all about?"

"You have no idea?"

"No, of course not."

"Your cooperation is most meaningful to us, Miss Caron. Please have a seat."

There was a hard wooden chair and a small table for four in the office. I took the chair. The other three men were seated around the table.

"Wilcox will take some notes. Are you ready to begin?"

"Yes."

"Do you remember attending the Queen's Ball this past week?"

"Yes. It was lovely."

"Can you tell me who escorted you to the ball?"

"Denton Brickman."

"How long had you been courted by Mr. Brickman?"

"About a month."

"Did you stay until the end of the ball?"

"No, we left early."

"You weren't having a good time together?"

"We had a lovely time together."

Lang was clearly prepared. He knew the questions he would ask me without referring to notes. And I knew he was studying me, noting my mannerisms and judging whether he thought I might be lying to him.

"Did you want to go somewhere to be together, as lovers do? Is that why you left early?"

"No."

"Nonetheless, you left quite early for your home?"

"Yes."

"Did you feel well? Did he?"

"Yes to both questions."

"Did you plan to do something, is that why you left early?"

"No." Lang's eyes held mine for a long moment, then he looked down at his notes.

"Did you have plans to become intimate that evening with Mr. Brickman?"

"No. We left early because I was tired from dancing."

"Where did you go when you left the dance?"

"To my manor."

"Did you stop anywhere?"

"We went directly to my home."

"What happened when you arrived there?"

"Denton got out of the carriage and helped me step down. Then he gave me a kiss. Upon my cheek, of course."

"Of course."

"He thanked me for a wonderful evening."

"And then what happened?"

"We spoke for a few minutes. His driver left the carriage to give us privacy—I believe he went to the stable. I thought I saw something in his hand. Perhaps a bottle."

"And did you see the driver after that?"

"No. I heard he got drunk in our stable, but I don't know that firsthand."

"And what did Denton do? What happened next?"

"Denton kissed me a few times at the door, thanked me again and again, and returned to his carriage. I didn't look closely. He must have gotten fed up with his driver and driven the carriage home himself."

"Did you sleep at your manor that night?"

"Actually, no. I'm usually excited before a trip and have insomnia before my travel. I make sure there are clear instructions and expectations for my servants during my absence. And when I feel there are no loose ends, depart for my journey."

"When did you leave your manor?"

"When?"

"Yes, when."

"You mean day or night?"

"I mean the time."

"I have no idea about the time. I'm not very good with time. So many others pay attention to time, but I don't even carry a timepiece and have few clocks in my home."

"Was it in the night?"

"Well, no, actually it was morning."

"You didn't leave in the middle of the night?"

"No, I left in the morning. For certain."

"Was it dark out?"

"If it was dark, it was light in just a moment."

"Why did you come here?"

"I had a friend who told me Glastonbury was a lovely town. And she was from here."

"What friend would that be?"

"Elizabeth."

"Elizabeth who?"

"I never did catch her last name. We met briefly on a train one day, and she talked of Glastonbury."

"Which train?"

"In London. Just a short train ride within London."

"Like from Piccadilly to somewhere?"

"I believe it was Queen's Crossing to Hyde Park."

"And when was it that you were in London?"

"About six months ago."

"Do you remember the dates of that London trip?"

"No."

"Did you take the train in?"

"We took a buggy. Marie and I."

"I see. Well, London is quite exhilarating, isn't it?"

"We had a lovely time."

"Where did you stay?"

"With friends."

"Their names?"

"Is there a reason that you're inquiring about my ancient travel plans?"

"Yes, there is."

"Sanford. Their name was Sanford."

"They have a home there?"

"Near Hyde Park."

"Why did you leave so early on your trip to Glastonbury? Why not have a night's rest and depart later in the morning?"

"I mentioned that I suffer from insomnia. I often take afternoon naps and turn my day around. I took a nap before the Queen's Ball and wasn't tired at all. I thought I could make good time on the road by leaving early and arrive during the day to secure a room."

"So you were sufficiently tired from dancing to leave the ball early but not too tired to leave early on your trip. Did you know people in Glastonbury before you came here?"

"Not really, but Elizabeth told me so many stories about the townspeople, I felt as if I knew several of them already."

"Why didn't you take Marie with you?"

"She was sleeping. I simply let her sleep. The plan was for her to join me after she'd finished some tasks at the manor."

"What kind of tasks?"

"She was taking care of the linens and getting my winter wardrobe ready for me."

"Did you stop along the way?"

"I stopped for a small breakfast Marie had packed for me."

"What did she pack?"

"I believe it was a lovely pastry, an apple, and some wine."

"Any grapes in the basket?"

"No, I didn't have any grapes."

There was a faint knock on the sheriff's door, and it opened slowly. It was Marie. Lang walked over to her.

"Miss Caron, gentlemen, let's take a few minutes' break. Marie, let me walk you out for a moment."

Marie and Lang stepped outside. "We may be another hour. Marie, can you find something to keep you busy for a bit? I'll tell Miss Caron where you'll be."

"I'll wait for her at Miriam's, then."

"Very well. By the way, Marie, she mentioned why you didn't come with her when she left for Glastonbury."

"Yes, I'm an early riser. She's up so late. I was sleeping."

"I see."

"And I had to get the wardrobe and linens prepared for the next season before I left."

"So she said. She appreciated the lunch you packed with her favorite things for the trip."

Marie smiled at him. "She does enjoy that pastry. And I packed a bottle of wine for her."

"Oh, yes. With the grapes. They're quite a delicacy around here."

"But they're her favorite—she won't be without them."

"I don't blame her. Thank you, Marie."

Lang almost felt guilty for tripping up such a nice little maid, but it was his job. And there was that tingle he always felt when his cleverness elicited information from people who didn't realize they were being interrogated.

Jackson walked back into the room, looking pleased with himself. His cool demeanor had an inverse reaction on me. I felt my body temperature rise and the wetness of perspiration under my arms. I fixed my arms tight to my body. *Let me go. Please let me go.*

"Marie will wait for you at Miriam's, Miss Caron," he said.

"Very well."

"May we resume?"

"Of course."

"Let's see here, where were we? Do I remember this right? You stopped for breakfast outside of town and had a pastry, wine, and some grapes?"

"No—pastry, wine, and an apple."

"I could have sworn you said grapes."

"Actually I don't care for them."

"I see. As you came into town that morning, did you see anyone on the road?"

"No."

"Did you meet a man named Frederick Bothem?"

"No."

"So when I ask you if you've ever seen Mr. Bothem, you don't even know who I'm talking about, do you?"

"No."

I felt less worried at this point in the interrogation—. He'd tripped me up on my being tired, but I didn't think he really had anything on me yet. I had an answer for all his questions. And they were good answers. He didn't have any proof that I knew Frederick at all. Or that Denton hadn't died miles from my home, when I was nowhere near his moment of death, much less its cause.

I was not relaxed, but I felt strong—until I looked in the mirror across the table. It was mounted within an old horse collar. And in the mirror *an outline formed of my dead lover Oliver.* I turned away.

"Sorry. I drifted a moment. What did you say?"

"I don't mean to bore you, Miss Caron. Just a bit longer."

"Of course."

"I need not ask you more questions about Frederick, since you don't know who I'm talking about. And I don't have a photograph, unless you'd like to come with me and pay your respects to the former constable."

"It's not necessary."

"Well, let me just have you take a look over at Benson's. You may recognize him."

"I think not." I was terrorized by the thought of having to face my poor victim in his disintegrating state.

"Come along—it should only take a moment." *No, you can't make me. I won't go.*

But Jackson crossed the room and lifted my elbow up so firmly it brought me to a stance. Then he held on tight and forced me outside. Though he made it look like a cordial escort, I was captive in his strong hold.

We all walked across the street in a kind of morbid parade to the undertaker's. Instead of leading me into the reviewing room on the main floor, Jackson took me to the staircase to the cellar.

"What are you doing?"

"We're going to look at Frederick Bothem and see if you recognize him."

"I'm sure I won't. Isn't he dead? I don't want to go with you."

"It will take only a moment."

I stood at the top of the stairway. I could smell a foul odor rising from the cellar, and my throat constricted from the stench. I locked my legs—refusing to go farther. But Jackson Lang wouldn't let me decide my next move.

"If you're afraid you'll trip on the stairs, I can help." And he picked me up and carried me down the steps. He set me down only a few feet from Frederick's nauseating corpse.

I couldn't breathe. I was so close to retching I could barely stand.

I looked at the blue-gray shell of death and imagined an animated, kind, friendly Frederick.

"Do you recognize this man, Nicollette?"

Wide-eyed I stared at the stiff man. And then *Frederick's corpse lifted his head and looked at me.*

Good morning, to you, beautiful lady, the dead man said. *Am I dreaming you, miss? If I am, it's such a lovely dream that you mustn't wake me.*

I was sick, overwhelmed, and unable to stand. I screamed and fell.

"Good work, Jackson," Wilcox said. "We'll remember to use this brute tactic again."

"Well, I had to try something."

"We'll get her." Peavey spoke as if the recruits were taking ownership of the fallen doll. He and Wilcox protectively carried Nicollette up the stairs to fresher air.

I came to in Dr. Ignat's office. I sat up, felt dizzy, and lay back down. I could see a desk, an eye chart, and a small price sign I couldn't read. My dress hung on a coatrack, and I wore only my corset and bloomers. I tried to cover myself. The doctor had a board with a clip and was studying a paper.

"I'm Dr. Ignat. I think you may have fainted, Miss Caron. You were unconscious quite a few minutes. Have you been to a doctor before?"

"I've had no need to go."

"That's fortunate. I took the liberty to check out a few things. First I checked you for fever, and you have none."

"Yes."

"You knew that?"

"Yes."

"Then I listened to your chest, and your lungs are clear."

"Yes."

"You knew that, too?"

"Yes."

"Did you know you have the fastest-beating heart I've ever heard?"

"No."

"Your heart beats so fast I could hardly measure it. Over two hundred beats per minute."

"Is that so very fast?"

"Miss Caron. The beat of your heart is the number of times blood is squeezed from the heart to the lungs. Normal is about seventy beats per minute. Your rate is three or four times that fast. Probably closer to a rabbit's heartbeat—which may be about three hundred."

"Well, it must work for me."

"Perhaps, but it may not work the same for others. As I was testing you, I felt my own heart increase its rate, and I began to sweat. My heart rate increased to almost two hundred. Not until I walked outside and sat in a chair away from you did my heart return to its normal rate."

"I don't understand."

"I think, Miss Caron, that you might be able to elevate the heart rate and blood pressure of someone close to you. You may not be aware of this, but you should consider it. Now I want you to listen to your heart through this instrument. It's called a stethoscope. You can hear how fast your heart is beating. There— do you hear?"

"Yes."

"Now listen to mine. Can you hear the difference?"

"Oh, yes."

"Hold it here on your neck and feel the pulse. I want you to count the beats. We'll count the beats in ten seconds and multiply by six."

"All right."

"Count the beats. Begin now."

I counted the beats as best I could until he told me to stop. "I think I counted forty-five, but I missed some."

"Now check mine."

I held my finger to the doctor's neck as he had showed me and counted about thirteen beats.

"You see, Miss Caron, I think close enough proximity to a woman with your condition might kill a man. It could stress his heart."

I began to cry. "Dr. Ignat, please don't tell anyone about this—that I'm not normal. Please, Dr. Ignat."

"My dear, be assured that I won't. I'm your personal physician, and what passes between us is confidential."

I looked into his kind, bespectacled eyes and took both his hands in mine.

"Our secret, Miss Caron," Dr. Ignat said. "I have no reason to tell anyone about this phenomenon. Inspector Lang wanted to be notified when you were better. I'll tell him I've ordered bed rest for you and will have you sent home. I have a spare stethoscope. You may keep it to test yourself periodically."

"Thank you, Dr. Ignat. For everything."

CHAPTER 23

A Gift from Marie

I DIDN'T WANT A MIRROR NEAR ME. HOW COULD I LOOK IN a mirror and see a killer?

A piece of my puzzle was now found, but it was a horrid detail to know—and one I wanted to forget. But I knew that my denying my deadly effect wouldn't neutralize it. I was confused and filled with self-hatred. I didn't know what to do with Dr. Ignat's discovery.

I truly was a murderer. A murderer without ill intent or motive, but no less a murderer.

Now that I knew for certain I was the cause of my lovers' deaths, I was more tormented by guilt. And how would I deal with this deadly force in my future? I think it was this guilt that made me feel weak as I left the doctor's office. I inhaled the fresh country air and began to improve when I saw Bertrum pull up in Blake's carriage.

"Good day, Miss Caron. Lord Baston sent his carriage for you."

"Good day, Bertrum. How thoughtful of him."

Bertrum cupped his hand around his mouth and let out a melodious birdcall aimed across the street. Through a window I saw Blake seated with several men at a large table in the Glastonbury city office. When Bertrum's call reached his ears he stood to leave his meeting and, with just a few long strides, crossed the street and helped me into the carriage.

"Nicollette, I heard about your fainting spell. I'm quite concerned." His arm gently surrounded me.

"Thank you, Blake."

"Would you like to go back to Miriam's? Or if you're feeling better, we could go to my manor and play doctor. I see you have part of the equipment there," he said with his eyes on my stethoscope.

"If I were the doctor, would you be—my patient?" I asked.

"A woman doctor? Not likely."

"Maybe one day."

"That I'd have to see. Women don't like blood."

"There could be a woman who might be able to handle it."

"All right, I concede the point. Yes. There very well might be a female doctor one day."

"Thank you. And now I'd like to go to Miriam's to bathe and change."

"May I offer my complimentary bathing services?"

I tossed my head with a laugh, then saw a flash of white to my left and turned to see the beautiful Pegasus hitched to a post near the doctor's office.

"Oh, Blake, isn't he a lovely horse?"

"That he is. I saw him perform—he's quite spectacular." We exited the carriage and moved closer to the horse.

"He looks like he has silver threads in his mane and tail. And his eyes, Blake—they're so intelligent. The horse has such presence. As if he understands his greatness."

"I think he may. Why was his owner questioning you, Nicollette?"

"I was the last person to see Denton Brickman alive. He escorted me to the Queen's Ball and was in some sort of an accident shortly after he delivered me home."

"Well, you can't be held accountable for an accident. Were you there when the accident occurred?"

"No. But they suspect his cause of death to be murder. Inspector Lang thought I might be able to shed some light on his death, but as it turned out I was unable to give him any helpful information. And oh, Blake, he also asked me to look at the corpse of another murder victim, to see if I recognized the man—which I didn't. That's when I fainted."

"It seems Inspector Lang is a high-handed fellow. Nicollette, you may be grateful for my training as a barrister. I don't think you should talk to him again unless I'm present. There's Lang now, let me have a word with him."

Lang stepped out in the street to find Lord Baston studying Pegasus. Nicollette was inside the carriage.

"This is quite a horse, Inspector."

"That he is."

"Would you like to sell him? Name your price."

"He has no price."

"Every horse has a price."

"Not Pegasus. To me he's priceless."

"How about in exchange for land, or a manor?"

"No price, Lord Baston. You can save your breath. One hundred thousand pounds wouldn't part me and this horse."

"Then two hundred thousand pounds?"

"Nor that."

"I understand you took Miss Caron to view a corpse today?"

Lang nodded. "Does that trouble you?"

"Are you finished with your interrogation of her?"

"No."

"I want to be present whenever you speak with her. I'll be her solicitor, until she hires another."

"Very well."

"Let me know if you change your mind about Pegasus. I'm quite interested."

"I have a waiting list for him."

Blake stepped into the carriage to return me to Miriam's.

"I've made it clear to Lang that I'm to be present anytime you're questioned," he said.

"Thank you, Blake."

"I believe they're after you, Nicollette."

"I'm afraid so."

"That's preposterous. You've done nothing wrong. A simple evening out with maybe a dance or two—that was all it was, wasn't it? You certainly did nothing more than that with the gentleman, did you?"

Blake was suddenly questioning me with a jealous heart—and so I merely calmed it. "No, of course not. Nothing happened."

All day long I felt like a baby sparrow on the edge of a branch that was being cut down. Any breeze, any movement, wobbled my branch—I had flightless wings and feared falling to my death. I was grateful for Lord Baston's strength.

The new constable summoned Lang and his assistants to his office. "I thought you might want to see this telegram," Niles said.

TO: GLASTONBURY CONSTABLE
               GLASTONBURY, ENGLAND

FROM: RANDALL DAVIS,
               LONDON, ENGLAND

DATE: AUGUST 8, 1891

SUBJECT: OLIVER DAVIS

BROTHER OLIVER WAS EXPECTED HERE FOR VISIT STOP

NOT ON TRAIN AS SCHEDULED STOP

PRESUMED MISSING STOP

COULD YOU PLEASE INVESTIGATE THIS FOR US STOP

PLEASE ADVISE STOP

WITH CONCERN
RANDALL DAVIS

"Inspector," Niles said, "I saw Oliver at the Foxhunt Club dance and learned that he went on a buggy outing the next day with Nicollette Caron."

Lang looked thoughtful before he spoke. "Just a hunch. Follow me."

All four men rode east with Pegasus in the lead. He appeared to know exactly where he was going.

I took a healing lavender bath while Lord Baston had tea with Miriam. I tried to imagine that the warm water was somehow flowing through my body and soaking away the pain of my losses from every cell of my being.

Perhaps if my story should ever be told, its hearers might not

understand how I could fall for men—*so many men*. Some
women believe the fairy tale of having a twin soul to find and
cleave to forever. And in my story, they might wonder how I
could cleave unto each one. And when a lover fell terminally still,
how I could move on.

When I thought about it, it made me wonder, too. Perhaps
my being young and still hopeful made me reluctant to give up
all yearning for a lover who might sustain me, and I him.

But first he would have to survive. What precautions could I
take? I said no, and they didn't listen. But I wasn't saying no to
Lord Baston—the attraction was too strong. He was the sun, to-
tally in control of his small moon, and he had me in his orbit. I
was merely in harmony with his path, to play when he played, to
dance when he danced, to sleep when he slept, and to be his love.

"Miss Nicollette, rise up," Marie said, urging me from the
tub. "Your handsome suitor awaits."

"Help me, please." Marie handed me a towel to dry myself,
then helped me dress and prepare for my outing with Blake.

"Lang isn't our friend," Marie said when I was ready. "He
should never have taken you to the undertaker's horror downstairs."

"Marie, I think I'll be leaving soon. Perhaps tonight. Maybe
for your safety, it would be best if you stay behind."

"I want to go with you. I'm sad without you, Miss Nicollette.
I feel I belong at your side."

"I'm thinking of your health, Marie. Your sweet neck, my
dear friend."

She looked at me tenderly, clasping both hands to her throat.
She pretended to lift it and hand it to me. "I give you my neck.
Now I have none. I'm just your dear friend and dedicated maid
who feels most complete when she's with you. Life is so dull
when you go away, Miss Nicollette."

"Dear Marie, I don't take your pledge lightly. I pray to save you from my nightmare. But I worry for you. Clearly, the queen has an affection for executions. And I feel the breath of her power at my back."

"Take me with you."

I nodded. "Very well, Marie. It will soon be dusk—pack our things. We'll leave tonight."

Chief Bart Marshall was escorted into the queen's chambers at Buckingham Palace. Queen Victoria sat in a purple robe with gold trim and a matching dress, a departure from the dark frocks she had worn on most occasions since the death of Prince Albert thirty years earlier.

"Your Royal Majesty. May I say your robe is extraordinarily becoming?"

"Purple is my favorite color—I'm happy to have a chief with a keen eye. Now share with me your progress on the murders."

"Since we spoke, there's another dead man near Glastonbury. Frederick Bothem, the constable. And I just received a telegram moments ago that Oliver Davis, a horse breeder and derby winner, is missing."

"Ambassador Davis's son?"

"Yes, Your Majesty."

"Has Davis been sent word?"

"Yes."

"This is very sad news indeed. I remember his lad."

"We have a suspect. A Frenchwoman named Nicollette Caron. Oliver Davis was last seen in her company. We have also heard from the police in France that she's a suspect for four murders in Nice and just missed the French guillotine. In northern Italy, she's a suspect in another murder."

"Bring her in for trial."

"My finest, Inspector Lang, is investigating her. He won't fail."

"Jackson Lang?"

"The same. He's gathering evidence for his case. He'll bring her in. He always apprehends his criminal—this case will be no different."

"Miss Caron. Is she a harlot?"

"Difficult to answer, Your Majesty. To many she may be. Apparently she falls in love with them all."

"And how does she kill them? Do you know this?"

"We're still investigating. We'll have an answer for you soon."

"Very well."

"Anything else, Your Majesty?"

"I heard a rumor, but I didn't understand the word. Can you explain priapism to me?"

"I think I ought not, Your Majesty. I'd be a bit uncomfortable. May I tell one of your attendants or a nurse who might pass along the information?"

"I appreciate your quandary, Sir Bart. Why don't you tell my prime minister? Through him the details can be passed along to me, for I must have them. Do you understand? It isn't for my amusement."

"Of course, Your Majesty."

She motioned for a guard to fetch the prime minister, Robert Gascoyne-Cecil, Marquess of Salisbury, so that Sir Bart could share the information about the case with him. Salisbury would in turn tell his wife Georgina. She would then tell the nurse, who would tell the queen. Though this five-channel process spared any embarrassment to male or female, neither Salisbury's wife nor the nurse was noted for her discretion—in fact, they were the most frequent conduits of information about the queen's business to the public.

In a matter of days the new word "priapism" would be familiar to most of England. In pubs there would be jokes about stiff Irishmen, Scots perpetually aroused under their kilts, and the Dutch boy who no longer relied on his thumb to plug the dam. All kinds of jokes, whispers, and rumors about a woman who caused this effect would be shared across the country.

CHAPTER 24

Sanctuary

Lord Baston and Miriam sipped tea in Miriam's parlor. They were engrossed in a conversation over the city-planning meetings Lord Baston had attended earlier in the day.

"We need to expand, Miriam," Lord Baston said. "Glastonbury is going to grow, whether we accept it or not. We might as well change with the times."

"But we have to keep the town's quaint atmosphere, or we'll end up with all the crime and other problems of London," Miriam said.

"Or are you concerned about other inns giving you competition?"

"Well, yes, of course I am. I have only my small business to support me and my staff."

"Excuse me, Miriam, I see something beautiful in your home."

"You mean that picture on the wall?"

"No, the woman on the stair."

• • •

Blake took my hand when I stood just three steps above him. The extra height aligned our eyes. And I paused, as he made no movement to bring me farther down the steps.

"My lord, what are you thinking?"

"A man has secrets."

"Tell me."

"Thirty-two. I'm thinking thirty-two."

"I'm not. I'm nineteen years old."

"Well, then, I was thinking twenty-two."

"I thank you. That's better than thirty-two."

"Then a one hundred fifty-six."

Ah. He was referring to the numbered positions from the erotic book he harbored in his study.

"Lord Baston, you're a rogue, aren't you?"

His eyes danced. "And I'll top it off with a five-twelve."

"Five-twelve?"

"Yes. I think I'd do that twice."

I laughed so loud, Miriam had to be wondering what comedy was playing on her stairs.

"Twice. Could I handle twice?"

"No, Nicollette." He sighed. "I don't believe you would let me go in that case."

"You mean never let you leave my *bed*?"

"Bed? I said nothing about a bed. Five-twelve takes place in a tree fort."

Oh, how I enjoyed the teasing ideas of a powerful man at play.

"Walk with me," he said.

I took Blake's arm, and we walked across the street to the small park, with its lovely white bench.

His glistening eyes peered deeply into mine, and I closed

mine to relish the moment. He made me feel as if I were champagne inside, full of tiny bubbles just floating through me. There was nothing to ground me or hold me. Unless he held on to me, I would rise. I was lighter than air, even mixed with the air. He could breathe me in and out. *In and out. In and out.*

Nothing hurt with him, and everything ached. The world was full, and in it there were just he and I. Jackson Lang was but a troll near a faraway bridge. And I pushed him to the other side of the world.

In my dream there was a magical land of love in which Blake and I danced. It had a sky full of stars, the moon, and the sun—all in a heaven that was filled only with our love, high above the earth.

Blake and I were dancing in that heaven when *I saw Robert appear with his blank stare, followed by Collin, Oliver, Frederick, Denton, and ten other men, all with the same pasty white lifeless expression.*

Dead lovers reached for me in the clouds. They tore Blake and me apart and pushed my head down in the clouds. The fog blinded me. I couldn't see. I called inside my mind for Blake, but he was gone. There was just me in the clouds. Surrounded by my dead lovers. Oh, God, help me. I searched their ghoulish eyes but only felt them tear at my soul. Help me.

"Help me!"

"I'm trying, Nicollette. What can I do?"

"I don't know how to tell you."

"None of your schemes will get rid of me, Miss Caron. I'll duel all your suitors."

"Blake, I need to tell you something. I must find an honest stand for us, in the web of my deceit."

"What if I don't need to hear it?"

I began carefully, unsure how deeply I could share my truth.

"Blake, I have a condition."

"What kind of condition?"

"I don't understand it."

"Perhaps it's nothing at all. You look quite well, Nicollette. Have you been misdiagnosed?"

"I'm not explaining this as I should, Blake. Only one other knows of it, please listen to what—"

"Nicollette, I don't care what you perceive to be wrong with you. I see only what I see. Your great beauty, and wit, and soul. I don't need anything more." He stood up and paced a few steps away from me. "Nicollette, there's nothing wrong with you. Perhaps this thing is only within your—"

"Would you like to make love with me?"

"Well, that's quite silly, Nicollette. I and any man in all of England who's seen you wants to do that."

"What if you knew that when we did make love, you would die?"

"What are you talking about?"

"I'm trying to tell you, there's something wrong with me."

"You're too lovely to have anything wrong with you. I can see this for myself."

"I have a curse. Something I can't control or change. Something I don't understand."

"I've heard of people dreaming up maladies. Hypochondria, they call it."

"You don't understand. This is real. You must believe me."

"All right, all right. I'm sorry. I see you quite believe in this, this . . ."

"Curse. I have a rabbit heart."

"Yes. Well. Can you tell me any fact about your, ah, rabid heart?"

"It's a rab*bit* heart."

"Like a garden bunny? I'm quite tall, but this is a stretch even for me."

"You mock me? I can't tell you, Blake. You'll think horribly of me, and I can't bear that."

"Oh, sweet Nicollette—nothing you could say or do, nothing you could tell me that you've ever done, could lead me to think ill of you."

"Except for this. You'd have a ruined image of me. Your thoughts of me would forever change."

"Tell me."

"It's a morbid curse, Blake."

My head fell limp, and tears crowded my eyes. Blake held me lovingly without any public shame. I found myself trying to withdraw some invisible nourishment from his touch, for I felt no strength or pride in myself after my words to him. He held me a long time.

Then I looked down the road—and thought I saw Jackson Lang and his men riding into town, with *Oliver's body thrown across one of the horses.* I stared at what I saw, terrified that Jackson would trot down to me and arrest me on the spot.

"Nicollette," Blake murmured.

Then Jackson and his men rode closer. I wanted to run, but I was motionless.

"Nicollette. Speak to me."

I saw them come after me. It was time for my arrest. They had proof of my kills. They knew of all the blood on my hands, they would bind my wrists, blaming me for the beautiful dead men they'd say I had left with no mercy or conscience. But as I prepared my mind for capture, Jackson and his men, upon their horses, melted before my eyes. A young handsome male tourist stood captivated by me in their place. He smiled and tipped his hat to me.

Blake took a few steps away from the bench. "If you won't talk to me, Nicollette, perhaps we need a rest from each other. For I won't be ignored for some other man you watch on the street. Good day, Nicollette."

I had paid no mind to the man in the street, as he claimed. Only to my delusions and fears, which chose a bad moment to haunt me. There had been no discovery of Oliver, but I felt my vision to be a premonition of the future that would unfold before me. Though the day was warm, a cold blast of air shot through my body, and I shuddered.

Blake didn't escort me back to Miriam's. Nor did he look back.

"Good-bye, my lord." But if he heard me, he paid me no mind. The bubbles inside me were flat. I walked back to the inn, feeling dejected, but couldn't keep my mind from plotting.

Miriam was sitting in a rocker, darning a sock. Her servant cleared the silver service that had served Lord Baston and left with a brief curtsy.

"Miriam," I said, "Lord Baston mentioned that Wilcox and Peavey had asked for you. The gentlemen wondered if you wanted to join them for a drink before dinner at the pub. They're there now."

"Oh, really? I shouldn't disappoint them."

"No, and you look lovely in that gray dress."

Miriam hurried down the street to get the buggy, and I returned to my room. Marie and I readied ourselves to leave.

I left Miriam a note expressing my gratitude—with a bonus, though I was paid up. I left her a signed note giving her the stabled horse and buggy I left behind for her warm hospitality. I hid the note in my sheets so she wouldn't find it until she changed the bedding. And just as the moon rose, Marie and I took our buggy quietly down a back street and out beyond the town. We went east until there was a fork in the road, then stayed left to drive north just before Lord Baston's property line.

The horses and buggy were going so fast that we were flying over the divots in the road, and the bumps threatened to bounce Marie and me out of our seats. We held on as I drove my horses with no mind at all for what lay ahead, only hoping that we would find our safety somewhere, anywhere.

"You must pray for us, Marie. I'm tired and confused, and I have no ideas for us. I can only think to run and only hope that they forget us. And I fear that's not likely."

"I pray, Miss Nicollette."

In the darkness up ahead we saw a carriage on the road driving slowly toward town.

"Keep your head down, Marie. We'll sail by him." I slapped the reins harder on the horses' rumps.

The driver was yelling something to me, but I didn't want to stop. He saw this and blocked the road.

"Miss Nicollette! Miss Nicollette! Stop! I'm to pick you up!"

"What?"

I slowed my buggy when I saw it was Blake's carriage. Blake stuck his head out. I went around the carriage and continued to fly down the road past him. But in my haste I dropped the reins and lost control of the horses.

Looking back, I saw Bertrum unharness the carriage's lead horse and Blake mount the horse. He chased down the road after our runaway buggy. When he was alongside my carriage, his horse parallel to my forward horse, he jumped from his horse to mine. Pulling on the reins, he slowed my buggy, and my horses surrendered to a stop.

He straightened the reins and held them firmly as he climbed in the seat next to me.

"Nicollette, you're quite anxious to leave our town."

"I'm sorry, Lord Baston."

"Lord Baston? What happened to Blake?"

"I've no time to explain. I fear there may be someone after me."

"What if I could hide you somewhere comfortable, somewhere you couldn't be found?"

"Could you do that?"

"If I helped you, how grateful would you be?" he said with a wicked smile.

"Very grateful."

"Trust me, Nicollette. Follow me."

He remounted his own horse, and Marie and I followed in my buggy.

"Bertrum," Blake said when we reached his carriage, "please take Marie with you and meet us at Shepherd's Grove. We'll be staying there this evening. You must talk to no one, and don't let anyone see you. Look for my hat along the way. I don't want to leave it behind." He dismounted and assisted Bertrum as he harnessed the horse into position.

"Marie," Bertrum said. "Lovely to see you." He tipped his hat.

She smiled like a schoolgirl. "Good evening, Bert."

"I've a bit of a confession."

"Oh?"

"I've missed you, Marie. And thought about you."

"Really?"

Then Blake lifted himself into the buggy and took the reins from me. He said nothing as he put my horses into motion. Riding with him took away the fever and the fear I'd felt when I held the reins. I felt calmed. And although I was still not sheltered safely, I knew I soon would be.

I looked at him as he drove straight ahead, watching the road. His hair was tousled, and he looked quite dashing in the breeze.

"You're a fascinating creature, Nicollette."

"And you, Lord Baston."

"Blake."

"Blake. It's a lovely name. I have a fondness for it."

"I love more than your name."

"Well, I might love more than your name, too. Where are you taking me?"

"I have a cottage on my property that I use only for hunting. You'll be safe there. Hardly a soul knows of it. It's secluded deep in the woods."

"That sounds perfect."

"Do you plan to always run from town to town?"

"I don't want to talk about it."

"If you do, I'll be able to help you."

"I doubt it."

"Perhaps I'll understand."

"I don't think so. You didn't this afternoon. And you only knew a little."

"We may surprise each other."

We rode the rest of the way in silence and turned down a long dirt road that led into the woods. We reached a secluded cottage estate buried in the thick woods, and Blake stabled the horses as I waited for him near the threshold. Marie entered the cottage shortly after us, followed by Bertrum, who held Blake's hat in his hand.

The cottage was rustic, yet warm. Cozy blankets were strewn about the furniture to wrap yourself in, and their presence provided a loving touch to the home. Each element of the decor showed the same eye for detail that I'd seen in Blake's manor. It was well lit when the lamps were ignited. And he had a games area with a large ornate chess set.

We were a bite reserved at first. But then the more informal setting of a hunting lodge allowed us to relax.

We scrounged through the pantry for canned items, wine, and dried goods. Then Bertrum and Marie creatively made a meal of jerky and the contents of various jars, which filled us. The two of them had great fun working in the kitchen together, and their laughter warmed our ears.

Blake and I were now beyond the smiles of new love. We had to be. I was in survival mode. I was not playing the game of marrying the richest man in the land. My game was deadly serious. How could I wake up tomorrow morning as a free woman? How could I avoid prison? How could I save my neck?

"Our royal system won't dissolve," Blake said. "Our tradition is too strong, and the queen is too rich."

We talked through the night. The more I listened to him, the more I wanted this man in a different way. He fascinated me, and he never looked away when I spoke.

"Let's play a game," he said.

"What game?"

"Truth. I ask you a question and you answer me."

"I've been honest with you—more honest than most women. You know I'm nineteen, for instance."

"I need to know more. Why is the law suspicious of you?"

"I told you, I was with Denton the night he died."

"But you weren't with him when he died?"

"Perhaps it is better to leave some females with their mysteries."

"Then I must be a sleuth at heart, for I like the truth."

"I think you're looking for reasons not to love me."

"Ask any man. We don't need to find reasons. Can't you see, being a bachelor is so much easier?"

"Easier, how?"

"No one to answer to, our life our own, no expectations of monogamy and the like, not to mention the nagging."

"Oh, so now I'm a nag, am I?"

"That's not what I meant—some women are, though."

"Some women are shrews, and I'm not that either, Blake." I reached up and let my long hair down. It fell to my waist, and he stared at me.

"Blake, I'm a bit bored with truth. Can we play one of my games now?"

"What is it?"

"I call it kiss."

"Do I need to bring my checkers for this?"

"No, you only need to bring your lips."

He crawled on the floor next to me. "I brought my lips. How do I play?"

"Well, first you search the room for someone you'd like to kiss. Do you see anyone?"

"Yes. I'm fairly certain that I do."

"Well, you have to ask permission of the person. Anything you want to do with that person, you have to ask permission."

"I see. Miss Nicollette, I believe I'd like to kiss you. May I?"

"Yes, you may."

Blake licked lightly around the rim of my lips, then kissed me with a tongue that probed me and simulated the sexual thrusts of lovemaking. I found myself getting lost in the kiss. I felt as if I were an instrument he was playing.

"I've kissed here for a while," he said. "May I kiss your neck?"

"Yes, you may."

Blake slowly nibbled and kissed down my neck, sometimes breathing lightly in my ear or kissing my ear lobe. I felt my body readying itself for penetration as he smoothly played me.

"I've kissed here a while. May I kiss your bosom?"

"Yes, you may, my lord."

I sat up for him as he undid my dress and my laced corset. He pulled my clothing away so that I was bare to him from the waist up. And he drank me in. Even without his touching me I could feel the pleasure he took in the sight of me. And he reached for me with a forceful kiss and brought a hand down to fondle my right breast.

"I'm sorry, Blake," I said, trying to pull away. "You didn't ask for permission to touch there, just to kiss there."

"Well, I need to—I mean, may I . . ."

He kissed me overpoweringly as he fondled my breasts. And the thrill of his touch made the evening in his den flood my head. All the desire and passion we had restrained ourselves from during the day became unleashed and startled every cell of my body. I kissed Blake back with equal passion until he stopped, and muttered, "Game over. I win."

Blake was a kinetic lover. He moved me from one position to the next, never staying in one position for more than a few seconds. At one point he sat in a large overstuffed chair and had me lean over him so he could suckle my breasts.

The blood rushing throughout me, the sucking sensation, and his touch all ignited me with overwhelming heat throughout my body. I did not feel any coolness of the air, only the passion we were stirring in each other.

We had started so late in the night, I hardly noticed the sun was coming up, and Blake had spent the better part of our lovemaking on kissing me, fondling me, and attending in all sorts of ways to my upper body. Now he slid his hand up my dress as a tease and lightly massaged my pubic area as I moaned to his touch.

Daylight was breaking. And as the sun came up he wanted to look into my eyes and hold me. I let him do so for a time, but then I turned so that my back rested on Blake's front to make sure that I did not kill my lover.

His lovemaking had a message for me that I understood. He was saving our most intimate union for a later time. It would not be tonight.

And though we were both full of our want for each other, we rested, too, because we feared what could happen after the sun was up. We both knew the threat of the law was upon me.

Bertrum and Marie had gone to their separate beds in the adjoining room. They were exhausted, and wiser than we were for getting their sleep.

CHAPTER 25

Lang Presses On

❧

"I have no idea what happened to her," Miriam said. "She left without a good-bye, Inspector. No note. Nothing."

"Was she seen going somewhere?"

"Sam Benson saw her last night heading east with Marie. The buggy was in a hurry."

"She left nothing behind?"

"I don't believe so, no."

Miriam's maid entered the room, "Ma'am, I found these in her bed, and this near the dresser." She handed over Nicollette's note, a hankie, several English pounds, and a small book entitled *A Rabbit Heart*.

"May I?" Lang asked.

"Of course."

He opened the folded note:

Dear Miriam,

I regret that I don't have the opportunity to speak personally of my gratitude for your hospitality. We had an urgent

*telegram, and I'm being called back to my home in Nice. A
dear family member has fallen ill.*

    *I know I have paid you for my stay. This is a gift of my ap-
preciation along with my second buggy and horse. I'll cherish
your friendship and seek you out whenever I return to Glastonbury. Your direction led me to wonderful friends and loving days.*

    Please remember me well, as I you.

    With warmest affection,

    Nicollette

"Well, she was quite generous to me. She enclosed a large tip
also."

"What is this book?"

"She must have been reading it."

"And the hankie?"

"Isn't it beautiful? Look at the delicate flowers embroidered
all around the 'N.' And it smells of Nicollette. You may keep all
this if you like, Inspector."

"Thank you, I'll keep it for evidence. Now we'd best get an
early start."

"If you wait a moment, we can pack you some lunch and a
bottle of wine for your trip."

"I'd be most grateful, Miss Bestell."

"You and your assistants may visit anytime."

Lang tipped his hat. "I'll look forward to seeing you again,
ma'am. Good day."

It was a sunny day, with just a hint of coolness. And sunlight
shimmered through the trees, casting shadows in their path as the
three men rode out of town. They made slow progress until they
headed east and found the buggy's tracks. One of the back right

wheels had a nail mark on the rim, which showed up every two meters in the track. The men followed the tracks to the fork and saw that the buggy had turned north.

"Before we head north, let's make a stop first."

Lang and Pegasus led, with Peavey's and Wilcox's horses in a steady gallop behind the white champion. They turned down the long drive and knocked on Lord Baston's door. Clive answered.

"Good day. I'm Inspector Lang. This is Peavey and Wilcox. We're looking for Lord Baston, is he at home?"

"I can check, but I don't believe so." Clive clapped his hands. "Roberta?"

She appeared from the kitchen. "Yes, sir?"

"Do you know where Lord Baston has gone?"

"No, sir."

"That's odd, Inspector—she's the one who best knows his schedule. But we can ask around to see if any of the other servants know."

"Yes, thank you."

Clive went out the front door and rang a large bell. Servants from all over the grounds flocked to the foyer area. Lang counted twenty-four when all of them had appeared.

"I'm sorry to interrupt your work," Clive said, "but Inspector Lang and his men are looking for Lord Baston. Do any of you know where he may be found?"

No one knew.

"How many think he could be in London?" All raised their hands.

"How many would bet their salary on that?" Every hand went down.

"Inspector, I'm afraid they don't know. Bertrum may be with him, if that helps you."

"Thank you." Lang eyed the grounds. "This is a beautiful property. How extensive are Lord Baston's holdings?"

"Very extensive, he's the largest landholder in the area, sir. But these are not my affairs, sir."

"Who knows of this?"

"I'm afraid my knowledge of his wealth would be only what is public knowledge."

"Yes, of course. You've been very helpful."

"I have, sir?"

"Quite."

The three detectives mounted their horses and left the estate.

"Now what, Jackson?" Peavey asked when they stopped near a clump of trees surrounded by the gentle green hills.

"I'm hungry," Wilcox said.

Lang reached in his saddlebag and took out the lunch Miriam had prepared for them. "Now let me hear your thoughts—no idea too ridiculous. Just say it, it may trigger other ideas not so ridiculous."

"We could follow her from town to town, collecting the bodies afterward."

"Yes, but then we don't prevent any deaths."

"We could give the stories and her photograph to the papers. A reward would assure her being found."

"We don't have her photograph," Lang said.

"She can't hide for long."

"She's being harbored by Lord Baston and his driver," Lang said. "I'll lay odds on it. I saw the driver and Marie talking together near the kitchen on the night of Lord Baston's party."

When the detectives had explored and discussed all their options, Lang said, "Let's go back to town."

"But shouldn't we pursue them?"

"We need to think before we hunt."

•   •   •

Lang entered the one-room doctor's office. There was an un-framed degree nailed to the wall over the doctor's desk. There was an open notebook, its pages filled with health notes on each of Ignat's patients. Scattered on nearby tables were cotton balls, tongue depressors, porcelain pans, and a few miscellaneous knives and tools.

There was a shelf near a sink loaded with small jars contain-ing a pickled finger, a toe, and various innards. Lang found Ignat's belief that such items made a beneficial display for his doctor business amusing.

"Good day, Doctor. I wondered if I could get you to look at a cut," Lang said. "I could use a bandage on it."

"Of course, let me have a look. Where is it?"

Lang rolled up his shirtsleeve. "My forearm."

"It's healing fine. But it could use some salve and a bandage to protect it."

"That would be good."

"Want me to check your feet or fingers for infection?"

"No, thanks, I think I'm all right there."

"Every toe or finger I take off pays for a day of my office ex-penses. If I get an arm, I can live a week on it. Want me to whack off that ugly forearm for you? It's your left. You don't use it much."

"I like it for balance when I ride."

Ignat put some salve on Lang's cut and taped a bandage in place.

"Got a favorite jar up there?" Lang said.

"Probably Mrs. Tweeter's Thing."

"What is it?"

"I haven't a clue. I did abdominal surgery on her and the Thing didn't look right in there, so I took it out."

"How's Mrs. Tweeter doing?"

"She died a couple of days after surgery. So I guess she needed it. I think the family was upset with me—I was upset with myself."

Lang saw him glance at the jar. He was silent for a moment, then he said, "Sidney, I need your help. We—"

"I can't tell you anything, Inspector."

"Call me Jackson. How did you know what I was going to ask?"

"Top of my class, remember?"

"I need to know about her."

"I can't tell you. Patient-doctor privilege, Jackson."

"You know, it's the end of the day. Let's have a drink and chat about a hypothesis. You don't have to tell me anything personal about her. Just give me a hint."

"I'd better not."

"Do you get free offers for alcohol every day? If I were looking at pickled jars, blood, and unknown body parts, I guess I'd need to forget occasionally."

"Very well, I accept your offer."

Sidney Ignat was a cheap drunk. Two drinks, and he was bemoaning the lack of high intelligence in Glastonbury and his desire to meet a woman, any woman.

During the third drink Lang said, "Sidney, you know, even in small towns unusual things are observed by physicians that win them attention—even fame."

"What do you mean?"

"Mrs. Tweeter's Thing, for instance. Perhaps you're the first to come across this rare condition. And a medical journal could honor you."

"Go on."

"I'm not a physician, but I have a hunch Nicollette has a medical condition that may be unique."

Ignat said nothing.

"And you, Sidney, are the only physician who knows about it."

Quiet.

"I see medical journals, conferences, and recognition."

He was listening. Through his whiskey glass, but he was listening.

"I wouldn't doubt that the queen would ask you for a command performance to find out what you've uncovered."

"Command performance?"

"Certainly. Queen Victoria has taken a particular interest in this case. So when Nicollette's brain—"

"You mean her heart."

"Sorry, I mean her heart, slows down—"

"No, it speeds up. It's way too fast."

"That's what I suspected," Lang said.

"More than two hundred beats a minute. Not normal at all. Actually, three to four times faster than a normal heart rate. And just listening, my heart began to beat unnaturally fast. Her heart has some unusual factor that causes it either electrically or like a tuning fork to race another's heart to resonate with hers."

"I thought that could be it." Lang pulled out the copy of *A Rabbit Heart*. "I was reading about the condition in this book. Do you think a death, such as Frederick Bothem's, could be caused by Nicollette's abnormality?"

"Well, for that to be the case, she'd have to be very close to the man. I don't think she knew Frederick."

"We can't be sure of that. And she knew Oliver, and was last seen with him."

"Yes, but she's a lovely girl. I'd hate to think she's your killer. I just don't believe she would willingly hurt a gnat."

"Perhaps she doesn't—on purpose," Lang said.

"Of course not. She's a lovely woman."

"That she is."

Lang realized he had gleaned about all he could, and the inebriated doctor had tears spilling down his cheeks. Then he let his head drop to his chest, shoulders shaking.

"Sidney, what's the matter?"

Ignat lifted his head up. "I cry for Mrs. Tweeter. I should have known she needed that part of her innards. Oh, my God, I killed her. You should hang me now."

Jackson felt sorry for the man, but out of his element in the presence of so much emotion.

"These things happen in our professions," he said. "We can only do the best we can. You're a sensitive man—it must make you a fine doctor. Buck up, Sidney. We all have our time to go."

The doctor stopped crying and looked around, as if suddenly embarrassed by his inappropriate display in a public place. Lang looked at the lonely doctor and had an idea as to how he might help him.

"Sidney, if you don't let on how you came by the information, I know a woman in Glastonbury who has quite a crush on you."

"On *me?* Who?"

"If I tell you, you would have to be a gentleman, and act upon it."

"Of course I would."

Lang walked over to a table where Peavey and Wilcox were seated and whispered a task to Peavey, who left the pub.

"Who?" Ignat said when he rejoined the doctor.

"What, Sidney?"

"Who's the woman? I'll court her with all my heart."

"I can't believe you didn't think of her. I thought of her for myself, but with my schedule, it wouldn't be fair to such a woman."

"Who is she? I'll marry her, if she'll have me."

"Miriam Bestell."

"She's interested in me? She's a fine-looking woman."

"Oh, yes. You're all she could talk about on several occasions."

"Good evening, Miss Bestell."

"Mr. Peavey. Hello. Would you like to come in?"

"Yes, thank you once again for the invitation to Lord Baston's. We all had an enjoyable evening."

"Thank you for being my charming escorts."

"Our pleasure. I hope you don't mind, but I have something quite personal to discuss with you."

"Please make yourself comfortable."

Peavey took one of her parlor chairs and set his hat in his lap. His long legs dwarfed the chair a bit. "Normally we would never get involved in this sort of thing. But there's a man who's smitten with you, and when Inspector Lang learned of it, he thought you should know."

"Oh, my."

"In case you should like to act on this information. The gentleman is quite renowned, and unmarried, and thinks of you for his bride."

"I've longed for a partner, but I'm way past marriage age."

"He doesn't see it that way, Miss Bestell. He longs for you."

"He does?"

"He's a man of means and great intelligence. And respect in the community. He's been a bit sheltered in studies and may not be as socially skilled as those who've taken the time for parties. But he has heart and soul for you."

"How do you know this?"

"He's down at the pub now with Inspector Lang, only talking of you. Perhaps I shouldn't tell you."

"Oh, you should tell me. I should know."

"It's just that this man we hold dear to us. We wouldn't want to see him get hurt."

"Oh, Mr. Peavey, I assure you that when I love, I love with my heart and soul. I wouldn't let this man go if he were to commit to me."

"The man is Dr. Sidney Ignat."

"I never go to him, but I know of him. He keeps to himself. You say he's at the pub now?"

"This very moment."

Miriam grabbed her hat and whisked herself out of the room. Sidney Ignat never saw love coming. Miriam took his breath away.

Constable Niles Morgan appeared as the three detectives mounted their horses.

"Inspector Lang, you might want to come with me. I've got a hunch."

The detectives followed the constable riding east until they arrived at the scenic creek side. After less than an hour's search, they found the nude body of Oliver Davis, not far from where Frederick Bothem had been found. All around the ghastly pale corpse, there was a beautiful arch of wildflowers.

"What do you think of his memorial?" Jackson asked his recruits.

"Quite artistic."

"A feminine touch. I doubt there's a man in the county with such an eye for decoration."

"Yes, look how someone has begun with reds and purples and gone purposefully lighter with pinks and yellows at the top."

"Very good, gentlemen," Lang said. "Even more care has been taken here than at the spot where Frederick Bothem was found."

Again there were no marks on the young man, nothing to indicate the cause of his death. And Lang noted the same engorged penis, the flushed face that suggested a cardiovascular problem, and that frozen smile.

"He was last seen taking Nicollette Caron for a buggy ride," Niles said. "She told Miriam he took the train to London. So she lied."

"We need to find this woman quickly," Peavey said.

The men rode back into town to check out of their hotel. Lang wanted to question Miriam. But first he sent a telegram to his chief:

TO:	BART MARSHALL, SCOTLAND YARD
	LONDON, ENGLAND
FROM:	INSPECTOR LANG
	GLASTONBURY, ENGLAND
DATE:	AUGUST 9, 1891
ADDENDUM:	OLIVER DAVIS FOUND DEAD STOP

SAME CONDITION AS CONSTABLE FREDERICK BOTHEM STOP

LAST SEEN WITH NICOLLETTE CARON STOP

INSPECTOR JACKSON LANG

The queen had received two men in her private chamber—her prime minister and advisor, Salisbury, and Sir Bart Marshall.

"A rabbit heart?" Salisbury said. "She must be tried."

"Without any mention of her condition?" Sir Bart said.

"Of course," the queen said. "Young men are being killed. I'll have no problem watching her lose her neck for that."

"Justice will decide her fate," Sir Bart said.

"Justice? My concern isn't mean-spirited. I'm concerned for something far greater than one woman's fate—the moral confusion of Great Britain. The very desecration of our ethical fiber."

"She's well liked, Your Maj—"

"No matter. The newspapers will incite outrage for her murders once they have her story. She's immoral. She's a loose woman with a deadly weapon. She's not a woman for a proposal and a white dress. She's shameless in all her adventures without marital union, and she must be stopped."

"Of course," Salisbury said.

"Sir Bart, I rely on you. Find her at once. I want this menace to England arrested. Her trial must be prompt."

"Yes, Your Majesty. Jackson Lang is in frequent touch with me. I'll hear from him shortly."

"Support him with as many men as he needs. You may go."

Sir Bart bowed to the queen as he left, and the queen beckoned to Salisbury.

"Salisbury, send a message to Sadi Carnot, the president of France. Tell him I need to borrow a guillotine."

"We decided not to use the device here, Your Majesty."

"Yes, but for a French temptress who just missed her French sentence, it will be appropriate."

"She hasn't been tried or found guilty. . . ."

"We should be prepared, Salisbury."

"Yes, Your Majesty."

He picked me up and set me on a stack of hay bales. "You shouldn't travel alone, Nicollette."

"I could ride to Wales. It's not far."

"Stay with me," he whispered. Then, to the group, "Everyone has the plan."

"I smell the hunt, Lord Baston. I need to go. I sense they're close."

"Nicollette, stop this talk. I won't let you go alone. I have a map inside, we can discuss this further."

Inside the cabin I renewed my plea. "None of you has done anything irreversible—you need to let me go. I can't bear to stay when I know Jackson Lang is so close on my heels. I must run—please, understand. I don't want to. I *have* to."

Finally, Blake conceded a bit. He agreed that I could take my lead horse and he would take his. Bertrum and Marie would follow.

He gathered provisions and a map for our journey. He stood by the window and watched a small opening through the trees that allowed him to see anyone who might be approaching the lodge via the road.

He saw a small flock of birds squawk and fly from a tree. "They'll be here soon—we don't want to meet them in the road, so we're going into the stands. Nicollette, Marie, take off your dresses. It's time."

We took off our dresses. We wouldn't be able to climb up to the stands in them, and their color in the trees could make us easier to spot. We folded them up and carried them with us.

Now Marie and I wore only our bloomers and corsets as we climbed out the back window. We were bent over in half with our fannies protruding—objects of much interest to the men below. I looked back and caught Blake's and Bertrum's eyes fixed on our undergarments at this critical moment.

CHAPTER 26

A Step Ahead

Nicollette, Blake, Bertrum, and Marie patrolled the lodge's grounds just past sunrise. In the areas where the foliage was thickest on the grounds of Blake's hunting property there were several hunting stands, each a flat wooden platform designed to fit into the shape of its tree.

The stands were big enough for one or two men to sit quietly and blend into their environment until an unsuspecting deer or other prey stepped into range. There was another guest cabin northeast about 150 meters from the lodge. And a small stable and corral near the lodge.

"If we know they're coming," Blake said, "while they're out front we can come through the stable and stow away in the stands. If they're on another part of the property, we'll be able to take our horses and go."

"They'll know we're here," I said. "They'll see our horses."

"Perhaps."

"I think I should leave now, my lord. It'll be easier for all of you."

"Men!" Marie said.

"We were gathering our things," Blake said as he moved back to the window to watch the road. "Weren't we, Bertrum?"

Bertrum grabbed an ashtray and slipped it in his pocket. "Yes, I didn't want to leave this *behind.*"

I had a retort ready, but all thought of their childish behavior was driven from my mind with Blake's next words.

"It's Lang and his assistants," he said. "Just the three."

We slipped out the back, through the stable, and climbed into the stands. Bertrum and Marie hid in one stand, Blake and I in the other. I lay in the middle of ours. Blake covered me with his body and pulled a blanket over him.

His body was almost directly over mine, heart to heart.

"Nicollette, this feels wonderful. You give me certain thoughts—even at a time like this."

"What kind of thoughts, Blake?"

"I'm thinking five-twelve, the position in a tree fort."

We were pressed close enough that I could tell he was aroused. "Blake, we shouldn't lie this way." He drew in a deep breath. "Blake, turn, so we're head to toes. I'm worried about your heart. If you'll just—"

We heard a door close. Blake could peer through the foliage. He motioned to us: Jackson was searching the grounds, looking at our horses as if hoping they might reveal our whereabouts.

We heard Wilcox's voice. "Jackson, there's a man in the window of that cabin just northeast about a hundred meters. It looks like Lord Baston is down in the other lodge. We'll go look, they must be there."

I could feel Blake's heart pounding so hard it was a wonder Jackson couldn't hear it. It beat faster, harder.

I sensed as I touched Blake that his blood raced within his veins. I knew he was aroused, but he held his body strong and quiet in wait of Jackson's departure. I couldn't move. The area was too small and Jackson was close enough to hear the slightest movement. I feared for Blake's life. I could see his hand change to a reddish color.

I knew what happened next to a man in this condition—and so I trembled. I tried to stop my heart. Slow its pace. Change my being so Blake wouldn't feel the effect of my heart so close to his.

I had warned him. And still he lay next to me—perhaps nearing the end of his life. *Leave, Jackson. Please leave us alone.*

He must have heard my prayer, for he said, "Wilcox, I'll go with you."

The detectives mounted their horses and rode down to the other cabin, just the other side of a rolling hill that blocked their view of our stands. As they disappeared over the hill, we scrambled down from our perches. Marie and I put on our dresses.

Blake struggled to regain his normal blood pressure, his breath labored with the simple act of mounting his horse. But all of us mounted our own horses, and we rode off.

"I know a shortcut," Bertrum said. He turned off a road, and we ran through a creek, several times crisscrossing the stream. We arrived at a fork in the road and headed due west.

When we saw other travelers on the road, we rode into the woods to avoid them. Our goal was to reach the coast. We feared the main bridge to Wales might be blockaded for us—a telegram might tip them off. We were going to have to find another way to Wales.

"Follow me," Blake said.

The road forked just ahead of us. There was a carriage on one path and a peddler wagon on the other, both several furlongs down each road but headed in our direction. To avoid them we turned into a nearby woods. Blake's horse swiftly moved under his lead. My horse followed, then Bertrum's, then Marie's.

The first three of us ducked under a large branch in our path.

But Marie made the mistake of looking back to make sure the carriage was gone and didn't see the branch.

It hit her broadside across her forehead and knocked her off her horse. She landed on the ground with a thud that sent Bertrum flying to her side. Blake and I missed the cadence of hooves behind us and doubled back to find Marie unconscious, cradled in Bertrum's arms.

"Oh, Marie, Marie," I cried out. "Dear sweet Marie, please speak to us." I knelt next to her. "Oh, Bertrum, please tell me she's going to be all right."

"I don't know, miss."

Blake knelt beside her and began to rub her hands.

"I found this in the trash." Wilcox waved a crumpled paper.

"What is it?" Lang said.

"Looks like their getaway plan," Peavey said.

"Let's have it, then."

"They're going to Sussex, by boat to Germany, down the Rhine, looks like there's a Joseph and Anita Hofer they'll visit in the Black Forest, then on to Switzerland."

"Convenient that they left it for us, wasn't it?" Lang said.

"Well, there are some things scratched off. Maybe they rewrote it."

"Maybe they set us up."

Lang and his men had searched the grounds and the small cabin only to find that what looked like Lord Baston in the cabin window was a makeshift mannequin dressed in his clothes. They returned to the lodge and found the horses gone. The ploy had given the fugitives a thirty-minute lead.

"We'll find their tracks," Jackson said. "Let's be off."

The three men struggled with the deciphering of the trail. The tracks appeared sporadically and danced in and out of the creek. Finally, finding a strong trail, they continued west.

Lang refused to torment himself over being so close to his quarry and losing them. He would keep his calm logical mind switched on and not let his emotions get the upper hand. Angry reactions made for mistakes when he was in pursuit. And he knew from the past that he need only stay persistent, focused, and single-minded to reach his goal.

It was not that emotions weren't involved. With each of his cases he felt a hatred for the criminal that compelled him like a lead hound on a fox scent.

Nicollette touched him differently. He wasn't sure how. But he felt his internal compass set for her, with the sole vision in his mind of riding back to London with Nicollette as his prize for the queen.

He had often brought in a husband for the murder of his wife. Or a family member for the killing of another family member. These were the most common cases. But to bring in a woman who had possibly killed men in three countries—this could earn him the widest possible recognition for his work.

It was best that he stop his thoughts when his mind wandered to his ambitions. He must remain focused on one single thought, the capture and arrest of Nicollette Caron.

Wilcox said, "I should have—"

"Don't look back in your chase, only forward," Lang said. "She's just ahead."

"There's a carriage—let's check to see if they saw anyone in the area."

The carriage halted for them. There was a couple in the buggy with an ancient driver.

"Good day, good people. We're in search of a party that may be just ahead of us. Did you happen to see anyone pass you—or on the road, heading west?"

"No, no, we didn't."

Lang tipped his hat. "Thank you for your time." And the carriage went slowly on its way.

Next they stopped the peddler's wagon. It looked a shambles, with wares hanging off its sides. DOCTOR OINTMENT'S MEDICINE FEATURING LEACHES was misspelled in paint on its side.

"Good day to you," Lang said. "Did any riders pass you on the road?"

"Haven't seen any all day."

"Are you certain?"

"Quite sure, sir. Well, good day."

"May we see your peddler's license? If we can't chase our criminals, we might as well pick up the tax for the queen."

"Wait. I didn't see anyone pass me, but there were four horses and riders that went into the woods back about a half mile behind me. Where the large marked rock is—with the drawings. They went in there. I thought you wanted to know if they passed me, and they didn't."

"How long ago was that?"

"I'd guess about ten minutes."

"What did they look like?"

"It was hard to tell, but I believe there were two men and two women."

"What color were their horses?"

"All dark horses."

"Very good. Thank you for your help."

They soon found the fresh tracks of four horses going into the woods. "We can't be more than fifteen minutes behind them," Peavey said.

CHAPTER 27

Icy Waters

T HE SECONDS DRAGGED PAINFULLY AS WE WAITED FOR A sign of life from Marie.

I began to sob, then Bertrum cried out, "Oh, Marie, don't do this to me!"

Blake and I were surprised at his outburst but apparently not so much as Marie. Because my injured friend gasped out loud as soon he said it.

"I'm here," she said in a strained whisper. "Bert, I do believe you are my rabbit's foot, my lucky star."

"Are you all right?"

"My head hurts."

"Marie, you frightened us terribly," I said.

"She had the wind knocked clean out of her," Blake said.

"You have such a wallop on your forehead," I said. "That branch barely missed your temple."

We all rested for a few minutes, pleased with her recovery but hoping she'd be able to ride.

Blake looked at his map. "I'm wondering where the best place to get across the Bristol Channel would be. We'll need a boat of some kind, a ferry to end up in Cardiff. But the Cardiff ferry is risky and doesn't leave often. Weston Super Mare, Wick St. Lawrence, or Burnham-on-Sea are all near the Channel and might have access. Perhaps they have a ferry for us. How much more time do you need, Marie?"

"I have a splitting headache—I don't think I could hold on to my horse. Could I have a few more minutes?"

Blake looked behind us. "I'm afraid we may be out of time." He helped me onto my horse and mounted his own. Again he looked back. We heard horses in the distant woods.

Bertrum reached down and pulled Marie behind him on his horse. "Hold on, Marie."

Our three horses tore off at a gallop through the trail that led deeper into the woods. The fourth horse followed us without a rider. We gripped our knees tight and artfully dodged branches, but we could hear the sound of the chase at our backs.

"Is it them?"

"It is."

It could have been anyone in the woods. But all of us knew it was our pursuers. And I couldn't, even in some corner of my mind, fathom my life should we fail to outrun them. It wasn't a thing I could accept or even envision, for I couldn't be caught. Capture meant certain death to me.

We were at the end of the woods, and a short run over a meadow brought us to our road. We continued west.

At the top of a rolling hill I looked back and saw the posse. It was indeed Jackson and his two men in hot pursuit. And they were close. A few minutes later I looked back again. They were the same distance behind us. Constant. Not gaining, not falling behind.

And then we saw a small sign that read north with a right arrow and south with a left arrow.

"Let's go south," Blake said.

But suddenly I remembered what Gabriella had told me: "Go north to the ferryman."

"Blake, we must go north."

He turned right and we headed north on the road. After a mile we saw a sign to a house that read, FERRYMAN.

We rode into his trail and down to the water's edge, where there was a flatbed ferry. Only large enough for our horses, the ferryman, and ourselves, who ran to us when Blake waved several pound notes at him.

We shoved off and were soon out in the water about a quarter of a kilometer into the Bristol Channel. The ferryman told us it was about thirty-two kilometers to our destination, since we needed to angle southwest to Cardiff.

I smiled at Marie, happy to have safely made the ferry and eluded our pursuers. But Marie seemed disoriented. Her eyes looked glassy, as if she didn't know or recognize me. Then, just as I realized she was in trouble, she swooned and fell off the back of the boat into the cold water.

"Wait, go back for her! She can't swim. Marie!"

The ferryman turned to Blake. "Are those your friends on the shore?"

"Far from it."

"If I go back for her, we'll be in gunshot range. I can't change direction so quickly."

"Go back," I said.

"Don't make your decision so hastily," Blake said. "Think of the implications of the rescue, Nicollette. They will save her." The ferry continued to move away from the shore, and Marie was floating farther away from us.

"I've decided."

"Nicollette, *it's your neck* if we go back for her." But in my mind's eye we were standing in my room at Miriam's, and Marie was offering her neck to me.

"I know, my lord."

I jumped off the side of the ferry, swimming awkwardly and slowly in my waterlogged dress toward Marie.

Slow movement. Short gasps. The frigid water chilled my body to the bone. I was afraid. Afraid I'd never reach her in time. Afraid she was already dead from her head injury. Afraid this was my end, as I saw Jackson Lang and his men on the shore.

Marie was floating facedown in the water. She began to sink, slipping down into the deep. Perhaps she was the lucky one, if this was to be her end. Her death would be a quick cold closure, as the mind becomes numb with the last thoughts of life. And for a moment I wished to close my eyes and sink with her.

Instead, I reached her hand and pulled her toward me. I rolled her over in the water and with her on my right hip turned her upright and had her rest on my side. My left arm churned at the water to pull us to shore.

I held my dear friend. Our dresses were heavy with water and dragged terribly in the sea's icy chill.

"Marie, breathe. Please breathe." But I felt only her dead-weight. And I knew if she were to survive, I had to bring her to shore. I had no choice. I couldn't stay in the cold water, I couldn't return with Marie to the ferry.

Jackson and his men moved so that they were in wait for me when we got near the shore. They took Marie from my grasp and lifted her away from the cold dark sea. I was exhausted from my exertions. I dragged myself out of the water and crawled on all fours to Marie.

I looked out over the water to what was to have been our freedom. Blake, Bertrum, four horses, and the ferryman were dark shadows in the setting sun.

I hovered over Marie, trying to bring her back. Jackson searched for her pulse. I shivered from the cold waters. But I held her.

"There's no pulse," Jackson said. "I'm sorry, Nicollette."

"No, she's alive. She's just cold, she—"

"Nicollette, she's not there. She's gone."

"No! She's here, she'll be fine. Wait."

I clutched my dear friend and hugged her chest to chest. She was cold and limp in my arms.

"I won't let you go, Marie. Don't go. Come back!" I rocked her in my arms. Tears ran down my face for the loss of my best friend in a chase that was for my life—not hers. *Oh, God in heaven, be fair. Don't take Marie from me.*

Jackson touched my arm. "Nicollette, you must come with us. We'll see that she's well attended."

"I tell you, she's not dead."

"Look at her color." He lifted her eyelids.

And Marie blinked.

"My heart—my heart . . ." Her hand moved to her chest. "My heart's fine, Nicollette, but my head throbs so."

"Marie needs medical attention," I said to the shocked men who'd witnessed her resurrection.

"She will have it. Nicollette Caron, you're under arrest for the murders of Denton Brickman, Frederick Bothem, and Oliver Davis."

I said nothing. I was turning blue with cold, and my teeth were chattering. I looked toward the ferry, expecting to see it as a dot on the horizon, but it was headed back to shore.

"Marie Tucci, you are under arrest for your assistance in the murder of Denton Brickman." Marie closed her eyes.

"You're going to be fine, Marie. Please, Marie, be strong for me."

I remained calm on the outside, but inside I was reeling. I was amazed that Marie had regained her senses. I wasn't sure of the part I had played in her resurrection, but I knew I had helped bring her around. I felt it happening as I held her in my arms.

The ferry arrived onshore. Jackson arrested Blake and Bertrum "for your harboring Nicollette Caron when you knew the law wanted her."

"Inspector, my good fellow, can't we discuss this?" Blake asked.

"Yes, we can," Jackson said. "And we will—back at the Yard. I want to hear all about it."

CHAPTER 28

Cold Arrest and Warm Bath

"Inspector, this is all a misunderstanding," Blake said.

"I don't think so, Lord Baston," Lang said. "But we'll hear your story. Ride with me, Miss Nicollette."

"I'm handcuffed, but I can still ride my horse," I said. I noticed that I was no longer "Miss Caron."

"You won't get far from me if we're on the same horse. Peavey, ride with Marie so our fugitives won't escape."

Wilcox checked her handcuffs to make sure they were secure, and Marie rode forward on his saddle as I rode forward on Jackson's horse. Blake and Bertrum were handcuffed on their horses under Peavey's close watch. The other two horses followed us. There was no chase or quickness to our ride to London—we had a long way to go and needed to pace ourselves. I was still so wet and cold that I shivered with each horse's step even though I could feel Jackson's warm body behind mine.

"Jackson, please may we stop for dry clothes and a bath? I'm chilled to my bones."

"I'm not going to take my eyes off you—even for a moment."

"Please let me get warm, Jackson. Wouldn't you hate to deprive London of a hanging because I succumbed to pneumonia? Hangings don't have the same effect when you wheel out a criminal already on her deathbed."

A moment of silence passed. Then Jackson called out. "Peavey? Wilcox? We'll stop at the next town."

In a half hour we arrived in Bristol, where there was a small hotel. Jackson approached the desk with me handcuffed to him as the others waited outside, under the watch of Peavey and Wilcox.

"Good day. Jackson Lang from Scotland Yard. May I buy the use of two hot baths and some towels from you?"

"How long?"

"Half an hour should suffice."

"Certainly," the desk manager said. "That'll be half a pound for the rooms, baths, and the towel use."

Jackson paid him. "May I have front rooms overlooking the street?"

"That's rooms two and three, and both are vacant. I'll have the help bring hot water up for you. Anything else, sir?"

"Yes, you can fetch a doctor for a head injury. Send him to room two."

"Very well."

"Is there a shop that sells clothing still open?"

"Just the one across the street."

"Watch them for a moment, Wilcox. I'll be right back."

Jackson crossed the street—faster than I could keep up, and so he dragged me a bit, as I dragged him back. We entered the store.

"Do you have ladies' dresses?"

"Sorry, sir. This is a gentlemen's haberdashery."

"Anything that would fit her?"

It took him only two minutes to make his purchases for Marie and me. We walked back across the street without a word.

He handed Peavey fitted black riding pants, white blouse, and a pair of brown riding boots for Marie. He carried the same for me. Marie was pale and shivering. She looked so weak and frail. I worried for her, and she saw my concern.

"I'll be fine, Nicollette. Don't worry about me," she said. I nodded to her.

Jackson told Wilcox to watch both men closely on the front steps of the hotel and not let his guard down. He changed the handcuffs so that Blake and Bertrum were cuffed left to right and right to left around a hotel post. Then Wilcox sat with his gun and a newspaper on the table. One eye was reading crime stories while the other eye was on his criminals.

"Peavey, about fifteen to thirty minutes should do it. I'll meet you back here."

All four of us climbed up the narrow stair single file. Marie and Peavey went into room two, Jackson and I went into room three.

When we entered the room I saw that it contained only a bed, a chair, and a dresser. There was a lightly curtained window that looked out on the street.

A knock on the door brought a large metal tub. Two men began pouring hot water into it. They set a bar of soap and towels on the bed.

"Jackson, I assume you'll be a gentlemen when I enter and exit the tub."

"And what would a gentleman do?"

"Why, he would look away, of course."

"I assume you're referring to a foolish gentleman."

"Why do you say that?"

"First, because you're a criminal, Nicollette. My job is to take you back to London for trial. You might run while I look away."

"But I won't run."

"You have before, Nicollette. Why should I believe you now? Second reason. To look away while you're bathing? That would take the kind of man who wouldn't want to see your body undressed. And I'm not that sort of man."

"Very well, Jackson."

The men returned with enough water to fill the tub. "Let me know when you're done with the room. We need to ready it for guests," one of the men said.

"Do you have any bath salts?" I asked.

"No, I'm sorry, miss."

I turned to Jackson. "Have you done this with other women before?"

"Done what?"

"Watched them bathe."

"Never."

I removed my wet boots and put my toe in the water.

"It's too hot. Or my feet are too frozen." I knew I'd have to wait for the water to cool down before entering the tub—so I took my time.

"Jackson, would you mind undoing my dress for me?"

"Certainly."

He was extraordinarily handsome, with a muscular build that couldn't be hidden by his clothes. I might have fancied that strength if our situation were different. But his crusade led me to my imprisonment. And I could not lose sight of my impending terror.

I could tell he was nervous. His sharp green eyes were on alert, as if he were photographing me and anxious not to miss anything in his recording of this experience. Suddenly he was not the confident man I knew.

I could feel his hands tremble as he fumbled with my dress buttons. I remained patient. Forgotten was our time limit. This moment, I decided, was about Jackson and me. The righteous man and his criminal, suddenly done with the chase—now connecting as man and woman.

There was a tension in the air. I admit to some of its being mine. But there was anxiety, too, and though I didn't bathe in front of near strangers every day, I sensed that most of the anxiety was coming from Jackson.

It dawned on me that he was dedicated to his job. He traveled quite a bit and had perhaps sacrificed marriage and sexual fulfillment to his demanding position. And when I decided that this might be Jackson's story, I realized what was before me.

A man who had the power to release me, a socially inexperienced lover, who might have wanted me from afar but would never act on his feelings. Now, suddenly, he was thrust into an intimate setting with the woman he desired. I was that woman. I saw it in his eyes.

Were he to act on his desire, I'd be free—one way or the other. He would release me, or he would die having me. Of course, I knew the chances were that he would not act. If only because he didn't have this path within him. He had only the righteous path of a straight arrow—yet I could try.

I slid off my dress and stood in my wet bloomers and bustier. They clung to my skin, cold from the sea. He noted the erectness of my nipples through the fabric—with intensity.

I slid out of my stockings and bloomers and wrapped a towel around my waist, then took off my bustier. Slowly. Jackson's eyes drank in my female charms, though I covered myself with the towels. Slowly.

I tested the waters again. The temperature was just right.

"What do you see, Jackson?"

"Many things."

"Such as?"

"I see Aphrodite."

"Thank you."

"Woman and temptation."

"Does this frighten you?"

"I see more."

"Yes?"

"I see killer and criminal."

I looked directly into his eyes. "I see a man, Jackson."

He didn't have a response. I think he was tongue-tied as I dropped my towels to enter the water. I leaned over toward him and slowly slid my toe into the water, then put both feet in. I covered my bosom with my arms crossed over my chest and bent over so that my personal area was difficult to see. Jackson sat up straighter, his eyes directed at my thighs and lap.

Every time I moved subtly as I adjusted to the warm water, he shifted his position. He moved the chair several times, trying to figure his best vantage point for observing me.

I thought I must take control, as forward as it might be perceived, for I had so little chance to save my life.

"Where is the soap?" I said. "Oh, on the bed."

"I'll get it." He half rose from the chair.

"That's all right, Jackson, I will."

I picked up my towels, but instead of wrapping them around me, I was bold. Without shame I carried them as I walked to the bed, where the soap was. I took my time. And even stopped a moment to run my fingers through my hair.

"It's better if I get the tangles out of my hair before I wash it."

Jackson couldn't take his eyes off me. So, I let him look.

"Oh, Jackson, there's a brush behind you. Could you get it for me?" I walked toward him—without hurry, without my towels, and without any shame.

"Of course." But he made no move, he couldn't turn his eyes

away from me. I was too close to him. His eyes were level with my bosom as I reached for the brush on the dresser behind him. Had I reached for a loaded gun left on the dresser from the previous tenant, he wouldn't have noticed.

I took the brush and handed it to him. I let my hair down. "Jackson, would you please brush my hair for me?"

"Yes," he whispered.

I sat on his lap and tossed my hair over my shoulders so that it hung down my back. He began to brush my hair, very gently.

"Jackson, I'm not fragile—you can brush it harder." He increased the vigor of his strokes. Long strokes.

He was making love to my hair. And as he was stroking me I shifted gently in his lap and could feel that Jackson was involuntarily aroused and pressing into my buttock through his trousers. As I shifted slowly, he would adjust himself to move a bit with me. And in the silence we moved together almost in a simulation of intercourse. It was not so obvious to be thrusting movements. Merely gentle movements that were my last hope of coordinating my release.

The man with the poker face showed a hint of softening, and I thought now might be the time to see if there was a way to earn his cooperation.

"Jackson . . ." I half turned to him. His eyes were full of desire for me, then he scanned my body as I turned to him.

"Is there a part of you that wishes you could set me loose?"

"I can't answer that." He was quiet for a long moment then let out a long sigh. "Nicollette, you should finish your bath," he said.

"Of course."

I got into the tub, but it was shallow. There were no bubbles, and so Jackson continued to get his eyeful. The water warmed me throughout, and I was grateful for this simple pleasure.

He pulled his chair up behind me and helped me wash my hair. Jackson used the soap bar to generate some lather, then would rub my hair in small circles. He had a sensuous touch, and I closed my eyes and let my head fall back close to almost being in his lap, but still resting at the edge of the tub. I closed my eyes to let him know that I was enjoying it. But I did this to give him permission to study my body.

I felt his eyes poring over me. I could almost hear his heart beating for me, and I had already felt his pants throbbing for me. He wanted to take me, but he didn't dare. I know he felt the devil telling him to love me—but he fought it, and in doing so only made the situation even more combustible.

I had to admit I was aroused from the attention. The role of being the object of his desire. My nudity stroking him further into a foreplay just as much as if I were touching his manhood.

He would reach down and bring the soap down to my hair that hung past my shoulders and rub the bar of soap around my breasts. It teased me and pleased him, and so I let him fondle me in the warm water.

All the while with my eyes closed in a state of bliss, all the while allowing him to roam my body without conversation, without any accusation, without any discouraging remarks. And as he was allowed the liberties, he continued by taking more.

He moved his chair to the side of the tub so that he could rub soap into the hair that straggled down my front. As he did, he rubbed the soap in a sensual circle around my belly, coming closer to my private area. Even feeling his nearness, I did not move. I kept my eyes closed and said nothing.

"Am I hurting you?"

"No, I'm enjoying every sensation. I'd love to be bathed like this every day."

Still keeping my eyes closed, Jackson glided the bar of soap down my front, then parted my legs slightly for his hand to massage me, and a finger to ever so gently penetrate me. If I had not been extremely sensitive, I might have thought he didn't actually do that—but he did.

I wanted the man. His sensuality had my body screaming for a union. By the time he slid his finger in and out of me, I rocked myself up and down, trying to draw the man into me deeper. My eyes were closed still, and he had unlimited view of my nakedness.

He enjoyed his task. He could look over my body with my cooperation and without shame. So he made no move to change his position as he continued to please me. And then I felt a shudder throughout my body, and I cried out from the unexpected flood of pleasure.

He leaned in to hold me tightly—without thought of my wetness or the bathwater. I rested a while longer in the water before we spoke.

When we did, we talked easily of many things while he sat vigil over my body. And when I had soaked long enough to wrinkle my fingertips, and the water had cooled, I stood up in the bath. His eyes were still memorizing my details.

"Would you hand me my towels, Jackson?"

"Yes." He went to get the towels, put them over my shoulders, and began drying off my body slowly. Lovingly.

"Jackson, you will be my last opportunity to be with a man. Would you love me?"

"Not unless I was ready to die, Nicollette. And I am not."

"That's rather cruel, Jackson. You've already tried and convicted me?"

He couldn't deny that his hands were lingering on my bathed body. He slid them down my back and rubbed my behind, all in the guise of drying me—*when he had no towel in his hand.*

He slid his hands down the side of my bosom, into my curves and down my hips, his hands taking a joyous ride over my skin. And then, as if he didn't think I watched or was even present, he reached for my breasts and cupped them in his hands. He kneaded them softly as he stood behind me fully dressed— pressed against my nudity. I said nothing. For my body was enjoying every moment of the exciting overture.

He might deny his interest in our intimate union, but he was in no hurry to leave the room. And I stayed with him in that moment and let him yearn for me. Some might judge me wicked to have enticed my policeman when my lover was handcuffed because of me—just beneath my window.

But men and women have all kinds of attractions and alchemy, I believe. Blake and I had a sexual and spiritual attraction. Jackson and I had a mental attraction. Ours was the game of cat and mouse. That of a cat playing with the mouse until the mouse plays with the cat.

But our moment had come—and passed. I dressed in the clothes Jackson had bought for me. A white poet's blouse with ruffles on the sleeve and a tie at the throat, tight black riding pants, and brown boots just below my knee. I took my wet dress with me, and we left to join the others.

It was dark outside. The atmosphere was tense, even hostile. Blake had questions for me. Peavey and Wilcox were concerned that we had been gone more than two hours.

Jackson said, "She fell asleep after her hot bath. I let her sleep."

Wilcox gave him a penetrating look. "Was there a struggle inside, Jackson?"

Was there a struggle? My, God, yes! If you only knew what your colleague just endured.

"No. She just passed out from exhaustion."

Blake said, "Nicollette, are you sure you're all right?"

"Yes, I feel fine."

"You didn't have a union with him, did you? Did he force himself on you?"

"Blake, of course not. *Nothing* happened."

We mounted the horses, I, once again with Jackson, and we rode into the night.

"Harlot!"

"Whore!"

Eight hours after we left the hotel in Bristol, we rode into the city. I saw that the London townspeople heard I had been captured, and the streets were lined with crowds taunting me.

"She's the devil's mistress!"

"Scum!"

"The harlot wears men's trousers. What kind of woman is she?"

I did my best to ignore them, yet I cried even as I tried to hold my head high. I looked to the heavens, but the sky was dark, with no hint of light behind its clouds.

After so long in England's countryside, I had forgotten the grit that hangs in the city's air. It made me breathe shallower, quicker. Or was this just my fear, and I with no right to blame the air for my suffocation?

I had been jailed a year earlier in Nice, France, when they suspected that I was a killer in my former lovers' murders. I had a clear idea of what I might expect before my death. And imprisonment would surely be but the horrific prelude to death.

We rode through the streets to Scotland Yard, where we were put into an interrogation room. All four of us were handcuffed to hard wooden chairs. The metal cut into our wrists. Marie seemed only partially recovered from her injury. She was still pale from her drowning, tired from our eight-hour evening ride, and fearful of our interrogation and our fate.

The Scotland Yard chief came into the room. "Four of you? Too many to deal with at once." He took out a key and released Lord Baston. "The queen knows you've been arrested. She said you're a barrister, and she has fondness for you. Neither she nor the legal bar wishes embarrassment to your profession. You're free to go."

"Not without the others."

"Step into the hall, Lord Baston."

We could see and hear them through the doorway.

"Lord Baston, all of you have been arrested for murder or abetting murder. The penalty is to hang. You're being given a gift, a onetime shot at your freedom. Tomorrow morning we press irreversible charges. Do you want to leave here with or without your neck?"

"Bart, I can't live without this woman."

"You won't be able to live at all, if you stay here," said Jackson, who had joined them in the hall.

Nobody spoke for a long moment. Finally, Blake said, "Then give me Bertrum and Marie."

"No," said the chief. "You alone."

After five minutes, Blake had pleaded and won Bertrum's life. But Marie and I would have to stay for trial.

"Let me talk to Nicollette."

"No, there's the door. I'll release Bertrum behind you."

Blake said nothing. Through the door I saw he hadn't moved.

"I won't be here longer to hear your words, Lord Baston," the chief said. "Don't be foolish about the regifting of your life." He stepped to the door. "Peavey and Wilcox. Bring Bertrum here."

They released Bertrum from his restraints and took him into the hall.

"Escort the two of them to their horses and don't listen to their pleas," the chief ordered.

Blake called out to me. "Nicollette! I'll use my freedom to gain yours. I swear to you, Nicollette!"

The detectives forced Blake out the door, but when they pushed him, he hit Peavey in his left eye and shoved Wilcox into Jackson's chest. He then seized the opportunity to run back in the room and reach for my hand.

"Nicollette, I promise I'll get you out. No matter the cost, you'll be free."

Jackson and his assistants burst in to drag Blake from the interrogation room.

"Kindly leave before you disgrace your profession any further, Lord Baston," Jackson said. "We were generous with you. Don't abuse your privilege."

"How do I look?" Peavey asked, when they had left. He blinked his bruised eye at Wilcox.

"I think you'll have a black eye tomorrow."

"Outstanding. I was going to meet Millicent for tea. Whatever will she think?"

"I think she'll be glad you showed up. You'll look rugged, Ulysses. Some women like that."

"Will this go on my permanent record?"

"I don't think so—it wasn't your fault. That fellow packs a wallop. But you'd think he would have been a little more grateful not to hang, wouldn't you?"

CHAPTER 29

Nicollette's Trial

"I HEARD SHE WORE PANTS INTO TOWN SO TIGHT YOU could see the outline of her legs."

"A woman like that is asking for her comeuppance."

"I heard she sucked their blood as they lay dying."

"No, she mutilated them like a werewolf."

"Oh, my Lord!"

Murder and other major trials took place at the Old Bailey, which was the Central Criminal Court. The judge was George Tareyton, the longest-serving judge in the court system. At age seventy-nine, he was also the most conservative.

The court doors were forced open. And the townspeople pushed tightly against each other to hear the court's activities. Those that could hear would often turn and share information with those less fortunate crowding the streets.

"They say she wanted to fornicate several times a day—and that she did it with other women's husbands."

"I heard she put a spell on the married men."

"Married men? She should hang for her flagrant adultery, then."

"Hang her!"

Spectators stood as Judge Tareyton entered the court. The aged man walked slowly, with a gold cane that looked more like a scepter. He was out of breath as he climbed the steps to his chair, his gray curly wig leaning to the right. A guard assisted him to make sure he reached his destination without injury, then unobtrusively adjusted the wig. Though he was all business and above reproach in his court of law, Tareyton had an interesting eccentricity. He wore lipstick, and rouge that pinked his cheeks noticeably.

He was known as a fair but firm judge. He believed in the death sentence for every guilty killer. So once he tried a murdering criminal, the defendant was certain to hang. He had great respect for Jackson Lang's ability to capture and charge the criminals, so he acknowledged Jackson and his recruits in their seats near the prosecution's table as he approached the bench.

He silenced the room as he sat on his chair. There was not so much as a rumpled handkerchief rustling once the judge pounded his gavel. Even the crowd in the street became hushed, waiting for information to be passed along.

The men in the street couldn't wait to have a look at this temptress who was so beautiful that she was sure to become a legend. The women in the street could have hung Nicollette without the bother of a trial.

"Even if *one* of the rumors about her is true, she deserves to hang," a female spectator stated righteously.

Judge Tareyton studied the defendant as she stood with her defense counsel. Lord Baston was a formidable man, dressed properly in a black robe and wig for the court.

Nicollette Caron wore a soft pink dress that her barrister had arranged for her. A custom design of fine fabric and a flattering neckline with ivory lace trim around the neck, sleeves, and waist. The judge was quite taken by her—even though he knew he was an old man. She had large brown doe eyes that looked directly at him. And he knew their wonder.

She was looking to him for benevolence. He knew as he sat in his chair for this moment in time, he was her God. He could make the godlike decision that would end her life, or allow her to live. He saw the plea for him to be a benevolent god, and show her mercy. But she didn't know that, most often, benevolence was a foreign path for him.

"Rise."

Nicollette, Blake, and Marie all stood before the judge with earnest expressions.

"Nicollette Caron, you are being tried for the murders of Oliver Davis, Denton Brickman, and Frederick Bothem. Do you understand these charges?"

"Yes, Your Honor." Her voice was soft and melodious, and the spectators strained to hear her words.

"How do you plead in the murder of Oliver Davis?"

"Not guilty, Your Honor."

"And in the murder of Denton Brickman?"

"Not guilty, Your Honor."

"And in the murder of Frederick Bothem?"

"Not guilty, Your Honor."

"And you have counsel for this trial, and confidence in your counsel?"

"Yes, Your Honor."

"And sir, you are?"

"Lord Baston, Your Honor."

"Very well."

"Marie Tucci," the judge said, "you are being tried for your assistance in the murder of Denton Brickman, and for conspiracy to cover up your knowledge of the murders of Frederick Bothem and Oliver Davis. Do you understand these charges?"

"Yes, Your Honor," Marie said.

"How do you plead in the murder of Denton Brickman?"

"Not guilty, Your Honor."

"And in the conspiracy of the murder of Frederick Bothem?"

"Not guilty, Your Honor."

"And in the conspiracy of the murder of Oliver Davis?"

"Not guilty, Your Honor," Marie said.

"And you have counsel for this trial, and confidence in your counsel?"

"Yes, Your Honor. It is Lord Baston."

"Very well."

"Prosecution, would you please go on record with your name?"

"Reginald Holcomb, Your Honor. I'll be representing Her Majesty, Queen Victoria, in this trial, as the crimes at issue here have taken place in different cities but all within England."

"Very well. Proceed."

Holcomb was not a charismatic man. He was not elegant in his dress—if you inspected the seams of his suit closely, you would see their fray. He was a stout man, with a mustache and outdated muttonchop sideburns. He wore glasses that he kept adjusting as he began in court. But despite his unimpressive persona and lax courtroom protocol, his ability to incriminate those who stood weakly at the other side of the courtroom was unparalleled. He couldn't remember when a guilty defendant he prosecuted had been allowed to go free—and they were all guilty so far as he was concerned.

Holcomb held his lapels firmly and paced back and forth near his seat. Then, when he had gathered his strength, he slipped on his wig and his robe and took his seat and waited for the judge to direct him. When he spoke, he began in a booming voice that sounded as if God himself was on the side of the prosecution.

"Miss Nicollette Caron is a harlot. By *anyone's* standards, she has indiscriminately bedded men. Though this is distasteful to most enlightened people, we do not find ourselves in a serial murder trial for these transgressions against mankind's *natural* monogamy.

"Nicollette Caron has murdered three gentlemen with malice, with purpose, and with secrecy—which crimes she has attempted to cover up. The prosecution will show that she has a history of events that cause death to men. That she continues to proceed in this same serial process. Murder after murder after murder.

"I'll prove that she's an uncaring sort, without conscience, a menace to our modern society. And that, should she ever be allowed to walk our streets a free woman, the entire population of England wouldn't be safe from her crimes.

"Miss Caron has fled after every one of her killings. The authorities in both France and Italy want her for questioning in four murders prior to her arrival in England. Ladies and gentlemen of the jury, Nicollette Caron must be stopped and punished for her crimes against her innocent victims, and for the safety of all people in the British Empire.

"I shall further demonstrate to the court that Marie Tucci was her accomplice in committing the treacherous crime against Denton Brickman, and assisted in the mock accident to hide his murder. Lest you think her an *unwitting* accomplice, she didn't disclose her knowledge of his death to the investigating authorities when given the opportunity to do so. She, too, should be punished to the full extent of the law, for her support of the murderous crime against that victim. Thank you, Your Honor."

Holcomb took his place at his table. He scanned the judge, some spectators, and the jurors as he sat. Then he looked over at Lord Baston, as if measuring his competency against that of the defense counsel.

Lord Baston held his gaze confidently upon his opponent. He had solicited several young barristers to interview witnesses and help him prepare for the case. He had studied every past court ruling in which the defendant's life was spared. He had been approached by Inspector Lang and informed of Nicollette's condition. He had been up day and night searching out any information he could find that might help him defend his client.

Judge Tareyton looked over and eyed the handsome defense counsel. "Lord Baston, we're ready for your opening statement."

"Your Honor, Nicollette Caron isn't the monster the prosecution would lead you to believe. She is not a malicious woman. She is not a purveyor of death and evil. Nicollette is a warm and tenderhearted person. She is a woman of beauty, a woman who loves, a woman who lives life to its fullest.

"I shall demonstrate that she does not deserve a penalty for her actions. I'll educate you about a rare, even tragic condition that plagues her. And in the end, you will find my client not guilty in your court of law and release her to her freedom.

"In your understanding of the chain of events that have brought Nicollette Caron to this court, you will come to realize that Marie Tucci is only guilty of performing her duties as Miss Caron's personal maid, and is in no way guilty of a punishable crime."

"Very well." The judge seemed uncomfortable. He rubbed his left shoulder, then regained his direction. "Esquire Holcomb, you may begin."

"I call Miriam Bestell to the stand."

Miriam was dressed for the event in a new blue dress and,

though a bit nervous, enjoyed the crowd's attention. She swore her oath on the Bible, rustled her dress in the witness chair until she found a comfortable spot, and moved the locket on her neck, actually adjusting her neckline just a bit.

"You are Miriam Bestell of Glastonbury, owner of Miriam Bestell's Cozy Inn?"

"Yes."

"Did Nicollette Caron ever stay as a guest there?"

"Oh, yes."

"Can you tell us which day and what time she arrived?"

"It was on the fifth of August. Late afternoon."

"Do you remember, Miss Bestell, anything extraordinary that happened on this day?"

"Frederick Bothem, our constable and a dear old friend of mine, went missing."

"I see. Was it usual for Mr. Bothem to leave town without informing his family of his plans?"

"Objection, Your Honor," Lord Baston said as he rose from his seat. "Miss Bestell was not sharing a home with the Bothems, so she is in no position to make judgments about Frederick Bothem's habits."

"Rephrase the question."

"I withdraw the question. Did you go with Nicollette Caron to the Foxhunt Club dance?"

"Yes."

"How many men did she dance with at the affair?"

"Ten to fifteen."

"Do you know what Nicollette did on the day after the dance?"

"Yes, she went for a buggy ride with Oliver Davis, one of her dancing partners."

"And did you or anyone see Oliver Davis after the buggy ride?

"He disappeared after the buggy ride."

"Did Nicollette tell you anything about his disappearance?"

"She said he dropped her off to shop in Glastonbury, and she also told me he was on his way to the train to London."

"She told you both stories?"

"Yes."

"Your Honor, I enter into the court documents the rail records for this day as the people's first exhibit. There was no train ticket sold from Glastonbury to London on this date. Now, Miss Bestell, can you tell us anything else Nicollette did that day?"

"She took a bath when she returned—it was her second of the day. She also bathed earlier that morning."

"Did you find that unusual?"

"I try not to judge my guests."

"But in the years of your boarding house, have most of your guests bathed twice a day?"

"None of them have."

"She stayed several days with you."

"Yes."

"So was she cordial in her departure when she left?"

"I didn't see her leave."

"Did you find this odd?"

"Yes."

"Your witness, counsel."

Lord Baston approached the witness with a cordial smile.

"You mentioned in your testimony that Frederick Bothem was a dear friend of yours for thirty-five years."

"Yes."

"Were you ever romantically involved with Mr. Bothem?"

"For years Frederick courted me. He was my first love."

"But you never married?"

"No. He chose to marry Mamie."

"Had you stopped loving him then?"

"No."

"You continued on as his friend for the years subsequent to his marriage?"

"Yes."

"And during those years you knew him, was he the kind of man to have an affair with a woman other than his wife?"

"Not ever. Frederick would never have had an affair."

"You sound quite certain of this. May I ask why?"

Miriam squirmed in the chair. When she spoke, her voice was low. "Because I loved him all those years, and we had feelings for each other. I'm not proud of this, but I'm unmarried. And, well, I've been lonely, and have hinted to Frederick that he might share my bed on several occasions—and he never would."

"So he was such a man of principle that he wouldn't go into your bed."

"Yes."

"Miriam, I hope you don't mind my being straightforward, but you're a lovely woman. I find you quite a temptation."

"Thank you."

"But Frederick didn't see the temptation?"

"He saw the temptation, but told me he wouldn't violate his vows."

"Well, he was a strong man to resist you, Miriam. I'm amazed at his fortitude."

"Thank you."

"Were there any other women in town who might have invited Frederick into their bedroom?"

"Yes, there were others. He was our constable. Everyone adored Frederick."

"Interesting. If he's a man who resisted the woman he cared about for thirty-five years, who resisted other overtures made to him, how do you think Frederick would act with other women?"

"Objection," Holcomb cried. "Calls for speculation."

"Rephrase."

"Miriam, how likely is it that Frederick, who wouldn't bed you or other women, suddenly would have an intimate union in the woods with a stranger, before the woman even arrived in town?"

"Objection. Calls for speculation."

"Miss Bestell is an *expert* witness on this subject. And I am asking for a probability, not for her opinion."

"Very well," the judge said. "You may answer the question."

"I don't think it was in Frederick's makeup to have a love affair outside of his marriage."

"Thank you, Miss Bestell."

"Do you wish to cross-examine, Esquire Holcomb?" the judge said.

"Yes. Miss Bestell. You testified that Frederick wouldn't violate his marriage vows?"

"Yes."

"What if the man were forced with a weapon to cooperate? Is it possible that Frederick could have been made to undress and cooperate, or be forced against his will?"

"That could happen to anyone."

"Thank you. And did you ever see erratic behavior from Nicollette Caron?"

"Erratic?"

"Yes. One minute this, another minute that?"

"Well, she decided not to go to the dance, then she changed her mind. And then she was going to rest, and the next minute she left for good. That kind of thing."

"Yes, that would be erratic. One minute sweet, the next violent. Thank you. You may step down."

Lord Baston stood up. "One moment. Have you ever changed your mind in your life, Miss Bestell? Thought you would do something, then decided not to follow your plan?"

"Yes."

"Have you known other women friends to do this, at one time or another?"

"Yes."

"May I remind the court that it is a woman's prerogative to change her mind, and that to do so is quite a common occurrence for our gentle female gender? It is a captivating factor that keeps men alert and on their toes, at their women's slightest whims. I am done. Thank you again, Miss Bestell."

Holcomb spent the rest of the morning with his witness list of who's who in London, all prominent people who said they'd seen Nicollette with Denton at the Queen's Ball, including Dr. Ian Lindsey's wife. They testified that Denton had been so captivated by her that he seemed to be under her spell, that he treated her as if she were royalty—when she was a common woman, from France, no less. Though they had nothing further to say, the sheer presence of so many powerful people made an impact on the jury.

Lord Baston tried to undermine their effect.

"Mrs. Lindsey, you informed the court that you saw Nicollette Caron and Denton Brickman together the night of the Queen's Ball. Did you see Nicollette Caron harm Denton Brickman in any way?"

"No."

"Did Brickman look to be in pain?"

"Well, no."

"Others said he looked enraptured with the woman on his arm. Would you agree?"

"Yes."

"Let me make sure that I have this right, Mrs. Lindsey. You witnessed that Denton Brickman and Nicollette Caron were at the Queen's Ball."

"Yes."

"And that you saw firsthand that Nicollette and Brickman danced, that Brickman seemed proud of Nicollette and, in fact, quite happy."

"Yes, he appeared so."

"And that at no time did Denton Brickman appear to be in pain or in harm's way, is that correct?"

"Yes."

"Thank you, Mrs. Lindsey, for taking part in this trial."

She smiled to the audience.

"Though I'm without a clue as to why you have taken the stand."

Mrs. Lindsey stepped down sheepishly. And Lord Baston returned to his table.

No hard evidence was introduced until Holcomb brought out the fact that grape stems had been found near Frederick's body and Miriam, recalled to the stand, testified that Nicollette had offered her grapes the next morning. Holcomb also called the fruit vendor who had sold the grapes to Marie, claiming she was a frequent customer because her mistress loved grapes.

Holcomb called witnesses who testified as to dates and whereabouts that proved Nicollette was in the vicinity of each of the murders.

Lord Baston whispered to Nicollette, "Something's not right. He has nothing. He must have something else up his sleeve. No matter, so do I." With that, he returned to his position in front of the jury.

"Your Honor, in his opening, Esquire Holcomb implied that it was not for the bedding of several partners that Nicollette Caron stands trial here. Indeed, if such were not the case, the courts wouldn't have time for its true criminals. That Miss Nicollette Caron may have had more than one partner isn't in question, or of any concern either to the court or the prosecutor. We are sophisticated people here, so it's best to concentrate on the serious matter at hand. I call to the stand Mademoiselle Bebe Kiley."

Marie whispered to Nicollette, "Who is she?"

"I don't know," Nicollette said.

A small dark-haired Frenchwoman approached the witness chair with slow arthritic movements. She wore an oversized scarf that draped her head and was folded several times around her neck and under her chin. She laboriously swore her oath on the Bible and moved without ease into the witness chair.

"Mademoiselle Kiley, where do you live?" Blake asked.

"Nice, France."

"Do you know Nicollette Caron?"

"No, not really."

"What do you mean, not really?"

"I don't know Nicollette Caron, the woman. I only knew her as a baby, upon her birth. She—"

"Objection," Holcomb said. "This has no relevance, Your Honor. That she was born isn't at issue here."

"Your Honor, I said I would educate the court about Nicollette Caron's condition, which has critical bearing on this case. Please allow me to do so."

"Very well, proceed," the judge ruled.

"You say, Mademoiselle Kiley, that you knew her upon her birth. Can you give us the background and circumstances of that birth?"

"I was the personal maid to Nicollette's mother, Michelle duBois. She was a beautiful courtesan, mistress to a French diplomat, Jean-Jacques Beaumont, who was married to Dorothee Royer, a French heiress and a depressed recluse."

Holcomb shifted and leaned toward the judge. "Objection— irrelevant."

"Nicollette's condition dates from her birth, Your Honor. We are about to hear of that birth."

"Overruled."

"Please tell us the story, Mademoiselle Kiley," Blake said.

The small Frenchwoman looked at the jury and judge before she began. "We lived in Nice in 1870. Jean-Jacques and Michelle loved each other deeply, and when she became pregnant, they were pleased with their news. But just before the child's birth, Jean-Jacques was sent as an ambassador to America.

"I was to assist with the birth, but he wanted Michelle to have male protection. He hired a man recommended to him by a colleague, and this man had a partner. Neither Michelle nor I trusted the men, so we sent them away immediately. We allowed them to keep their pay for the promise of their absence.

"That December night Michelle retired early, exhausted from her burden. There was a knock on the door later that evening that we chose to ignore. The two hired men broke into the house, tied me up, and bludgeoned me with a board. When I tried to protect myself with my arms, they broke my arms in several places. And when I fell, they gagged me, used the board on my head several times. They raped and sodomized me, then pushed me into the closet.

"I listened helplessly from the closet as I faded in and out of consciousness. Whenever I came to, I'd hear the horrific beating that no woman should experience—and no pregnant woman could survive.

"Michelle duBois was stripped, beaten, and raped by the men. The rape triggered her labor. And the men saw this, and left her in her time of need. In their haste to leave they left the door slightly ajar during their escape, and an unusually cold wind blew in with great force.

"I tried to shout out to Michelle, but my teeth were broken, my mouth swollen, and my jaw unhinged. I couldn't talk with the swelling and pain. Michelle's sounds grew weaker and weaker. She didn't cry out like a woman about to give birth, she could only whimper. Her sounds became fainter and fainter, and I feared she was dying.

"I had two broken arms and was in too much pain to move. Michelle continued through her labor without help. She was wounded, and I could only hear her muffled moans through her gag.

"I tried to pull myself out of the closet, but the pain was too great. I heard a thump on the floor, and a baby's cry, then I passed out.

"When I came to, I realized I had been unconscious for a long time. With great effort I opened the closet door and dragged myself out. The blood had dried around my eyes, and I could barely see. But I struggled to squint through the slight vision in one eye. On the floor before me was a baby girl—still attached to her mother by the umbilical cord.

"I could see that the baby was awake and calm, and that in the cold night air she was not alone. Live warm rabbits had come inside from the cold to lie near the infant. There was a whole circle of rabbits around the baby and two small rabbits on top of her, their soft fur keeping her warm.

"One little rabbit sat perched on her chest—not skittish, as a rabbit usually would be. And the largest rabbit covered the umbilical cord. The doctor later said this prevented the baby from bleeding to death and thus saved Nicollette's life.

"I was finally able to crawl out of the closet. I couldn't pick up the child; my arms were useless. I called to Michelle but there was no answer. No movement. No breath. And I knew that Michelle was dead.

"I screamed and cried for help for a long time before neighbors came to the door. They detached the baby from her mother. The band of rabbits were not timid with humans. They looked at us with intelligence and understanding. They had a wisdom and compassion that struck me as profound. How very strange when they are most often our food. They didn't leave until the cord was cut and Nicollette was laid in safe arms.

"A doctor said the baby would have died from exposure to the cold or have bled to death were it not for the rabbits. He checked her vital signs. All were normal—except for her heartbeat. Instead of a normal human beat, her heart is three times faster. The infant had the same heartbeat as the rabbits that had saved her life.

"I was tended in a monastery as my injuries healed. The child couldn't be acknowledged as that of her noble father's blood, nor did he know of her survival. He was told that mother and child had died at childbirth. He never knew that the men he hired for protection were his lover's murderers. I thought it best not to tell him, and have never spoken of these events until the Nice police asked about Nicollette's background.

"Nicollette Caron is a special woman who comes from beautiful parents. In France a courtesan isn't so unusual as here. There's a respect for the woman who may be loved more than a wife in many cases. As was Michelle."

"And what became of the infant?" Lord Baston asked.

"She was taken to the church for adoption."

"And you lost touch at that point?"

"Yes. Until now."

Bebe Kiley looked upon Nicollette with great affection, and tears welled in her eyes.

"She looks just like her mother," she said.

I returned Bebe's gaze, my eyes blurred from the tears that filled my eyes. I had so many questions about my parents, so much more I wanted to know. I'd always wondered what my mother was like, who she might be, and where she was. I had yearned to find that she was alive and living in some nearby city I could travel to. We would meet, and she would tell me, "I've longed to hold you, Nicollette, all these years." Now I was filled with sadness—my mother had lost her life, horribly, with my birth, so I would never meet my mother, and she would never hold me.

I was stunned to learn about the rabbits and how they helped me survive. Simple animals had come to my aid. Bless them for this, but then perhaps it was that very saving act that had made me as I am, had led to my standing trial before God and the world.

I felt orphaned, wretched, and alone. I was anguished by my mother's cruel fate and angry that I wouldn't be allowed to speak with Bebe—perhaps the only person on earth who might help me make sense of my life—and ask personal questions about my mother. I stifled my sobs for the loss of the mother I'd never known, would never know.

"Thank you," Lord Baston said. "Your witness, Esquire Holcomb."

Holcomb rose and walked slowly to stand in front of the witness box.

"In England," he said, "we lock up those out of touch with reality, Mademoiselle Kiley. In France, perhaps, they don't have our civilized ways. So you want us to believe this rabbits' tale you've told us?" He walked to the jurors' area and shrugged with a smirk on his face.

"What proof can you possibly show us that there's any particle of truth to your fantastic story?"

Bebe Kiley glared at him.

"Anything at all—to substantiate even a piece of your story?"

She stood up and removed her jacket, slowly. Her dress had a sheer sleeve, which she rolled up. Both arms had bones that pushed the skin out in several places. So deformed were her arms that it hurt to look at them. The court drew a collective breath, and muttering arose through the room.

Slam! went the judge's gavel.

The witness spoke. "I have not been able to pick up anything that weighs even a stone since then. These are some of the scars I carry from that night. My one eye has no vision. I have scars on my head, hidden by my hair. My jaw didn't heal right." She reached up to remove the scarf that shrouded a deformed jaw.

The spectators gasped.

"And if you look into my soul, you'll see that I'm a woman of my word and quite in possession of my faculties. I'm in tune with God, and I'm respectful of this court, and of my homeland, France, and of the royal country of Great Britain. Though you may question my voice, I know of this young woman's privileged heritage. I can't say more to persuade you, sir. I can say no more than the truth I have already told you."

"No further questions."

Mademoiselle Kiley left the stand slowly, still suffering from her injuries of long ago. The spectators and jurors were spellbound watching her depart the witness stand. And I reached out wanting to know her and talk to her as she passed. But a guard blocked us, and she walked out still looking back at me.

"Lord Baston, call your next witness."

"I call Dr. Sidney Ignat."

Ignat swore his oath on the Bible and took the stand. Lord Baston established his name and credentials.

"Dr. Ignat, in the month of August did you have cause to examine Nicollette Caron?"

"Yes, I did."

"Did you learn of her medical history or experience with other physicians?"

"She didn't believe she had ever been to a doctor."

"Why did she come to you?"

"She didn't, she was brought to me in need of medical attention. Inspector Lang showed her Frederick Bothem's decaying corpse, and she fainted."

"Was her general health good?"

"Yes."

"Did you find anything unusual when you checked her out?"

"Yes. I found that her heart beats about three times faster than a normal human heart. It beats like a rabbit's heart."

The crowd murmured all the way back into the street. As those in the back couldn't hear and each before them passed on the words. "She has a rabbit heart," echoed throughout the Old Bailey.

Slam! "Order in the court!" the judge shouted.

"Did you notice anything unusual in yourself?"

"I noticed that my heart rate accelerated from being near her."

"Did this alarm you?"

"Yes, to the point that I distanced myself from her."

"Did you note this phenomenon because you're a doctor?"

"Not really. I started to feel light-headed and flushed. I think anyone would have noticed."

"Objection. Irrelevant."

"Your Honor, Dr. Ignat is testifying about a condition that is beyond Miss Caron's control. It has every bearing upon this case."

"Objection overruled."

"What do you think, Doctor, might happen to a man who willingly had intimate relations with a woman with the malady of Miss Caron?"

"Objection. Calls for conclusion."

"Your Honor, I am asking a doctor for a medical conclusion, but I'll rephrase. In your medical opinion, Doctor, do you think it would be possible that in that union, a man's heart could quicken three times its normal rate, causing cardiac arrest?"

"Yes."

The spectators became loud with their whispering opinions.

Slam! The judge threatened to clear the room and gaveled it into silence.

"I understand that you examined the corpses of Frederick Bothem and Oliver Davis. Did you find similar symptoms of their deaths?"

"Yes."

"Can you explain?"

"Well, the appearance of both their deaths were symptomatic of cardiac arrest."

"Was this unusual to you?"

"Yes, because both were healthy gentlemen with no previous medical conditions."

"Could you tell us about anything else you noticed in your examination?"

"Both men had cases of priapism."

"Priapism. That's a new word. Can you define the medical term so that we may all understand it?"

"Yes, priapism is a serious, rare condition in which the blood flow from the male organ is blocked."

"Can you explain, Doctor, what this would look like, then?"

"There are women in the court."

"Yes. Please proceed, Doctor."

"Well, the organ is still engorged with blood, and appears to be in an aroused state."

Slam!

"You observed this condition in both Frederick Bothem and Oliver Davis?"

"Yes."

"Can you tell us more about this condition?"

"There's not much known. It requires immediate surgery. In the case that was in our medical journal the patient died from the condition, which was complicated by an overdose of a cocaine-based elixir."

"To your knowledge did either of the victims have cocaine elixir?"

"No."

"Would you say that the priapism might have contributed to these men's deaths?"

"It very well may have."

"Did you see stab wounds on their bodies, Doctor?"

"No."

"Gunshot wounds?"

"No."

"Bruises? Had they been bludgeoned to death?"

"No."

"So other than the heart and male organ, everything else was fine in each of the victim's bodies?"

"Yes."

"Thank you, Doctor, nothing further. Your witness, Esquire Holcomb."

"I have no questions for this witness." Holcomb signaled the judge. "Your Honor, may we approach the bench?"

"Yes."

"I have another witness we believed couldn't be found, but he has been located and his testimony is critical."

"Do you object, Lord Baston?"

"Who is the witness?"

"Wilbur, Nicollette Caron's servant at her manor. He's the last witness I will be calling except for Inspector Jackson Lang."

"Yes, I object," Lord Baston said. "I've had no chance to interview him. He should be disregarded."

"I'll allow it."

"But, Your Honor—"

"I'll allow it." The judge looked overexerted and red-faced. Lord Baston knew to drop his protest. "Let's get on with the trial," the judge said. "I'm not getting younger."

Lord Baston returned to the defendant's table. "Nicollette," he whispered, "will Wilbur say anything to incriminate you?"

"Yes, Blake. He will."

"What? Whisper to me."

Nicollette whispered. And as she whispered, the light went out of Lord Baston's eyes.

Wilbur entered the room looking as though he'd been beaten. He had a gash on his chin, a bruised cheek, and swollen eyes. He swore on the Bible and took the stand.

"Wilbur Rodham, you worked for Miss Caron this past summer?"

"Yes, I did."

"What was your job at the manor?"

"I was her foreman. I was her top hired man."

"On the evening of August 4, do you remember that night?"

"Yes, sir."

"Can you tell us in your own words exactly what happened? And may I remind you that you're under oath?"

"Yes, sir. I went to sleep early, but Marie woke me at about two-thirty in the morning. A gentlemen by the name of Denton Brickman had died while in Miss Caron's bedroom."

The crowd murmured. The gavel slammed.

"Was there a chance the man was still alive?"

"No, he was dead—and getting cooler."

"What made you think that?"

"Because I could see . . ." he mumbled inaudibly.

"Can you speak up, sir? The court has to hear you. How did you know Mr. Brickman had been dead for a while? Was it because he had been dead long enough for the women to complete a task?"

"Yes."

"Can you tell the court what the task was?"

"Yes. I understand that Miss Caron and Marie had broke the dead man's neck."

"Did I hear you right? Denton Brickman was dead, and the women broke the dead man's neck?"

"Yes."

"Why would they commit such an atrocity on a dead man?"

"They said they needed to make it look like an accident."

"When you heard that, did you think he had died of natural causes and now they wanted to cover his natural death?"

"No. I didn't think."

"Did you think they had killed him, and now they wanted to make it look like an accident?"

"Objection. Asked and answered. He said he wasn't thinking about it."

"Rephrase your question."

"Did you help the women with their dilemma?"

"Yes."

"Did you want to?"

"No."

"Why did you, then?"

"Marie told me if I wanted to keep my job, I had to help."

Holcomb drew from Wilbur the rest of the story. How Denton was put in the road, and how Wilbur ran over him with a carriage to make his death look like an accident.

"You didn't want to defile the dead man's corpse, did you, Wilbur?"

"No, sir."

"Did any part of this malicious plan please you?"

"No, sir. I ain't slept a wink since."

"After the murder of Denton Brickman, what did Miss Caron do?"

"She fled to Glastonbury."

"Why?"

"Objection. Calls for speculation."

"I'll allow it. The witness may answer."

"She was afraid of being questioned about the man's death."

"Thank you. Your witness, Lord Baston."

"You make this sound like an awful event, Wilbur. Poor, poor man, unable to sleep for so long. Did you confess this to your priest?"

"No."

"Did you share this information with Inspector Lang when he came to question you?

"No."

"Why not?"

"I was ashamed."

"Maybe you were the one who killed him, Wilbur."

"No."

"Wilbur, did you make a trade with the prosecuting barrister? Your freedom in exchange for your incriminating testimony?"

"It's the truth."

"But you will be free after this?"

"Yes."

"You carried a dead man from his death scene. Drove his corpse two miles to lay him in the road. Drove your carriage over him a few times. And kept this a secret for months. These are crimes, yet you'll be free to go. You do *fine* work, Wilbur. No further questions."

Jackson Lang was sitting near the prosecution table with Peavey and Wilcox. Peavey leaned over, and said, "Good work, Jackson."

"It's not my doing," Lang said.

"At any rate, Wilbur just hanged them," Wilcox said. "I can hear the creak of the gallows."

Esquire Holcomb said, "Your Honor, may we have a brief recess?"

"You can take twenty minutes."

During the recess many people remained in their seats, fearing a momentary departure might cost them their view of the proceedings.

Sir Bart found Lang among the spectators leaving the room and pulled him aside.

"I've had a meeting with Queen Victoria. She wants to knight you. She'll make an announcement after Nicollette's hanging."

Lang's face was expressionless.

"Smile, Jackson, it's what you wanted. Congratulations."

"Thank you."

Jackson Lang waited outside the courtroom and watched as Nicollette, chained at her ankles and wrists, hobbled by him. At first she didn't see him, and then at the last moment she turned and smiled at him. He winced to see such a beauty in chains.

The barristers who'd left the courtroom, the defendants, the jury, and the court spectators returned to their places. Judge Tareyton wobbled slowly to his perch and slammed his gavel. He looked paler as the day wore on.

"Esquire Holcomb, you may proceed."

Holcomb stood. "I call to the stand Inspector Jackson Lang."

Lang's expression was guarded as he stood up to take his oath. And he walked stiffly to the stand.

"Inspector Lang, you've often been honored for your investigations which have led to the arrest and conviction of numerous criminals, is this correct?"

"I've been fortunate in solving the crimes I am assigned. And I've received recognition for it."

"Can you tell us how you first were pulled into this criminal investigation?"

"My recruits and I were assigned the case by Chief Bart Marshall the late morning of Mr. Brickman's death. The CID had received an anonymous tip of a dead man in the road."

"And did you investigate the scene?"

"Yes, we documented how we found the body."

"Can you tell us why you did that?"

"We thought it might not be a death from natural causes."

"What did you do with Mr. Brickman's body?"

"We took it with us to Scotland Yard and had a physician examine it for cause of death."

"Which doctor?"

"Dr. Ian Lindsey."

Lang's eyes searched the room and came to rest on Nicollette. She was looking at him intently.

"And did Ian Lindsey indicate that Brickman had been murdered?"

Lang paused. "No, he couldn't be certain."

"Could he tell the neck was broken?"

"This was not confirmed."

"Nicollette Caron went to Glastonbury the night of the murder. Did you question her?"

"Yes. When we arrived at Glastonbury."

"Did you catch her in any untruths?"

"I found her quite forthright."

Holcomb's mounting frustration showed on his face. Clearly Lang was not responding as they had rehearsed before the trial.

"Do you believe Miss Nicollette Caron is our serial killer?"

"I bring in the facts and let the jury determine guilt."

"May I remind you, Jackson Lang, that you are under oath in a court of law? Can you tell me without a doubt that she's the killer?"

Lang looked at Chief Bart Marshall, his men, and other CID officers he knew in court.

"I can't say without doubt," he said. "There have been no witnesses to any of the murders with which Miss Caron has been charged."

"You mean no survivors?"

"I mean witnesses to an extinguished life."

"Extinguished life? What do you mean by this?"

"A hastened death."

"Your Honor, I have under oath a detective who apparently does not know the word 'murder.' May I approach the bench?" Both barristers came closer to the judge.

"Your Honor, Inspector Lang has compiled an extensive file on Nicollette Caron identifying her as the murderer. I don't know why he's not testifying to that effect, but he borders on perjury or treason here. I won't go on further with my questions to hear his bogus answers. I withdraw further questions and submit that I'll have assistant detectives Peavey and Wilcox testify. I was not planning to call them but have no other choice."

"Very well. And Lord Baston, if you or your client is exerting undue influence on Inspector Lang, you are in contempt."

"I swear we are not, Your Honor."

Holcomb said, "No further questions, Inspector. Your witness, Lord Baston."

"Inspector Lang, could you explain for us the circumstances under which you captured Nicollette Caron and Marie Tucci?"

"Marie and Nicollette were on a ferry with their horses. Marie fell off the ferry. She was unable to swim. Nicollette jumped into the frigid waters and brought her safely to shore. Directly to us, so we could help her."

"This person in flight from you—swam right to you?"

"Yes."

"And she saved a life, rather than took a life?"

"Yes."

"What was Marie's condition when she was brought to the shore?"

"She was dead."

"How did you determine this?"

"She was not breathing. She had no pulse."

"And what did Nicollette Caron do upon being told she was dead?"

"She bent down over Marie and begged God for her friend's life."

"What did you do?"

"We confirmed that she was dead and tried to reason with Miss Caron."

"Did she resign herself then to her friend's death?"

"No. She held Marie as if she were holding her most beloved person in the world. And then she laid her heart upon Marie's heart."

"Did you know why she did this?"

"I thought she was lamenting the loss of her friend's life. But the act of laying her heart to Marie's heart apparently restarted the dead woman's heart."

The crowd gasped and muttered.

Slam. "Order in the court."

"Can you tell us how you perceived this act?"

"Frankly, I thought it was a miracle that Nicollette resurrected her friend. Perhaps she has a miraculous gift—perhaps she's a healer, a gift to mankind," Lang said.

"Inspector Lang, do you like Nicollette Caron?"

"Yes."

"Do you believe Nicollette Caron is a threat to society?"

"The more I know her, the less I think so."

Sir Bart leaned over to Peavey, "Why has he gone soft on us?"

"Sir Bart, he's honest to a fault—he must be telling his own truth."

Peavey and Wilcox testified next, and the young fresh-faced inspectors gave evidence of the sort Lang had failed to supply. How Marie had hidden the facts of Denton's death. How Nicollette had fled the scene in fear of being questioned. How the day Nicollette arrived in Glastonbury, the constable died from the same unusual cause of death as Denton. How Nicollette had lied about putting Oliver Davis on the train for London. How she had lied when questioned about her taste for grapes, whose stems were found near Frederick Bothem's body though there were no grapes in Glastonbury at that time.

Peavey was the most factual and straightforward in his presentation. Wilcox presented the stack of logical evidence compiled against Nicollette.

The spectators who listened so intently to Esquire Holcomb's and Lord Baston's brilliant summaries were of the opinion that neither would change the mind of any juror who had followed the proceedings. Wilbur Rodham's testimony had made the odds in the street seventy-five to twenty-five, then Peavey and Wilcox swung the odds to 95 percent for a guilty verdict. Marie and Nicollette would need an act of God to save their necks.

The old judge looked exhausted. The whole trial had taken just one day. But by the looks of him, the long process of weighing each word and its life-or-death import had burdened him greatly.

Now his part in the proceedings was over until the critical moment when he passed sentence—that is, assuming the jurors found Nicollette and Marie guilty.

CHAPTER 30
The Verdict

Judge Tareyton used his gavel frequently. Each time he slapped the wood for order, I didn't expect that loud sudden bang—and I jumped. Wood on wood. It made me think of the sound of a trap dropping on a hangman's platform. *Wood on wood.*

As the trial drew to its conclusion, the judge raised the gavel and slammed it down. And with that slam, he gasped for air. He clutched his chest, held his left shoulder, then smashed into the side of his desk and fell to the floor.

"Is there a doctor in the court?" Holcomb cried out.

Dr. Sidney Ignat was still there. He carried his medical bag to the fallen judge. He put smelling salts under his nose, but they did nothing to bring the old man around. His face was contorted in pain and bluish in color. His breathing was labored, and then there was no breath. Dr. Ignat pronounced the judge dead at 4:20 P.M.

"May I try to help?" I asked. I felt strangely compelled to protect the old man, no matter the outcome to me. The drive was coming from my inner core. I felt impelled to do something. I had never deliberately attempted to heal someone, yet I knew I must try.

Blake said, "It's a mistrial if he dies. Let nature take its course, Nicollette. Perhaps this is God's will."

"But we have free will."

"Forget your free will. Set your *neck* free."

"I must try."

Blake saw that he couldn't stop me. And he spoke up for me. "Let her help."

I went over to the old judge and touched his hand gently to let him know I was there. Then I laid my chest on top of his and put my arms around him.

I whispered to him, "Your Honor, don't leave us."

The old judge didn't move. He remained cold and still.

"Your Honor, please come back."

The fates were kind to the old man. Within moments, the heart beneath mine began to beat. The judge gathered all the oxygen he could with each inhalation, one breath after another, until the cadence became more even and his breathing returned to a normal rate. His blood had resumed its flow, returning a light pink color that overcame his deathly pallor. He rested a moment, aware of his close call.

He reached for my hand. "Thank you," he whispered.

"Peace to you, Your Honor."

He didn't take his eyes from me as he was being carried to a medical bed to stabilize his condition. I had never saved anyone before Marie. Now this. I wondered about my new power to bring back life—why hadn't I been able to resurrect my lovers?

It was different. Marie had merely taken in some water and had a lapse in life to start again. With the judge I could sense a failure of the heart. Some temporary beat missing that just needed a start to get it going.

But my lovers had experienced a more drastic attack to their hearts—an explosion of sorts. When I thought about it, I knew I wouldn't have been able to do anything to save them.

I had suffered such remorse for the loss of my young lovers' lives that it had become my haunt each day and night since their leaving. I was growing mentally exhausted by my dead lovers' appearances, yet the terror of a cadaver's cold touch could not distress me so much as did my guilt.

Marie and I were taken to a holding cell to await our verdict.

"Marie, there are no words to thank you for all that you have done for me. I would have been lost without you."

"You don't need to say anything, I can feel your gratitude," she said.

"Marie, are you sorry that you ever joined me in Glastonbury?"

"I have not regretted one moment of our time together," she said.

The jurors were out for less than an hour. In the street we knew the townspeople were gossiping about Wilbur's testimony. And though many undoubtedly knew of my miraculous healing of the judge, they wouldn't know how to react to an event that so contradicted their impression of me.

How could a harlot have a gift to resurrect the dead? It was apparent that they had already cleared a path for Marie and me to their gallows. And they chose not to see the healer within me, as their cruel taunts of me continued.

"We find the defendant, Nicollette Caron, guilty, Your Honor."

"Unanimously?"

"Yes, Your Honor."

Judge Tareyton straightened his spine, as if the true judgment he was about to pronounce had somehow righted his aged bones, the same way a guilty verdict had as far back as he could remember. But the judge's hands began to shake as he looked at the paper tally, and he put off the moment by clearing his throat, as if he might choke on the simple words.

"Nicollette Caron, please rise for your sentence."

I wobbled to a standing position.

"Nicollette Caron . . ." The old judge paused to review the paper, taking the time to reread the note several times.

"You have been found guilty of three counts of murder and will be sentenced to death." The courtroom erupted in chaos. Cheers echoed in the streets.

The judge slammed his gavel. "Quiet! Order in the court!

"Because you are a Frenchwoman, you'll have a French ambassador represent you through your penalty. He has assured us that beheading is more humane than hanging, and the queen has arranged for a guillotine to be brought here on your behalf. Therefore, you are sentenced to be beheaded after three Sundays have passed on the morning of Friday, September 25, 1891."

I fainted. No one ran to catch me. I just dropped to the court's cold stone floor. Someone put ammonia salts under my nose, and I came around.

They made me rise to my feet, propped up by the guards' shoulders. But I couldn't feel my legs. They no longer tolerated the duty of holding me up. I felt as though I were shutting down, overloaded with my despair over the verdict.

"Marie Tucci, you have been found guilty of one count of assisting in the murder of Denton Brickman. You will hang by the neck until dead after three Sundays have passed on the morning of Friday, September 25, 1891."

Marie crossed herself, and then her knees gave out. The guards caught her and held her up. Then I saw her try to hold her shaking body taller and appear unafraid.

Oh, that I could be so brave. But I'm not. I'm not sure what lies ahead for me when I lose my neck. Do I burn in eternal hellfire? Or is my God an understanding God? He did create me, after all. And I'm not a treacherous person. I haven't maliciously killed men—I've loved them.

I turned from my tormenting thoughts to look at Blake.

His face was frozen. I couldn't read his thoughts, couldn't see his love for me. Perhaps, after Wilbur's testimony, he had lost his feelings for me. I wouldn't blame him. *Blake, I love you. Can you hear my heart call to you?*

He gave me a single nod. *He must have heard my soul crying for his. Or did he merely give up on our ill-fated love and nod to say: So be it?*

"May the Lord have mercy on your souls and grant you peace. This court is adjourned." The judge slammed his gavel a final time. People rose as he departed, then fled into the streets to share the news.

CHAPTER 31

Newgate

My feet and wrists were still shackled. Four large men came to lead Marie and me to our cells.

Then Blake was there. Trying to talk with me, but they were shoving me away from him, farther out the door.

"Wait," I said. "Please. Let us talk."

"You'd only kill him while we looked on," one of the men said.

I glared at them.

"Blake." They pushed me farther. I smiled at him through my tears, and then I fought them. They swiftly overcame me as I cried out, "I love you, Blake!" And then I could no longer see him, nor he me.

The four men led Marie and me away, dragging our chains through the tunnel that connected the Old Bailey courthouse to our prison cell at Newgate Prison. Leaving behind my heart and my hope. Lost in some game where the loser is beheaded for loving.

I cried piteously. I replayed in my mind all the things I had done wrong. The men I allowed to court me, the intimacy I allowed while I had an awareness of what could happen, and with each death, the inevitability of the next. Perhaps if I had been more forthright and not hidden my plague, the people might not have blamed me. They might have seen that I suffered from each lover's loss.

No. Not in Victorian England. They had ruled upon it. For I craved the intimate unions that Victorian women feared and tolerated. Only Marie had come close to understanding me. And now she would die for her compassion.

My musty, dark, cramped cell at Newgate Prison reeked of human odors not properly cleaned. When I was first thrown into it I curled up in the far corner, crying. I looked only at the wall. I heard a man enter but I didn't look up.

"Don't be afraid, miss."

I cried harder with my eyes closed to the wall. I didn't want to see my surroundings.

"London's famous Newgate Prison has a history dating back to 1188, when two carpenters and one smith built the prison for three pounds, six shillings, and eight pence." He spoke as if he were trying to calm me with a child's story.

"It's quite an interesting piece of Great Britain's history, miss. It has housed London's worst prisoners through the years. In 1236, 1422, and the late 1500s it was reconstructed. Then it burned in London's Great Fire and was rebuilt in 1672."

I didn't want to hear the story he told. But there was something soothing about his voice, a kindness in its tone. And it did calm me.

"In 1770 Newgate was torn down and reconstructed. After the new facility was completed, rioters broke into its gates with crowbars, tore open the roof, and set the prison on fire. During this attack several hundred prisoners escaped within an hour." *I could pray for a fire to enable me to escape.*

"It was rebuilt again by 1783, the scaffold erected in front for the condemned to hang." *Stop. Don't talk about the hangings.* "Good money was paid back then to watch the hangings, which were popular events for the lower classes, who cheered or jeered them.

"Newgate's interior has poor ventilation and dark, gloomy cells. Its inadequate water supply and its stench—the jail fumes—spread what the prisoners know as jail fever, a disease related to typhoid fever. Even some of us guards have been lost to it. Newgate's a place of misery and hardship, of spiritual as well as physical and mental torment. I tell you this so you know to be strong.

"Women are kept in a solitary cell, as are the men. Sometimes the prisoners barter for favors. Half-clothed women are common here, and some guards force themselves on them. Pregnancy isn't uncommon because of the rapes. I'll try to protect you, Miss Nicollette—but I'm not always here at the prison."

I knew that this soft-spoken introduction was the best I could have hoped for in my hellish surroundings. I looked up at the man leaving my cell. I could see him drag his clubfoot as he crossed the stone floor and let himself out. Exhausted, I laid my head on the cold floor. But I couldn't sleep with the chants I heard through my small window near the ceiling.

"Death to the tramp!"

"Harlot!"

"Devil's vixen!"

"Murdering hussy!"

"Murderer!"

I tried to blot out their voices, but I could not. I was to learn that they began their shouts at five in the morning and continued throughout the day, even beyond the midnight hour. Building to crescendos as the crowds built up at different hours of the day.

I'd cry at their cruel taunts, for I knew their jeers would be the last words I heard from my fellow humans on earth.

The first day of my imprisonment, I felt rebellious. I tried to be hopeful that there was yet an escape. I had a sense that I had more life to live, that it couldn't end with my head detached from my body. The queen would come to her senses. Or Blake would use his power to free Marie and me. Or the guards would protest my captivity, revolt, and free me.

But as night fell that first day and I lay on the cold stone of my cell, I listened to the rats, and I knew none of these things was going to happen. And I knew that I must accept my fate.

I even began to wonder if killing me wasn't the right thing for society to do. If perhaps I wasn't the menace to mankind they believed me to be. And when I had these thoughts, when I lost my belief in myself—that was the moment of my first ghostly visitor.

From a shadow, he appeared. *Denton's phantom body was a bluish gray. His frame was outlined with a bit of a glow. And his empty eyes widened as he came closer to me.*

"Denton? Denton, I'm so sorry. Denton, I didn't mean to hurt you."

It was pitch-dark, three o'clock in the morning. I pleaded to him through the night for forgiveness.

The next day I heard keys jingle, and my door opened to admit the guard with the clubfoot. The crippled man had a crooked smile he tried to cover with a red untrimmed mustache and beard, a grooming trick that didn't accomplish its end.

"Miss Nicollette, you should eat something. I don't believe you've taken a bite since you've been here."

He held a cup of fresh water for me. I hadn't been drinking the water, fearing cholera. But he approached me with a kindness

I'd not been shown since his first visit. And after all, dying of cholera might be preferable to losing my head.

He held the cup for me and encouraged me to drink.

"Who are you?"

"Alfred, ma'am."

"Thank you, Alfred." I looked at him as if he were the most handsome man in the world. For at that moment he was beautiful to my eyes. And though he was dusty from his job in these dank caverns, he smelled as sweet to me as if he were fresh from a spring meadow.

"Miss Nicollette?"

"Yes?"

"I ain't ever seen a woman as beautiful as you before."

"Thank you, Alfred."

"And I never had a pretty woman talk to me before, ever. They don't come here too often, you know."

"I'm flattered, Alfred."

"You're like a beautiful bird that shouldn't be caged," he whispered. I could see how much he wanted to let me out. "Is there anything I can do for you, Miss Nicollette?"

"Yes."

Alfred smuggled me pen and paper, which I hid behind a loose stone in the wall. I wrote to Blake. Alfred promised me he would try to get my letters to him.

My Dearest Blake,

    Thank you for your fine representation in court. The case was an impossibility to defend. I knew this long before my trial, so please do not feel any guilt.

    No one could have defended me with more heart and more conviction. And I appreciate all that you did.

    My darling, I pray we will meet again in a happier time,

*you and I. And that we still have our same desire, and that it
is only for each other.*

*There's a window near me, and the townspeople taunt me
without ceasing. I don't sleep here. I count down the hours to
the ending of my life. If I could choose my death, it would be
to leave as I rested in your arms.*

*I wish you continued greatness, and if I can look down
upon you and tell you heaven is real, I surely will.*

Kissing you with the enchanted wing of my rising flight,
I love you, Blake,
With all my heart,
Your Nicollette

I folded my letter, and when Alfred brought my daily watered
lard, I handed it to him. As I looked at him, I saw an outline by
his shoulder. It became more defined as I squinted my eyes. It was
*a full-bodied Oliver outlined with a white light and a bluish gray
translucence to his body.* He wore the clothes he'd had on the day
he picked me up for our buggy ride.

"Oliver."

"It's Alfred, ma'am."

"Oliver, I'm so sorry, I didn't mean to hurt you." I reached my
hand out to block the ghost. But *Oliver stood there with his
deathly stare, just beyond Alfred.* Denton had been confused that
he was on the other side looking at me through a veil, yet *Oliver
stood a silent commentary that only taunted me.*

"My name is Alfred, ma'am. And you didn't hurt me."

Was Oliver angry with me? Was he upset that I had hastened
his death from a beautiful life? Was he lost? Or was I? Was this my
fate—imprisonment in the dark with silent ghosts who once
loved me but now haunted me?

Oliver's ghost gave a sudden start and took steps toward me.

"Oliver, forgive me." *He came closer to me.* And suddenly in the room *Collin's ghost stood with flowers from our courtship on the hill, Robert twirled a long willow reed, Frederick held some grapes, and Denton tipped a top hat, as beautiful as he looked when we went to the Queen's Ball.*

The men stood with soulless stares on their faces. I couldn't tell if I feared their danger or their anger, but I hated seeing them in this altered state. I wanted them alive. I wanted them all to be the living, breathing, charming men they had been. I didn't want to die for their deaths, when all I'd done was love them and make them happy.

Oliver walked closer to me. He reached his arms out to me, and I trembled.

"Forgive me!" I cried. *Closer.* "Please forgive me," and I sank to my knees on the stone, as *Oliver walked through me. He moved subtle inches into me, mixing the particles of his ghostliness with my live flesh.*

I shuddered as I felt his coldness and the icicle air that surrounded him. I turned my head as the ghosts reached out to touch me, to draw me into their ghastly world. Even through my chill I was sweating, which somehow made me colder still.

"Please. I didn't mean to hurt any of you. Please. You must understand." *Ice. Ice shooting through my spine.* I was shaking, then I screamed. I could take no more. "Leave me, leave me—I don't want you here."

"Very well, Miss Nicollette," Alfred said.

And I fell into blackness. Was this their world? Were they taking me on a trip to preview hell—before my death? Dark caverns turned into a tunnel without light. I tried to feel the walls, but they were moving beneath my fingers. Something alive was squirming on the walls wherever I put my hands. Sometimes a long rat tail. Sometimes a face, or fur, or an animal's sharp teeth.

I could hear the hiss of snakes and smell the must of decay. I closed my eyes; I didn't want to see what I moved through.

Oh, my dear God, surely this is a hell for a woman. There are endless tunnels without any end in sight. And only beasts and horror surround me as I walk. Oh, my dearest God in heaven, remember the Nicollette who played with dolls, who enjoyed rolling a hoop down a sandy road, and searched for rabbits in the meadow to spy on their softness. Remember that Nicollette. Oh, God, please save me. Please, God—

I opened my eyes. The ghosts were gone. Only Alfred knelt near me. He stroked my hair and pressed a cup of water to my lips. He lifted my head to help me drink.

"I don't leave the prison or the grounds much, but because it's you, I'll try to find Lord Baston for you."

"Thank you, Alfred."

"I hope you don't go through anything like that again, ma'am."

He looked back one time at me, then closed the door behind him. But as I looked over his shoulder, I saw Denton's ghost. *He walked through Alfred and approached me from my right side.*

"Denton, you must go. Go away, Denton. No, go!" But *he kept coming toward me.* I put my face in my hands to hide the hideous vision.

"Oh, my God, please help me. Make him go away." I prayed every prayer I could think of in hope that when I opened my tired eyes Denton would be gone and I could lie down to escape in sleep the jeers that were in full force outside my window. Breaking the silence with the knives of a hundred tongues, clamoring for their harlot's demise.

"Die, devil's vixen!"

"Death to the whore!"

I finished my prayers—my most intimate conversation with

God. Though my neck could no longer take the strain of holding my head high, somehow I lifted my head to look up. *In time to see that Denton had not disappeared but had now been joined by Oliver, and Frederick was manifesting before me.*

The ghosts were all coming toward me. Reaching for me. Trying to touch me—as if they wanted to make love again. They touched my sack dress and rubbed my body, and I felt their coldness throughout my being as my other lovers loomed in my cell. More ghosts coming toward me with their black eyes. Reaching for me. Some horrific wanting that continued from death's other side. Some ghoulish motive that wouldn't allow them to rest behind the veil.

I tried to block their touches, my two small hands trying to defend my honor, but there were so many hands reaching all over for me. Some of the ghouls began at my ankles and rubbed up my legs, going higher with their demonic tease.

Others pawed at my breasts, and Frederick's corpse leaned to kiss me.

"If I just kiss you, perhaps that will satisfy me," he said.

And I screamed, with his monstrous dead face looming above me, I slapped their ice hands, but they had no solidity and continued without the obstacle.

I tucked myself and tried to roll on my side, but the movement exposed my derriere to their efforts, and they began to rub underneath my sack dress, and I screamed and cried out from the ghostly foreplay that penetrated my soul. And when I couldn't think of another thing to do to overcome my tortured horror—I screamed again.

As the days of my imprisonment wore on, I found myself floating between sanity and insanity. I learned that my time with sanity could be lengthened if I stretched myself to write, for the moments when I committed myself to paper were the moments when I felt most myself behind bars.

Yet when I'd put down my pen each evening, my madness would return. I heard the sound of tortures so piercing that I thought they were happening to me. But they were not. The painful cries were from other cells that were not in sight, and the blindness of their occupants' fates rattled my mind's imagination even deeper.

Sometimes the tortures were served with a warrant, but sometimes they were carried out at the sadistic whim of the warden or the guards.

Often groups of three to five men would come to torture and rape the female prisoners, and I could hear them doing it. I heard them flogging their victims, I heard the women cry out in pain— until they begged the men to rape them to stop the beatings.

But it was not only the women prisoners who cried out, for I heard victims with deeper voices. There were guards who brutally tortured the male prisoners. I heard them with various devices, crushing the prisoners' limbs, breaking their teeth. Sodomizing them.

There was a mother named Abigail Morse in a nearby cell, jailed for six months for failure to vaccinate her five-year-old child, Tory, who died of a fever. She was flogged often—I heard her cries. Sometimes I couldn't tell where Abigail's cries or mine began and ended. And I could not decide if her cry was the saddest of them all—or if it was my own, echoing against the stone walls in the night.

I prayed for someone to shelter me, yet no one came. Then, knowing the tortures that could be mine, I prayed for my solitary nights. I hoped to be alone, if there was to be no one to protect me. But late one afternoon Emil Hatchett, the warden's aide, came to my cell.

"You're very pretty, Nicollette. Tonight we'll see just how pretty you are."

I awaited my attack, as if I could hear a clock ticking out the seconds. And later that night I could smell ripe body odor outside my cell door. To my senses, this rancid smell was quite different from the other prison odors. The iron key jiggled my lock open, and three men entered.

Emil stood forward, as the leader. He was an unkempt man missing one front tooth, and another was made of wood. He had bushy eyebrows that almost met over his nose and plentiful facial hair that looked as though it had never been tended. He wore slightly finer clothes than the other two guards, although that was not a compliment to his attire. Just that the other two men wore clothing of near rags.

"This here's Michael and Terrence," Emil said.

Michael was tall and skinny, with wild red hair and big lips. And Terrence, a rotund man with greasy black hair, had an unhealthy-looking growth on his face.

"Nicollette," Emil said, "we've come to play a game with you."

"I'm quite fond of games," I said. The men approached me to tie my hands. "Wait. Before you do this, explain the game. I have rules of my own you may like better."

"I see no reason not to hear them," Emil said, "since we know *you like it so.* All right with you, men?"

"Sure."

"Fine with me."

"Very well, Miss Nicollette. We usually undress you and tie you to the wall. Where we will flog you—with this, or that." Emil and Michael held up their flogging weapons.

"Do you have a warrant for my torture?"

"Sure. Of course, we ain't got it with us. Trust us, all the papers are in order."

"Of course."

"And we'll stop your torture and climb on you—when you ask to have us."

"Actually, I like you to beg for me," Terrence added.

"I like that, too," Emil said.

"Thank you for explaining the game to me," I said.

"Emil. My name's Emil."

"Yes, Emil. I have some other ideas."

"We'll hear 'em, Miss Nicollette."

"You see, I'm not a woman who wants to be like your others. And I want you to be different, to be a memorable experience for me. Can you understand this? You may be my last taste of a man's flesh before I lose my head."

I thought I saw Terrence drool as he listened.

"So may I say that the flogging isn't necessary? I already want you now. Not just you, Emil, I want all of you. One at a time, of course."

"Of course."

"So I ask for all of you to please take me tonight. I want you each to have the ride you seek—and will remember always. I offer myself willingly to you. Though I ask for a promise that you tell no one that you've had me, because surely the queen would be displeased should this knowledge become public. And to tell even another guard could risk this message becoming too loud for you or me. So I ask that what happens here remain between the four of us in this cell—*our secret.*"

"You have my word," Emil said. The other two men nodded. They were staring at me, fascinated by my words and manner.

"Good sirs, I imagine that women may misunderstand you completely," I said.

All three men nodded vigorously.

"They do," Emil said. "After we have 'em, they fight even harder the next time."

"Aye, why don't they want us?" Terrence asked, obviously pondering his technique with women for the first time.

"This is a simple thing to fix, gentlemen. It isn't your fault at all. Apparently no woman has taken the time to show you some gentle arts that will make them putty in your hands."

"You mean—a woman would *want to do it?*"

"If you will let me show you."

"Oh, yes."

"Yes."

"Yes."

"But first I must warn you, as I've warned my other lovers. There are men who expire when they have me. I don't understand it. Perhaps they were just too weak, not as strong as you men."

"I can handle it," Emil said. "I'll even set my pipe down to handle it."

"That's rare. Emil is always smoking his pipe," his friend spoke up.

"I expect you can, Emil. I can see you're the leader. You're the one with the strength and the good ideas."

"I'm the warden's right-hand man. I actually run *everything* around here."

"I can see this. Would you like to be first, then?"

"I reckon I would. Yeah, first is better."

"Please set down your equipment there. You two gentlemen, would you like to leave or watch?"

"We want to watch."

"Then sit against the wall, gentlemen, and move your lamps, so you can see. And allow me to be like a schoolteacher to you about love."

"Aye. A teacher."

"Emil, would you take off your shirt?"

"I don't need to take off my shirt, what I got is in my trousers."

"Yes, but remember, I'm the teacher."

"All right, then." He took off a vest and his shirt. I opened my dress to my waist and stood half-naked before him. And his eyes nearly bugged out of his head as he tried to reach for me. But I stepped back.

"Wait. This is the time to arouse and excite. You must ready yourself with your vision of your woman. You should take time to let your body become pleased."

"I'm pleased now. I want to unbutton my trousers."

"Not yet."

"But I'm burning up."

"That's good. This is a stage. Have you done it with the woman on top of the man?"

"Everybody knows the man is always on the woman."

"Oh, gentlemen, that's heavy for the woman. I'd like to show you a way for the woman to be on top."

"That's not natural."

"You said you wanted to learn."

"All right."

"Emil, lie down on the floor."

"With my pants on?"

"They'll come off soon enough."

Emil lay down on the floor, and I lay on top of him. We were heart to heart.

"That looks good," the voyeurs said. They reached down to adjust the tightness in their pants.

"I want you to think about the excitement of my bosom against your chest. Do you feel the excitement building?"

"I feel it, all right." Emil was breathing hard and had started to gasp. "When do I poke you?"

But he was gasping harder and struggling to breathe.

"Oh, my." I sat up and looked down at Emil as he writhed on the floor. He clutched his chest. He was unable to speak, just a surprised smile upon his face as he stared at my bosom. Then he stiffened and was still.

Michael sprang forward to inspect his still accomplice—suddenly afraid to touch him.

"Oh, my God, Terrence—he's dead!"

I held up my hands. "I don't know what to say. I did nothing—you saw this. Did you know of his health problems? Oh, well, gentlemen, which one of you is next? I hope you two are in better health than poor Emil."

Michael fumbled to unlock my cell door, and both men tried to fit through the door at the same time, tripping in their haste to leave.

"Gentlemen, would you mind removing his body? I rather like a tidy cell. And remember our pact. This is all between us. Please feel free to visit anytime. Either of you can be next."

"Yes, Miss Nicollette."

They dragged Emil across the floor so quickly that they forgot their flogging whips. I hid them behind some loose bricks— Michael and Terrence would have two less whips for their abuse.

Emil was not missed, as no one questioned me about his death. Nor did anyone return physically to torture me at night, and for this I was grateful. My tortures remained the apparitions of my past loves.

CHAPTER 32

From the Heart

My Dearest Blake,

I awoke a few days ago to someone suffering a torture. I wondered if it was my own.

When I learned it was not I was reminded of my real torture, that of waiting just a few more days for the guillotine. I began to take short, rapid breaths. As if my body didn't want to gather its air to go on. As if it were trying to shut down my involuntary breathing functions to extinguish my very life. That would be so much easier than what I face.

I think the queen comes to me today. What, pray tell, can she say to me? "Good day, Miss Nicollette, I've always wanted to kill a saucy Frenchwoman," or "Lovely frock you have on today, Miss Nicollette, you must tell me who designs the prison attire," or "Miss Nicollette, is everything to your liking?" Oh, my darling, she's killing someone who only loved men. Who warned them that loving me might mean their deaths.

Oh, Blake, I miss you so. I close my eyes and see your face. I dream of what could have been, so that my mind will focus on my dreams and not the torture in my near future.

Oh, Blake, tell me that you can visit me. I long for you so. Do you miss me? I receive no letters from you. They must not give them to me. And this is worse torture than the bars, this prison, or my fate. I love you, Blake.

With all my heart,
Your Nicollette

"Sir, she has responded to your request," Bertrum said.

Lord Baston sat in his study with his head bowed, Nicollette's letter on his lap. Her words tore at his heart. There was little time before her execution, and he was forbidden to see her. He held his head up with his hands, as if his neck lacked the strength to keep it erect.

"My lord, I said she has responded to your request."

Lord Baston looked up. "Yes, Bertrum?"

"The queen said she would see you. I'll bring the carriage around for you, sir."

"Thank you, Bertrum."

Lord Baston had dressed himself in a brocade waistcoat and other attire appropriate for a royal audience. Bertrum and another driver helped secure a gift for the queen to a large flatbed wagon.

"Your Royal Majesty, I'm Lord Baston," Lord Baston said as he practiced the sound of his voice in the carriage on the way to Buckingham Palace. How could he make his presentation to plead for Nicollette's life most effective? He rehearsed in his head how he would word his request. And how he thought Queen Victoria would receive the plea.

•   •   •

Lord Baston bowed low to the queen, who was seated on her throne. "Your Royal Majesty, I'm Lord Baston."

"Of course I know who you are, Lord Baston. You're on my list for possible appointment. I've thought of you for an ambassadorship."

"Thank you, Your Majesty. I'd be honored to serve England as you choose."

"Very well."

"I've brought you a gift. A life-size horse made from ivory and lapis and thousands of hand-set precious and semiprecious jewels."

"Is this a bribe to me, Lord Baston?"

"Certainly not. While in China I bought one for my manor's entry, then decided it was such an unusual item that perhaps my queen would enjoy its mate."

Her response was a stern look.

"Your Majesty, the horse was carved by hand. Thought to be part of the Tang Dynasty in about A.D. 625. It was buried for years until it was recently uncovered and became part of my recent acquisition of Asian antiquities."

"I see."

"The gift comes without strings, Your Majesty. England has been very good to me. Please consider this a separate matter from the purpose of my visit."

Lord Baston's drivers brought the large horse in with the assistance of the queen's attendants.

"Very well," the queen said. "I graciously thank you for your very generous gift to England."

She rose and walked over to the horse to inspect the jewels. "Very lovely. It has sapphires on the saddle with ruby trim. Did you say you had two of these? A matched set?"

"Yes, Your Majesty."

"A pair would make a more dramatic presentation, don't you think?"

"Its mate is yours, Your Royal Highness. It will be my privilege. I'll have the other horse delivered to you in the morning."

"Thank you." She walked back to her throne and shifted upon it until she was comfortable. Then, as if her resumption of the throne had created some internal change, her voice became low and throaty. "But what you are about to ask me for—I can't grant."

"I plead for your mercy."

"There's no chance of mercy, Lord Baston. Nicollette Caron has been tried in our highest court and sentenced. The courts and I have given opinions. And if you have any question as to the public's sentiments, just stand beneath her window and hear their cries." Two attendants entered the royal chamber. "Excuse us, Your Majesty. We have an emergency and request your presence in the Grand Room."

"Can't the emergency come to me?"

"Not this one, Your Majesty."

"Lord Baston, you will excuse me. I won't be long."

"Certainly, Your Majesty."

The Grand Room had a stage and a closed curtain. A thin, eager Frenchman stood at attention as the queen entered.

"What is it?" she said. "I'm not accustomed to being asked to leave my throne without knowing why."

"It has arrived, Your Majesty." The curtain was pulled to reveal a large guillotine. "Would you like a demonstration?"

"Yes."

"I'm Monsieur Paul Delage and I represent the fine—"

"Don't sell me, Monsieur Delage. This isn't a peddler's call. But you may demonstrate your machine."

"Of course. Let me use, as an example, this melon to show the strength and accuracy of this finely crafted machine by the—"

"I don't listen to peddler's talk. Say nothing. Show me."

The trembling Frenchman had shoes that didn't fit. His feet were too long for them, so he curled his toes and stood as though he were on tiptoe. The queen thought this odd, but held her tongue.

He set the melon in the wooden stockade, then slipped a gripper down the other side of the stockade to lock in the melon. Above it hung a sharp-angled blade of iron, polished to such a high gloss that it sent reflections of light flickering across the room.

Once he had secured the fruit he reached for the rope, unfastened it from the side, and dropped the heavy blade down on its target. The melon was sliced so quickly that the eye could hardly see it. Its two halves fell with thuds to the floor.

"That will do very well, Monsieur Delage."

"This is a new guillotine—would you like to test it on a prisoner you have no need to maintain?"

"I have no need for any of my prisoners, Monsieur Delage, but I quite trust that the apparatus will operate at its moment. You will see to that, or I'll share my dissatisfaction with your president."

"Yes, Your Majesty."

She made her exit, leaving Monsieur Delage still shaking in his ill-fitting shoes, and returned to Lord Baston.

"I'm sorry, Lord Baston, for the interruption, but there are many things happening in our world. I have no more time today, and regret that I cannot help you."

"Your Majesty, if I may—"

"I'm sure she's a charming woman. She's quite lovely, in fact, but she has been sentenced to her death for good cause. And you, my good fellow, must come to grips with that reality."

"Never."

"Then you will be sad indeed when you face the real world."

Lord Baston bowed his head. "May I see her?"

"I am not without mercy, Lord Baston. I am not so cold as to not see an affection and understand the depth with which it resonates within a heart."

Lord Baston looked up at the queen, his eyes bright with hope.

"But in this case I feel your affection is misdirected, Lord Baston. No, you may not see the harlot. I say this in protection of you, your life, and your soul. Now leave me to my affairs of state with more importance than a doomed woman in Newgate Prison. But please feel free to return for her beheading. I wouldn't want you to miss this; it should be well attended."

Lord Baston dipped a small bow toward the queen and left in silence.

My Dearest Blake,

Another day went by. I hear the cries of other prisoners in the night, and I've become used to it, as if it were the sound of the rooster in the morning or something I am to accept. But it is the mourning of human beings who go unanswered in the night, and their tortures by day. Sometimes it is my tortured cry that is the loudest.

The queen comes tonight, I am told. I don't know why. Perhaps she has the same morbid curiosity as the townspeople who throw sharpened sticks into my cell. Perhaps the queen will bring her own stick to poke me.

I am falling. Finally, after three days awake, I feel sleep may be within my reach.

Good night for now, my darling. I pray that I'll wake in the morning and my nightmare will be gone, and you will come to bed with me, as it should be.

Good night,
I love you, Blake.
With all my heart,
Your Nicollette

CHAPTER 33

A Visit from the Queen

I WAS TRYING TO SLEEP ON MY STONE FLOOR, FIGHTING the ghosts that filled my cell, when an aide to the queen stepped forward in the middle of the night.

"Her Majesty is here to see you."

I stood as she entered my cell. She was a rather large woman, with such rich details on her dress as I might have dreamed about in another day. The cloth was so brilliant that I could glimpse fine golden threads in the dark. And yet I sensed that had she been wearing a sack dress like mine, she still would have emitted a grand power. There was something charismatic about her, something that commanded respect, even reverence.

Queen Victoria sat on a bench the aide found for her. She was barely able to fit her large backside on it, and she studied me for a moment.

Then she said, "I have children, you know."

"Yes, Your Majesty."

"Nine heirs. I am not the Virgin Queen."

"No, Your Majesty."

"So, the union of man and woman isn't unknown to me. I have mothered the little snots through their colds and fevers. I have tried to steer them into decisions that have fostered some success. And my husband, Prince Albert's death ended my marital union years ago. I don't long for another man to fill his slippers."

"Yes, Your Majesty."

"You can't blame me when I rule a powerful country that depends upon my word."

I curtsied to her. "Your Majesty, I understand. I am but a servant to you. I'm privileged for your visit."

"Sit, Nicollette. I wish to speak with you."

"Yes, Your Majesty."

"I have questions for you. Most women suffer through their unions. They bed their husbands, hoping that tonight won't be a night of tribulation, as their husbands have their way with them. But I hear that you actually enjoy having a man upon you. Is this true?"

"Yes, Your Majesty."

"Do you think there are other women who feel this way?"

"Most certainly."

"This worries me. I am trying to envision a world in which women desire to have unions—and what it would do to men. Might they think that all women feel this way, and force themselves upon women who don't? Would women want to have a second partner or even a third? Would men have to please women more, lest they lose them to another? Or would women have to please their men lest they stray, thus breaking up a family?

"Would there be unwanted children? Unknown fathers? Would people stop their work? There would be no control. That way is lies and chaos, Nicollette."

"But that way lies happiness, Your Majesty. It's more joyous to share in the power of a beautiful union. To not just be willing—but filled with true desire for it, and true fulfillment when joining together takes place."

"I cannot envision such a world, Nicollette." The queen paused, a severe expression on her face. Then said eagerly, "Tell me more of it."

"Gladly, Your Majesty. Today a husband believes he has to finance his home and family and contribute nothing more. His wife must clean, and launder, and cook, and birth and tend the children. In addition she's to be available at his whim in the bedroom, though she gets nothing from the experience but notice of the ceiling's paint."

"All this is true."

"Perhaps women will want choices in the future. What if they didn't choose to marry?"

"We have that now. They are spinsters."

"Those we pity, for no man has selected the spinster for the privilege of marriage. Women feel they must marry if they have an opportunity, whether they want to act on it out of love or not. They fear their solitude, when they might choose it."

"You mean a woman might deny marriage offers and remain single by choice?"

"Yes, Your Majesty."

"Well, I don't know who could respect such a woman. People would see her as unable to secure a man in her life. They would judge that."

"And what if they didn't? What if we allowed men and women to enter into relationships as they please? And when it's over, they might find another more appealing."

"Even when out of their courting period? They have three years."

"What if they had their whole life to search and discover others?"

"Oh, but think of the children, the broken families. As I said—chaos."

"Think of the happiness."

"And then what are you saying? Man or woman could dance hellishly in the bedrooms of many other partners?"

"Possibly."

"May the heavens strike me before such days arrive." The queen took a fan from her bag and applied it vigorously. "I suppose all these women would enjoy their unions?"

"Yes, Your Majesty. They would learn what ignites their passions and share this knowledge with their partners."

"Oh, goodness."

She was in no hurry to leave and asked me questions at length about my ideas. She listened attentively.

Finally I said, "Your Majesty, may I beg you for my life? I meant no harm to any of the men who lay in my arms. I couldn't help what happened to them."

The queen looked at me for a long moment before she spoke. "Nicollette, as a woman I'd surely release you. But as queen of England, I cannot. I don't want this world of which you speak to come to England. And your free spirit for women must be erased. I believe you understand me. Kneel before me, child."

I knelt. She laid her hand on my head.

"I give a promise to you, Nicollette. You and your assistant, Marie, will have a speedy death. We will see you are laid to rest as soon as possible. This is all I can grant."

And then she left my cell. Her powerful energy had drained me, and I was able to sleep.

When I awoke I had less than a day before my execution.

"Alfred, did you see the queen last night when she visited?"

Alfred looked at me, concern evident upon his face. "Miss Nicollette, I was near your door all night. I didn't leave. No one came to your cell."

My Dearest Blake,

They came to me to see if I had requests after my death. They told me that heads are no longer displayed, but the queen has had so many requests from the people for mine that she intends to oblige them. They will display my head for three days upon the scaffold, and then my wishes will be followed. After Marie is hung, she will be displayed hanging from a tree outside Glastonbury as a warning for those that ride by that crime doesn't pay.

I wish my head and body to go to you. Will you take care of this for me, my darling? I pray that you will.

And please take care of Marie also, if you don't mind, when they take her down. Perhaps you will find a suitable place, such as your hunting lodge property? We were so happy there. If you can't comply, then I'll be buried in a pauper's grave. I leave this to your choice.

And don't dwell on your decision, as I won't be in either piece of my body but quite intend to take flight to a greater place, where I await our meeting.

I love you, Blake.

Love with all my heart,

Your Nicollette

CHAPTER 34

Lord Baston's Plan

"I've come to see Nicollette." The man wore a disguise.

"I'm sure it would be better if you didn't, sir," Alfred said. "She isn't as you might think."

"Whatever her condition, open her door for me."

Alfred opened the cell door and let the man in.

His quick eyes searched the cell and didn't find Nicollette where he thought he might. And when he did find her, he ran to her in the corner. She cowered in his arms, and they held each other throughout the night.

The man wouldn't let her go until Alfred came in. "Sir, you must leave, it's time soon."

He turned to go. Before he left, he whispered, "Nicollette, trust me."

Bertrum had been to see the warden two days earlier. The warden didn't recognize him as his former prisoner from years ago, because Bertrum had changed his appearance with one of Lord Baston's disguises—long muttonchops and a beard. He brought along a beautiful pewter plate, as a sample of the fifty plates he offered for the price of twenty-five. He further promised a roast pig for the prison guards, and another to be delivered to the warden's wife and children.

" 'Tis the extra pig for my dame and brats that sways me."

"You know, sir, the hanging will be a big day here. Why don't I deliver the pig fully prepared on execution morning, and you can feast on your banquet that day? I'll have the plates with me for celebration."

"You're easy to do business with, Osker," the warden had said, pouring them both a goblet of wine.

"I hate to have a finished pig go to waste. When I make your delivery in the morning, will I have trouble gaining entrance?"

"When will you arrive? I'll inform them, so they expect you."

"We should allow plenty of time before the special event, perhaps as early as an hour before daybreak."

"Very well." The warden lifted his glass to toast his good fortune.

Inspector Lang stayed in town during these days. He rode Pegasus up and down the streets, sometimes flanked by Peavey and Wilcox. Sometimes putting on a brief show with Pegasus for the crowds, but always patrolling the grounds near Newgate Prison.

"Jackson," Peavey said the day before the execution, "let's go out to Blackpool for the murdered woman found under the pier."

"Perhaps you should go do this one on your own, as part of your training."

"You mean by ourselves? You wouldn't come with us at all?"

"Yes."

Lang dismounted and wrote out a note to Chief Bart Marshall to ensure they'd have provisions for their trip. The detectives mounted their horses and trotted down the street.

Alfred sat on a crate in an alley a couple of blocks away from the prison. He stood up as he saw Lord Baston approach him on foot.

"Good day, my lord," he said.

"Don't let me down, Alfred." Lord Baston passed a money bag to the guard.

Jackson Lang, who was on his horse at the end of the alley, saw the transaction. So did Peavey and Wilcox.

The young recruits rode down the alley and arrested Lord Baston on suspicion of plotting Nicollette's escape. But Alfred got away, and they couldn't describe the nondescript man they'd seen take the money.

"He was the kind of man you pay no attention to as you pass him on the street," Wilcox said.

They took Lord Baston to Scotland Yard, where the chief interrogated him.

"We believe you're involved in a plot to rescue Nicollette Caron," Sir Bart said.

"No, sir, you're mistaken. In fact I have no intention of watching the execution. I'm leaving tomorrow on holiday to Italy."

"Peavey and Wilcox saw you handing money to a man in the alley near the jail."

"There was a beggar there, I gave him money when he sought my favor."

"We saw no beggar," Peavey said.

They questioned him until Sir Bart, who believed Lord

Baston's story, had the young detectives step into the hall for a private conversation. Lord Baston overheard them.

"Sir, we swear we saw him hand a bag of money to someone. Not an amount you'd give a beggar. He's lying, sir."

The chief looked at both men. "Where there's a confusion, I try to err on the generous side when it involves a barrister. I tend to believe the man if he has an honorable reputation. And his story is credible; there are beggars who work that area."

"I swear, Chief. There's too much to risk if he's released to his plot. We must keep him sequestered until the deed is done."

"Very well, keep him here through the night. We can release him in the morning. When you hear two trumpets, you'll know that Nicollette will be on her walk, and it will be too late for rescue."

"Very good, sir."

"Can you stay up through the night?"

"Certainly, sir."

Peavey and Wilcox went back into the room. "Lord Baston," Wilcox said, "you've been left in our charge, and we'll ask you questions until we're satisfied with your answers."

"I've told you the truth."

Wilcox didn't think so. He also thought it prudent to tie Lord Baston to the chair.

At four in the morning, Lang found Peavey and Wilcox in an interrogation room with Lord Baston. Peavey was still slightly alert, and Wilcox had his head on the table asleep.

"Gentlemen, can you leave me with Lord Baston, so I may question him?" The recruits left.

Lang came out of the room after only a few moments.

"He confessed nothing to me, just keep him here. You can release him when the horns have sounded. Nicollette's execution is scheduled for six in the morning."

"Very well, sir."

"Good job, men. Very bright of you to bring Lord Baston in when you had questions."

Lang walked out, mounted his horse, and pranced down the street as though an audience were watching.

He and Pegasus rested near the London Bridge. At the water's edge, he dismounted and shared with his brilliant beast the view of the gaslights that still lit the city. He stood before Pegasus and searched the horse's eyes.

"I've come to you with my puzzles. Great horse, you've served me well."

The horse seemed to understand.

"But you have no answers for me, do you?"

Lang reached in his pocket and retrieved the small book Miriam had given to him, *A Rabbit Heart.* He lit a candle and reread the book and watched the city's reflection in the water.

Man and horse remained still together until it was five in the morning. If he strained his eyes, Lang could see a hint of daybreak on the distant horizon. The guillotine blade would drop in an hour.

Beyond the tower's walls he could see people beginning to stream toward the prison walls. Now he and Pegasus fell into the crowd arriving on foot, on horseback, in buggies and carriages.

He left Pegasus at the post reserved for him. And then, as the townspeople swarmed the area, he merged into the crowd.

CHAPTER 35

Good-bye, Cruel World

MY PRIEST ARRIVED IN A WHITE-AND-GOLD-BROCADED robe with a miter on his head. He looked majestic, but he was not.

"I'm late. I'll have to cut this short for us to stay on schedule."

I had been in a fetal position for days, but I sat up for him as he entered.

"Remember that your body has been claimed by the medical school that won the bid. After your display period, the school will fetch you for dissection. This should cause you relief, in that you needn't trouble yourself about a resting place. Murderers quite foul a cemetery, in any case. Do you understand and accept this?"

"Lord Baston was to care for my body. And also Marie's."

"He cannot. Both your bodies have been bid upon and sold."

"Please, can you inform Lord Baston for me?"

"Lord Baston will find this out as soon as he tries to claim your bodies. Now, then, I was going to read something from the

Bible, but I'm sure that would be of no use to a woman such as you. Scripture is reserved for holy souls. You, Nicollette, must be clear as to where yours will reside, as you'll be in hell for eternity. Do you understand and accept this?"

I said nothing.

"I always like to cheer prisoners and leave them with a hope. May I do anything for you? Our time is up, but I'll try to respond to your requests."

I said nothing.

"Now let me give you some tips when you're on the scaffold. The magistrates appreciate *a beautiful execution.* Everyone likes to witness repentance and remorse, so my suggestion is that you demonstrate both to your audience. And if you could do this in such a way that we feel *almost sorry* for your death, your memory will be less dishonorable. And frankly, without your repentance, you will be jeered horribly. Do you have questions about this? Do you need tips as to how to beg forgiveness? Or advice about your remorse or your repentance?"

I said nothing.

"Do you have any requests?"

"Yes, two."

"Very well. Be quick about it, we're on a schedule."

"Tell Marie she was my dearest friend and that I regret with all my heart the sad turn our lives have taken. That surely she will rise in heaven and sit with God's angels."

"It shall be done. And?"

"Tell Lord Baston that I love him and will search for him again one day."

"Of course. Now, would you like to say the Lord's Prayer with me?"

"No. I'll say it to God all the way to the scaffold." I was not going to pray with this ungodly hypocrite who posed as a priest.

He hustled from my cell without concern, compassion, or warmth.

The first of three trumpets sounded, to signal that the priest had finished with me and that the event was about to take place. Another robed man waited outside my cell.

"Did she have any final requests?" he said.

I heard the priest's voice. "None."

Two female attendants had been summoned to prepare me. A fresh muslin gown was put on me, the first I had been given during my stay. One of the women combed my hair with great care.

"Thank you. I must look dreadful."

She tried to reassure me with a gentle smile, but both of us knew I had been in prison long enough to lose my glow. I had absorbed the stench of Newgate's walls, the terror in its air, the ghosts that haunted my cell.

But she said softly, "You have beautiful hair."

I wanted to believe her. I wanted to believe that in all the hell of being caged, I could still be a pretty woman.

My face and hands were washed of their grime. A black hood was brought in to me, with eyes cut out and an airhole for my nose.

The attendants left me when they had done their work, but not before they shared a tear for me. They were young sweet spirits, and though they had somehow found their way to accept this prison fee, I sensed that Newgate's hellishness was far from the goodness of their hearts.

The guards arrived to shepherd Marie and me to the scaffold. The trumpets sounded a second time, to signal that the procession had begun from my cell. Marie walked ahead of me. We were both hooded as we began our final journey to our destiny. Our hands shook, but the hoods didn't allow spectators to see the terror on our faces.

It would take almost five minutes to walk us to our stage. And it felt more like a stage than a platform, because the event seemed unreal to me—like a tragic play. As I walked, I wondered.

Does God feel the torment of those of us destined to dreadful deaths? Does he feel the chill, as the river of the blood stops its course through our veins?

Or does he weep for us all and welcome us with open sympathetic arms, lifting our spirits to rise and sit with him in his heavens?

And if he does, do I just look for his arms to lift me to him? Where I can rest, and where he will shelter me? And if so, will he explain to me why the cost of love was so high? And why I had to pay its price with my head?

CHAPTER 36

Hoods, Ropes, and Horror

ALFRED STAYED BEHIND. MANY OF THE OTHER GUARDS left their posts to join with the crowd in its excitement. The circus was about to begin, and the guards didn't want to miss the big show.

Alfred was praying when the hooded women stood before him. He reached to touch them with affection. "God bless you." He bowed his head. "I can't watch."

The women touched his cheek and continued on, led by three somber guards. The group walked through the jeering crowds and suffered the occasional toss of a rock or a piece of rotten food.

"Here ye! Hear ye!" the royal guardsman read from a scroll.

The two hooded women stood on the platform with the executioner and other attendants crowding the platform.

"In that Great Britain has found that Nicollette Caron is a convicted murderer with guilty verdicts for three murderous events for the lives of Oliver Davis, Frederick Bothem, and Denton Brickman, we do hereby declare her sentenced to be be-headed on this morning for her crimes.

"We also find Marie Tucci guilty of her assistance and the hid-ing of the murder of Denton Brickman. She will be hanged until she is dead on this date Friday, September 25, 1891."

"Marie, before we hang you for your crimes, do you have anything you wish to say?" The hooded woman shook her head.

"Nicollette Caron, do you have any last words before you are guillotined?"

The hooded woman shook her head.

Near Nicollette's abandoned prison cell, Alfred sat with his head bowed in prayer. But he heard a sound, and a figure appeared down the hall. It came closer to him.

"Hello, sir, you must hurry. Her door's open."

I didn't know what was going on around me. I knew I should be walking with the procession to the guillotine, but someone had taken my place, and I was not on my path. Then a man entered. I was astonished to see him.

"Nicollette, come with me. Hurry. But quietly. You must be ready to ride as you never have."

"What of Marie?"

"She's right here."

As we hurried through the prison chambers, Bertrum was un-loading a roast pig carcass. Marie crawled into a buggy and lay down behind some pewter plates. Bertrum covered her, stacked the plates next to the pig, and took off slowly.

The man took my hand and led me through a secret tunnel out of Newgate and into a fog-shrouded world.

"Get ready to ride your fastest," the man said.

My legs suddenly felt stronger—they were free, and ready for a dash on horseback.

Outside the door was a horse for me, and I was boosted to its back. My horse tore off in the lead, with my hero rescuer in a gallop behind me. He shouted directions, my horse followed, as if the horse knew exactly where he was going.

The courtyard was filled with spectators, the air with a fog so thick that it threatened to hide the executions from view. Vision was impaired at fifteen feet, and images were lost in the airy white mass.

"Executioner, it's time," Queen Victoria said. But as she did, she found her stumpy shoe heel became caught between the floor's planking.

She leaned forward around her protruding belly, which was not an easy effort, but one she would suffer for her own pride. The movement meant that her head was duck-downed and she could not see the platform with the sentenced women. She would have removed the shoe if she could have reached it or had it not been buttoned so tight, but she had not fastened her shoes for herself in years.

The executioner was over six feet tall and weighed as much as two men. This giant of a man stood before the first woman and lifted the hood to check the prisoner's condition. The crowd gasped.

"This isn't Marie Tucci," an attendant said.

"She's the mother who didn't vaccinate her child!" someone in the crowd shouted.

Abigail Morse stood bravely—defiantly—on the platform. "Hang me. Please hang me. I beg you."

The executioner looked at her, confused, then turned to the other prisoner and pulled off her hood.

"This is the wrong woman also!" he cried. "What do I do, Your Majesty?"

The townspeople close enough to see erupted into chaos.

Prime minister Salisbury stood nearby and picked up on the opportunity. His queen was still bent over and nobody realized the queen was—stuck, unable to pull herself upright in her chair.

"Let the townspeople decide. You must vote your judgment. Do you vote to death or not?" Salisbury cried out, inciting the audience.

"Hang them!"

"Hang them!" The people shouted in cadence.

"I know her—that's Carrie McMurray!" someone called out.

As the news spread through the fog, two people on horseback rode by outside Newgate's walls.

"There she goes!" the guards on the tower fence shouted, pointing to the road.

"She's on horseback!"

"After her!" A posse of men galloped off within minutes to capture Nicollette for her punishment.

The executioner looked to Queen Victoria as she awkwardly tried to pull herself up. "Your Majesty, what am I to do with these wrong women?"

The great queen was about to dismiss the people, but unaware in the commotion, Salisbury took it upon himself to give the order.

"Execute them. Execute them for their cooperation. Execute them for their folly."

"You don't get paid, Executioner, if you don't do your job," Salisbury said.

Part of the crowd cheered. Abigail did not falter as she stepped forward with her neck stretched and head held high.

"Tory, my son, your mother will find you," she said as she tilted her black-hooded head to the sky. "I'll see you in heaven."

A lethal noose was put around Abigail's neck, and the floor dropped from beneath her. She dangled and swung as the crowd stared at the spectacle.

Carrie bent over the guillotine, knelt with her head in its stockade. The executioner untied the blade to let it drop, but the blade didn't reach her neck.

The executioner looked at the queen, wondering if divine intervention was involved. The queen glared at Monsieur Delage, who tripped over his poor shoes to fall flat on his face. Then she turned.

The giant man reached for another noose and slipped it over Carrie's head. He pulled the long wooden lever to the hatch and opened it. She dropped through the opening and hung with her limbs dangling at her side. Her feet twitched in a kind of jig.

The two women hung from each side of the scaffold for several minutes of nervous jerking motions before their bodies finally came to a rest.

Someone asked, "What did they do? Does anyone know?"

A guard spoke up. "The deaf woman was a cocaine addict. She stole a horse and got all the way to Glastonbury before she was caught. The other wouldn't vaccinate her child. They'd both been in prison the past few months and prayed for their quick deaths."

"Salisbury, what were you thinking?"

"I thought only that we had a crowd that could get boisterous if they didn't see an execution, Your Majesty."

She turned to the royal documenter, whose duty was historical accounting. He sat near the queen with a poised pen ready to document the women's executions.

"This did not happen. History cannot record this moment," she said.

"Yes, Your Majesty."

My horse's mane blew beautifully in the wind. The smoothness of his ride was like no other. For this was not just any white horse that I rode, this was Pegasus. My accomplice galloped behind me on Peavey's dark horse. For it was Jackson Lang, my captor, who had come to my rescue.

We rode for miles, to a steep cliff overlooking the ocean, and when we were on the bluff, Jackson stopped my horse with just a verbal command.

I dismounted, as did he.

"I don't know how to thank you, Jackson."

He only looked at me with eyes that showed something between love and shame.

"Remove your dress," he said.

"Now?

"Remove your dress, Nicollette. They're after us, it's the only way."

"But—"

"I tell you, it's the only way. How I wish there was another!"

I removed my dress. He took it from me and began to mount Pegasus. And in that moment, I grasped his plan.

"Jackson—please no, you mustn't do this!" I tried to block his mount by wedging my body between Jackson and Pegasus.

"It's the only way to save you, Nicollette—and I only know I must save you."

Blake rode over the hill and stopped to watch us.

"Oh, Jackson, I beg you, *don't do this!* I can't bear it!"

Jackson stroked Pegasus's neck and gazed a moment into his eyes. Then he pushed me aside and mounted the horse. I tried to cry out, to dissuade him further. But my voice was not there. I couldn't speak. I could only watch in horror as he began to ride Pegasus straight at the cliff.

The beautiful mighty horse galloped without any falter to his stride as he obeyed his master's direction. Jackson jumped off just before the edge of the cliff, catching himself on the bluff's ridge. But as he jumped, he had issued the command: Pegasus took flight and leaped off the cliff. Like the performer he was, he kicked back his legs to show off the flying horse he'd been bred to be.

My dress, on the back of the saddle, trailed like a kite tail attached to the magnificent stallion. Pegasus in his death flight had a proud demeanor, as if he were doing one of his usual stunts that would end with applause. Instead, there was the sound of a sickening thud on the rocky shore.

My dress floated above the water, marking the spot near where Pegasus had crashed on the rocks. I heard a horse approach from behind me. It was Blake, who dismounted to assist Lang as he pulled himself up the side of the cliff. I ran to them.

Pegasus neighed a terrible cry. It tore at my heart.

"Jackson, why, *why*? Any horse would make them think me dead. Why Pegasus?"

"Should they suspect my part in your escape, Nicollette, only the death of Pegasus would make the accident believable. For in my chase after you, surely I would have saved my horse if I could."

The horse continued with its death cries. Jackson dropped to his knees hearing his horse's pain.

"Oh, my God, Jackson—I'd rather have had my life be lost."

I couldn't look below. I heard Pegasus writhing. Perhaps struggling to extricate himself from rocks or perhaps to hurry his death.

"Jackson, you must," Blake said from his horse.

Jackson couldn't move.

"He has no chance. He's in torment. You must help your animal, or I will."

Jackson walked back to the cliff.

I had never heard such agony as I heard in the horse's cry. I had never seen such agony as I saw on Jackson's face.

"Jackson," Blake said. "Get on with it."

But Jackson froze. As if he felt his suicidal command had been enough of his part in his horse's kill. He seemed unable to complete the task.

Lord Baston drew his gun. "Jackson, I'll shoot with you. Shoot to kill. Your beast deserves your love for him—now."

Still Jackson didn't draw his gun.

"Jackson, did you hear me? Years from now, you can't remember that you couldn't help your horse. Be a man. Take care of your beast."

Pegasus neighed again. The sound had lost none of its agony, but it was fainter.

I ran to Jackson and stood behind him. I drew the gun and put his hand on it.

"Please, Jackson, you must do this for me. Please."

I clasped his hand with mine on the gun.

"If you love him, shoot him. Please." He looked over his shoulder at me. I saw the anguish on his face. I saw within him the young boy in love with a horse. I saw the horror of a child learning for the first time that a beloved animal is lost to death. I saw his horror. I saw the anger we all hold for death when some being we love leaves us.

I clasped his hand with mine on the gun.

"BAM!"

"BAM!"

Both Blake and Jackson shot together, and the horse was silent.

Jackson dropped to his knees in his anguish, and I fell with him.

I looked into his eyes to thank him. He looked back with a tortured face that couldn't conceal his feelings for me.

"Go, you must go," he said. "There's no time for good-byes. Take her, Lord Baston."

Blake mounted his horse and lifted me to him. I wrapped my arms tightly around his waist, staring back over my shoulder at Jackson.

I'll never forget the tormented look in his eyes. Or my feeling of love and tenderness for my captor.

CHAPTER 37

Mourning

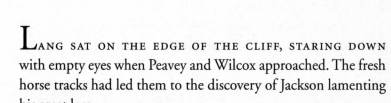

Lang sat on the edge of the cliff, staring down with empty eyes when Peavey and Wilcox approached. The fresh horse tracks had led them to the discovery of Jackson lamenting his great loss.

"Have you seen Nicollette?" Peavey asked him.

"She was killed when she hit the rocks, but she was taken out to sea with a wave. There's a strong undertow—I watched her disappear."

He pointed to the water below, where Nicollette's dress floated in the rough waters. They saw the wreck of Pegasus upon the rocks.

"I'm sorry, Jackson. That's your stallion, isn't it?"

"Yes."

"Should we try to find Nicollette's body?"

"I don't expect it will be found. Leave it for the sea animals. Once down there, we'd have trouble getting it out, and it's too rocky for a boat."

"I believe you're right, sir."

Lang mounted behind Wilcox to ride back to town. He was grateful that neither of the recruits could see his face.

The ten strong workers Lang had hired climbed down to the shore where the horse's body was dashed and built a makeshift raft from lumbers and rope. The men lifted Pegasus's carcass onto it as they watched Lang cut a piece of the horse's mane for his remembrance.

They covered the horse with kindling and saturated the kindling and raft with lamp oil. And they shoved him off into the water as the sun set—burying him at sea, like a Viking king. A flaming arrow ignited the funeral pyre, which burned for hours. By dusk the deed was done.

Jackson paid and dismissed the men. He stayed at the edge of the water, watching, as the great horse burned at sea.

I was in a hideaway lodge near the water with Blake. Bertrum and Marie had joined us as part of the plan. We were safe. I looked out the window, saw fire on the water near the beach where Pegasus had died, and knew what Jackson must have done with the horse's carcass. I wanted enough ether to put me under. For how could I revel in life with the blood of other beings on my hands? Beautiful men dead, and now a beautiful horse's life sacrificed for mine.

And then I learned of Abigail's and Carrie's deaths from a trusted stableboy who brought Blake provisions. Bertrum had visited Carrie in prison and learned she wanted to die. She was suffering from the tortures in prison and begged Bertrum to let her take Nicollette's place on the gallows, and when Abigail was asked, she also begged for Marie's place. In exchange Lord Baston made sure their families received a generous anonymous donation of gold.

It was their idea to take the places of Marie and me. I protested. I told them I would never allow it. When they realized I was so insistent, they assured me they would only be returned to their cells. That taking our place for a short time would just be a ruse to allow time for Marie and me to escape.

I whispered at them through walls when the prison was most quiet. I insisted they must not attempt to take my place, because I feared for their lives. They promised me they wouldn't. *They promised me.* I had no way of knowing these women *chose* to walk to their deaths. Oh, my Father, in heaven, please help me.

I started crying and couldn't stop. All the emotions of living in a dungeon with the haunt of ghosts, the narrow escape of a blade on my neck, and the horrific sacrifices of those around me pushed me over the edge of sanity. Blake held me tight as I sobbed, hours past midnight. Finally, I quieted and fell asleep in his arms, exhausted from my breakdown.

CHAPTER 38

Branded

T HE CHIEF WALKED INTO THE INTERROGATION ROOM THE
day after Nicollette's escape. There were two men guarding Jackson Lang.

"Leave us alone," Sir Bart said. The men nodded and left.

Lang sat in the interrogation chair unrestrained—*except for his mind's chains*. His shoulders and body were slumped. His eyes gazed upon the plain concrete floor as if he hoped to find answer there.

"We know you were gone the evening before," Sir Bart said. "You didn't show up at your boardinghouse all night. Where were you, Jackson?"

Lang was silent.

"We know that an unknown man was seen entering Nicollette's cell and holding her on her last night. Your horse was outside the nearest entrance to the prison."

Lang was silent.

"Help me out here, Jackson. Where are your denials?"

Lang searched the floor again, but the floor was blank. *He thought a red hand might reach up and pull him underground—to finish the job.* He had lived his life to do the right thing, with the knowledge that rewards and recognition would follow. He had taken an oath to uphold the laws of England. And here he sat, a traitor. He would be lucky if they didn't hang him. *The red hand didn't reach up for him. Instead his conscience would wrap around and around him, and wring out his true self.*

"We're starting to put the pieces together. We found her dress but not her body, so we assume she's escaped. But there's one thing we don't understand about the whole thing, Jackson. We know how much you loved your horse. We didn't think you would dash Pegasus to the rocks for a woman you were not to have, let alone a murderess, let alone a convicted criminal you entrapped."

Lang looked away, not wanting the chief to see his face.

"Jackson, you are our finest at Scotland Yard. You tried to help her at her trial. If you helped her escape"—he leaned in close to Lang, his face inches from his—"then you must have fallen in love with this woman." He looked deep into Lang's eyes, searching for his answers. But he already had them.

Lang said nothing.

"You've been a brother to me, my most trusted lieutenant on crime, my closest friend. And now . . . your offer of knighthood has been withdrawn. As a friend, I know you wanted this most in your life." Sir Bart slammed his good hand hard on the table, not caring that he might injure it.

"I don't know why you've done this, Jackson. But as my gesture of brotherhood, and because I don't want to incriminate the CID in this scandal, I'll cover you. They want to question you. I'll vouch for your innocence. I have your file of letters of reference with one from me dated a week ago. Because I could have written that letter then, but I couldn't today."

He pushed an envelope over to him. "Here's your last salary

and an undeserved bonus for your capture of Nicollette. Lastly, I give you a one-way ticket out of the country and an order for you to leave London immediately.

"I don't know the man you are today. I only hope you go away and find that man of integrity who has been lost. The honorable man we respected and the master of criminal puzzles."

Lang sighed. "How can I thank you, Bart?"

"By journeying within your core and destroying the wrong within you. I have placed my neck on a block for you, at my own career peril. Everything in your office remains. When the door closes, don't return without an invitation."

Lang tried to embrace his friend, but Sir Bart recoiled.

"Lest you think you were the only one smitten with Nicollette, Judge Tareyton assigned her a trusted guard so that her escape would be allowed and made sure her guillotine was inoperable—in case the escape plan failed.

"Apparently he was most grateful for his resurrection. The queen has asked Tareyton to resign his post and has left his punishment up to her prime minister."

Lang extended his hand, as if asking for at least this sign of forgiveness.

"I can't, Jackson. Peavey and Wilcox will see you off."

Peavey, Wilcox, and Lang rode to Southampton, where they stayed at a hotel for the night before Lang's departure the next day. Peavey and Wilcox chose not to dine with Lang, though he said he had something to discuss with them. So he ate alone, while his former apprentices dined just tables away from the shunned inspector.

The next morning they rode with him to the boat. Their assigned duty was to take possession of the horse Lang had borrowed and make certain that he left on his one-way trip.

Though not as sincere as they might have been, both recruits shook Lang's hand. Peavey broke the silence. "Thank you, Jackson."

"She's beautiful," Wilcox said. "We fell in love with her, too."

Lang looked like a surrendering general. As well he might, with the loss of his career, his unrequited love, the death of Pegasus, and the banishment from his country.

"All aboard. All aboard. All aboard for America."

"We appreciate all you taught us," Peavey said.

"We're grateful to you for having been our mentor," Wilcox said.

Lang looked at the two recruits as they stepped away from the boarding area.

"Which one of you turned me in?" Lang asked.

"I noticed Pegasus outside the prison," Peavey said. "Why did you leave us the clue, Jackson? Was it intentional?"

"You made it too easy for us," Wilcox said. Lang stared intently at them. He noticed they had dropped the "sir" as they addressed him. And why not? He was no longer their superior. He could have walked away and not asked the question. But he had to know.

"What did you recommend as my fate?"

The men didn't want to answer to his face.

"It's all over now. Tell me."

"Jackson, you dishonored Scotland Yard. Though people may not know the truth. We thought you should hang for your treason."

"Good. Then I've trained you well. Now I have one final thing for you. I've done some work on my own on our killer, Jack the Ripper. You may have my notes. The identity of the criminal is not far off, if you'll follow my trail. Perhaps this will win you two even better favor with the chief." He reached out and pulled a piece of paper from behind Peavey's ear, as a mockery to his coins-in-the-ear trick, then handed Wilcox the notes.

"Thank you, Jackson."

Lang reached in his breast pocket for his ship pass. He suddenly felt the burden of his dishonor on his shoulders, and his body felt the age he had never noticed before.

"You're good men, and fine detectives. It was a privilege to work with you."

He boarded the boat without looking back at the recruits. He moved slowly, like a much older man. The detectives stood near the dock and watched as the large ship embarked on its voyage.

The starched purser reached for Jackson's ticket and read his name. "Lang. Oh. Jackson Lang. We have a letter in our custody for you, sir. Someone has gone to great lengths to reach you. A personal carrier has delivered it to our captain. I'll get it."

"Thank you."

The young purser returned with a sealed envelope marked TOP SECRET and Jackson tore the letter open. It read:

Dear Inspector Lang:

I am writing to offer you a position as detective with the New York City Police. Our force is in need of a detective with your skills. We have a series of murders at the docks, a most baffling case, and many others arise that would challenge your expertise.

The position we are offering is a solid job with genuine benefits you may not expect. It is not without danger but would pay you twice your last salary, with horse, and all your expenses.

A particularly fine horse awaits you here. She's a rare one selected to sway you to accept our offer: a Lippizan mare, yours to keep if you take the job.

You may wire me at the return address on this envelope. If you are interested in taking the position, I will meet your ship when it docks.

I look forward to the opportunity of working with you.

Sincerely,

Detective Superintendent Howard Duke, 23rd Precinct

CHAPTER 39

On the Sea

B<small>LAKE AND</small> I <small>WERE IN A SITTING ROOM ON THE OCEAN</small> liner. Marie and Bertrum had joined us, and we hugged and talked like long-lost friends. I was not sure of our destination. It didn't matter to me, so long as I'd be far from London. So long as I was not going to be hunted like some fox pup, pursued by horses and dogs and guns.

Bertrum gathered food and wine and brought it to us each day. We decided that since there were other Londoners on board, we should not take the risk of leaving our cabins. Though small, they were luxurious compared to the quarters Marie and I had endured, and there was a romance to our confinement.

I *wanted* to be in close quarters with Blake. And Bert and Marie's romance was developing, so they enjoyed their close quarters. I did think it had probably been a long while since Bertrum had courted a woman. His clumsy attempts to charm Marie were comical, if quite touching.

He brought back a rose to her. Instead of telling her that the rose reminded him of her beauty, he handed it to her, and said, "Here, Marie, this was on the banquet table, so you can have it."

Instead of asking her to come sit closer on the settee with him, he said, "Sit on this chair, Marie, it's the most comfortable. Unless you'd like to sit somewhere harder." Then he laughed at his own joke.

But Marie just giggled, and before long, Blake and I saw her flirting overtly with him.

There was one point where Blake had poured the last of the wine in our glasses, and Marie turned to Bertrum with tears in her eyes.

"Bert, you're so gallant. That you risked your life and picked me up in my eleventh hour, just moments before my neck was broken, I can never forget. You planned for my safety, sheltered me in my escape, and have me now in your care and protection. I don't know how I can properly thank you. You are my hero, Bert. May I kiss you in a show of my gratitude?"

"I believe so," he whispered. And they disappeared into the adjoining cabin. Blake and I smiled at each other as we watched Marie and Bertrum begin their courtship, then we retired to our own cabin.

Our rooms were for ship's officers, who for a generous amount of cash had sold Blake their private quarters and doubled up with other officers for the voyage. This meant we didn't have to sleep with other passengers, who might recognize Marie and me.

Once alone, Blake and I kissed. I stood on my tiptoes, and my lips parted for his. And then he picked me up and carried me to the bed. He was propped up against the pillows, and with both of us fully clothed, I rested against his chest. Feeling protected from anything that could harm me.

"Where are we going, Blake?"

"To America."

"Isn't it all renegades and cowboys and the like?"

"There are cities. We'll be landing in New York City."

Nestled against Blake's strong chest, I couldn't believe the good fortune that had turned my life around. And though we were both exhausted, he kept kissing me, and our passion kept building to such a heat that I had to gasp for air.

So with poor timing I excused myself to cool myself near the hand bowl. I searched the mirror as I splashed my face. But I saw *Denton's ghost reaching for me. Trying to touch me, then there was Robert and Frederick* and I wanted to fight them. I wanted their chilled touch to leave me alone. I wanted their haunt gone from my life.

This time I closed my eyes. I decided to surrender to their touch, to their ghostly demands that I continue our relationship through death's veil. I kept my eyes closed and tried to feel nothing. But I did. I felt their cold unearthly presence—so cold, and yet I achieved a level of bliss surrendering to their touch. And without making a sound, from the depths of my being, *I cried for help.*

And when I opened my eyes, I saw the outline of a woman, a flowing form in the mirror. She was a beautiful vision who looked similar in face to myself. Her hair was long and with a curl like mine. Yet it had an iridescent aura as it floated airborne above her shoulders like it was carried by the wind—but there was only the indoor stillness.

Somehow I knew that she was my mother. And then she did an astonishing thing: she reached out for the hands of the ghosts that swarmed around me.

They turned to her eagerly, as if captivated by some heavenly communication or motion invisible to my eye. She raised her arms, ruffled her hair, and moved her hands over her breasts and down the curve of her hips.

And then she began to retreat, very slowly, with the ghosts in pursuit. I watched her back up, step by step. I watched the ghostly apparitions follow her, one by one—through the portal window on our largest wall.

And I felt a sudden peace deep within my soul, for I knew they wouldn't return.

Blake walked over to stand near me. He looked at me, his face questioning whether it was acceptable for us to make love. And with renewed energy I reached up to remove his cravat. I opened his shirt, and he lifted my dress with such finesse that I felt as if it dissolved from my body. He picked me up and lay me down on the bed.

He undid my corset, moved down the bed to remove my stockings, and when I was naked before him, he let me know of his approval. I had never seen an Englishman move so fast and recklessly—he threw his jacket across the room and hurled his shirt to a corner. He stood and took off his trousers next to the bed, and I looked at him shamelessly, as no Victorian woman should. But I did. And I smiled.

He looked so ready for me.

"Nicollette, my Nicollette, I have longed for this moment."

It never occurred to me to warn him. For he crawled into the bed next to me and was doing things to me no man had ever done before, and the sensations were so thrilling that I was incapable of thought. Yet my lover had some sort of photographic memory, I'm convinced. He had no need to use his book, *777*. He had memorized every position and had them all on call for our pleasure.

"Turn over, Nicollette," he said, and I did as I was told. I learned that he was the most inventive man I had ever known in bed, a true maestro of sensual choreography.

"Nicollette, darling, please bend forward."

"Blake, I don't know what you mean."

So he showed me, with the gentlest of movements. And soon I was cooperating with him as if I were a prima ballerina who couldn't move wrongly. Every time I moved, he had something new to teach me. Soon I spoke up, "Blake, could we try walking the wall?"

"I thought you'd never ask." He smiled at me. And he picked me up and put me upon three pillows on the edge of the bed. While still standing he entered me as I walked my feet up his chest, slowly, until I found the angle that pleased me most, before moving on to the next positions.

We completed our acts, then again later that night, and again, we went through many different positions without once making love heart to heart in the usual way.

There were times when he took me to a place where I couldn't catch my breath as my female areas raced faster than his movements. And I knew I had finally met my match.

"Nicollette, I'll be yours forever, if you'll have me," he said.

"I will," I said. And then he fell asleep in my arms. Never had I had a man fall asleep near me, and I loved it.

He turned slightly, so that we were both on our sides and the length of his front was pressed against my back. I felt his arousal nestled in my curves and his long arms wrapped around me. I felt as though nothing could hurt me so long as I wore this man as a shawl.

I lay asleep in his arms for a moment. I knew my lover could come alive at any time to begin again. And I felt at peace.

The prison of rats and sorrow was long ago and far away. The guillotine, no doubt, was on its way back to France. I had found a man who could survive and thrive in my love, and a whole new future was before me. I could begin again with a fresh start in a wild new country.

I kept my eyes closed, and Blake reached for me again. And

he kissed me with the softest kiss, a kiss I had waited for forever. It tasted so sweet that I didn't want the kiss to end. I kept my eyes closed and the ghosts didn't haunt me. We loved throughout the night in such a way I'm sure has never been done in England.

I drifted into sleep. And when I awoke, I knew that anyone's past could leave her with haunting images that must be put aside. And I can either choose to live in that world or move on and seize the moment I have today.

I choose to live in my today. To know that my world in England is a chapter in a book I choose not to reopen. And that my ghosts and memories will be buried at sea. I'll build a future so full of excitement, adventure, and loving, that I will ignite and excite others who share their moments with me. And in the dark, when I'm alone, I will not worry. I'll just close my eyes until my mind is filled with my life with Blake. Dear God, I pray this to be so.

Epilogue
Message in a Bottle

"Do you mind if I sit here?" A woman with violet eyes and a heart-shaped beauty mark thought to flirt with the handsome man on deck. But he lifted his head up to squint at her in such a way that she immediately abandoned her plan and hurried back to her father's side.

"Father, I thought that man there was Jackson Lang. But he didn't recognize me, and now I'm not sure."

Dominic Dabber looked at the scruffy man tipping a bottle of whiskey to his throat.

"No, Daphne, he's not clean-shaven and he's had those clothes on for days. He's just someone who looks like him."

A Vixen's Lament

If love is to unite a man and a woman as one,
Could we have one man for the dark, and another for the sun?
Might we taste each other's skin in the early morn?
Without a lady's reputation being torn.

Acknowledgments

With gratitude to two writing gods who have had great impact upon my work in very different ways. Bestselling author Bryce (*Power of One*) Courtenay, for his encouragement, coaching, and respect for my writing—at a time when I most needed professional accolades and a boost; and renowned author Tom (*Without Remorse*) Clancy, for his assessment on sixteen lines of my writing and spying the "perfect pen" within my work. His distribution of millions of copies of my poem *Ascension* has yielded me touching letters and stories around the world, for which I will be forever grateful to him.

Writers can't share their work with the public without a network of people who encourage us. And I could not do it without the time and assistance of many people. Special thanks to all the writers and friends who have taken the time to read my work in its various evolutions, including screenwriter Gary Ruben; friend and former producer Deborah Stack; childhood friend Barbara Jahnke; fellow screenwriter Mark Vashon; dear friend Roxanne Wongdock; fellow writer Julie Percell; funnyman Ernie Witham; my recently departed cousin, Joyce Opheim; and Vera Magnuson, who at eighty-five did not live to see the book in print, but read my manuscript in one day and was so sad that the story ended that she read it again the next day and the next, and many others.

To New York surgeon Dr. Dirk Bogart (pseudonym) for serving as my medical consultant in the writing of this book. To Ted Knuckey, former rodeo cowboy turned policeman, turned lawyer, turned judge, turned writer, for his judicial counsel and fellow writer's support. To Jason MacKenzie, my weapons expert. To the numerous librarians and subject experts on England, Glastonbury, prisons, and punishment who helped me in my research for this book. And to Nigel, my Great Britain expert.

To my special professional friends who take their time to read my work and coach me, including Kate MacCallum, film producer and creative director with Wolf Films; Chip Diggins, former vice president of production, Paramount Pictures, Inc.; and other writers such as Judith Guest, Terry Brooks, Don McQuinn, and Robert Morris.

To Shannon and John Tullius, founders and hosts of the Maui Writers Conference. They've not only created a mecca for writers and a breeding ground for better writing, but a Shangri-la writers' network where a writer can find a family.

Major publishers craft books with a team of professionals that discovers new writing talents, and I'm most grateful to be in their company: Pocket Books, a division of Simon & Schuster, and the talented creative staff, who brought *Rabbit Heart* to the public; Maggie Crawford, editor extraordinaire, who not only makes the decision to buy, but steers the project with her steadfast focus and editorial talents; my agent, Mel Berger, who is a titan in his field and has the power to ignite others about an unknown writer; and my editor and angel, Renni Browne, who saw the originality in *Rabbit Heart* and polished the diamond in the rough, and whose word mastery helped me discover my writing voice.

And to Gary, for his love and support.

With gratitude,
Colleen Hitchcock